A Stranger On Board

Cameron Ward had the good fortune to be born to a teacher and an editor in a house full of books. A philosophy graduate with a professional background in IT, he has worked in both publishing and the public sector. His previous published works, under the name Adam Southward, include the Kindle-bestselling Alex Madison series. He enjoys beach walks, paddleboarding, and stealing superyachts.

Eight Days In

At this time of night, and in other circumstances, the superyacht Escape *should have been illuminated with a dazzling array of lighting — a shout-out to surrounding vessels, to aircraft, and to the crew and guests. Spotlights, deck lights, LED walkways. Underwater lanterns and multicoloured lasers, turning the water every hue under the sky. Fireworks were a regular evening spectacle on a yacht this size, though perhaps not in weather like this.*

Tonight, the only glow was from a dying flare — the last one, launched in desperation. It glided towards the water, dancing as gusts of wind took it this way and that, before it was extinguished, unseen, under the black water of the Atlantic.

The superyacht drifted, thousands of miles from land, rising and falling in the white-crested swell. Water crashed over her bows and stern, swamping the lower decks, swirling into every corner. The metal hull shuddered under the strain, vibrations travelling deep inside the vessel. Thunder rumbled as wind screamed across every surface, with no sign of relenting.

Inside, on the main deck, the chandeliers should have been casting their sparkle over a room bursting with smiling crew, relaxing into the leather sofas, enjoying the splendour and isolation of the voyage. Their glasses should have been full, along with their stomachs.

But the chandeliers were dark, the only lights battery-powered, emergency use, already fading. The lower decks were pitch black, the upper decks lit sporadically, many of the torches extinguished on purpose as the crew took refuge in the darkness.

Glasses lay strewn across the floor of the lounge, contents spilled into the thick carpet. Empty bottles of wine and beer rolled to and fro, dropped as their owners hurried outside into the night, climbing as high as possible.

Trying to get away.

Outside, battling the wind and rain, a solitary figure crept along one of the side decks, pausing to peer into the swirling waters below, holding tight to the rail. The floor was slippery, the yacht's motion uncontrolled, unpredictable. They shivered against the wind, tasting the salt spray, feeling the drop in temperature the storm had brought with it, tugging at the zipper on their jacket. Was that movement — footsteps, a splash in the water? In this weather, it would be a miracle to hear anything useful at all.

The figure remained motionless for a few seconds, ensuring they kept to the darkness, out of the range of any feeble lanterns swinging in the windows, avoiding the probing search of a flashlight from above. Satisfied, they headed forward, ducking inside, towards the stairwell.

Three decks above, the crew huddled together in fear. Most had sailed through far worse storms than this. The motion didn't bother them, and neither did the wind and the rain. On a yacht this size, none of those things would normally pose a threat.

And yet, they were terrified.

The crew had shut themselves into the enclosed cocktail bar, a room some thirty feet across and twenty deep. The bi-fold doors were closed and locked. A distant flash of lightning illuminated them, just for a second, but long enough for all to see the smear of blood on the glass, and the crimson stains on the floor.

The single staircase down to the bridge was barricaded, covered over by a fridge, of all things, pushed across the doorway and wedged at the corner with a fire extinguisher. They didn't put much faith in it. But it was all they had.

The storm raged. Dangerous and violent. They were at least three days from land, but with no way of contacting the shore.

One of the crew wept, legs tucked against her chest. Another tried to comfort her, but without much conviction. There was nowhere to go. No reassurance to give.

It wasn't the storm she was afraid of.

I

Two weeks earlier

The smell hit me before the noise. Salt, diesel, the bitter tang of chemicals in the air. It was followed by the low thrum of a busy port, distant and relentless. I'd followed the directions Mitch had given me, through the centre of Southampton, past the port towards the Ocean Marina, where he based his offices. I pulled up outside a squat brick building with bars on the windows.

'It's me,' I said, holding down the intercom button, catching my reflection in the dirty mirrored glass of the door, wondering if I should have made more of an effort. Too late now.

I heard a grunt, followed by the click of the lock. I took a swift breath, sucking in another lungful of fumes, before pushing open the door.

The office was cramped, but clean, professional. Freshly painted walls lined with pictures of Navy destroyers, a few private yachts to break things up. A photo of the winner of last year's America's Cup hung behind the single desk, along with a collection of framed military credentials. Mitch sniffed and grinned, pushing himself out of his swivel chair. His dark hair was longer now, as was his beard, both neatly groomed, finished off with an expensive suit. Civilian life suited him.

'Sarah,' he said. 'Great to see you.'

'You too, Mitch,' I said.

I didn't have many people I could count on, but Mitch was one of them. We shared an awkward hug, my stomach performing an involuntary flutter as his arms embraced me. He patted me on the back, punched me on the shoulder, indicated for me to take a chair. He slumped back into his, its frame creaking in protest.

'You look . . .'

I stared down at my vest top and jeans, thrown on just half an hour before. Tatty trainers completed the look, poking out on to his nice clean carpet. I made a show of patting my hair.

'Perfect?' I said, baring my teeth.

Mitch laughed. 'As always.'

He tapped the desk with a huge finger, unable to keep the grin off his face. I looked down.

A photo covered half the desk, a set of blueprints to the left, a thick wad of technical manuals and construction information to the right.

'This is what you called me about? You're kidding,' I said, staring at the picture of the enormous superyacht. The shot had been captured from a helicopter or drone, showing off the multiple decks, the jet skis, the hot tub. A smiling family dressed in white, waving for the camera. The name of the yacht, *Escape*, was stencilled in striking titanium against the pure white of the stern. A delicious and grotesque monument of wealth. I leaned over to examine the image, kicking the chair to one side.

Mitch shrugged. 'I can get you something smaller, more local,' he said, 'but not for a few weeks – probably

6

guarding some boatyard, charter stuff in the Med, that sort of thing.'

My heart thudded. Twelve days' passage. That's what he'd said on the phone. Time to get my head together. I couldn't do that locally, didn't want some local job baby-sitting rich shits and their jet skis off the coast of Ibiza. I wanted as far away as possible. This was perfect. Just . . . unexpected.

'Who owns it?' I said.

'We don't get to know,' he said. 'Superyacht owners, ones who can afford these,' he touched the photo, caress-ing the fine lines towards the bow, tapping the expanse of mirrored glass on the lower levels, 'don't advertise them-selves. It's another level. Proper money. I'm talking Abramovich and Bezos. The level that gets you assured privacy.'

I nodded. Another level. Another life. And the security detail that comes with it. Assholes, probably, the lot of them.

'And it's just a delivery?'

Mitch nodded. 'It's in Majorca for a refurbishment, but the owner wants it moved to Antigua for final fittings. Skeleton crew, straight A to B, no passengers. No hassle.' He sniffed and leaned back. The chair gave another squeak of protest. 'They decided at the last minute they wanted a security detail. Something about insurance crossing the Atlantic. You're it.'

I could see the beginnings of a belly poking over Mitch's belt. Too long out. Letting the training slide. He saw me looking.

'You OK, Sarah?' he said, sucking his gut in.

I hid the smile in time. I nodded.

'I know this is a little rushed,' he said, 'but you're one of the most qualified on my books. It's why you joined me, right?'

Joined him and his security company, providing military-trained personnel to private and commercial industry. Mitch was ex-Royal Marines too, we shared that as a bond, and when I came looking, he snapped me up.

'Fuck, Mitch,' I said. 'It's perfect. I guess I should thank you.'

He laughed, a deep bellow, genuine. 'You guess? Look, this is the job, Sarah. With your skills you can do this in your sleep and take home four times the salary. It's good work.' He patted his stomach. 'So good, a man can go a little soft.'

I couldn't hide my smile this time. My own body was only three months out, and my training hadn't relaxed one iota. I didn't leave because I wasn't fit enough. I was in perfect shape; killer shape. I knew it, Mitch knew it.

'You just wait,' he said, reading my expression, looking a little hurt. 'A couple of weeks of lazing around on that thing, those cute jeans won't fit you any more.'

I shook my head, laughing. 'There's a gym on board, says so here.' I pointed to the blueprint, tugging it out from under the photo.

'And three kitchens and four bars,' he countered, 'not that you'll be drinking. But tonic water is full of calories, you know?'

I relaxed, knowing we could banter all day. It was one of our tricks, learned through hours and days of operations skin-to-skin. Nothing more with Mitch, though, he wasn't

8

up for that, and neither was I. We were pros, ex-pros, at least. And this was a decent way to make a living, after everything. He'd called me yesterday, told me he had a job, something right up my street. He knew what had happened, why I left, why I needed to do something to keep my mind sharp. He'd seen what happens when ex-soldiers are left to rot. He wasn't going to let it happen to me.

'So get your shit together,' he said. 'We'll do the full brief on Monday; you fly to Palma on Wednesday. Immediate departure.'

I tried to look like I was considering it, like I had a load of shit to get together. I didn't. This was pretty much it, here in this office, in a small industrial park in the Port of Southampton.

I carried all of my baggage inside.

I sat in the car for a few moments. It was Amy's, loaned on the condition I didn't add to the scratches or dents. Don't worry, sis, if anyone dents your car, I'll dent them. It's what I do. Did, anyway. Amy hadn't asked for all the details yet, why I left in such a hurry. But she would. It's what sisters do.

The house was empty when I pulled up. Amy might still be at work, her shifts twelve hours long – sometimes she slept at the hospital, sometimes she made it home. I breathed out, feeling the tension, sitting with it, knowing it had nowhere to go.

'Hey,' I said, stepping out of the car, spying Wilfred, her ginger tabby. He crept out from the garden hedge, rubbed against my leg. I crouched, scooping him into my arms, pushing my face against his warm fur.

'Hungry?' I said.

We went inside. Wilfred bolted his dinner before curling up on the windowsill, staring out into the back garden, a long narrow wilderness full of unsuspecting prey to be watched and judged. I cleared up, wondering if the ready-meal I'd grabbed from the freezer had more or less nutrition in it than the dried cat food. I decided I wasn't that far gone, not yet, and threw it back, grabbing some veg out of the fridge, putting a saucepan of pasta on to boil. I eyed the rack of wine bottles for a few moments before taking a can of Diet Coke.

The front door slammed.

'Only me.'

'Through here,' I called, grabbing another bowl, adding more pasta to the pan. The least I could do was cook for her. She'd refused rent, so far. With this job I'd be able to pay her back and then some, start looking for a place of my own. She didn't deserve all of my crap on top of her already stressful life.

'How'd it go?' Amy asked, dropping her coat over a chair, kissing me on the cheek before pulling a bottle of Rioja from the rack. She studied the label, her face twisting as she evaluated it.

Her profile was similar to mine, with the same dark complexion, but her features were more refined, gentle, with welcoming brown eyes and a perfect bob, cut to emphasize her delicate chin, which she jutted out just the right amount to convey the strength of her feelings at any moment. Shorter than me, her frame was nevertheless cut from the same cloth, though she hid it under hospital scrubs.

I paused, smiling – a kiss on the cheek from a loving

sibling. Life was made of such moments, and they should be cherished.

'Good,' I said. 'I'm taking the job. He's paying me part up-front, so I can give you all the back rent –'

'I don't want your money,' said Amy, popping the cork, grabbing a glass.

She glanced at me and I gave a small shake of my head. No alcohol. Not for me. My body is a temple, *blah, blah*. The truth is, it made the dreams worse.

'I'll pay you,' I said. 'It's not fair.'

'Sarah, I won't take it,' she said. 'I don't need it. All I want is a bit of time with my little sister, who I've hardly seen for three years.' She took a swig of her wine. 'So what's the job?' she said. 'Pretend I understand.'

Pretend. My sister, the consultant oncologist, with a brain the size of a small planet and a heart to make it work. She'd got the brains and I'd got . . . well, an athletic body, a temper, and a constant sense of restlessness. We both picked what we thought were the correct career choices. She got hers right.

I'd pay the rent into her account. She couldn't stop it. She wasn't clever enough to break the banking system.

I gave her a sinister smile. 'A delivery,' I said, followed by a quick relay of most of what Mitch had told me. There was nothing confidential – I hadn't been *told* anything confidential, and it made a refreshing change, being able to talk about my work.

'A Russian oligarch?' she asked, laughing. 'Or a narco? No, wait, an oil baron?'

I shrugged. 'A fast-food tycoon. In his sixties with a hairpiece and an eighteen-year-old wife.'

'Pharmaceuticals,' said Amy, decisively.

'That's the same as a narco. Plastic surgeon?' I offered.

'There's money in that,' she said, laughing, draining her glass and refilling it.

I tried not to raise either eyebrow. The shit she must deal with every day, if this was her way of winding down, it was fine by me.

'Nearly two weeks at sea?' she said, her face twisting in concern. 'An Atlantic crossing is tough, isn't it?'

'I've done much longer,' I reminded her, 'been much further.'

'Yes, but that was . . . you know. A Navy warship is pretty safe at sea.'

'And so will this be,' I said. 'It's huge. A floating palace. It's got a gym and an art gallery on it, Amy. It's safe.'

'Because you're on it,' she said with a sigh. 'I know. You can't stop me worrying, though. I insist on it.'

We ate. She drank. She pried gently around the edges, not too much, just enough.

'Hey,' she said, between mouthfuls of pasta, 'maybe you'll meet someone. Sex on a superyacht!' She wiggled her eyebrows.

I swallowed. Memories of Kay jumped out, brief stabs of pain, longing and regret. The moments we shared – at the time so dangerous and erotic and so alive, they scared the hell out of me. We'd lie awake at night in secret, my skin all goosebumps, anticipating his touch.

He'd make his move, rough, uncoordinated, but never clumsy. I'd shiver, burning as he knelt between my legs, eyes watching me, sparkling. I begged and writhed and when I was done and completely exhausted, I'd ask for more.

The memory slunk away. Amy's comment was innocent, and not altogether crazy. Perhaps that was exactly what I needed. For the last twelve months, sex was something I read about in novels. Perhaps it would be nice to have some of it leap off the page.

'You're thinking about it,' she said.

'I'm not!' I said, feeling my cheeks flush, confusion mixed with guilt.

'You are. I'm a doctor. I see these things. Maybe a dashing captain, or a rugged engineer?'

'Jesus.'

'I'm just saying. How many people are on board?'

'I don't know,' I said. 'I'll find out on Monday. Ten, maybe fewer. The essential crew, plus me.'

'You're essential.'

'I'm a last-minute addition.'

'An essential one.'

'I guess.'

'Ten possible playmates.'

'Amy!'

'What?' She cackled, refilled her glass, pushing her bowl to one side. She let out a huge sigh, leaning back, massaging her neck. 'I miss this.'

I finished off my Coke, crunching the can, dropping it in my bowl. So did I. Life could be this simple, for some people. Sleep, work, eat, drink. Repeat. I wish it *was* enough for me, but it never had been – and now, it never would be.

We cleared up and Amy went to bed, pausing to hug me so tightly I swear I heard a rib crack. I checked in on her a few minutes later and she was fast asleep, curled into a foetal position, the alcohol and fatigue sending her under without a moment's pause. She looked small in the king-sized bed, the bed she should be sharing with her husband, Rob. Except Rob had cheated on her and been booted out six months ago. She'd decided to keep the house, paying the mortgage on her own. Four bedrooms wasn't so lonely, she said, not now she had her favourite sister coming to stay. Rob was lucky I hadn't been around when he'd cheated. The blood would have been tough to wash out of these thick woollen carpets.

I lay in bed and prepared myself for the opposite of sleep. If I managed to doze off without the tablets, it would be interrupted, sweaty, restless. I used the techniques the shrink gave me – visualization, distraction – but I couldn't make any of the images stick.

I tried to imagine my next job, standing at the bow of the huge yacht, watching the hull cut through the limitless ocean, the stern waves betraying our passage, hearing the low throb of the engines propelling us along, observing the bustle of the crew keeping it all running in perfect harmony. All those things I was so familiar with, yet each of them conjuring waves of anxiety.

I pictured the lavish expanse of polished decks and soft furnishings, the yacht wrapping its protective luxuries around me. The alien glamour of a billionaire's plaything, beckoning me on board, welcoming me into their world.

I tried to picture the crew. Imaginary faces, imaginary

personalities. The people I'd be spending the next couple of weeks with.

But that was a mistake. Because then the real faces started to appear – the one I couldn't shake. The one that kept me awake every night, and had done since I'd been discharged three months ago.

2

The Southampton dockside was busy, the lunch crowds descending to the waterfront cafes and bars, fighting for the best tables, the clearest views of the water and the various motor craft packed in like sardines along the pontoon. I reckoned the average cost of the smaller motor yachts came in at around £500k, the larger ones topping £5 million. But that was still small fry compared to the *Escape*. Mitch assured me that once I reached Palma, the wealth would hit a different level. I took his word for it.

I was the last to arrive, though rigidly on time. Mitch had booked a table at one of the better restaurants near his office, a private booth overlooking the water, with a glass shield which did an impressive job of dampening the noise. The meeting would only take twenty minutes, he said, but appearances were important, and I had to be there. The captain and the owner's rep were both still in the UK and wanted to see us before flying out to Palma. Mitch had told me to smile and not talk. I told him what he could do with that advice.

I approached our table. Mitch gave me a wink before introducing me to the two men already seated.

'Sarah. This is your skipper, Greg Mayer,' he said, indicating the man to his left.

That ruled out the 'dashing captain', Amy's words

flashing to the fore. Greg was maybe fifty, with a receding hairline, a red nose and a body that hadn't seen a treadmill in a few decades. I probably wouldn't be looking to bunk up with him. Still, at least his smile was genuine.

'And Jason Chen,' said Mitch, indicating to his right, 'is a VP in our client's company. He'll also be on board.'

Jason's smile was reserved, unable to hide his surprise. He looked me up and down with the sort of disdain I'd grown used to as a female soldier, pausing in all the wrong places, as if I'd struggle to fight off a period, let alone a heavily armed aggressor. Yes, Jason, soldiers have tits, too. These are mine. Fuck you.

I smiled. 'Pleasure to meet you both,' I said.

Jason cleared his throat. 'And you're . . . um?'

His accent was clipped, American, coastal. I reckoned New York.

'Sarah French. Ex-Royal Marines,' I said. 'Served for five years, in Afghanistan twice, plus various places I can't tell you about.'

'Oh, right. Well . . .'

'I nearly shot this guy once,' I added, pointing at Mitch. 'Because he looked at me the wrong way. Like I didn't belong there.'

Mitch snorted, biting down on his laughter, looking as though his cheeks might explode. He threw me a pleading look.

Jason narrowed his eyes. I'd made my first friend on the crew. Great.

But a sideways glance at Greg showed the captain was equally amused. I'd misjudged his appearance, a bad habit of mine, but the man seemed the polar opposite to Jason.

He stood, placing his napkin to one side, and extended his hand, looking me squarely in the face.

'Pleasure to meet you, Sarah,' he said, his handshake firm, but lacking the squeezing insecurity of a man who had something to prove. 'I've only sailed with a security detail twice before, and neither were as qualified nor experienced as you.'

'That's what sets us apart,' said Mitch, obviously anxious to keep things friendly. Jason represented a valuable client. He wanted to make sure I didn't piss him off too much before we sailed.

'And it's why we cost twice as much,' added Mitch, with a beaming smile at Jason, who scowled, turning back to the table, and the array of paperwork covering it.

Greg was still grinning. 'I'd love to hear some stories, Sarah,' he said, 'perhaps when we're under way. I've always been merchant, private, never military, though I've sailed close to a fair few warships in my time. Too close, on occasion.'

'We'll swap stories,' I said, nodding. I'd checked Greg off as a good guy. I could see the wisdom of a few decades at sea behind his eyes. We'd get on just fine.

'Where in Germany are you from?' I said, trying to place his accent.

He smiled. 'I was born in the UK,' he said, 'but my parents are from Munich. I grew up there.'

'And you came back?'

'I go where the work is,' he said, laughing.

'Down to business?' said Jason, looking impatient.

We ordered drinks and huddled over the schematics of

the yacht. It was even more impressive when displayed in blueprinted detail.

Jason gave us some limited detail on the client – bar anything that could identify him or her – and a briefing on the crew. Greg was recruiting a core team who would meet us dockside in Palma. He paused before describing the *Escape*.

Three thousand tonnes, three hundred feet long, forty-five feet wide. Bigger than plenty of naval craft I'd been on – and I suspected a tad more comfortable, if the cabin layout was anything to go by. Six decks in all, with a central spiral staircase connecting them, as well as fore and aft stairwells and lifts. In accommodation terms, that meant six guest suites in addition to the owner's vast cabin, covering a deck of its own including stateroom and office, plus a further ten crew cabins.

'Jesus,' I said. 'It's a floating hotel.' I glanced out at the boats in this marina. They were caravans in comparison.

'A private one,' said Mitch.

'It's better than a hotel,' said Jason. 'It's a palace. We've got everything. Indoor and outdoor hot tubs, sauna and steam rooms, a massage room, a sky lounge, a cinema, a beach club, a playroom, four bars, two dining rooms, a library and an art gallery. All of it wherever we want in the world.' Jason reeled it all off, looking very pleased with himself.

'Infirmary?' I asked.

'Of course.'

'You didn't mention it.'

Jason huffed. 'I didn't mention the laundry either.'

'Oh. Has it got an engine room?'

Jason's smile thinned.

'Somewhere to keep the jet skis? I read the brochure.'

'We'll give you the full tour before we depart,' said Greg, 'today is to check what, other than Sarah, we need on board.'

'Why am I on board?' I said, ignoring the polite daggers from Mitch. 'I mean, this is all lovely, but passage from Palma to the Caribbean is all blue water sailing, friendly states.'

'Insurance,' said Jason, cutting in front of Mitch, who looked poised to answer. 'They insisted on it.'

I looked for more, raising my eyebrows at Jason.

'The times we live in,' he offered. 'You never know.'

'Never know what?' I said, glancing at Mitch. 'Because if —'

'Our company gives owners the peace of mind,' said Mitch, 'that should *anything* at all happen, we'll protect their substantial investment — and the crew on board — from harm. It's what my business is built on. The one you work for, Sarah.' Mitch's voice was gruff; his eyes still sparkled but his expression was a little strained.

I tried to wind it in a bit. *This is what you do, Sarah.* I heard my ex-CO's voice in my head: *You push it a little too far, masking your insecurities by attacking.* He was right. I should be able to deal with people like Jason without getting so wound up.

'Gotcha, boss,' I said, taking a breath. 'So . . .'

'We have a range of lethal and non-lethal deterrents that we can deploy,' said Mitch. 'I have a list of my recommendations here . . .' He rummaged around in his open briefcase, producing several copies of a spreadsheet, handing them to Greg and Jason. 'I already have suppliers in Spain for everything – these items can be on board in less than twenty-four hours.'

I half listened as Mitch described what we had, my attention drifting, staring out past the glass and the passers-by and the small boats bobbing restlessly in their moorings. I reminded myself that the grey water of this harbour would soon be replaced with the aquamarine of the Mediterranean, the British clouds replaced with the blue skies of warmer latitudes, the city smog replaced with pure ocean air.

But none of it helped. I couldn't dislodge the rock in my gut, soothe the ripples of guilt, the knowledge that I deserved none of it.

'Fine,' said Jason, his voice bringing my attention back to the discussion around the table. 'This meets the brief. I'll call the insurers this afternoon. I think we're done.'

He scrawled his signature at the bottom, and on another two sheets of paper that Mitch produced. Turning to me, he smiled. 'We depart Wednesday. See you in Majorca, Sarah.'

I could see Mitch's shoulders relax. Contract signed.

And me signed up with it.

I hung around afterwards, walking through the car park towards Mitch's office. Jason drove off in a Maserati, Greg in a Ford Mondeo. It surprised me – skippers on this circuit tended to earn big bucks. You didn't let any old sailor take charge of a £200 million vessel, and the one you chose was compensated well.

'You still here?' Mitch loomed over me.

I nodded. 'Sorry,' I said.

'For what?'

'For being me,' I said. 'Jason just . . .'

'Jason's a complete arse,' said Mitch, 'as are a lot of my clients.' He shrugged. 'But . . .'

I winced. 'I know.'

'I'm trying to build this company,' he said. 'He's a VP of one of the biggest investment groups in Europe, he came to us at short notice, last minute, blank cheque – he could have gone anywhere. And this level of business . . . it's a small world. I want to grow our reputation as the best, with the best people, providing the best service.'

I shook my head. 'Then this was a mistake.'

'Bullshit,' he said. 'Look at me.'

I turned away, feeling the nerves biting, the blood rising.

'*Look* at me, Sarah,' he said.

I turned back.

'You don't have to grovel, serve, laugh at his jokes,' said Mitch. 'Hell, you don't have to be *nice* to anyone. But you can't be nasty. OK?'

I swallowed. Coming across as nasty was the last thing I ever wanted. Despite my career path, I was never the sort to go looking for fights. I just can't help my tongue sometimes.

I could jack it all in, let Mitch down, crawl back home and rethink my employment prospects, or I could suck it up and give it a chance.

I nodded. 'I'll try.'

Mitch examined me for a few moments before his beaming smile returned.

'Of course you will,' he said, slapping me on the shoulder with such force I staggered to the left, bracing myself against the doorframe. He still didn't know his own strength, despite years of his fellow soldiers telling him not to hit them so hard.

'To address your earlier concern,' he said, his smile fading. 'The biggest risk you face is boredom. But what you will have is time. Time to think, to heal, to get over what happened. That's what you wanted, so it's what I'm giving you — and paying you handsomely for it.' He handed me an envelope.

I opened it and stared at the payslip inside, frowning. 'This is —'

'Your fee.'

'This is *way* more —'

'You're way more capable than most, plus it's all up front. Bank it, spend it, whatever. Just know you're worth it, OK?'

I swallowed an uncomfortable lump in my throat. This type of kindness was rare, in my experience. Mitch was too good for me. This job was too good for me.

'Now scoot,' he said. 'You're making the place look untidy. I've emailed your flight details to you. Wednesday first thing. Don't miss it.'

I folded and placed the envelope in my pocket, giving Mitch a tight smile before walking away. I managed to keep the shakes at bay until I reached the car.

3

My crack-of-dawn flight to Palma departed twenty-three minutes late, packed full of unbearably cheerful holiday-makers. I hunkered down in the window seat, thinking I'd been on military transport planes that were less raucous. The two hours dragged, but there were no further delays and I pushed my way through to baggage reclaim as soon as we landed, grabbing my trusty bergen off the conveyor belt and heading towards the exit.

As the glass doors parted, the island humidity embraced me like a suffocating blanket. The Spanish sun was dazzling, intense, the sky a deep blue, drenched with colour. It was already pushing thirty degrees, and by the sweat forming on the back of my neck, I reckoned near one hundred per cent humidity. I paused, sucking in a few deep breaths, thinking how I couldn't wait to get out on the water.

I checked my watch, approaching the first taxi in the queue.

'Club de Mar Mallorca, *por favor*,' I said, referring to the name of the private marina where the *Escape* was berthed.

The taxi driver raised his eyebrows, nodding, impressed, but not without a flash of confusion as he looked me up and down, watching me shove my tatty backpack on to the seat. I glanced down at my vest, already dark in patches, sticking to my skin. My appearance obviously didn't tally with the normal fares who would be heading to such an exclusive marina.

'Crew,' I said.

His confusion disappeared, replaced with understanding, perhaps even a flicker of sympathy.

The short trip through Palma city centre, the so-called 'Pearl of the Mediterranean', blurred as I felt the nerves bite. I focused on my breathing, suppressing the nagging doubt that lodged just below my chest, where it sniped and grumbled at me. I was doing the right thing. I just needed to convince myself of it.

'Air conditioning?' I asked, waving my hands at my face.

The driver nodded, played with the controls.

'*Gracias.*' I felt a waft of mildly cooler air as we bounced along, past the old town, its streets heaving with sunburned visitors and working locals.

The tourist traffic was heavy, refusing to thin out even as we left the market town behind and approached the sprawling marinas and shipyards that lined the west side of the bay. But soon, the crowded pedestrian streets disappeared and my view became dominated by a swathe of private yachts of every shape, size and colour. If the marina near Mitch's office had a few million pounds' worth of craft in it, it was loose change compared to this lot.

I spied small sailing vessels at first – forty-foot single hulls and catamarans, old and new, packed in tightly, masts swaying, halyards clanking by the thousand. As we continued, the masts disappeared and rows of motor yachts came into view, squat and gleaming in the morning sun, fast, sleek, the daytime playthings of millionaires – but so far, predictable.

That was, until I looked past them, to the outer jetties, to the berths that could accommodate craft of several hundred feet in length. And there, gleaming hulks of metal rose above the rest. Monuments of maritime design forged with unlimited budgets. The superyachts, the mega-yachts. The property of the one per cent of the one per cent.

In amongst them was the *Escape*. My home for the next two weeks, give or take.

The taxi slowed, pulling up in front of a tree-lined entrance to the marina, security gates barring the road.

'Club de Mar Mallorca,' he said, pointing. '*A través de allí.*'

Through there.

'*Gracias,*' I said, tapping my credit card on the payment terminal, grabbing my bag, stepping into the heat.

I approached the gate, waving my passport at the reception window of a small guard box. The woman inside checked my name lazily against a clipboard, nodded, waved me through.

I checked my directions. Fourth pier along, the furthest from the entrance. The private club buildings were quiet at this time in the morning, restricted, exclusive. A man and woman passed me, coming from the direction of the jetty, arms linked, the gold on their necks and wrists contrasting perfectly with their deep tans, dressed in white linen that perfectly hugged their expensive bodies. I tried not to stare as they entered one of the exclusive waterfront cafes.

I kept going, past the buildings and on to the jetty walkways, staring out at the bay, again feeling the nerves teetering in my chest and throat, forcing them down.

To my left a small pilot boat trundled across the harbour, coming close to the pier, engine belching smoke into the clear air. It contrasted with the clean lines of the huge motor yachts; grubby and industrial, distinctly out of place. A group of men stood on the deck, busily packing holdalls and boxes. They looked like seasoned sailors, wearing black offshore jackets and trousers, and heavy boots. Tall, with thick beards, weathered faces. Fishermen? Coastguard? No, their gear looked too new, neat and expensive. Their appearance caused a pang of memory, of military preparation before setting off on a mission, the mental 'get your shit together' strength I'd worked so hard to perfect. Could I conjure it again?

One of the men saw me looking, meeting my eye, holding it for a moment before turning to the man next to him, speaking into his ear. The second man gave me a quick glance before ducking away as the boat rumbled off and out of sight.

Mitch's photos hadn't done the *Escape* justice. It was far better in real life.

At the end of the jetty, backed against the largest berth in the marina, was the gleaming expanse of the three-hundred-foot status symbol.

As long as a Premier League football pitch, or the length of Big Ben tower, if you were to topple it, the sleek hull of the enormous yacht appeared to be skimming the water's surface, perpetually in motion, the designers having created an optical illusion, a vision that stopped most people in their tracks for a second look. Which was exactly the purpose of such creations – to make people look at you.

The glare of the hull forced me to squint, nudging my glasses back down, the polarizing lenses causing the mirrored windows on the upper decks to glimmer with a rainbow tint.

It was bigger in real life, too. I'd sailed on plenty of huge ships, but they were big for a purpose – war machines designed to circumnavigate the globe, remaining self-sufficient in times of conflict. They cost billions – but that was OK, because they were necessary.

Yachts such as the *Escape* were excessive. Nobody *needed* one of these. It was pure want and greed – by far the biggest toy I'd ever seen.

Entrance was via a passerelle from the jetty on to the main deck at the stern, and I could already see several people moving around, stowing equipment, pushing boxes to each side, stacking them with care. On the lower deck I spied a couple of jet skis under covers, ready to be moved into the garage – the rear storage area which housed the tenders and other watercraft: surfboards, diving equipment and whatever toys the owner had requested. A pair of water scooters were lashed to each other – small, hand-held propulsion units that could pull a swimmer through the water at a fair rate. We used them extensively in the Marines for rapid underwater approaches or egress. The bright yellow ones on the *Escape* would be used for far more leisurely activities – lazy snorkelling and scuba diving. Not much chance to play with them on an Atlantic crossing, but they were part of the delivery.

Looking up, I noticed a flashing from the bridge deck – interior lighting being switched on and off. It was too early for a party, so I assumed perhaps an electrical test following the refurbishment. Mitch had mentioned something about the work being incomplete, but we were leaving regardless, the owner impatient and demanding to get his yacht to the Caribbean as soon as possible. 'What the owner wants, they get,' Mitch had said, 'and besides, it's all the same to us. If the sauna doesn't work, you'll survive.'

I checked my watch. Despite the delayed flight I was bang on time. Time to go and make friends. I grabbed my bergen. The rest of the security systems were already on board. Mitch had texted me the thumbs up earlier that day, and told me to call him from the hot tub once we were under way. I'd responded with the middle-finger emoji.

'Sarah French?'

The voice belonged to a woman perhaps ten, fifteen years my senior. Home Counties accent, she was uniformed – first mate, according to her epaulettes – with an open, friendly face. Her dark hair was tied back, her posture relaxed but professional. As a woman of rank, she had my immediate attention.

I nodded. 'That's me,' I said, giving what I hoped was my most genuine and least threatening smile.

'Karis,' she said, matching my smile, stepping on to the passerelle, offering to help me across.

'Thanks,' I said.

29

'This is yours,' she said as I stepped on to the deck, handing me a hard, locked case. 'I was told to hand it over to you on arrival – you'll lock it in your cabin?'

I took the small but heavy case from her. It contained my firearms – a Glock 22 pistol and a Swiss-made APC9K sub-machine gun, both lightweight and reliable, approved by Mitch's suppliers and cleared by police and port security last night. The case would be chained to my bunk and locked until we docked in Antigua, when I'd need to declare it to Customs and offload to a partner company, who would arrange shipping back to Europe.

It was nothing but a box-ticking exercise, but that was the job – I needed to keep reminding myself.

Karis was looking me up and down while trying not to. She bit her lower lip. 'I think it's awesome.'

'What?'

'Having you on board,' she said. 'A woman who's tougher than all of the male crew put together.' She laughed.

'Well, I . . .' I frowned.

'I mean that in the professional sense,' she said. 'When they said security, I thought they meant another tough-guy deckhand armed with a taser and an ego problem.'

'Oh.' I shrugged, glancing at the case. 'Well . . . we do have tasers, but better things, too.'

She smiled.

'I *do* have an ego, though.'

'Good. And the experience to back it up,' she said. 'Greg told me about you. He was impressed. Reckons you're gonna trade stories and give him the inside info on all of your military operations.'

'He seems like a nice guy.'

'He is,' said Karis.

I saw her eyes sparkle as she said it, her thoughts drifting for a split second. So at least somebody was bunking in with Greg. Or wanted to. Not the best way to run a ship, but who was I to judge?

'I'll take you down to the crew cabins,' continued Karis, 'show you where to stow your gear, then I'll get somebody to give you a tour. I would do it myself but I'm wanted on the bridge – Greg is already complaining that things aren't as he wants them.'

'Skipper's prerogative,' I said.

'Indeed.'

We weaved our way across the deck – an immaculate wooden slatted floor running almost the full width of the yacht, some forty feet, sheltered by the overhang of the owner's deck above. A collection of outdoor chairs and loungers were stacked along the port side, the rest of the space was given over to loading – I saw boxes of perishable and canned food, several cases of wine and beer, along with a stack of huge plastic crates cable-tied at the top.

We headed inside, stepping over the threshold on to polished hardwood.

'This is the main deck lounge,' said Karis, pausing to let our eyes adjust, 'and dining area through there.'

I took it all in, managing to stop the string of expletives jumping from my brain to my tongue. 'It's . . .'

'Impressive?' said Karis. 'That it is.'

The similarity with any Navy ships I'd sailed on ended here. I'd walked into a room that would pass as a luxury lounge in a five-star hotel. The hardwood flooring soon gave way to thick pile carpet; there was a row of three cut-glass tables surrounded by stitched-leather sofas, cavernous brown Chesterfield armchairs and chaises longues designed to fit the room. The ceiling was high, painted white, but stepped towards the centre, giving the illusion of more space. Dozens of spotlights provided a warm glow, fading as they neared the windows – also oversized, with delicate shutters. I felt the cool blast of the air conditioning, the vents hidden, the air filtered and fragrant.

A grand piano stood to my left, the stool intricately carved. Every surface was peppered with abstract pieces of art, cut flowers and orchids – their colours matching the throw cushions. Bright flashes of colour were framed on the walls, enhanced by deep-purple crystal panels, along with long mirrors placed at strategic intervals, creating the illusion of even more space.

'Are those walls made of –'

'Amethyst, yes,' said Karis. 'They're back-lit. I think they cost around a quarter of a million pounds each.'

I shook my head, keeping my lips sealed.

Beyond the lounge was the dining area – more wood, high-backed chairs around a fourteen-seater table, with a retro cocktail bar to the left. Not one but two glittering chandeliers hung above the long table. The colour scheme shifted, the bold colours of the lounge giving way to creams and browns. They probably had names like Sussex Cream and Amalfi White – I imagined the designers laying out colour charts in the same way Amy had done when she decorated her house. I remember her showing me over a Zoom call – *No, it's not just paint, Sarah, interior design is what normal people do.* I'd feigned interest. Amy had laughed and said she'd paint the bathroom in Angry Sarah Pink.

At the end of the dining room was a set of double doors leading to the central foyer and spiral staircase.

'Is it all like this?' I asked Karis. It was the sheer scale that shocked me – the room was cavernous, and this was only one half of one deck.

'No,' she said. 'It gets better. The private rooms and owner's stateroom are another level.'

'F—' I bit it off in time.

Karis laughed. 'I know, right?' she said. 'You get used to it, although the effect never entirely wears off.'

I wanted to say it was grotesque, an insult to the 99 per cent, a waste of money and natural resources that could be used for far better things, and yet, part of me wanted to bask in it, jump on the sofas, roll around on a carpet that cost more than my annual salary. Perhaps dance on the table, lean on the bar, put some fingerprint smudges on the crystal. I could see why Mitch was so enthralled when he first showed me the pictures. I couldn't deny it. Being a billionaire looked like fun.

'It's *nice*,' I summed up, twisting my face as I said it.

Karis nodded with a shrewd smile. 'Nice. It's nice.'

She led me to the corner stairwell on the port side – there was one on each side, repeated at the front of the yacht. These, combined with a central spiral staircase, gave multiple routes through the yacht – essential for crew who needed to move around almost 25,000 square feet of interior space without disturbing the guests.

We headed down.

The smell of paint and new furnishings was even

33

stronger on the lower deck, hot too, as the air-conditioned luxury gave way to naturally ventilated passageways. As I jumped off the last step, I detected a hint of motion, the yacht shifting in its moorings. At sea it would be stable, designed for comfort as much as speed, although I suspected a decent Atlantic swell would still spill some drinks on that posh dining table.

'Engine room through there,' said Karis, walking a narrow corridor. 'Then we've got laundry and infirmary, steps down to the tank deck, engineering – generators, electricals, monitoring.' She pointed to another stairwell.

We passed through a thick bulkhead, well soundproofed to keep the engine noise from the cabins, emerging at the bottom of the spiral staircase.

'We've got the six guest suites here,' she said, pointing at the doors leading from the lower foyer. 'Then the cinema and spa, and further forward are the crew cabins.'

I nodded.

'All the guest suites except one are empty for this trip, but we're not allowed to use them.'

'Who's the lucky one?'

'A guy called Jason, the owner's representative, or something. He gets the luxury of a guest cabin and full service, which at least gives the stewards something to do.' She didn't look too impressed. 'However, we *can* use the cinema if Jack can get it to work.'

'Jack?'

'Jack Foster, chief engineer. Great guy. Australian super nerd. Keeps himself to himself, unless you want to talk about politics, then he'll chew your ear off.'

'No thanks.'

'That's what we all tell him.'

Karis took me through another set of doors, the decor changing to functional, clean, unfussy. The central corridor narrowed and the lighting dimmed, small doors leading right and left. I detected more movement; my inner ear was getting used to stepping off land. I'd always been sensitive to motion, but never sick with it – which turned out to be a rather big asset in my line of work.

Out of one of the crew cabins stepped a tall man with bleached-blond hair and a bronzed face. He turned towards us, smiling, revealing teeth so white I thought I might need my sunglasses again. To match his teeth he wore a white polo T-shirt and chino shorts, both a size too small. I couldn't help the image of Barbie's boyfriend Ken springing to mind – I remembered the doll well from my childhood because Amy used to steal him from me. I'd never seen one in real life.

'Hi, Dan,' said Karis. 'This is Sarah, our security guard.'

We shook hands. He tried to squeeze the life out of mine. I didn't let him. His smile didn't waver as he puffed his chest out.

'Dan's the chief steward,' said Karis. 'He takes care of the interior of the *Escape*, and, when we have guests, ensures they get everything they need.'

Dan wiggled his eyebrows. '*Everything*,' he said. 'You wouldn't believe how neglected some of the rich totty is. But don't worry, I take care of them.'

Why he thought I'd find that funny was beyond me. His voice was public-school posh, like some of the officers I was used to, but without the gravitas. He made a point of looking at my body as he spoke.

Karis snorted, 'You wish, Dan!' But I could tell she was a little embarrassed.

Dan kept his eyes on me, grin fixed, blocking the corridor, legs wide apart. I could tell his alpha-male brain was in overdrive already, probably struggling with seeing someone who also had muscles on show.

'Army, huh?' he said.

'Nope, Navy,' I replied. 'Royal Marines.'

He shrugged. 'Whatever. I guess the *Escape* is nicer than anything you would have been on? Proper beds, hot running water, soft furnishings?' He laughed. 'It'll be a nice change for you?'

I smiled for as long as I could, clenching my jaw until I was worried I'd crack a tooth.

'You're right,' I said. 'Everything looks softer here.'

He nodded, giving me a slow blink.

'Even the men,' I added.

Dan frowned, his face twisting into a brief scowl, which he hid well. He paused for a second, perhaps thinking of a suitable retort, before clearing his throat.

'Nice to meet you, Sarah,' he said, 'I'm sure you'll fit in well.' He turned and headed away from us. I heard a door slam at the end of the corridor as he exited the crew quarters.

Karis laughed. 'Told you this would be awesome. That put him in his place.'

It did. But I wished I hadn't snapped quite so readily. Dan fancied himself, but I could have let him be. He *was* pretty – and, no doubt, harmless. Plus talking about my squad triggered a whole raft of dangerous memories, always eager to bubble up and ruin my day. I forced them back down.

'I'll apologize later,' I said.

'To Dan?' said Karis. 'No you won't. He'll get over it, and he'll try to sleep with you, anyway. He does with every young female on board.'

I grunted. 'I hope, for his sake, he doesn't.'

Karis led me further along the corridor. 'This is you,' she said, pushing open one of the doors, letting me go first.

I smiled as I entered. The cabin must have been ten feet by six, the size of a small single bedroom. Two bunks on one wall, another doorway through to a small en-suite containing toilet, basin and over-shower. Sunk into one wall was a wardrobe with drawers. On the other, a single porthole above the water level. The room was finished with an eye-watering smell of paint. The contrast between the crew quarters and the luxury elsewhere was extreme, and the tales I'd heard – of yachting crew getting sick from lack of fresh air and the ultra-high temperatures on board – seemed to ring true.

'At least you get it to yourself,' said Karis, looking apologetic. 'Most of us share. You can use one of the bunks for your bag.'

The size of the room didn't bother me in the least. As Dan had eloquently pointed out, I was used to it, although it was hard to understand why the designers couldn't have afforded a little more room for the crew. Sharing a room this small with your life partner would be difficult. With a relative stranger it was a recipe for stress and discontent.

Karis's radio hissed with static.

'*Karis? Where are you?*' A deep male voice.

Karis tapped the radio microphone pinned to the collar of her shirt. 'What is it, Luan?'

'*You're not going to like this.*' The voice sounded tentative, strained.

'What?' Karis frowned, glanced at me.

'*We have a guest. Says she's here to stay. You'd better come up.*'

4

'What do you mean, Luan?' said Karis, her frown deepening. 'What guest? Who?'

'*A Miss Harriet DeWitt-Fendley*,' came Luan's voice. '*Says she's the owner's niece.*'

Karis mouthed the word 'shit' at me.

'What does she want?'

'*By the look of her luggage, a holiday. Says she's coming with us, taking the owner's stateroom.*'

'Is she with you now?'

'*No. She's already gone up, put in a drinks order and slammed the door to the bedroom. I'm staring at her suitcases.*'

'Does Greg know?'

'*Not yet. I thought you'd like to tell him.*'

Karis closed her eyes for a few seconds. 'Thanks. I'm heading to the bridge.' The radio bleeped off.

'Trouble?' I said.

'Who knows?' said Karis. 'But if anything else can go wrong on this yacht, it bloody well will.'

I looked quizzically at her, but she shook her head.

'I'll try to send somebody for that tour,' she said, 'but feel free to have a wander around on your own. I think we all trust you won't get into any mischief.'

I thanked her as she left, seeing the strain in her eyes, hoping she wasn't in for a hard day. I liked Karis – she seemed ballsy and straight-talking. I doubted I could help with this particular issue, but I'd offer anyway.

The first thing I did was lock away the firearms case. A pair of armoured cable locks secured it underneath the lower bunk. I shoved it out of sight and heaved my bergen on to the bunk.

My luggage was modest for the twelve days I'd be away. Amy had insisted I pack a selection of 'appropriate' summer clothing, a lot of it from her wardrobe, along with my more functional items. I tried to emphasize to Amy just how cold it might be mid-Atlantic, but she didn't listen. The bikini and flip-flops would stay in the bag, as would the summer hat. I grabbed a black cap and slipped it on, pulling my ponytail through the back.

I tucked my washbag against the shelf under the vanity mirror. It had a zipped compartment inside. I'd checked it before I left home, but pulled it open now, poking my fingers inside, feeling for the small blister pack of Zopiclone. Two should knock me out for eight hours straight – at least, that's what the doc told me. He also said prolonged use might reduce their effectiveness, and no, that didn't mean I could double the dose. I zipped it shut, hoping it would remain that way.

Last thing out was a thick ring-binder holding the yacht's security assessment and notes from Mitch. I'd read through it once, but all it did was confirm my original conclusion – my presence here was a box-ticking exercise from some over-zealous insurance company. I probably *could* lie around in a bikini for the duration and it would make no difference to anything. I wondered what I would do to pass the time.

Think, Mitch had told me. *Reflect. Perhaps forgive yourself for something that wasn't your fault.*

If only it was that easy.

I stepped back into the corridor, pulling the door shut behind me. It closed, the latch clicking. I felt a cool draught, and at the same time the lights flickered, then switched off. Must be the engineer, Jack, tinkering around again. I paused, letting my eyes adjust to the temporary darkness, but as I did so, I felt the familiar tightening in my chest, the onset of an attack. They were still regular, triggered by the most unlikely of events, but often quite mundane. I could feel it, taste it, the surge of memory, looking for a way in, my subconscious using the lighting as a distraction, a connection.

The psych said it was normal, understandable. It would take time. It was just my brain's way of dealing with the trauma.

But that explanation, rational though it was, didn't stop it.

I pushed my back against the wall, feeling the space close in, the air squeezing from my lungs. My vision tunnelled and the interior of the *Escape* faded.

I breathed. Four in, hold, four out, hold. Square breathing. Control the physical and your mind will follow. Slow your heart rate, Sarah, you can do it.

I slumped to the floor, my back against the wall.

A shadow in the darkness.

Four in, hold, four out, hold.

He came out of nowhere.

My chest screamed at me. My ears popped.

Except he didn't. Your room. Your fault.

Gunshots in the dark. A scream. My scream.

I turned my head, left and right, shaking myself back from the brink.

Four in, hold, four out, hold.

My vision flashed. Repeating. The memory faded as quickly as it had started. The narrow corridor of the *Escape*'s crew quarters blinked at me, the lights coming back on – and with them, my senses.

I stared at the opposite wall, waiting for my heart rate to settle – which it always did, in rapid fashion – before pulling myself upright.

I tugged my phone out of my pocket. Counted to five, then dialled.

'*Sarah. How . . . are you OK?*'

I shook my head, sucking in a long breath, letting it out slowly, quietly.

'No, Mitch,' I said. 'This was a mistake. I'm not ready.'

'*Sarah –*'

'I can't.'

'*You can.*'

'You don't know . . .' Shit. He didn't know what? What I was going through?

'*I do, Sarah,*' he said, reading my mind. '*Your burden is my burden. But quitting isn't going to help it.*'

'I'm not quitting. I'm just . . .'

'*Delaying. We've been through this. Until when? This job is the best way to get your head together, and you know it. It gives you a taste of the familiar, a sense of purpose, all wrapped in cotton wool, billionaire-style.*'

I was still shaking my head. 'I appreciate what you're doing, but –'

'*But nothing.*'

'I'm not —'

'*What would Kay tell you to do?*'

The name hit me like a bullet. My throat constricted. Fuck. How dare he? The anger rose, my heart leaping back into action. That was low . . . wasn't it? Shit, I didn't even know. What *would* Kay tell me? Thanks for fucking everything up? Thanks for ending it in such a perfect mess? Thanks for going on without me, cruising off in some megapimp's boat?

No. Because Kay didn't have a mean bone in his body. He'd tell me to do whatever it took. He'd tell me to save myself, one step at a time.

Mitch was right. I needed to do this.

'You're an asshole,' I said.

'*It's why you like me.*'

I banged the back of my head against the wall, then again. A third time for luck.

'I'm not calling you from the hot tub,' I said.

I heard him laughing as I hung up.

5

The clock was ticking, one hour until we departed. I didn't wait for the guided tour, heading forward until I found one of the stairwells, then upwards for some fresh air, wondering what Karis had meant by things going wrong. I tried to keep my bearings as I walked, but it was easy to get lost on a new ship, particularly one as large as this. I wouldn't sweat it. It wasn't as if I had my CO screaming in my face or a practice drill thumping in my eardrums.

I emerged on the main deck near the kitchen. The surrounding bar and serving area were decorated in white marble with an Art Deco theme. I smelled citrus and something warmer – perhaps the walls were perfumed?

Despite my initial reaction to the extravagance of the yacht, I couldn't deny it helped lift my mood. Being surrounded by so much luxury stimulated a primitive part of my brain, creating a comforting sense of security and self-importance. I was sure that was the idea, the designers knowing what they were doing when they made their first brush stroke on the blank canvas. The location didn't hurt, either. The intensity of the Spanish sun was kicking my mood up a level, the bright blues and greens bathing my eyes in dazzling comfort.

I poked my head around the corner, only to find a couple of new faces.

The first, a woman in dress whites – presumably a

stewardess – was leaning over the serving counter into the kitchen. She looked young, perhaps early twenties, with pale skin, neat blonde bob and a delicate body, her attention absorbed by the chef who was unpacking crates of food and storing it away in two stainless-steel fridge-freezers. I saw several kilos of vacuum-wrapped steaks, countless chicken breasts and legs, lumps of other unidentifiable meats shimmering with frost. The smell of fresh fish wafted out from polystyrene cartons. Whole cheeses were stacked in the corner, plus jars of olives and pickled veg. The sight of it all made my stomach rumble, and I regretted skipping breakfast, a habit of mine before setting off on a trip – keep the butterflies from having anything to churn around.

We definitely wouldn't starve.

The chef looked a little older than her, a stocky black guy with thick stubble. Already in his chef's tunic, he looked like he'd been working for hours, sweat glistening on his forehead. The stewardess was distracting him, but he seemed to welcome it, his eyes sparkling when he addressed her, his body language awkward, flirty but reserved. She mirrored his movements, leaning in at the right times, flicking her hair, subconsciously playing through all of those primal reactions we're all slaves to under the same circumstances.

I couldn't help but smile as I watched the two of them, remembering how Kay and I used to behave. A glance here, a cheeky smile there, flirtatious comments filled with innuendo. It all created such wonderful energy, leaving each of us with a bounce in our step as we faced our separate days.

My chest tightened a little. A reminder. I drifted, unaware the conversation had stopped and they were both staring at me.

'Sarah?' The young woman waved in my direction.

I headed towards them, letting the stairwell door slam behind me. I shook my head, dispersing the memories. 'Yes,' I said. 'That's me.'

'I'm Lily,' said the young woman, stepping forward and embracing me. It was unexpected – I was used to grunts, thumps and playful insults from my colleagues, not hugs. She kissed both of my cheeks and stood back; her pale blue eyes were full of warmth. 'Sorry,' she said, 'I was on my way to fetch you. Karis asked me to give you a tour. I got, erm –'

'Distracted,' said the chef. 'My fault. Name's Elijah.' He leaned over so I could shake his hand. A more familiar gesture, at least. His palm was rough, chapped, hardworking, his accent deep and friendly, Jamaican, if I wasn't mistaken. He held my gaze as we shook.

'Good to meet you both,' I said.

Elijah nodded and returned to his unpacking, giving Lily a raised eyebrow as he moved across the kitchen.

'So . . .' said Lily. She fidgeted with her hands, picking her nails. 'Where do you want to start?'

I shrugged. 'You don't need to,' I said. 'I can find my own way around. Honestly. You can carry on doing whatever it is you . . .' I looked across to Elijah, but he kept his head down.

'Oh.' Lily's face fell, followed by her whole body language. 'Oh,' she repeated.

She looked like a scolded puppy.

Be nice, Sarah. Would it kill you?

'Wait,' I said, forcing my own smile to match hers, realizing it wasn't difficult. I had nothing to prove in front of Lily; there was no one trying to catch me out. 'I'd love a tour,' I said. 'I didn't want to put you out. That's all.'

Lily's face lifted. 'You're not,' she said. 'We're crew. You're one of us.'

Lily took off at a pace, her walking matching the speed of her talking, gesturing wildly at our surroundings, taking particular pains to describe how the layout of this particular yacht was classic Benetti – the Italian yacht builder who crafted the *Escape* – but with a modern twist. I didn't want to point out Karis had already shown me the main deck, so I just nodded, smiled and followed. She described some of the yacht's structure in reasonable depth – she clearly knew her stuff, although her enthusiasm seemed mainly for my benefit. I detected a hint of weariness; here was someone who'd shown plenty of people around, and now struggled to get excited herself about it.

It wasn't until we reached the stern and climbed up to the owner's deck that she stopped talking, pausing mid-stride as the sound of raised voices echoed from the nearest stairwell.

Two men in a heated argument, snapping at each other, the thud of their feet on the metal steps. The men stopped on our deck, still inside the stairwell. Lily and I remained on deck, out of sight.

'We leave now or I find somebody else.'

I recognized the voice: Jason Chen, the American, his arrogant tone easy to place.

'What? Don't be ridiculous. You can't.' Captain Greg Mayer's voice. He sounded angry, surprised.

'I can,' said Jason. 'Read your contract.'

'But you heard Jack,' protested Greg, 'he –'

'The *Escape* is *fine*,' said Jason, 'And your engineer can leave too, if he insists on making trouble for us.'

They fell silent. I glanced at Lily, who shook her head, putting her finger to her lips.

'It's not that simple,' said Greg, his voice rising in pitch. 'We can't just –'

'Greg, look . . .' Jason's voice again, firm, but calmer, conciliatory. 'We've been through this a hundred times. Stay or go. If you stay, I'm willing to make an improvement to our offer.'

More silence.

'I know we said thirty. How about we up it to fifty, if you meet the brief? No pissing around. No more complaining.'

I heard a sigh from Greg. Fifty what? It was common practice to tip the captain and crew after a trip. Is that what he meant? Jesus.

'You *insist*?' said Greg. 'Even though –'

'We leave today,' said Jason. 'Final offer, take it or leave it, Greg. You're pissing me off.'

Another deep sigh. Greg stepped out of the stairwell on to the deck, in plain sight, though he still hadn't seen Lily and me. He paced, head down.

'Fine,' he said, 'you win. But stay off the bridge until we're under way.'

I didn't hear a response from Jason, just the sound of footsteps retreating downwards. Greg waited a few seconds before punching the wall in front of him, uttering a string of expletives in German.

I opened the nearest door, and slammed it closed, shuffling my feet in the process. Greg froze, turned, suddenly aware we were watching him.

'Sarah,' he said, straightening up, adjusting his collar.

'Good to see you, Captain,' I said, thinking it best if he didn't know he'd been overheard. It was none of my business, whatever it was. 'Lily is showing me around.'

Greg nodded, his forehead creased, skin clammy, but a look of relief passed over his face. 'Good,' he said, giving the briefest of smiles to Lily. 'I'm headed to the bridge. Join me for departure?' He spun on his feet, beckoning me to follow.

'Sure,' I said, before turning to Lily. 'Thanks,' I said, noting how Greg had dismissed her without a word. 'It was kind of you to offer – the tour. We'll continue it later. Once we're under way?'

Lily nodded, giving me a shy smile before heading back towards the lower deck. Whatever energy she had summoned for me seemed to have been sapped by Greg's appearance. I paused for a second before following our captain.

'Ten minutes,' called Greg, announcing our entrance to the bridge. I noticed a sweat mark down the line of his back and could hear the wheeze in his chest. Whatever had transpired between him and Jason had visibly shaken the man.

I stepped in behind, casting my eyes around. The *Escape*'s bridge was modern, consisting of touchscreens and soft furnishings, surrounded by panoramic windows. Karis stood at the centre, near the wheel and throttles, tapping at one of the screens, talking into her radio.

'Any luck?' called Greg, directing his attention to the floor, underneath the cockpit console.

A small wiry man pushed himself up. He was barefoot, in black shorts and a white polo shirt with 'Engineer' written on the back. He scratched the top of his head and rubbed his eyes. Jack, I guessed. When he spoke, his Australian accent confirmed it.

'I can't work out why the autopilot is tripping the main board,' he said. 'But it's staying on at the moment.' He tapped one of the touchscreens and it came to life.

Greg shook his head. 'Fine,' he said.

Jack looked about to say something else to Greg, but apparently thought better of it. He turned to me, hand extended. 'Jack Foster,' he said with a smile. 'Greg mentioned you.'

I shook his hand. 'Sarah French. Protect and serve.' I gave him a faux salute.

He laughed and slapped me on the shoulder.

As he stepped back, I noticed an odour, a waft of something on his breath. It was immediately familiar; I'd witnessed the same thing on several soldiers. Alcoholism was easy to hide from some, but impossible from those who'd been there, flirted with it, wrestled themselves away just in time.

'We have a few teething troubles,' said Jack, indicating his previous position on the floor.

'Oh?'

'All of the redundant systems are offline for this trip – waiting on parts in Antigua, which means we only have one of each of the major systems – main controls and monitoring, GPS, radar, autopilot, everything. And now those are on the blink. The autopilot keeps switching itself off and taking half the systems with it.'

He said it with the excitable charm only a geek could pull off, but I was immediately on-guard. A chief engineer with an alcohol problem was a liability. He could screw anything up. Perhaps he already had. Back in the forces this would be a no-brainer – he'd sit it out until he got himself some help, willingly or not. But ... I had to remind myself this wasn't the forces. This was civilian life, the rules were different, the responsibility wasn't mine – protecting the crew didn't extend to this, did it?

'That sounds . . .'

'Nothing I can't handle,' he said, although his smile looked strained. 'A yacht like this runs on a collection of black-box computer systems – self-contained, not user serviceable. If we have an issue, we swap the whole unit out – GPS, radar, whatever – it's the modern way of doing things. But they're just a bunch of computers. They're fallible, and at least we have manual systems for the basics – our engines and the steering hydraulics.' He shrugged. 'But I doubt Greg wants to hand-steer us across the Atlantic,' he added. 'My advice was to stay put until it's fixed. I was overruled.'

He glanced again at Greg, who was in deep discussion with Karis.

'She stays,' Greg was saying. 'Jason confirmed with the boss. If the niece wants two weeks on board, she gets it.'

They were talking about the latecomer, Harriet.

Karis shook her head. 'Have you told Dan? He'll need to prep for full service for *two* people now. I get the impression she'll be more demanding than Jason.'

Greg nodded. 'She's a spoilt brat, by all accounts, going through some drama, insists she needs privacy. I don't want her on my ship, but I don't make the rules when it comes to the owner's family, OK?'

Or about our departure schedule, I thought, remembering Jason's words. Greg's influence as captain was rather less than I'd expect on a yacht this size.

Karis put her hands up in defeat. 'On your head be it,' she said, turning back to the cockpit. 'OK then. Everyone at their stations?'

She issued a series of instructions over the radio. I heard multiple voices responding – the bosun and deckhands would be fore and aft, taking in the mooring ropes, calling distances, keeping a close eye on the *Escape* as Karis manoeuvred it away from the dock.

A single loud blast from the horn signalled our departure. I felt the subtle sideways shift as the thrusters pushed us away, followed by a deep, almost inaudible rumble as Karis engaged the main engines, propelling us forward.

6

I tensed, gripping the handrail, looking over the stern of the lower deck at the white backwash churning away from us, disturbing the steely blues of the shallow water. I tasted the salt in the air, the fine spray cool on my face, seeping into every pore. Any departure was an emotional event for me, a momentary beat to reflect on the voyage ahead – into the unknown, and a chance to reflect on what was left behind. Routine, perhaps, for many, yet each voyage was different, the ocean never offering the same experience twice, always keeping you on your toes, warning mere mortals that she was in charge, capable of either bearing you safely to your destination, or throwing everything she had at you.

My feet trembled with the vibrations of the metal hull, reminding me that the open ocean would be no more forgiving to the *Escape* than to the navy vessels in which I had travelled the world.

Day one. The calm aqua waters of the Med would last until we reached the narrow choppy seas of the Strait of Gibraltar, and beyond that the undulating dark swell of the Atlantic. One hundred million square kilometres of surface water, famously separating the 'Old World' from the 'New World', swallowing us in its grandeur.

It took a couple of hours for me to relax, to shake off the latent effects of my panic attack. I tucked myself away at the stern, and the rest of the crew gave me some space, perhaps sensing I needed it.

Think, Mitch had told me. *Use the time to clear your head.*

I had to admit, there were worse places on earth to do it.

I enjoyed the gentle pitching, the thrust of the powerful engines, the struggle of machine against nature. I looked for distraction, scanning the water behind us, picking out small passenger ferries, a cruise ship at anchor, and the steady stream of private vessels heading off all over the islands for summer cruising. In amongst the pleasure boats were freight and fishing craft of all sizes. I watched two identical trawlers heading back to harbour, low in the water, full to the brim. A small flotilla of sailing dinghies weaved back and forth, keeping a respectable distance from the larger ships that would cut them in half without even noticing.

Close behind, on a similar heading, was a smallish rust-red freighter, perhaps a little smaller than the *Escape*. The markings were obscured, but the name, *Nakatomi*, was clear on the bow. I could see crew on the bridge deck. They watched the seas ahead, binoculars to their eyes, scanning back and forth, pausing on the *Escape* for a few moments before moving on. The ship gradually dropped behind us, until it was lost in amongst the haze and the other boats.

I drew a few deep breaths of sea air, realizing how much I had missed it.

'Sarah?'

Lily sidled up to me at the rail. She was out of her dress whites, wearing the standard black T-shirt and shorts the crew were permitted to wear when not serving guests. I'd been given the same, and figured I may as well wear them. Those, my radio and my well-worn deck shoes were all I'd need in the current temperature.

'I hear you don't need a tour,' said Lily, with an accusing smile. 'The guys filled me in on your background. I had no idea. You must think me an idiot.'

'Not at all,' I said. 'They're wrong if they think I know anything about superyachts.'

Lily narrowed her eyes. 'Quite a few of the crew were surprised to have a Royal Marine on board, to be honest,' she said. 'You should have seen Camila's face when I told her!'

'Camila?'

'One of the deckhands. Friend of Arno's – the other deckhand. Greg hired her. French Canadian, I think. A bit too sassy for my liking – I'll need to keep her away from Elijah.'

She laughed as she said it, but I could see a brief flash of genuine concern.

'Fancy a stroll?' she said. 'I'm on a break.'

'Sure,' I said, not thinking of a reasonable excuse not to. Lily seemed friendly, open, vulnerable. The opposite personality to me in every way. But I liked her. I figured perhaps this was what normal people were like.

Careful, Sarah. If you're not sarcastic or blunt enough, you might end up with an actual female friend.

Mitch would never believe it. Neither would Amy.

I followed Lily all the way to the top – the sun deck, above the bridge – a smallish area, comparatively speaking, with a hot tub, several sunloungers, and indoor and outdoor bars.

There were two men by the hot tub, stowing chemicals away underneath. They looked similar, both stocky, one had a shaved head, the other floppy brown hair, both dressed in matching black T-shirts and shorts. They were deep in conversation – I picked up thick and cultivated South African accents.

The taller of the two, with the hair, glanced our way as we approached. I couldn't help but do a double-take, his rough appearance and tight body catching my eye. I reckoned he was a little younger than me, still with a hint of boyish mischief. He saw me looking and smiled.

'Hey, Lily,' he called, 'you going to introduce us?'

Lily waved, a little dismissively. 'Hi, Arno,' she said. 'And Luan. The Jacobs brothers. Meet Sarah.'

Arno dusted himself off and walked over. His brother, Luan, looked but didn't follow, carrying on with his work.

'So, the mystery woman,' said Arno, his accent strong, charming. He smiled, wide and goofy, and as he did so my heart skipped a beat. That striking, perfect contrast of rugged and comical. Different to Kay. Completely. And yet the similarities between them were unnerving.

I struggled to look away. 'That's me,' I said.

We shook hands. His grip was strong, hard, rough. I saw his pecs jump as he squeezed my hand. It did nothing to help the flushing in my cheeks.

He looked at me curiously, but not in the sleazy manner of Dan, or with the dismissive attitude of Jason, more like the way my PT instructor used to. I half expected him to comment on my posture or foot position.

'Royal Marines, huh?' he said.

I nodded.

He sighed. 'I tried to sign up, once. Back home. Too old now.' He flexed his arms and back, as if to demonstrate the point. All I saw was a toned physique. He was large, but trim, a perfect soldier's body. I wondered what had happened.

'Most don't make it,' I said.

'But you did.'

'I'm stubborn.'

'And young. Why did you leave?'

I swallowed; my face flushed again, but for a different reason. Shit. I should have a straight answer to that.

'I prefer superyachts,' I said. 'What about you? Why are you here?'

Arno shrugged, his smile twisting. 'You ask any member of the crew that question, they'll give you a different answer. Mostly lies, or they're kidding themselves. My current excuse? I'm saving.'

'What for?'

He shrugged again, and laughed. 'Nothing important,' he said.

I glanced over at his brother, who looked up at the sound of laughter. Still no smile though. He turned away.

Arno followed my gaze; his face fell a fraction and he tried to hide it. 'It won't happen now, anyway,' he said.

'What won't?'

Arno chewed his bottom lip, ignoring my question. 'Are you joining us tonight for dinner?' he asked.

I glanced at Lily. 'What dinner?'

Lily had a knowing grin on her face. 'First night,' she said. 'Tradition. We always get together, the whole crew. It'll be fun.'

An uneasy feeling settled in my stomach. Socializing, pretending I was normal, making friends . . . it was . . .

'You have to,' said Lily. 'Non-negotiable.'

Arno looked at me, perhaps sensing my discomfort. He gave us both a small nod and backed away. 'I'd better get back to work,' he said. 'If we get this deck tidy, Greg said we could use the hot tub this afternoon.'

Lily clapped her hands with glee. 'Perfect,' she said.

Arno saved a final smile for me. 'It would be nice to see you later.'

My stomach danced with butterflies; but the familiar guilt rushed forward to temper the flutter of interest. I forced myself to breathe, to remember what Mitch had told me, to focus on the here and now. *Shit*, why did Arno have to be *so* cute? I could hear Amy's voice in my ears, tried to shut her out. She didn't know the reason why this would be so difficult for me.

'Someone has an admirer,' said Lily, giggling as she opened the doors to the bar.

I followed her inside, feeling my heart pound in my chest. 'Don't be silly,' I said.

'You could do worse,' she said. 'Arno's an OK guy. He works for Pieter, the bosun – or would do, if Pieter were here – I'll tell you about *that* later. Anyway, the deck crew work for Karis, the first mate. They look after the outside of the boat . . .' She paused. 'You probably know this?'

I nodded, familiar with the hierarchy on a working yacht.

'I thought you would. Arno's brother, Luan, is the other steward with me, but . . . he's an arse. We both work for Dan, also an arse. He's chief stew, responsible for the *inside* of the yacht. He's close friends with Pieter and is still pissed about him not being here.'

I smiled, but saw how Lily screwed up her face at the mention of Dan. She didn't rate Ken-doll either. I tried to pay attention, thankful for the distraction, trying to remember the names and roles.

'Who else is there?' said Lily, 'Well, you've met our gorgeous chef – my Jamaican hunk of a man. I think he's looking forward to getting back across the pond – he doesn't *love* the European climate, though he made an exception because Greg asked him personally, and he's being hired the other end for the remainder of the season, along with the rest of us. He'll cook for crew and guests, three meals a day. He's amazing. The things he can do with a fillet of sea bass!' Her eyes sparkled.

I watched her drifting into some blissful fantasy as she opened the doorway into the stairwell and headed down again.

'I've only been on one charter with him before,' she continued, 'where we kinda hooked up but didn't. I'm not sure what happens next but, you know . . .' She wiggled her eyebrows.

We emerged at the back of the bridge deck, past a well-stocked library, furnished floor to ceiling with hardbacks, before stepping into another small lounge, the decor contrasting with the ones above and below, packed with a selection of garish green leather chairs.

I suspected it would be polite to probe Lily's relationship with her 'hunk of a man', but I always found this bit – the girly get-to-know-each-other bit – difficult. I'm crap at small talk, too awkward, too inept in social situations to know the right thing to say. By the time I'd thought of a witty remark, the moment would pass. Amy was the only female with whom I came close to talking about relationships. And I still hadn't discussed the important one with her.

'I met Jack,' I said, avoiding the topic.

'Right,' said Lily. 'Yes. Aussie, engineer. He was married once. She died, back in Australia, some tragic illness. Intense guy. Not sure what his deal is. Seems a bit . . . you know?'

I wondered if Lily had detected the same thing about Jack I had, assuming my hunch was correct. His wife's death might explain his addiction, but not excuse it. I didn't say anything more, and Lily didn't elaborate, taking off again, weaving across the interior, through the lounge, past another bar and another kitchen – empty this time. As tours went, it was pretty superficial, but I got the gist. The contents of each deck seemed of little importance until you reached the wheelhouse (on the bridge deck), or engineering (on the lower decks). The rest was just gravy, as Mitch would say.

'You've got the Wi-Fi code?' she asked as we walked, rummaging in her pocket, producing a scrap of paper. 'We'll be out of mobile phone range soon.'

I pulled out my phone and noted it down.

'One of the perks of having two guests on board,' she said. 'Greg will leave the VSAT on for the duration. Full internet, unrestricted. You can email, WhatsApp, do some Netflix bingeing if you get bored.'

I smiled. Satellite Internet was mega expensive, but then, so was everything else on this boat. I guessed the owner's niece wouldn't accept anything less.

'We're not used to being watched,' said Lily, changing the subject, striding forward once again. 'At least, not by a security guard.'

I lurched forward to keep up. 'I'm not paid to watch you,' I said. 'I hope everyone can forget I'm here. I've done my job properly if that happens.'

Lily shrugged. 'Did you hear we have a new guest?'

'I heard,' I said. 'Harriet De Something.'

She frowned. 'Nobody is happy about it,' she said. 'It means no shagging in the hot tub.'

I spluttered. 'Were you –?'

'It's nice to have the *option*,' she said, giggling.

I could see her mind drifting again, no doubt to Elijah, perhaps peeling him out of his chef's whites and into the bubbling water.

'Here, check this out,' she said, opening a door to her left. I peered in at a fully equipped gym. Long and thin; mirrors lined one wall, while the other was floor-to-ceiling windows with views out of the starboard side of the yacht. The running and rowing machines faced out to sea. I could see the shoreline in the far distance – the Valencian coast along the mainland, the jagged mountain peaks and swooping valleys giving way to hundreds of kilometres of white sandy beaches, secret coves and historic towns.

'Why do they need three weights benches?' I asked.

Lily laughed. 'If you're asking about *need*, you're in the wrong place,' she said, pulling the door closed.

Point taken.

'And this,' she said, stepping across the corridor, grabbing another door handle. 'Oh,' she said, wiggling it. 'It's locked.'

'What's in there?'

'The owner's private art gallery,' said Lily, rolling her eyes. 'Because they *need* one, before you ask. I saw them loading crates into it yesterday.' She laughed again, but it was thin, the weariness returning. She glanced sideways at me. 'Tell me something,' she said. 'How did you get into the military, Sarah?'

'Technically or . . .'

'I guess. Just . . . I had visions of seeing the world, and it led me here, more on impulse than anything else. You've obviously seen a lot more of it than I have.'

'Maybe. But with less champagne. And fewer cushions.'

She chuckled, but bit her lower lip. 'Was it the right choice?' she said.

I blew my cheeks out. Of all the ways I could answer that one. I managed to stop myself going there. Not now, not with a relative stranger, however warm and innocent.

'It made me who I am,' I offered. 'I don't regret it. Why?'

Lily stopped, leaning against the locked door of the gallery. Her face dropped a fraction, her smile wavering. 'Well, I –'

'*Lily. Come in, please.*'

A male voice on the radio. I'd clipped my own on after departure – Greg insisted the crew wore the earpieces at all times. The broadcast messages were how they kept in constant communication throughout the *Escape*. We also had private channels for engineering and watch duty – I'd been given all three.

'What is it, Dan?' she said.

'*Owner's stateroom, quick as you can.*'

'Be right there,' said Lily into the collar mic.

'Sorry,' she said to me, looking relieved, perhaps at not having to answer my question. 'Duty calls. Probably Harriet wanting me to plump her pillows or something. Meet us on the sun deck later, catch a few rays before dinner?'

'Maybe.' It didn't look as if I had a choice.

Despite Mitch's suggestion that I sit around on my arse for twelve days, I had work to do. Reviewing the security equipment, the plan of the superyacht, and inspecting various aspects of the *Escape*'s operations were all tasks I must complete and log, even if just for the insurance company. Mitch's contractors would have done the first pass in dock. I'd do my own tomorrow, then daily until we reached our destination.

But I should speak to the remaining crew and our new guest – make my face known. I wasn't sure about jumping in the hot tub, but dinner would be a good opportunity to say hello, even though I hated the idea of sitting around talking crap with a bunch of strangers.

I took a seat on one of the nearby deckchairs, turning my face to the sun, taking a moment to enjoy the heat. I reflected on my first few hours, Lily's warm welcome, Greg's argument, the subtle hints of dissonance I'd already detected. You grew a sense for these things, working in the military. If anyone had a complaint it needed to be out in the open, not hidden away, festering. It always came out, in my experience, in one way or another.

Perhaps it was just the fatigue of the day getting to me. Whether it was my lingering anxiety, or simply good old-fashioned sea air, I fell into a trance, gazing out at the waves, mesmerized by the way the sunlight glanced off the white water behind us. I used the opportunity to fill my lungs, reset my body, attempt to expel my stress.

I played a guessing game with the other boats I could see – their origin, their destination. I used to do it on guard duty in basic training to pass the time. The small craft were easy, the larger ones spawning a wider range of possible combinations, their names and types often giving them away. The mid-sized craft were hardest of all, their purpose known only to them; their destination could be the next port, or the next continent.

My eyes began to close. As I drifted off, I caught sight of the small freighter from earlier, the *Nakatomi*, cutting through the waves behind us, changing course, heading further south.

7

I heard a shriek as I climbed the exterior stairs. It was followed by a splash and a deep laugh. The afternoon waned, but the heat was intense and Greg had been as good as his word, allowing the crew to use the sun deck before dinner. Once we hit the open ocean this area would be closed off, battened down for the crossing. I respected Greg's motives – let them play while they can.

The sun hung lower in the sky, the sunset deepening, the horizon already transforming into streaks of pinks and oranges. Heat rippled up from the deck, the haze giving everything a surreal glow.

'Sarah!' Lily called across the deck as I poked my head up. Her smile turned to a frown. 'You're not in your bikini.'

I gave an apologetic shrug, taking in the assembled group. Lily was submerged up to her neck. Arno and Dan sat across from her. Elijah sat on the edge, feet in the water, towelling his face and head. To the rear of the hot tub was an infinity panel of glass, letting the occupants gaze at an unbroken view of the water behind.

The breeze hit me as I turned my head, the force of the sun blinding. I pulled the visor of my cap lower and let my eyes wander, mesmerized at the sight of Majorca dropping into the horizon behind us. We were sailing around the north of Ibiza, then we'd hug the coast of southern Spain – close enough to spy the resorts of Alicante,

Benidorm and the like. I wondered how many average Joes on the beaches would be looking up, seeing the *Escape* as she sailed past, wondering who we are, where we were headed. Did they know the majority of people on this boat were just like them? Or did they cast their stares with envy at the floating extravagance on the horizon, whose luxuries were forever out of their reach?

'Sorry,' I said, bringing my attention back to the crew, 'I'll have to sit this one out.' I had no intention of stripping off in front of this lot, not yet. The thought of prancing around in my bikini, pretending to have fun like some lurid spring-break party, made me cringe. That said, I couldn't stop my eyes meeting Arno's. He looked mildly disappointed, and it gave me an awkward thrill, even more so as he pushed himself out of the water.

'It's time to get moving, anyway,' he said, checking his watch. 'Captain wants dinner early. He's a bit of a grump today.'

'Spoilsport,' said Lily, splashing water at him.

I tried not to stare as Arno grabbed a small towel and rubbed at his tanned body, his eyes flicking to mine again.

'You missed the others,' said Lily. 'Camila and Karis dipped their feet in but had to go and take care of something. Greg might be in a bad mood but the rest of us are enjoying it while we can.' She stretched her arms and ducked her head under the bubbles, emerging to spray a mouthful of water at Elijah. He flicked his towel at her.

'Get a fucking room, you two,' said Dan, smirking. 'Oh, wait, you can't, because we've got *proper* guests.' He blew out his cheeks, looking sideways at me. 'Although some of us still get a cabin to ourselves, I hear.'

I turned to him, square on. He seemed to cower a little in my gaze, still struggling to assert his dominance, while I struggled to think of a retort that wouldn't alienate the rest of them.

'I've got much bigger guns than you, Dan,' I said. 'They need a bunk of their own. What can I say?'

I think I got it right. Arno and Elijah laughed, fist-bumped. Dan remained steely-faced, nodding his head as he climbed out.

I smiled, pulling up a deckchair, kicking my legs out and tucking my hands behind my head, wishing I felt as confident as I appeared. In truth, I hated this sort of gathering, the intimate social interaction with relative strangers. I could handle being arse-to-arse with other soldiers in a cramped ship, a barracks, even dug into a sweaty trench, but at least in those circumstances there was nothing to hide, no agendas to figure out. Here, it was different, the looks and nods, the winks and smiles that hid a shared history, a thousand words and motives. I struggled to keep up in these situations, tended to withdraw, and rather than work on my social failings, I avoided them.

I could imagine Mitch's assessment: *You're relaxing on the top deck of a superyacht in the Med, next to an infinity tub, surrounded by a bunch of young spunky crew who want you to party with them. You'll get served Michelin-star quality food for dinner, served on the finest crockery, drinking your Diet Coke from cut-glass crystal. Fucking enjoy yourself!*

I smiled, picturing Mitch's envious face. He was right. I'd try.

'So what's the deal with our mystery guest?' asked Elijah. 'Harriet? Is that her name?'

Dan snorted. 'Daddy's little girl,' he said. 'Or niece. Or something. Clicks her fingers and gets a ride on our yacht. Can you imagine?'

Elijah shrugged. '*Her* yacht. Anyone talked to her yet?'

Lily nodded. 'She's nice. Don't listen to Dan. I read about her – her family is in the Forbes rich list again this year. Billionaires. They own half of London, so it seems.'

'Only half?' said Elijah. He sighed. 'Which bits, exactly?'

'Property, stocks, art, gold. You name it. There was some drama about the family recently – I can't remember what about.'

'Dirty little secrets?' asked Elijah.

Lily shrugged.

'She's pretty hot,' said Dan. 'I'll offer some room service later.'

I glanced at Lily. She rolled her eyes, mouthing *wanker* at Dan.

Dan missed the gesture, instead listing the types of service he might offer his new object of affection, at the top of his voice.

I heard footsteps behind me and turned. Jack appeared through the bar. He stepped outside, squinting. I thought he looked tired, still strained, probably working all day on his growing list of problems.

'Keep it down a bit, yeah,' he said. 'I can hear you from the bridge.'

'Is she on the bridge?' said Dan.

'Who?'

'Harriet?'

'That's not the point,' said Jack. 'You shouldn't be talking about her.'

'She can't hear us,' said Dan. 'For fuck's sake, chill out, Jack. You've been uptight since we boarded.'

'Hey, calm down, chaps,' said Arno, walking over to Jack, grabbing him around the shoulders, giving his hair a playful rub. 'It's just a bit of banter. You OK, mate?'

Jack shrugged him off, rubbing the back of his neck. I could see the stress in his posture, his eyes. He shook his head, staring at the tub.

'At least that thing works,' he said, huffing before turning away, heading back through the bar.

Arno watched him leave, turned to Dan, and put his palms up as if to say *enough*.

Lily slid out of the water, gave me a small smile, nodding towards Arno. 'There's always dinner,' she said.

'About that,' I said, wondering again if I could still get out of it.

'Seven o'clock,' said Lily, shaking her head. 'And no, you can't.'

I snorted. 'That obvious?'

She pulled a sad face. 'Give us all a chance, yeah?'

I took a breath, wanted to say it wasn't them, it was me. That it was always me, and they'd have a much better time tonight if I stayed in my cabin. But Lily's creeping smile and unconditional offer of friendship was unwavering, and it broke me.

'I'll be there,' I said.

The view from the table was the best money could buy – the plush outside dining area of the owner's deck, third from the top. The sun was low, on our bow, spreading a glow over the deck and illuminating the water around us in shimmering sparkles of light. The sea was calm, reflecting the sunset in an array of reds and oranges, with bursts of yellow. The motion was hardly noticeable, the background thrum of the engines providing a gentle white noise, already drowned out by the increasing volume of the crew as they argued, gossiped and laughed. First-night nerves and excitement, old and new friendships, a couple with their heads bowed in thoughtful silence.

'Too posh to eat with the rest of us.' Dan stated his conclusion as he poured more wine, swirling it around the glass, examining the dark liquid with a critical eye before gulping it down.

He was referring to Harriet and Jason, who had declined to join the crew for the first-night dinner, instead demanding a separate meal in the stateroom.

'She turned you down?' said Jack, smirking into his own glass, taking a sip.

Sparkling water, it said on the bottle. I wondered.

'She didn't want your room service?' said Arno. 'Can't say I blame her. You're looking pretty rough today, mate.'

'Fuck off, the both of you,' said Dan, with a touch more menace than perhaps he planned. He shrugged, tried to pull it back with a smile. 'Her loss,' he said, to the table at large.

I'd changed into something a little less casual, appearing on the dot of seven. My eyes found Arno first, and his mine. He was dressed in a terrible Hawaiian shirt and white linen trousers, sunglasses wedged on to his forehead. His skin looked more tanned in the lower light of the evening, and his stubble thicker. He indicated an empty seat next to him and I took it after a microsecond of resistance, much to Lily's apparent delight, who took the chair the other side of me.

Two new friends. *Steady on, Sarah.*

I scanned the table, counting the assembled crew. Everyone had changed for dinner, the men in assorted garish shirts, the women taking more care, perhaps relishing the opportunity to dress up for a change.

Arno and his brother, Luan, to my left, Lily to my right, and next to her, Jack, our engineer, who slouched after Dan's rebuke, his grin more tentative.

Next to Jack was the only crew member I hadn't met – Camila, I presumed. She had a chiselled jawline and a flawless face of make-up, her dark hair slicked back into a bun. Her posture was relaxed, her clothes immaculate and expensive, the black fabric of her dress shimmering in the light. She gazed at her phone, scrolling with her index finger, pausing now and again to sip from a glass of champagne. She looked up at Dan's retort, glancing between him and Arno, a smile forming.

'I think you look gorgeous,' she said to Dan, her French accent soft and lingering. She gave him a wink and a pat on the forearm.

Dan gave her a sarcastic smile, snorting into his drink. He already looked half-cut.

Elijah would be in the kitchen, and when I saw Greg approaching, I guessed Karis was on the bridge. All accounted for. Except for our two guests.

Greg stood at the head of the table, casting his eyes over his crew, appraising them for a few seconds. He picked up an empty glass and tapped it with a fork until we fell silent.

'Welcome, folks,' he said. 'And don't worry, I won't make this formal.'

A small cheer went up from Lily and Dan. I saw Camila chuckle as she scanned the table, her eyes finding me. She smiled, gave me a friendly wave.

'As is tradition, to those who've sailed with me before, we start the voyage with the crew's dinner. Elijah is working his magic in the kitchen, and I know you'll all chip in and give him plenty of help clearing up afterwards.'

A small groan around the table.

'You'll give him more than that,' said Jack, nudging Lily in the ribs.

She turned bright red. 'I don't know what you mean.'

I heard Luan whisper something behind Arno. His accent was similar to Arno's but gruffer, deeper. Arno spun towards his brother. 'Shut it, mate,' he said, without a trace of humour.

Greg appeared not to notice, naming us all in turn with a nod, ticking us off as he went around the table. I tipped my glass to Camila as we were officially introduced, and as soon as Greg had finished talking, she slid off her chair and approached me.

'Camila,' she said, extending a hand.

I took it. It was rough – a proper deckhand's skin. I liked her already. 'Sarah.'

'Sorry we didn't meet earlier,' she said. 'I've been running around like a . . . what do you say . . . "blue-arsed fly"?'

I laughed. 'That'll do,' I said, watching her expression relax.

She shrugged, leaned in, out of Greg's earshot, and

explained, 'We're a little short staffed. Arno and I are picking up the slack.'

No shit. This was a huge yacht to be functioning on such a skeleton crew, even if just for a delivery run. Lily had mentioned something about the bosun not being on board. Another one of Greg's problems?

'It looks like you've got it under control,' I said. A platitudinous statement, which I didn't really mean, but it felt like the proper response.

'We will,' she said, rolling her eyes, before gliding slowly back to her chair.

Dinner was served, and Lily was right about Elijah – he was an exceptional chef, if the starter was anything to go by. The biggest king prawns I'd ever seen, cooked in a secret garlic sauce, and served with crispy mangetout. Second course would be a seafood buffet, allowing Elijah out of the kitchen to join us.

The drinks flowed to those who wanted them. The conversation warmed up, turning to previous trips and charters, memorable guests and absent friends. I watched and listened, letting the conversations flow over me, attempting to keep myself calm and composed, tongue in check. By nine o'clock I was proud of myself – I hadn't insulted anyone.

Arno kept glancing at me, and I resisted glancing back. I wondered if sitting next to him had been a mistake, giving a signal I wasn't ready to give. I was probably overthinking it, but started to feel uncomfortable. I checked my watch – how much longer before I could reasonably sneak away?

'Do you remember that singer on the Virgin Islands?'

Dan shook his head at the memory. 'What was her name? San Dee or something? Pieter and I found so much coke in her bathroom, we could have started a decent business.'

Greg smirked. 'That was the end of the charter,' he said. 'I remember. She was lucky I didn't call the coastguard.'

'I think Dan snorted half of it,' said Elijah, appearing behind us with a full platter, and to a collection of cheers and compliments. He nudged in opposite Lily. I saw their eyes meet; a brief moment passed between them.

'So . . . this Harriet,' said Luan. 'I'm amazed she's not interested in Dan, but what's her deal?'

Greg frowned. The collective mood dampened. I wondered if that was Luan's intention – one of many snarky comments he'd made thus far.

'Her family owns this yacht,' said Greg. 'She pays our wages. That's all we need to know. And she's suffering from seasickness – hence the no-show.'

'Sick in the Med,' said Elijah, rolling his eyes. 'Are you kidding? She knows we're crossing the Atlantic?'

'I've already had that conversation with Jason,' said Greg. 'She always gets sick in the first twenty-four hours. It'll pass.'

'I hope so,' said Lily. 'I have to clean her bathroom.'

Luan let out a cackle. 'Living the dream, eh, Lily?'

'Shut up, mate,' said Elijah. 'Lily likes this job, don't you?'

Lily shrugged. Another awkward pause.

I think Jack sensed it, too. 'Don't worry,' he said. 'I'll be spending most of my time in the bowels of this boat, fixing everything.'

I saw Greg throw him a look.

'I thought that was all sorted,' said Arno. 'What's up now?'

Jack shrugged. 'Everything,' he said, ignoring Greg. 'I was hoping to get the water maker working, but it's off until Antigua.'

'What? We don't have the water maker?' said Dan.

A few of the others sat straighter in their chairs.

'What are we supposed to drink – the rain?'

'We have extra fresh-water tanks installed,' said Greg. 'If anyone was paying attention at the departure briefing. We have plenty of drinking water.' Another glare at Jack, who seemed to get the hint this time, slouching lower in his chair.

Dan blew out his cheeks. 'Way to go, Jack.'

'It's not *my* fault,' said Jack.

'Miss DeWitt-Fendley enjoyed a thirty-minute shower earlier,' said Dan. 'Did your plans factor her in? Who's going to tell Little Miss Billionaire she can't do that every day? If we're running on tanks, you need to calculate fresh water per person, per day. Have you done that?'

'I think that's the chief stew's job,' said Greg, wading in, apparently deciding to defend his engineer.

About time.

'Or the bosun's,' hissed Dan, pushing his chair away, walking off in a huff. He took a stool at the bar, reaching over to grab a bottle of whisky. He broke the seal, pouring himself a large glass.

'Or a captain who knew what he was doing,' whispered Luan, under his breath.

I think only Arno and I heard him, but I was really

surprised – not just by the petty squabbling and backchat, but by the general lack of respect for each other, particularly Greg. The crew spoke to him with barely contained contempt. I could already sense that the *Escape* was far from a smoothly oiled machine, in both the literal and operational senses. This supposedly close-knit team seemed to be simmering underneath. It was disappointing, this early on, although I figured I wouldn't have to do this every night. I could ignore most of them for the rest of the trip.

'So what was in all of those crates?' said Arno. 'The ones I lugged to the art gallery earlier?' His deep voice had the effect of settling the outlying conversations, commanding attention – much more so than Greg, I noticed.

'I dunno, pictures?' said Luan.

'Funny,' said Arno. 'I mean what kind?'

Dan swivelled around on his stool. 'Let's pretend any of us understand art,' he said. 'Good idea.'

'Hey,' said Lily. 'Some of us have an education, Dan. Why wouldn't we understand?'

Dan smirked, flexing his muscles. I thought this evening's T-shirt was two sizes too small.

'There is an original Jackson Pollock and a Gustav Klimt,' piped up Camila, 'several pieces by an upcoming Italian artist who recently exhibited at the Hauser & Wirth gallery. Also a sculpture by Jeff Koons, I believe. Quite an eclectic collection.'

We all turned to her.

She pulled a pained smile, taking another sip of champagne, after she'd said it. 'We're not all ignoramuses, thank you.'

Dan looked incredulous, before raising his palms in mock submission. 'Okaaaaay,' he said.

Camila turned to the rest of us and whispered, 'Plus I read the cargo manifest. It listed everything – that's all I could remember.'

Lily laughed, choking on her drink.

'And there's more.' A new voice.

I turned to see Jason approaching. He was alone, a glass in one hand, barefoot, still dressed in his corporate suit. Decided to join the staff, I guessed.

'Twenty-eight pieces in total,' he said. He paused, watching Camila, swaying on the spot.

I wondered how much he'd drunk while keeping Harriet company.

'A pair of Rembrandts,' he continued. 'Full-length wedding portraits of Marten Soolmans and Oopjen Coppit in 1634, always hung as a pair. A late addition, not on the manifest. Ground-breaking works.'

We pretended to be impressed. I'd heard of Rembrandt and Pollock, but my art appreciation was about the same level as Dan's. Not that I'd ever admit it.

'Nice,' said Arno. 'I think I have one of those in my kitchen. Or was it an original Ikea? I can never remember.'

Luan snorted. A few titters. Jason's eyes narrowed, as he glanced around the table in disdain.

'These are seminal pieces we're talking about,' he said. 'They speak to what it is to be human. You should care. They . . .' He paused, a thoughtful look on his face.

'I care,' said Lily, glancing at Elijah.

Elijah shrugged. 'I could dig a Rembrandt,' he said.

Jason nodded to himself, before taking a breath. 'It doesn't matter,' he said. 'I don't expect –'

'Why should we care?' said Dan. 'What is it to us?'

I glanced across at Dan. He looked flustered, spoiling for an argument. His public-school accent seemed to intensify with more alcohol. Drunk and embarrassing. Lily was right – a total arse.

'Enough, Dan,' said Greg. He turned to Jason. 'Some of us have had a few too many. First night and all that. We weren't expecting you to join us.'

Jason stiffened, tilting his head back, looking down his nose at Greg. They stared at each other. Greg shook his head. Jason paused, nodded, seemingly as much to himself as to Greg.

'No . . .' he said, his tone softening. 'You're right. I'm sorry for interrupting.' He paused, took a breath. 'Good night, everyone,' he said, spinning on his heels, heading inside, through the doors into the owner's lounge. They slammed shut behind him.

'Off for a nightcap with the young lady,' said Dan, a little too loudly.

'Gross,' said Lily. 'She's half his age.'

'Sugar daddy?' said Elijah.

'But she's the rich one,' said Lily. 'Doesn't work. Does it?' She looked around for answers, but the atmosphere, such as it was, had soured with Jason's appearance.

Greg pushed himself away from the table, dabbing his forehead with a napkin, announcing he'd be joining Karis on the bridge for the rest of the evening. 'Radio if you need me,' he said, walking away. 'Emergencies only.'

The table descended into silence.

'Are they . . . you know?' said Luan.

'After what happened in Palma? I doubt it,' said Arno.

I raised my eyebrows at Lily, who leaned in conspiratorially, eyes wide.

'We shouldn't gossip,' said Arno.

Lily waved him away. 'It's not gossip,' she said. 'Besides, Sarah is part of the crew. She needs to know.'

'I really don't . . .' I began, but Lily had already tucked herself right up against me, ready to go.

'Karis and Greg started seeing each other, a few seasons back,' she said. 'He was married, still is, but it was complicated.'

Elijah laughed. 'Sordid affairs always are. Especially at sea.'

'Anyway,' said Lily, ignoring him, 'Greg wouldn't commit, so she broke it off and ended up having a fling with Pieter – the bosun, and one of Greg's core crew. He and Greg have been friends for years.'

'And Greg didn't know,' said Arno. 'About the fling.'

'No. He didn't. Not until last night.'

'Last night?' I said, watching their exchange like a game of tennis.

'Yep,' said Lily. 'Palma, at the club. It was already over between Karis and Pieter, but Greg found out about it and went ballistic. He sacked Pieter on the spot, booted him off the *Escape*.'

'None of us are supposed to know about this, by the way,' added Arno.

'She knows we know,' said Lily. 'She's not stupid. But they nearly came to blows dockside. Pieter has a legendary temper – apparently it's a Dutch thing.'

'It's not a *Dutch* thing, it's a spurned-lover thing,' said Elijah.

'*Whatever*,' said Lily. 'Pieter stormed off, making all sorts of threats.'

'I don't blame him,' piped up Dan. 'Greg's out of order, sacking him like that.'

'Is he? You're just sore because you and Pieter were best buddies.'

'So what if we were? He's a decent bloke. He deserved better.'

'Pieter really liked her,' said Elijah. 'He was smitten. As soon as Greg announces his divorce, suddenly Karis dumps Pieter and goes back to him.'

'That's not quite how it happened,' said Lily.

'Pieter looked ready to kill,' said Elijah. 'He made it clear it wasn't over.'

'So did Greg.'

'I feel for Karis,' said Lily. 'It all kind of blew up in her face.'

I agreed. Perhaps it wasn't the most sensible thing, flipping from captain to bosun, but I admired Karis's energy. 'Is she OK?' I said.

Lily nodded. 'She will be.'

'But the bigger issue,' said Arno, grabbing his beer, 'is that it leaves us without a bosun, which means Camila and I have to cover it.'

'We get to run the decks,' said Camila, who'd stayed out of the brief saga, sipping her drink slowly. 'It's not all bad.'

'Greg should appoint one of you,' said Lily.

Arno and Camila glanced at each other.

'It's all yours,' said Arno, raising a toast to her with his beer. 'I'd prefer to stay where I am, do as I'm told.'

I'm not sure if Arno expected Camila to reciprocate the offer, but she just shrugged, shook her head, chuckled into her glass. 'Let's see, shall we?'

Arno cleared his throat. The conversation died, replaced with the sound of gulls overhead and the steady throb of the engines. We sipped our drinks, stared at the water, the awkwardness extending towards the horizon. I decided it was time to turn in.

I could see those who were in it for the long haul, and those who would rather be anywhere else. Luan's face was set in a permanent scowl, and Arno seemed pre-occupied trying to placate him. Camila joined Dan, who was a good quarter of the way through the bottle of Johnnie Walker. Jack sidled over, an awkward third hand, and Elijah shuffled around next to Lily. There was talk of champagne in the hot tub, and perhaps a midnight movie. They knew to enjoy it while they could – the perks of crewing a yacht like this meant squeezing in the luxury whenever possible. Steal those moments, enjoy them, bank them. It isn't your life, not really, but you can pretend.

But despite Lily's best efforts to include me, I could already feel my chest tightening, the table feeling claustrophobic in the low light.

The sun had long gone, the sky offering only a faint glow to say goodnight. Arno's eyes were on me as I walked across the deck, his goofy smile edged with disappointment as I headed into the stairwell.

*

I only heard the radio because I nipped out to get some air. It was well past midnight, but I'd tossed and turned for hours, sleep elusive, so I threw on my jogging pants and padded along the metal floor in bare feet, away from the cabins, heading aft towards the storage and engine room, making for the rear deck. Amy had messaged me earlier in the day, asking how I was holding up, and I'd forgotten to text her back. Sending her a few words might help to settle my thoughts.

I paused in the central stairwell. The rest of the yacht was quiet, the dinner and drinking long finished, replaced with the constant throb of the engines, and the soothing friction of water against the hull.

But I heard it again, voices, hushed, broken. I couldn't make out the words, but each was followed by a burst of static. A radio, I guessed, one of the crew listening to whatever they could pick up along the coast, or possibly a VHF receiver, monitoring maritime chit-chat over the airwaves.

I continued aft, opening the door to the next corridor, which was lined with storage cupboards, expecting to find Jack or one of the deckhands, even Greg, perhaps taking a break from the bridge.

But the door clicked shut behind me, the sound echoing along the empty corridor, and the voices stopped. Abruptly, the radio, or whatever it was, silenced. I heard footsteps, light taps on the hard floor, but they too were distant – in the next stairwell, or perhaps the next deck up, hurrying away. Sound travels strangely through a yacht, particularly on the lower decks, and I figured it could have been my imagination.

I paused again, leaning against the wall, taking a few breaths, shaking off the unease, a sense of disquiet in the dead of night. All I could feel was the faint vibration of the engines, and my heartbeat against the cold metal.

I pulled out my phone and started typing my reply to Amy.

Don't you worry about me, sis. I'm fine.
Never better.

8

Day two at sea. I woke late, my dreams tenuous, dark and obscure, my body soaked with sweat. I'd shunned the sleeping tablets after returning to my cabin, hoping I might do without them – hoping the sea air and motion would do a good enough job.

I was wrong. My body shuddered with nervous energy.

My feet hit the ground hard as I stepped out of the bunk. The motion of the yacht was pronounced this morning, choppier than yesterday. I checked out of my window, and realized Greg must have been gunning it through the night, pushing the engines hard. The *Escape* was fast, designed for immense power if the owner needed it, with a top speed of well over twenty knots. We were already approaching Gibraltar – the sea was darker, greyer, the silt and sands whipping up to create a muddy mix of colour. The sky seemed hazier too, wisps of cloud streaming up high. We would soon be leaving the relative shelter of the Med, and it would only get tougher from here. It was still unbearably hot, though, the suffocating humidity below decks lingering, my skin struggling to shrug off the moisture. I wondered how our elusive guest, Harriet, was doing – I had some sympathy, even though I'd yet to meet the woman. Every sailor had at one time suffered from a bout of seasickness – the definition of misery for most people.

The huge rock of Gibraltar loomed to the starboard side, off our bows. Morocco would lie to port.

The two countries would be the last visible land for roughly eleven days – depending on how hard Greg pushed us, and what weather we encountered. It triggered both the primal thrill of being at sea, and the reactive fear of what it meant, to be so isolated, alone with my thoughts, my dreams, and a crew who I barely knew.

I dragged my eyes away, forcing my attention back inside the ship. I changed into my training vest and shorts, laced my trainers, and stretched against the bunk, feeling a pleasant tension in my hamstrings. A workout would clear my head, get the endorphins pumping – provide temporary relief.

Always temporary.

Those with hangovers were still asleep, and those without were on duty. I managed to avoid everyone as I jogged along the crew corridor and up the starboard stairwell, until I reached the bridge deck, second from top. Where the gym was located.

'Whoa,' said Jack, jumping out of the way before I ploughed into him. He looked terrible, huge bags under his eyes, unshaven, carrying a distinct odour.

'Sorry,' I said. 'You OK?'

'Yeah,' he said, grinning nervously. 'Late night.' He played with a bottle of water in his hands. His clothes were dishevelled, his shirt untucked. 'I had to see Greg. There's something . . .' He shook his head. 'No big deal.'

I watched him, making a point of it. He squirmed under my gaze. Surely Greg knew? This man was half-cut, whether through hangover or hair-of-the-dog.

'I need to go,' he said, sidling past me to the stairs. 'This ship won't fix itself.' He gave a small laugh and headed down.

I watched him leave, feeling torn about what to do. He was one of Greg's, a personal hire. Sticking my oar in might single me out as a troublemaker. I decided to keep my mouth shut, for now.

The bridge deck was oddly laid out, split into two sections. The front section held the wheelhouse and the captain's quarters, the rear section held the gym, art gallery, and another lounge area with a bar.

I emerged from one of the rear stairwells, pulling another stretch against the gunwale, taking a few moments of moist air, listening to the cries of the gulls that followed the *Escape*. They'd stay with us for the next day or two before dispersing.

'Excuse me?'

I turned, spinning on one foot, the other tucked against my rear.

A timid-looking woman approached, perhaps mid-twenties, her features delicate and manicured. No make-up as far as I could tell, and dressed in jogging bottoms and a hoodie – sensible at this time in the morning, though not what I'd expected from a billionaire's niece. As she got closer, I could tell there was little more than skin and bone under her baggy clothes. Her jawline was pronounced, her cheekbones high. Small piercing eyes appraised me.

'You must be Harriet,' I said, dropping my left foot and extending my hand.

She looked at it for a moment before shaking it with her fingertips. She nodded, staggering a little as the *Escape* rolled. Still getting her sea legs.

'Yes,' she said. 'Are you one of the crew?'

Her voice was soft, calm, upper class. She reminded me of a character out of one of Amy's favourite period dramas. Apart from the hoodie.

'Kinda,' I said.

'Oh,' she said. 'Oh, OK. What is it you do? Miss, uh . . .'

I cleared my throat. 'Sarah. Sarah French. Didn't Jason tell you?'

She shook her head.

'I'm the security officer for the yacht.'

Harriet's face twisted in surprise. She opened her mouth to say something, then closed it. 'Hmm,' she murmured. 'Is this to do with Nikolas?'

'Nikolas?' The name didn't ring a bell. 'One of the crew?'

'Oh,' she said, seeing my confusion. 'No. Don't worry. It's nothing.'

I smiled. 'I'm an insurance requirement, that's all,' I said, sensing I needed to put her at ease.

Harriet tilted her head. 'Interesting.'

She nodded to herself, her gaze drifting past me towards the water. Her eyes looked damp, perhaps just the breeze.

'So you fancied an ocean crossing?' I said. I could have just excused myself and gone for my workout, but I remembered Mitch's plea – people like this could make or break his company. I owed it to him to make an effort with the client.

Her gaze shifted back to me. 'Oh, not really,' she said, a small titter escaping from her lips, 'but I *did* want to get away. This seemed like the place to do it.'

I wasn't sure whether to pry or not. It looked like we

were both here for the same reason – though I presumed under vastly different circumstances.

'This is certainly one way to do it,' I said. 'Twelve days of staring out at that,' I indicated over the gunwale, 'will do wonders.'

She nodded, before taking a deep breath and turning away from the water, scanning the deck. 'I could do with some breakfast,' she said. 'How would I . . . ?' She raised her eyebrows at me.

I guessed our conversation was over. I was crew, after all.

I'd neglected to bring my radio, not expecting to need it in the gym. I peered across this deck, then stuck my head over the gunwale to scan the deck below. Perfect.

'Camila?' I called.

She must have been on early shift, tidying the owner's deck after the night before, no doubt finding a few too many corks and bottle tops. She looked at me. I assumed she'd been drinking with Dan and Jack all night, but she looked surprisingly fresh-faced.

'Could you come here, please?' I said.

She paused. Deckhands were the lowest in rank, but reported up their own chain. The exterior was their domain, and breakfast was definitely *not* their remit, but . . . she didn't know that's what I wanted, yet. She made the right choice, as far as I was concerned, and headed up.

When she emerged from the stairs she stopped, her eyes running over Harriet and me.

'Miss DeWitt . . . Fendley,' I said, struggling to remember the name, 'would like some breakfast. Could you help?'

Camila nodded, looking a little annoyed, and didn't come any closer. 'I'll wake the chef,' she said, turning to speak into her radio.

I heard her asking if Elijah was awake yet. She seemed to get a response.

'The chef will be right with you, Miss DeWitt-Fendley,' she said, with a brief smile, then without another word disappeared towards the gym.

'Efficient,' said Harriet, raising her eyebrows at me, 'and pretty. What did you say her name was?'

'Camila,' I said. 'They're short staffed, lots to do –'

'Oh, don't apologize,' Harriet said, dismissing my concern with a wave of her hand. She looked puzzled, deep in thought.

'I should go,' I said, deciding I'd spent the required amount of time being polite. 'Workout before work, you know . . .'

'Oh, of course,' said Harriet, who'd certainly never worked a day in her life. 'Please, don't let me stop you.'

'Lovely to meet you, Miss DeWitt-Fendley,' I said.

She nodded unconvincingly, before staring back out at the water, the creases of a frown set deep in her forehead.

I entered the gym, surprised to see Camila talking to Arno in the corner, behind the row of running machines. She must have headed straight there. Their faces were inches apart. He was towelling his neck, his T-shirt drenched in sweat; she was perched, left hand on hip, leaning in a little too close. Too close? Shit, what was that, Sarah? Jealousy?

They knew each other already, met in the South of France, so Lily said. He recommended her to Greg. Everyone knows everyone on these circuits. Had they dated? Harriet had called her pretty. I guessed she was. I watched the way she twirled a strand of hair, wondering if I should leave, or knock and re-enter. But she wasn't smiling. If anything, their conversation looked heated. Lovers' tiff? A morning after the night before? Christ. What was wrong with me?

I watched her body as she shifted her weight.

I had a body most fitness magazines would call *rigorously athletic*, towards the mesomorph end of the spectrum. What they meant, if they were honest, was muscle-bound. I was solid, my thighs defined, my stomach a washboard, my triceps visible from a hundred yards. My body had been honed through years of bloody-minded training, lugging the same loads as my male counterparts in the Marines, running the same distances, lifting the same weights.

It was a body to be proud of, yet that still didn't stop the natural wave of socially conditioned self-consciousness when faced with someone like Camila. Camila was athletic; Instagram-athletic, if I could coin a term for it. The sort of body that looked good in any outfit – even a crew T-shirt and shorts – all without trying. Along with that French accent . . . I wondered what Arno preferred.

I closed the door, hearing it clunk in its frame. They both turned. Arno swallowed. Camila smiled, stepping back from Arno, immediately heading towards me. Her hips swayed as she walked.

I watched Arno, waiting for the natural flick of the eyes

towards her, the way all men do. Except Arno didn't. His eyes were focused downwards, frown lines etched on his forehead. He didn't give her a second look.

'Was Harriet OK?' asked Camila, pausing at the door. Her eyes were honest, concerned, and I felt a little bad.

I nodded, glancing at Arno. 'Yes,' I said, 'and thanks. I know breakfast isn't your job.'

She shook her head. 'No problem. What the guests want, they get. Happy to help.'

She left. I waited until she'd closed the door behind her, before approaching Arno. He blinked a couple of times before looking up, meeting my gaze. The frown disappeared and his face was transformed with a smile. I noticed his eyes were bloodshot, puffy around the edges.

'You OK?' I asked.

'Yes,' he replied. 'Work stuff. Hangover doesn't help.' He rolled his eyes, but the humour looked insincere.

'She's nice,' I said, nodding over my shoulder. May as well go for it, Sarah. It'll bug you otherwise.

'Who?'

'Camila,' I said. 'Seems nice.'

'I guess,' said Arno. He gazed at me, the realization dawning. 'Oh. No,' he said. 'If that's what you thought? No. She's not my type. No way.'

He overemphasized the last point. Protesting too much? Or trying to make it clear to me? If the latter, what was I supposed to do? I heard Amy's voice in my head, tried to force it away. Was a mindless fling with a stranger what I needed? A relative toy boy at that? How would it help, other than to satisfy the physical urges that Amy insisted I had? To fulfil them was human, she said, and acceptable. *It's the twenty-first century*, she reminded me. *If you want something, take it.*

The sight of Arno soaked in sweat did nothing to help the case against her.

His face relaxed, his goofy smile appearing at the edges. That didn't help either.

'I prefer a bit more, you know . . .' he said.

Did I know?

'What?' I asked, feeling a tingling in my stomach.

His face flushed. 'I –'

The door to the gym opened. Jason strode in, head-phones on. He nodded to both of us and selected a running machine at the far end, starting it with a whir.

The moment evaporated.

'I should do the same,' I said, stepping on to the tread-mill in front of me. I didn't fancy Jason overhearing our conversation. 'Talk later?'

Arno nodded, glancing at Jason, grabbing his towel and drink. 'Or I could stay and watch?' he said, grin broaden-ing.

'Um, I . . .'

'I'm joking,' he said. His deep laugh broke through the remaining tension.

'Piss off,' I mouthed at him, starting the machine, feel-ing my own face reddening.

He left me to it, and I got into my stride, unable to wipe the small smile from my face, thankful I was facing out to sea.

It took thirty minutes of pounding before the mental triggers went off, my brain reminding me – a surge of guilt and regret. Arno's face blended into Kay's and my mood plummeted; my pace slowed. What right did I have to flirt and smile, after what I'd done? Twelve short months. Long enough, said Mitch, but he was wrong. It would never be enough. Not to forgive myself, not by a long way.

Arno was cute, but I must deny Amy her wish. Survival for me meant *just* me, no distractions, no temptation. No moving on.

I didn't deserve to.

I stepped off the machine, stretching for a few minutes, letting my heart rate settle, letting the feeling pass. It always did.

I watched Jason out of the corner of my eye, interested by what I saw. He ran with fervour – a concentration and stamina I'd rarely seen outside the military. Out of his suit he looked different, less corporate, more . . . human.

His attitude and behaviour sucked, but I was still curious about something. Given we were alone, I thought it worth a shot.

I stood next to his machine, indicating he take his headphones off. He glanced at me for a few moments before hitting the stop button, letting the machine slow right down before he slid the headphones on to his neck.

'Sarah,' he said, tilting his head. Still the management stiff, still looking down on me. 'Good morning.'

'Morning, Jason,' I said, keeping my voice upbeat. 'I wondered. Could you answer something for me?'

Jason shrugged. 'Greg runs this yacht,' he said. 'He'd be better –'

'I'm asking you,' I said.

A huff. 'What is it?'

'Why were we in such a hurry to depart?' I said.

Jason's eyes darted to mine. He rallied well, but I could tell my question caught him off guard. He grabbed his towel, turning his face away from me.

'What do you mean?' he said.

'I mean the *Escape* has issues, lots of them. Technical failures that would never pass an engineering sign-off. We left anyway. Why?'

Jason cleared his throat. 'It bothers you? I can assure you, the *Escape* is quite safe.'

'That wasn't my question. I'm not worried about the yacht.' It was true. I'd sailed on plenty of ships less seaworthy than this. As long as we had an engine and a rudder we'd get to our destination. But this was a superyacht. My own safety was not my concern.

He turned to face me, eyes searching. I could see his mind ticking over.

'You can trust me,' I said. 'It's better for me to know now than find out later.'

He frowned, but nodded.

'Is this about Nikolas?'

Jason's face darkened. He stared at me, eyes unwavering. 'Where did you hear that name?'

I shrugged. 'Harriet asked if I was here because of Nikolas.'

His face relaxed a fraction, but his frown remained. 'Did she now? Is that all she said?'

I nodded. 'Something I should know?'

Jason mopped the back of his neck with a towel, stretching his back, taking a deep breath. He glanced at me for a few moments. I found his eyes searching, unnerving.

'No,' he said, finally. 'But I'll tell you why we're in a hurry, if you don't spread it around the crew.'

'You have my word.'

Another frown. 'Tax management,' he said.

I raised my eyebrows. 'Tax what?'

'The owner needed to move their assets out of Europe. This . . .' he indicated the inside of the gym, 'is a two-hundred-million-pound asset. It had to go. We had a deadline.' He shrugged. 'Now you know.'

I watched his eyes, his poker face. Practised.

'So this trip is about tax avoidance?' I said.

'Management,' he repeated. 'We don't avoid tax. We follow the law and the advice of our accountants. It made no sense to keep some of our assets in the EU any longer. Now . . .' He looked at his watch. 'Time for a shower. And I need to make a call.' He nodded and smiled, exited the gym, leaving me perched against his running machine.

I decided not to challenge, press him, but something about his answer made me feel uneasy. It was reluctant, then rehearsed, followed by a swift exit. His drinks bottle remained in the holder, forgotten, and the moisture from his hand was still evaporating from the touchscreen.

I stretched for ten minutes before heading down to my cabin, daydreaming, wondering if I should have put in more effort on the treadmill. I had to keep my body tight and ready, no slacking, not even for a day. Once you lose that discipline . . . well, you end up with a belly like Mitch's. I chuckled to myself, feeling mean. Mitch was rock solid. He had a six-pack in there somewhere.

As I entered the crew corridor, I saw a flash at the other

end, the door slamming. I didn't see who it was – we all looked alike in the drab uniforms, and the lighting was so poor the figure was just a blur. But halfway along, my own cabin door swung on its hinges, slowly closing, until it clicked shut.

I walked up to it, twisted the handle, and pushed it all the way open. We didn't lock our cabins as a rule – the stews would be cleaning the crew cabins at least every couple of days, and the only valuable items in mine were locked away under my bunk.

My cabin was empty. I stood for a moment, checking my bunk, my shelves – not that there was much to look at. I crouched, ducked under the bunk, grabbed my phone and switched on the torch. My gun case was where I had left it, tucked against one wall, chained securely to the metal legs of the bunk. Had I left it against the front edge or the rear edge? The more I stared, the more I couldn't be sure. It may have shifted with the motion, anyway.

I checked the lock and stood back up. My wardrobe and drawers were neat, as I'd left them. My toiletries bag was tucked to one side, the zipper closed. The security folder and paperwork were stacked next to it.

There was nothing else to check, such was the expanse of my cabin, so I closed the door, stripped off my sweaty clothing and stood in the shower, enjoying the hot water cascading down my face and body, wondering why somebody would want to snoop in my accommodation.

Probably innocent – checking if my cabin needed cleaning. Or checking if I was asleep. I got that I was the new girl – most of the crew knew each other, had worked with each other, even slept with each other. Perhaps privacy wasn't a thing for the crews on these yachts. Some of them might have wanted to check me out, see what secrets I might be hiding, find my diary and have a good laugh. Unfortunately for them, I carried all the important secrets in my head.

I could go to Karis or Greg, but say what, exactly? That I saw my cabin door closing on its own? They might humour me, but there was nothing much they could do, and it would alienate pretty much everyone else.

No. I'd leave it, let it go. This time. No damage done. Nothing except a slight flicker of unease, a breach of my privacy. A slight wall of distrust, my natural protection rearing up.

But I could handle that. I was used to it.

9

The afternoon of the second day saw a fresh wind spring up, thicker clouds racing each other across the pale sky as we exited the Strait of Gibraltar. The heat clung to the air, but it was gradually being torn away as we left the shelter and protection of the mainland behind, leaving us exposed to the wilds of the open ocean.

The motion was pronounced, the bow pummelled by waves that had crossed thousands of miles before hitting our hull, a small fragment of their energy transferred to the *Escape*, the rest surging on and past us, before ultimately breaking against the shores that we'd departed.

It was a familiar experience – the rumble and chatter of the waves, the wind sweeping over the decks and snaking around the fittings and awnings, the myriad clinks and bangs as loose items found new corners to hide in. I'd check in with Karis or Greg later, see what the weather reports offered. I assumed we'd divert to avoid any squalls – though it didn't bother me either way. I'd been on Navy transport ships in force ten more than once. Uncomfortable, but survivable. Harriet would need looking after. I assumed Greg kept a ship's pharmacy – Hyoscine or Dramamine would help her, if it got much worse. Jason's comments also preyed on my mind. It wasn't my business, though it was odd he'd lie rather than tell me so.

Leaving Palma quickly was one thing. But was there any reason to maintain our hasty speed?

Despite the freshness, Harriet had commandeered the sun deck, waited on by Lily. The cocktails flowed and the chatter on the radio adopted a low-level hum as the crew conferred on how to keep her happy. Some grumbling was evident – without Harriet on board it might still have been the crew in the tub, soaking up the sun, basking in the billionaires' club. But it was lucky they remained out-doors, and I wondered if Harriet understood that her world would get smaller once we were out on the ocean, the decks closed, confined to the interior. The owner's stateroom was hardly restrictive, but it might feel that way as the days dragged on.

Jason already tended to stay indoors, alternating between the library, cinema and art gallery. I only saw him a couple of times, hurrying between decks. He shunned most of the service – which was fine by Dan – and seemed absorbed in his own world. A corporate world, I guessed, full of shareholders, profits, and perhaps a little tax once in a while. The world which kept this palace afloat.

I was headed to the main deck this afternoon. A storage room near the spiral staircase held all of the non-firearms security equipment. Mitch had loaded and checked it all, but I needed to give it a quick once-over, see what had shifted since departure.

Nipping back to my cabin to grab the equipment mani-fest, I heard raised voices coming from the back of the crew quarters, in the shared kitchen. I paused, not intend-ing to eavesdrop, but concerned. I tucked myself outside the kitchen door by the bulkhead.

'Let it go.' Arno's voice.

'I can't.' Luan's voice. 'He fucked me over, brother.'

'I know, and I'm as angry as you are, but –'

'No buts. He fucking deserves it. He did the same to Pieter. He's a fucking rat.'

'I agree,' said Arno, 'but I have another idea.'

'That's you, always full of ideas.'

'Trust me,' said Arno. 'Something's come up. Something new. Keep your head down, yeah? Don't cause trouble. Just smile and do your job.'

'What the fuck have I got to smile about?' said Luan.

'We'll both be smiling when I get paid,' said Arno.

'The only thing I see you smiling at is that new bit of ass.'

'What?' Arno's voice rose an octave.

'You heard.'

'Don't call her that,' said Arno. 'Who I talk to is none of your business.' His voice was trembling, his anger evident.

Whatever Luan said next was masked by a cupboard door slamming. I stepped closer, intrigued, but the two men had lowered their voices again, the words muffled. It was a heated exchange, back and forth, but one I struggled to make out.

'Just leave it,' said Arno.

I heard the fridge close and their footsteps approaching. I jumped away, nipping through the bulkhead door, out of sight. The brothers exited the kitchen and headed the other way, back to their cabin. The last thing I heard was Luan's voice.

'He's got it coming,' he said, opening their cabin door. 'That's all I'm saying.'

*

The argument had intrigued me, and brothers will fight, but Luan's final words were rather more concerning. Who did he mean? I mulled it over as I resumed my climb to the main deck. Perhaps I'd ask Arno about it, pry gently around the edges. The thought made me frown; the butterflies gave a small flutter in my stomach.

I opened the storage room door. First up were the stun guns – a case containing three Taser Pulse subcompact pistols. Short range, sometimes useful, though the conditions in which anyone would use them on board ship were limited. The batteries read as charged, so I closed the case and stowed it, checking off my list.

The next item was rather larger, one of Mitch's favourites, and useful, if we happened to be travelling through high-risk piracy areas such as the Horn of Africa or the South China Sea. Standing five feet tall on a tripod, the sound cannon's basic premise was to blast powerful sound waves at people. Technically called an LRAD, or long-range acoustic device, they'd been used by police forces across the globe for years for dispersing hostile crowds and rioters. Excruciating if you got hit, it was the sound equivalent of looking directly at the sun. Disorientation and panic followed. Most people lay on the ground and screamed.

The rest of the equipment was less exciting – some good old-fashioned nightsticks, plasticuffs and pepper spray – items you'd expect if settling a rowdy crew or passengers on a commercial outfit. Some extra backup disks for the CCTV – the main console was wired into the lower deck, in engineering. I made a note to ask Jack to show it to me asap.

Checklist complete, I headed to the bridge, finding Greg and Karis huddled over the cockpit screens. Jack stood to one side, arms crossed, fidgeting and shuffling his feet. The sky over the bow was noticeably darker, a wall of clouds now obscuring the blue, the horizon closing in. The sun still tried to stream through, but weaker, a far cry from our opening run out of the Med. I watched us rise and fall, pitching hard as we faced the swell. Our heading was clear – nothing between us and Antigua but three and a half thousand miles of unforgiving ocean.

'We're too fast,' said Jack.

Karis nodded. Her brow was furrowed. 'I agree,' she said. 'Greg, there's no need to run her at this speed.'

'We have enough fuel to run at seventeen knots,' said Greg.

'With little room for error,' said Jack.

'But enough,' said Greg. His tone was no-nonsense, his clipped German accent coming through stronger as he asserted his authority.

'We proceed at this speed,' he said. 'We're rhumb lining it. We'll be fine.'

Rhumb lining – the nautical term for a straight line between origin and destination, and the preferred route for large, powered craft such as the *Escape*. Smaller vessels would often take a different route, south towards the Canaries, across to Cape Verde, before a final long leg to the Caribbean. Our route took us well north of Madeira, but not far enough to avoid the huge low pressure visible on the screens. Karis tapped one of them. I edged closer. It was the weather radar, showing a good deal of activity to the south.

'We'll be skirting this,' she said. 'It'll get very uncomfortable, Greg. It's already rougher than I'd like.'

'I've checked with our *guests*.' Greg spat the last word. I assumed he meant Jason and Harriet. 'Faster the better. It's only a squall.'

'It's growing,' said Karis, 'and you know it'll be unpredictable – these temperatures, higher than usual for this time of year. A summer storm could be violent – we could have days of it. It could veer around and do a U-turn on us.'

Greg slammed his hand on the wheel. He took several deep breaths, before turning to her.

'Please, Karis. Stop questioning me,' he said. 'We must hit the schedule, that's all I'm trying to do. The owner says *sail*, we say *how fast*? That's how it works, and you know it.' He glanced over, seeing me for the first time. His expression changed; he gave me a small nod. 'Sarah,' he said. 'We were just discussing our route.'

I nodded. 'We aren't deviating for the weather?' I said, making it sound innocent, but backing Karis at the same time.

Greg shook his head. 'It would add days to our schedule. Not possible.'

Jack made a noise.

'You have something to add, Jack?' I could tell Greg's patience was already thin.

'The autopilot tripped twice this morning,' said Jack. 'Going through a storm . . . I wonder . . .'

'Noted,' said Greg, turning back to the screens. 'Is there anything else, Jack?'

'There was, actually, something with the . . .' He tailed

off, glancing at me and apparently deciding whatever it was, it could wait. 'No, boss,' he said. 'If you need me, I'll –'

'We'll come find you,' said Greg.

Jack sidled out, eyes down, like a hurt puppy.

Greg waited until he'd gone before turning to me, leaning against the wheel, folding his arms, perhaps sensing I needed an explanation.

'They're a good bunch,' he said, 'my crew.' He nodded to Karis, a smile curling at the edges of his lips. 'Solid, experienced, professional. Even Jack, despite his faults.'

I caught his gaze. Was he sharing what I already knew?

'This trip, as you've no doubt gathered, Sarah, was a little rushed in its preparation. We departed at haste, and I'm sorry you're seeing the after-effects – some tensions and strain amongst the crew. But rest assured, we know what we're doing. Once we get a couple of days out, it'll all come together. People will relax. You'll see.'

I glanced at Karis; her expression was softened, but conflicted. She watched Greg with undeniable affection.

I had to remind myself this wasn't the military. These crews ran with a degree of informality which, it seemed, was more akin to a squabbling family than a professional outfit. They fought, they made up, no harm done. Still, each seemed to know their job, and whatever my concerns, it wasn't *my* job to comment. *Suck it up, Sarah*, I imagined Mitch saying. *Jump in the hot tub. Relax.*

'I actually have one of our deckhands joining me on the bridge any minute,' he said, checking his watch, as if to emphasize his own care and attention to the crew. 'Camila – friend of a friend, working towards her advanced

RYA exams. I said she could join me on watch.' He turned to Karis. 'It might be handy, in fact,' he added for her benefit, 'gives us an extra pair of hands up here. I feel she's someone I can really trust.'

As if on cue, the side door opened and Camila appeared. She was in her working clothes – polo shirt and shorts, hair pulled back, make-up subtle. She paused.

'You said to be here at three?'

Greg nodded. 'Come on in,' he said. 'We'll start with our route planning. Tell me what you think.'

Camila nodded, throwing me a quick glance – a shy smile, wary. *Was* Arno in her sights, and she was sizing up the competition? Not that I was competing.

There I went again.

'You OK?' I said to Karis, leaving Greg and Camila to talk.

'Hmm,' she said, keeping her eye on Greg. 'I guess so.'

'Into the storm? Fun, if that's your thing.'

She nodded. 'He's in a hurry, all right,' she said, still gazing at the captain, shaking her head.

'Any idea why?'

'Greg's always in a hurry,' she said. 'Except when it matters.'

I waited. Karis's eyes darted to me. 'Sorry, I shouldn't have . . . forget it.'

I shrugged. 'You two . . . ?'

She nodded. 'We were. But the timing is *just* awful.'

'Pieter?'

Karis looked taken aback, blinked a couple of times. 'Who told . . . ?' Her shoulders sagged. 'Is the whole crew talking about it?'

I winced. 'No.'

She sighed, laughed. 'You can't hide anything on these boats,' she said. 'Especially not when your current partner and ex-partner are screaming at each other on the quay.'

'None of my business,' I said, agreeing. It would be hard to find much privacy for such things, even on a yacht this size.

And yet I still sensed secrets under the surface. I wondered what commitment looked like in this world of civilian yachting, what plans they'd make – what happened next. Did Karis dream of sailing with Greg until retirement, finally settling down on dry land, a cottage in the country perhaps, reminiscing with kids and grandkids? It was a nice thought, a warm future, except it jarred, a stab of pain, highlighting my own devastated future plans. There would be no cottage in the country for me. Not with Kay.

The rear door opened. Harriet stepped in, dressed in a robe, hair in a towel, a petulant expression on her face. Greg's bridge was a busy place.

'Um,' said Harriet, holding the wall for support. 'Nobody seems to be waiting on me.'

I hid my smirk. And the crew still had to deal with the guests.

Karis stepped forward. 'What can we get you?'

'My shower has stopped working,' said Harriet. 'Just . . . stopped. I was in it. Is that normal? I don't think it is.'

Karis maintained a perfectly professional tone as she responded. 'I'm terribly sorry, and no, it's not normal. I'll ask the chief stew to look right into it. In the meantime, please use one of the showers in the guest rooms. They are all made up.'

She tapped her mic. 'Dan, this is Karis. Come in, please.'

'*Go ahead.*'

'Miss DeWitt-Fendley's shower is broken. Can you take a look, please?'

'*Is she with you now?*'

'Yes.'

'*Please tell her I'll be there immediately.*'

Harriet smiled her thanks. She turned to leave, paused, stared towards Greg. She tapped an index finger to her lips, narrowed her eyes, tilting her head this way and that.

'Are you OK?' said Karis.

'Yes. Yes, I'm fine,' said Harriet, directing a beaming smile at us both, before gliding out of the rear door.

10

Day three, early morning. I was ducked down with Karis, picking my way across the slatted metal floor. The tank deck was industrial, a claustrophobic level dedicated to the mechanical apparatus of the *Escape* – engine room, generators, air conditioning and electrical relay points. The next room, through the thick bulkhead, housed the two diesel caterpillar engines. Beyond that, the tender and jet ski storage. The deck was alive with the sound of motors and pumps, the hiss of valves and the clicking of switchgear. Extractor fans hummed away in the corners, doing their best to expel the gases and chemical fumes – though some remained, tickling the throat, causing a dull ache in my nose.

We were below sea level at this point, and I could feel the water against the hull, the screeches and thuds revealing a world away from the luxury of the decks above, a world the guests would never see – and under normal circumstances, neither would most of the crew.

But when the chief engineer called the captain down to this level, you knew something was seriously wrong.

'How the hell did this happen?' Greg raised his voice over the background throb of the engines.

Jack stared forward. His fidgeting was worse, his face stricken and dishevelled. Despite Greg's words on the bridge yesterday, I wondered how long Greg could let him go on like this. I'd tagged along at Karis's request, hearing a brief exchange on the engineering frequency of the radios, offering my assistance.

Jack glanced at Karis, the four of us staring at the 4,000-litre fresh water tank. It was one of two – the second placed on the other side of the room, distributing the colossal weight equally across the beam of the yacht.

'Both of them?' said Greg, in disbelief. 'You're telling me both are empty?'

Jack knocked on the tank. The hollow sound answered Greg. 'Almost,' he said. 'Maybe fifty litres in the bottom. Same with tank two.'

Greg shook his head, palms to his cheeks.

'The problem,' said Jack, pointing to a neat collection of pipes snaking from the bottom of the tank up to a complicated set of valves, 'is these. They're shot to bits – jammed over into the purge setting. The taps are missing. They've been emptying since we sailed.'

'Emptying where?'

'Into the bilge,' said Jack. 'The pump has been on full whack – it's how I noticed the leak. It was overheating. Miss DeWitt-Fendley's shower stopped because the guest rooms' boiler draws from these tanks.'

'Eight thousand litres of fresh water pumped into the sea,' said Karis. 'Wonderful.'

I turned over the possible implications of losing the majority of our fresh water. None were good. I stepped forward, running my fingers over the valve caps. Paint had chipped away, like they had been struck with something. But they were brand new – the tanks installed just days ago, so it couldn't be wear and tear. I wondered how that might happen by accident. Jack's incompetence, the rush to leave harbour?

'How much in the standard tanks?' I said.

Greg looked sharply at me.

'Two thousand litres,' said Jack. 'Those tanks are fine.'

I nodded. 'So we have two thousand one hundred litres, give or take.'

Jack shrugged. 'A little less. We've been quite excessive over the first couple of days. Perhaps eighteen hundred.'

Karis paced up and down, then stopped, shaking her head. 'It's not enough.'

Greg frowned. 'Hang on.'

'It's not,' Karis insisted. 'Eighteen hundred litres between twelve of us, over nine, ten days. That's . . .'

'Roughly fifteen litres per person per day,' said Jack, '*if* we make our destination on schedule, which should be OK . . . I guess, given our faster speed.'

Karis laughed. 'No way.' She looked at Greg. 'You're not seriously considering that we keep going?'

Greg took a deep breath. 'It's plenty. Two litres a day – that's all people need.'

'Need? Christ, Greg. Two litres for emergency drinking rations. What about washing? Clean clothing, sheets, the ship itself? It's less than a fifth of our planned fresh water, we have two guests on board, and we're only two days from land. We turn around, fix the tanks – along with a bunch of other things – restart this trip in a week or two.'

I could see Jack nodding.

'We also have the bottled water, soft drinks,' said Greg.

Karis looked incredulous. 'Perhaps we could wash in beer?' she said. 'Brush my teeth with Merlot?'

'The water maker,' I said. 'Any chance you can get it working?'

'None at all,' said Jack. 'It's not broken, per se. It's just missing several parts. Essential ones. It was never installed . . .' He tailed off.

Whatever the cause, the decision was an easy one. Karis was right. Greg must turn the *Escape* around and head home, or at least to the nearest equipped shipyard.

It was a no-brainer.

'Gather the crew on the main deck,' said Greg. 'Jason and Harriet, too.'

Karis paused, watching Greg for a few moments before making the calls on the radio. We filed out in silence.

Karis took watch on the bridge, the remaining eleven of us huddled around the main dining table. The chandeliers sparkled, in contrast to the mood in the room, which simmered with unease. An all-crew meeting was never good news.

Jason stood behind Greg, to his left. They'd spoken outside for several minutes, keeping us all waiting. I noted Harriet, standing in the doorway, arms folded, eyeing us all with mild disdain. She staggered as the *Escape* pitched, forced to grab the door frame. Her eyes darted around, found mine. I gave her a reassuring smile.

'This morning we discovered another minor technical issue with the *Escape*,' said Greg.

I saw Jack raise his eyebrows. Mine did the same. Hardly minor.

'As you know from the departure briefing, the fresh water maker is out of action. Instead, we installed two additional fresh water tanks, giving us more than enough – within reason – for our trip.'

Nods and nervous glances from the assembled crew. Dan opened a can of cola, draining half of it in one gulp. I heard the gas escape from his throat. He glanced at me, a hint of arrogance. I stared at him until he looked away.

My eyes found Arno's. He smiled at me, winked. I narrowed my eyes at the gesture, but couldn't stop the familiar flush in my cheeks. *Dammit, Sarah. What's wrong with you?* Arno took the hint and averted his gaze, adopting a mock chastised expression.

'The tanks turned out to be faulty,' Greg continued, 'and the additional water has been lost – literally, drained. Which leaves us with one tank – less than two thousand litres . . .' He paused, as if struggling for words.

'So we're heading home,' said Dan. A statement, not a question. He crumpled the can of cola and flicked it on to the table. 'Great,' he said, drawing it out sarcastically. 'We still get paid.'

'It's the right choice,' said Luan, casting his gaze around the table, nodding.

Most of the others pulled disappointed expressions, but didn't disagree. I noticed Camila shaking her head, staring at Greg. Her face was fixed with a deep frown, chewing her bottom lip. Nobody was happy. It would be a shock for most of them, and me too, if I believed it. But Greg hadn't finished, and I had a horrible feeling I knew what came next.

'But,' he said, raising his voice, nodding over his shoulder, 'Jason and I have discussed the situation, and we've agreed to continue as planned, albeit with strict water rationing, we –'

Greg's words were drowned out by shouts of protest. Both Arno and Luan threw their hands in the air, shaking their heads violently. Elijah slouched back in his chair, folding his arms, swearing under his breath.

'You must be joking,' said Lily. 'Rationing? That's insane.'

'But,' Greg continued, 'with a ten per cent bonus on top of your pay. The whole trip's worth.'

The murmurs continued, but died down at the offer of money.

I glanced at Harriet, who looked like she wanted to speak. I waved to Greg, got his attention, and pointed to Harriet.

'Miss DeWitt-Fendley,' said Greg.

The crew stopped talking at once. Eyes were on the billionaire, who they might reasonably guess would have the final say in what happened.

'I . . . I just wondered,' she said. 'What does rationing mean, in practice? How much are we talking?'

Greg glanced at Jason. 'You and Mr Chen will have enough for personal washing and a shower every other day. I guarantee it.'

Jack cleared his throat. 'That's not going to –'

'The crew will have eight litres per day for washing and drinking,' said Greg. 'Plus whatever we've got in the bar storage?' He glanced at Dan, who shrugged.

'A couple of hundred bottles,' said Dan, 'plus a few hundred soft drinks, soda, tonic. We have beer?'

'Right,' said Greg.

Each person did a mental picture of eight litres, realizing it wasn't much, not if you drank two or three of them, and were expected to keep some modicum of cleanliness. I watched the reactions unfold with faint amusement. Water rationing was second nature to me, and I had no qualms with eight litres a day. Greg was right – two was enough to keep you hydrated, and we could wash with seawater if we had to. It was only nine days – fewer, if Greg maintained the increased speed. I'd spent that long in a hole in the jungle before. Now *that* was dirty.

But Greg's decision still amazed me. This was essentially a toy ship, not a navy at war. Why take the risk of an ocean crossing, with rationing from the outset? Jason and Greg obviously had their reasons, and Greg was receiving a hefty bonus for his cooperation. But they weren't telling the truth.

Bite your tongue, Sarah. It's not your call.

'How do the, um, toilets work?' asked Harriet.

Good question.

'It's a closed system,' said Jack. 'Black water . . . that is, the flushed water, er, is processed, cleaned, used again.'

Harriet looked at him in horror.

'For flushing,' he clarified. 'Just for flushing.'

She nodded, looking quite perturbed.

'And we can flush with seawater,' he added. 'If that system breaks. Not that I expect it to.'

'Mr Chen, may we have a moment?' said Harriet.

Jason and Harriet filed out into the next room. The table fell quiet, a hush of uncomfortable silence, several suspicious glances directed at Greg. Arno played with a bottle of mineral water, stared at it for a moment, before tucking it carefully into his pocket.

'We should vote,' said Luan.

'This isn't a democracy, Luan,' said Camila.

Luan looked incensed. 'Why aren't we turning back?' He glared at Greg. 'Why?'

Greg sniffed. 'Because we do what the owner wants,' he said. 'That's why. Schedule is dictated by the owner, through Jason. We follow it. It's in your contract. I have a copy if you'd like to read it.'

I chuckled under my breath, watching Greg repeating the line Jason had given him before departure, during their argument. *Read your contract.*

Luan clenched his jaw, looked set to boil over. Arno nudged him, whispered something in his ear. Luan shook his head but shuffled back, taking a few deep breaths.

'What the hell am I supposed to cook with?' said Elijah.

'You'll have enough,' said Greg. 'I'm sure you'll figure it out.'

Luan snorted. 'Won't be any worse than the usual fare,' he said.

'What the fuck did you say?' said Elijah, clearly in no mood for the joke.

Luan mumbled something.

'Enough,' said Greg. 'Luan, the decision is made. Deal with it.'

Luan stood up, shoving his chair into the table. 'It's a shame we don't have the full crew,' he said. 'Karis and Pieter could have saved water by showering together.'

Lily nearly choked. I saw Jack's eyes widen. Camila shrank into her chair. Greg stopped, mouth open, processing the insult. He narrowed his eyes, his expression twisting, cheeks flushing. I felt for him – his business with Karis and Pieter had spilled over into his professional life – but Luan was bang out of order, whatever the circumstances. That kind of insubordination would have landed you in deep shit where I came from. I was amazed Greg managed to keep his cool.

'Dan,' Greg whispered. 'Please find something for your stews to do. The interior needs a complete wipe down, top to bottom. Every deck.'

Luan looked about to protest further, but Dan shut him down.

'Yes, Captain,' he said, ushering Luan out of the room. 'Move it, Luan, for fuck's sake,' he hissed. 'And leave Pieter out of this.'

'Hang on –' began Lily.

'No more discussion,' said Greg, swallowing, keeping his eyes on the table. 'Dismissed, all of you. Get back to work.'

He nodded to himself a few times before heading in the opposite direction, into the nearest stairwell, towards the bridge. Towards Karis.

I grabbed Jack as the others dispersed in a series of grunts and expletives.

'You OK, Jack?' I said.

His eyes said no. 'Sure,' he replied. 'Fine and dandy. Why wouldn't I be?'

'It's bad luck, that's all.' I kept eye contact as I said it, searching.

He pulled a curious expression. 'Sure,' he said. 'If you say so.'

Interesting. 'What do you mean?'

He paused, sighed. 'Nothing,' he said. 'This yacht is a steaming hulk of bad luck.'

'Could be worse,' I said. 'You only need one litre of water a day to stay alive. Short-term, anyway. We've got seven extra to play with. I might save it up and have a bath.'

Jack snorted, laughing before it shifted into a coughing fit. He turned away, but too late to stop me smelling the alcohol on his breath. He saw my expression, his eyes darting to and fro.

Should I say it? If I didn't, would Greg? Did I trust Jack's assessment of the water tanks, or the installation of them? We only had his word they were full when we left port. And the damage to the valves . . . a manufacturing defect, or inflicted post-installation? Something didn't sit right.

'I had a few last night, *again*,' he said, by way of explanation. 'Camila and I . . . we . . .' He wiggled his eyebrows half-heartedly, trying to deflect my scrutiny.

'Really?' I was surprised.

'Well . . .' his face fell a fraction. 'No. But we had a drink. She was asking all about my job, the different engineering functions, anchors, hydraulics, you know – taking an interest. I think she has some exams or something when we get home.'

Could I picture Camila with Jack? Not for a second. But I didn't blame her for taking the initiative. Perhaps she *was* aiming for the bosun job.

'And you're *sure* you're OK,' I said. *One last chance.* 'I've known friends – soldiers – that, you know . . .'

Jack sniffed. His gaze wouldn't settle. He looked past me, outside. 'What do you mean?' he said.

Should I spell it out? *Jack, you're an addict and I see you?*

I sighed. 'You can talk to me,' I said. 'If you wanted to. That's all.'

He ran his tongue around the inside of his mouth, nodding, appearing to contemplate my offer.

'Thanks, Sarah,' he said, with a little too much enthusiasm. 'Right. Back to work. We'll be running out of fuel next, given the captain's schedule.'

I think he meant it as a joke, but he spat the last bit out with uncharacteristic bile. Then he spun on his feet and left.

I stared after him, thinking about what he'd said – or rather, hadn't said. If I believed the water tank failure wasn't his fault (a big if), and if it wasn't *bad luck* – as he seemed to intimate before hastily changing the subject – what did that leave?

11

I watched the darkening skies, two hours before sunset, hiding high on the sun deck – the only place I could find a modicum of peace, even with the wind starting to whip up. The hot tub was covered and the sunloungers stowed. Harriet had reluctantly been ushered inside, joining Jason – forced to make do with the opulent interior of the owner's stateroom. The last I'd heard she was watching reruns of *Sex and the City*.

The deck was bare. The indoor bar was closed and shuttered – I doubted it would get used until we hit the Caribbean.

Over the bow was darkest of all, the squall we'd seen in the south gaining energy and speed, now wholly visible with the naked eye. The *Escape* headed along its edge, aiming to charge across without changing course, if Greg's dubious predictions held.

But the sea conditions continued to deteriorate, and we were already hitting uncomfortably high waves. They might settle, they might worsen. We'd ride through it regardless.

Nearly four days in, and while the unexpected distractions were useful, I was no closer to thinking my way through any of the baggage I'd arrived with.

I'd tried. Not very hard, but I'd tucked myself away on occasion in an attempt to let my mind relax, taking a novel, a magazine, or even the security manifest. I'd mingled, observing the crew's habits, keeping a cautious distance.

My cabin remained untouched – whoever had poked around seemed to have been satisfied, although the niggling feeling remained, exacerbated by the claustrophobia of the crew quarters, the thin walls failing to mask the grumbles and animosity, albeit mostly directed at our captain.

Thankfully, the crew were still given freedom to roam the yacht, provided Harriet and Jason were taken care of. They watched movies, read books in one of the many lounges, or hit the gym while not on shift – their private lives no doubt continued behind closed doors.

But the fundamentals of my mood persisted: the deep, dragging sensations of grief and guilt, the dreams waking me in the early hours. I'd resisted the sleeping tablets so far, but I couldn't go on like this – I needed to block out his face, the sound of his voice, the feel of his skin.

Kay's presence was overwhelming, and yet I'd never see him again.

The thought took my breath away, and time stopped, my mind's cogs grinding to a halt. I'd stopped telling myself it wasn't my fault. I'd stopped lying. But where did that leave me? Was it a sign to move on, or to wallow forever in my failures?

I wished Amy were here to tell me, though I suspected I knew what her answer would be. *Grab the nearest cute guy and treat yourself*. Did I want to go there? If probed, my careful wall of defiance was at risk of crumbling. Each time I saw Arno's goofy smile and piercing eyes, I asked myself whether resistance was necessary, or useful to my current state of mind. He clearly wanted more – to talk, to have a drink, whatever. Since we'd spoken in the gym, I'd avoided him, obviously so. He'd laughed it off and kept asking. I was scared of being alone with him. Scared I might let him in.

Scared I *could* move on. Because where did that leave my guilt? My responsibility?

A freak wave jolted me into the moment, the *Escape* shuddered, thousands of tons of steel vibrating in protest, deforming a fraction, rebounding as the wall of water passed under the hull. I staggered to the left. Kay's face vanished.

I checked the time, wondering where to go. Since the water tank discovery, the atmosphere on the *Escape* seemed to be deteriorating as fast as the weather, the glamour of the Mediterranean a distant memory as we ploughed into the grey waters, my attention shifting from polite curiosity to a more critical analysis of the crew and the guests' activity.

I was almost certain Jack had something to do with the water. *Almost*. Carelessness, lack of attention to detail, deflecting blame. It was entirely possible he'd wrenched those water valves off himself, and blacked out afterwards. I could list the traits of an addict in my sleep, I'd seen it all before.

But Greg must know about Jack's addiction, and it wasn't my place to drive a wedge into that relationship. If Greg wanted to hold Jack to account, he would. Perhaps he already had, in private?

I heard a noise on the deck below. Karis walked towards the gunwale, rested on it for a second, head down. I assumed she was looking for the same thing as me, and I would have let her be, except she turned and saw me.

'Hey,' she called. A warm smile. She ducked out of sight and reappeared on the sun deck with me, grabbed two chairs and sat in one of them, staggering a little as we rolled to starboard, grabbing the chair to stop it sliding. 'Got five?' she said.

'Of course,' I replied.

We settled with a view over the stern, sheltered from the wind. Karis looked tired, older in this light, a long shift perhaps, but also something else.

I waited until she was ready.

'So, Greg and I aren't getting on so well,' she said.

I nodded my sympathy, but thinking she'd got the wrong person if she wanted relationship counselling. Where was Lily when you needed her? But I mentally chided myself. Karis was one of the good ones. How she worked with some of the idiots on this yacht was beyond me.

'Do you want to talk about it?' I said.

She turned to me, laughed. I think she saw straight through me. 'I won't bore you with the mushy crap, Sarah.'

'No, I . . .'

She raised her eyebrows.

'Honestly,' I said. 'Give me the mush if you like. I can't promise any good advice, though.'

She sighed. 'It's too late for that, I think.'

'How did he find out?'

Karis shrugged. 'I don't know. But I managed to hurt both of them.'

'Luan was quick to snipe at Greg about it in front of the crew,' I said. 'You want to watch that one.'

Karis nodded. 'Luan can be an arse; on that we agree. But the brothers come as a pair, and Arno is invaluable.'

'Does anyone on this crew like each other?'

That got another laugh out of her. 'Some,' she said, glancing at me. 'Crewing on these things – it's like family. Long histories, flings, friendships, fights . . . and like family, you don't always choose who you crew with. I thought it must be a bit like the military?'

Maybe. Though with a lot more tolerance for insubordination.

'You're one of the popular ones,' she said, with a wink. 'Particularly with a certain young deckhand.'

'Hmm.' Reading my mind. My turn to deflect. 'So what's the deal with Pieter, then?'

Karis blew out her cheeks. 'How long have you got?'

I checked my watch. 'About nine days, give or take.'

Karis chuckled, pulling her jacket tighter, zipping it up. I felt the cold at the same time, the wind sucking the heat from my skin.

She shifted in her chair, nodding towards the bow. 'See those clouds?'

I squinted, making out the towering plumes in the distance, anvil-shaped at the top, menacing. I should know the answer.

'Cumulonimbus?' I guessed.

'Correct. And why do we not like those?'

Thunderstorms, that's why. Violent electrical discharge looking for the tallest point to hit, heavy rain, and hail. I brought my gaze back to the *Escape*, to the metal hull, the masts and radar domes.

I smiled. 'We'll be OK,' I said, as the deck tilted to a

sharp angle, the hull struggling over a rogue wave, rushing down the other side. It creaked and groaned deep down, complaining at the stress. I looked out at the water, dark, almost black at this time in the evening. Menacing.

Karis chuckled. 'You'd hope so. But every day Jack seems to find another thing wrong with this luxurious hunk of crap.'

'That he does,' I said.

'But Greg insists we plough through,' said Karis. 'It's crazy. Never in the ten years I've known him would he go straight into a storm like this.'

I thought of all the storms I'd been through, without any choice in the matter. Hailstones the size of golf balls hitting the decks, so slippery you had to be tied on to avoid smashing into each other. Ships could take it; crew could take it. But you needed a good reason. I hoped Greg's was good enough.

'Decisions like this will be the death of him, one day,' she said.

I watched her. I think she needed to get something out, whatever it was. She'd called me over the deck, asked *me* to sit down. If talking about it was important to her, then it should be important to me.

'Pieter. You didn't answer me.'

Karis sighed. 'Pieter and Greg have been friends for years, although I think he and Dan have ended up closer lately. Started working together on charters in the BVIs.'

'Fun.'

Karis screwed up her face. 'Not really,' she said. 'It's a slog. Long shifts, shitty guests. But it builds your hours.'

I chuckled. I'd done my fair share of shitty hour-building at sea. Some of the boats even had cabins.

'So how did it all . . .' I struggled.

'Go wrong?' said Karis. 'I don't know. Or it's too much of a cliché to describe. I was Greg's "bit on the side", the difference being that his marriage was already on the rocks – spending most of your life at sea a thousand miles away from your wife will do that to a relationship, I don't care who you are.'

'Fair enough,' I said, wondering if Kay and I had been posted to the opposite ends of the earth, whether it would have mattered. Of course it would. But I'd like to pretend it wouldn't have.

'So we enjoyed each other to the point where I wanted more,' said Karis, turning to me. 'That's the cliché bit. Sorry. The mistress wants to be the wife. I got to a certain age and . . . well.'

'Happens all the time. You're just describing it wrong,' I said.

'Oh?'

'How about, you met a man in an unhappy relationship, and decided to sweep him off his feet, make him yours?'

Karis nodded, impressed. 'You're right. That does sound better. And it's what I did.'

'But he wouldn't leave his wife. Now *he's* the cliché,' I said.

'Exactly. I waited. And I waited.'

'And you're a professional woman who knows she's worth it,' I said, seeing the flicker of emotion in her eyes, the hurt and frustration.

'Damn right,' she said, sniffing.

'And if he couldn't commit, then you had needs. And you took care of them?'

Karis nodded, smiling. 'That I did. Rather too close to home, though.'

I glanced around, indicating the deck, the yacht. 'How far can you get from home mid-season? Plus I imagine you already had Pieter's eye.' I winked at her. 'He would have pounced the second he saw the opportunity.'

Karis cupped her face with both hands, rubbed her eyes. 'He did. But I knew what I was doing ... It didn't last long, and I figured we wouldn't get caught.'

'You're human.'

'I'm a yachtie. Just about human on a good day. But Pieter was so angry after Greg fired him,' she said. 'I've never seen him like that ... I worry what he'll do.'

We stared out at sea for a few moments, letting the motion settle our thoughts.

'But you don't want the top job?' I said. 'Captain Karis? Surely that's what you're working towards?'

She sighed. 'I *do*. It's my dream. *Was* my dream. But ... I'd still pick a future with Greg over it. You can't have two captains on a ship, Sarah.' She said it with a touch of bitterness.

I nodded, wondering how many women give up their careers at a similar point. Never hitting the top jobs they were destined to have. It pissed me off.

'So where does it leave you?' I said.

Another shrug. 'Pieter was exciting, passionate, *unreliable*. You never quite knew what he was going to do next. Greg is dependable, my ... I don't know. Soulmate? Does that sound like another horrible cliché?'

'Not at all,' I said, trying to avoid the instant lump forming in my throat.

Soulmate. I had one of those, once. But Karis still had the chance of a future with hers. What seemed like a major fracture in their relationship was insignificant in comparison. It could be fixed, forgotten. The future could be theirs.

I remembered Kay talking about a career after the Marines, buying a farm, his reason being that any farm would be about as far away as he could get from barracks. He'd gladly replace his brothers in arms with a stable full of farm animals – he reckoned it would be more peaceful. He hastily added that I'd be there with him, that we'd enjoy the peace together, perhaps on the hay bales, in the fields – creating plenty of animal noises of our own. Importantly, it would be our own little world. I knew he was joking, but it didn't stop me dreaming about it, creating my own fantasies of a life together afterwards. After the war, after the death and the resulting trauma that we'd forever carry. Such thoughts kept me going, in the darkness, in those moments when none of what we did seemed worth it.

But all those dreams had been extinguished in a heartbeat. I had nothing planned now, and I dreamed only of the past.

'If Greg's the one,' I said, 'he's worth fighting for. Don't throw it all away for one mistake, however hard it might seem right now.'

Karis looked at me, through me. I saw her understanding, also the pain of the chaos created by a wandering mind – the what-ifs, the lack of certainty about your own destiny.

She checked her watch. 'He's pretty mad right now, but . . . you're right. I'm not giving up. Thanks for . . . this. It's nice to have a new ear to chew.'

'Pleasure,' I said. 'It's my turn, next time.'

I wondered if I meant it. Would talking help? It was something I'd resisted, throughout my therapy, my friends' best attempts, my sister's relentless questioning.

It might be just what I needed.

I went to the crew kitchen, looking for a snack before bed. I found Arno.

'Hey,' he said, his eyes lighting up, the goofy grin present and correct.

I grabbed a banana from the counter and some muesli from the cupboard. Breakfast before bed – an old habit from my training days. Why stop now? I held the bowl carefully to stop it moving around. The rest of the plates and cups clinked in their fixtures, sliding as we rolled.

'Budge up,' I said, sliding on to the shallow sofa.

Arno shuffled around, dropping his *Men's Health* magazine and folding his arms. He must have known it was a good look for him – his biceps struggling to stay put, pecs stretching his T-shirt. I made a point of staring over his shoulder at something.

The crew kitchen was rather basic – a fixed table and sofa, one wall covered in kitchen units, with a microwave, fridge, toaster and kettle. A pod coffee machine was unplugged and shoved to one side – nobody could get it working, and the coffee from the main deck kitchen was better. The walls were plastered with printouts of the deck plan, fire procedures, radio frequencies and a framed chart of the Caribbean. A smallish TV tilted down from a wall bracket. It was switched off.

'Busy few days, huh?' said Arno.

'I guess,' I said, shovelling the cereal into my mouth.

He peered at me. 'I guess you've seen us at our worst.'

The milk ran down my chin, and I wiped it with my sleeve. 'It's not what I was expecting,' I said.

Arno nodded. 'You're settling in OK, though? We've barely had a chance to talk.'

His expression was one of mild accusation.

'Yeah,' I said. 'Sorry. I've been too busy watching you lot tear shreds off each other.'

He laughed, a little too loudly. 'Not me,' he said.

'Oh?' I raised my eyebrows.

The goofy smile twisted into a frown. 'What do you mean? I had a go at Greg, sure. But we're all a little mad about the water.'

'I meant Luan,' I said. I wasn't sure whether to push it, but I figured part of my ruthless commitment to avoid Arno should involve finding out a little more about him. Perhaps I'd find something I detested – a porn addiction, or a cult membership. A psycho. Something I could draw a line with.

Because as it stood, in close confines, I'd only be able to resist that smile for a little longer.

'What do you mean?' he said again. His grin wavered. I'd hit a nerve of some sort, but he wasn't going to admit it.

'I overheard you,' I said, peeling the banana, pausing for a second before breaking a piece off and shoving it in my mouth. 'Arguing with him, yesterday.'

Arno's turn to flush. 'What did you hear?'

'All of it,' I said, suddenly intrigued. What family drama had I stumbled into?

Arno deflated, his chest shrinking. He closed his eyes for a second before placing his palms on the table.

'He didn't mean it,' he said. 'Luan is angry, and rightly so. Greg totally screwed him over with that loan reference. It meant our business start-up would be sunk. I was just trying to . . .' He caught my puzzled look.

I winced, quickly breaking off another piece of banana. 'Keep going,' I said, with my mouth full.

Arno's mouth dropped open. 'You little . . .' he said, grinning. 'What *did* you hear?'

'Not that,' I said. 'But thanks.'

Arno shook his head. 'Fucking Marines,' he joked. 'You're cunning.'

'So you may as well tell me the rest,' I said.

He chuckled. 'That's it. Luan and I are starting a business – a charter company, back home. The marine mortgage required employer references. We just found out Greg's was awful and obstructive – he recommended against the bank lending to us.' Arno shrugged. 'The references are supposed to be confidential. The bank let it slip.'

'And Luan wants to say something?'

'Oh, Luan wants to say something. Trouble is, Luan often speaks with his fists. I had to stop him. We were already committed to this trip and I figured we'd try and prove ourselves to Greg, rather than fight him. I think Luan had other ideas, along the lines of marching up to the bridge and pushing Greg's face through the window.' He sniffed. 'Either way, I might have figured something out.' He pushed himself away from the table and made a point of checking his watch. 'Shift starts in ten,' he said. 'How about we continue this tomorrow?'

I wondered exactly *what* he'd figured out. 'This . . . ?'

Another shake of his head. 'This getting to know each other,' he said. 'Tease me all you like, but I'm not giving up yet. We South Africans are made of stubborn stuff.'

I kept any further sarky remarks to myself. Truth was, I didn't want him to give up. The banter was fun, and harmless. And I could stop it at any time.

'Maybe,' I said. 'I'll check my schedule.'

His laughter echoed in the corridor as he headed off.

I stayed for a while, grabbing another bowl of cereal, reflecting on what he'd said. Another argument. Another minor transgression, perhaps amplified by the confines of living in the same yacht, night after night. It might be called the *Escape*, but nobody could, not from each other. Not out here. But I hoped Arno had a tight leash on Luan. Luan had sounded frustrated, furious, ready to blow. Despite Arno's assurances that it was over, Luan's final words repeated in my head.

His words meant for Greg.

He's got it coming.

12

The siren pierced my dreams, a repeating high-pitched scream that grabbed my consciousness and dragged it kicking and screaming into reality. I opened my eyes, confused, mind groggy from the sleeping tablets, my heart hammering at the shock.

A moment later, someone thumped the outside of my cabin door. Twice, three times more, then the call.

'*Fire!*'

Lily's voice, urgent, on the verge of panic.

My cabin quickly came into focus, I kicked off the sheets, took a few breaths. Prepared myself. Checked my watch.

Five a.m. The morning of the fourth day.

A fire at sea is catastrophic if not contained quickly. All crew are trained in how to respond, and I knew the standard drill like the back of my hand. I needed to get my arse out on deck and follow instructions.

I put on the first thing I could find – my joggers and a vest from the evening before – opening the door to find Lily hammering at each of the crew cabins, repeating her shouts. She ran to me. I couldn't see any smoke, but a faint acrid taste tickled my throat – it would be circulating through the air ventilation system by now – which *should* have shut off when the alarm triggered.

'You know the assembly point?' she said.

'Yes. Are the rest of the crew out?'

'Nearly.'

'Harriet and Jason?'

'Karis has gone for them,' said Lily. 'Elijah is already suited up.'

'Where?'

'Aft of the stairwell, this deck,' she said.

This deck, the lower deck. Must have been something in the engine room, or electrical. Lily shouted again, repeating her call. Luan jumped out of his cabin, Arno following. They cottoned on immediately, didn't say a word, grabbed some basic clothing and headed my way.

Lily checked the remaining cabins and called out, 'All clear.'

I paused . . .

Arno and Luan rushed past, knowing I was right behind. But Lily's words stabbed at me. *All clear.* A statement of safety, of completeness. An acceptance of responsibility.

The same words I'd uttered all those months ago.

The memory shot to the fore. My dreams, my nightmare. The timing couldn't be worse.

The corridor shrank before my eyes, my vision tunnelling. My chest constricted as if a boa had grabbed it, my heart thumping painfully, my breath coming in gasps.

All clear. I'd called it, on that fateful day. My call. My responsibility.

The panic grabbed me and wouldn't release.

I saw it as if it were yesterday. Most buildings were cleared without a single shot fired. By the book, clean and easy. I entered one of the last. It was dusty, a narrow corridor with three rooms leading off. Hazy sunlight filtered through from the left; dust motes danced as I crept forward. The first two rooms were empty. In the third, a man and woman sat at a wooden table, food prepared, laid out in front of them. They cowered, eyes down, raising their hands. The man muttered something in Pashto, but there was no threat. I lowered my rifle, calling the all-clear.

All clear.

All clear.

'Sarah?' Lily's voice broke through. She had me by the shoulders, shaking me.

Arno stood behind her; brow creased with concern. 'What's the matter, Sarah?' he said.

I blinked, the memory fading, shuddering out of existence like a stop-motion film, the dusty compound in Afghanistan replaced with the narrow corridor of the crew cabins, the firm ground underfoot replaced with the unremitting motion of the *Escape*. I had my back against the wall, legs bent at the knees, still hyperventilating.

'What's wrong?' Lily's concerned voice seeped through the haze. She shook me again. 'Sarah. I said everyone is out. Go to the stern, assembly point, main deck.'

I focused on her face, then Arno's. He grabbed me by the arm and dragged me along the corridor to the background piercing scream of the alarm, into the nearest stairwell.

We stopped.

Smoke billowed out towards us, black, acrid, burning my eyes. I didn't see any flames, no heat.

'Back,' said Arno, pushing me back along the corridor towards one of the side stairwells.

Upwards, Arno's hand on my back, the smoke mixing with fresher air as we climbed.

The sprinkler pipes and red nozzles on the ceiling caught my eye.

'Why aren't the sprinklers firing?' I shouted.

Arno shook his head. We stood aside as two fire-suited crew – I thought Dan and Jack – raced past with extinguishers. Another figure followed close behind. It was Greg, gasping in the full suit, oxygen mask tugged over his face.

'Out!' he shouted.

We obeyed, on the main deck now, weaving through to the relative safety of the outside deck. It was crisp, a strong wind, the air noticeably colder than yesterday. I gulped a few lungfuls of fresh air.

The short snap of activity had woken me from my memories, banished my demons – I was alert, tense, ready. I scanned the deck, the assembled crew, Jason behind them – Harriet tucked against him in shock. I counted – six, including me. Lily appeared behind me. Seven. Four inside. Lily had said Elijah had gone straight to the tank deck.

'Who's missing?' I said.

'Karis went to the bridge,' said Lily. 'She'll only leave it if we . . .' she paused, gulping at the thought, 'are forced to abandon . . .' Her eyes widened.

It was my turn to reassure her. Her assertiveness and prompt actions had roused us all and got us out to safety.

The adrenaline was catching up. 'It won't come to that,' I said, gripping her arm. 'We'll control this.' I looked towards Arno, who was pulling another suit out of the fire lockers at the side of the deck. 'Get me one,' I shouted.

'You aren't part of the fire crew,' said Arno, shaking his head, pulling the trousers on. 'I'll do it.'

'Give me a damn suit,' I shouted.

'You haven't practised the drills on this yacht,' said Arno, grabbing the fireproof jacket, mask and oxygen bottle. 'Stay here,' he ordered.

I didn't argue – it would only waste time – but hovered by the rear doors instead, trying to peer back in, ready to run in and grab anyone who needed help. I was fit, strong, my lungs could take it, which is more than I could say for Greg or some of the others.

The next few minutes were painful. Over the sound of the wind and sea, I heard the extinguishers firing on the lower deck, short blasts, Greg and Jack calling to each other, but no shouts for help. The main deck was clear, but thicker black smoke poured out of an open door on the deck below – it was a positive sign, the fire must be small, contained. I hoped. A gust of wind caught the smoke, lifted it up and over the assembled crew. We coughed, eyes burning.

Across the lounge, Greg appeared, the others close behind. Last out was Elijah, who dumped his extinguisher on the side and ripped his mask off, sucking in air.

I ran over, held him up. 'You OK?' I said. 'Take it slow, deep breaths.'

He nodded; the mask had done its job. If it hadn't . . . well, I could have been pulling his body out at this point.

There wasn't much I could do, other than wait for the four of them to strip their suits off – they were left in a pile for cleaning – and have a drink of water. Rations were ignored as they tipped the bottles over their heads and faces.

'It's out,' said Greg, wheezing against Dan, the two of them staring at each other. Greg took a moment, before slapping Dan on the shoulder. 'Thanks, mate,' he said.

'No problem,' mumbled Dan, wiping his eyes – his were streaming, as were the others'.

I could still see the animosity between the two men – I assumed Dan wasn't forgiving Greg for Pieter's dismissal – but at least they'd pulled together when it counted. We'd need some decent observation on the four of them for the next twenty-four hours. Smoke can have delayed effects, particularly on the heart and lungs.

I waited to one side, watching Jack and Greg talking. It became heated, Jack putting his hands up and walking off.

Greg turned to us all, his eyes wide, bloodshot, surrounded by a line of soot where the mask had met his face. He looked at us each in turn.

'Debrief, one hour,' he said, before walking off.

13

We'd have to wait for answers. The fire fighters went back to their cabins to wash and change, Karis giving them each a quick medical once-over, though there was a limit to what she could do – minor burns were one thing, lung function tests would have to wait.

I went outside to get some air and a couple of laps of the side decks, keeping my eye on the undulating seas, the limitless horizon. The waves were dark, grey-blue with white crests that nipped at each other as they surged across our path. The occasional ray of sun sparkled off a brief swell, only to be lost as the clouds fought back. I tasted the salt in the air, a snap of anxiety, of isolation – helplessness perhaps. We were so alone out here, the contrast between facing inwards at the man-made crises and outwards at the harsh environment, so extreme.

I found Camila at the bow, staring out, face to the wind. I approached, hearing her muttering to herself.

'*Merde*,' she exclaimed, kicking the gunwale.

'*Merde*, indeed,' I said, startling her.

She turned, appraising me, her eyes performing a quick assessment, followed by a thin smile. I think she did it to everyone, just her way.

'Sorry, didn't mean to sneak up on you,' I said. 'I think I had the same idea.'

'Just letting it all out,' she said. 'Better here than around the others.' Her voice was smooth, deep and passionate, but she was wound tighter than I'd seen her before. Her knuckles were white against the railing.

I shrugged. 'You're not alone,' I said. 'That was a near miss.'

She laughed, shaking her head. 'This yacht . . . *morceau de merde.*'

A 'piece of shit'. I nodded, not sure I disagreed at this point. 'We don't know what caused it yet. Something in engineering.'

She nodded. 'It could have been so much worse, yes?' she said, clenching her jaw, averting her eyes.

I saw her take a couple of deep breaths; the fear evident, but also anger. I'd seen it a hundred times before – sometimes from a relatively small event, but nevertheless one which had the potential to be life-threatening. I'd seen soldiers throw their guts up after a near miss, collapse in panic after an inconsequential moment of stress, punch a brick wall in fury. The body and mind react in mysterious ways, some of them essential for survival, some of them downright useless.

'A little different to peaceful charters off the south of France?' I said. 'Don't worry, whatever this *piece of shit* yacht throws at us, I'm sure we can handle it.'

That got a smile. 'The south of France is full of just as much shit,' she said. 'Rich shit. Obnoxious shit. The *crème de la merde.*'

She turned to me, placed her hand over mine. 'Thank you, Sarah,' she said, her eyes darting again across my body until they rested somewhere around my mouth. 'You're right.'

Her hand trembled slightly on mine, nervous energy. She was putting on a brave face, but needed a little more time to settle – and she wasn't the only one.

'Let's head back?' I suggested.

She sniffed, still not meeting my eyes, but nodding. 'Sure,' she said. 'Lead the way.'

We all assembled again in the lounge an hour later, huddled around the dining table. Greg stood at the head of it with Jack, who placed the charred remains of what looked like a desktop PC on to the table, protecting the expensive wood with a thick cloth.

'Right,' said Greg, his face red, still simmering, even an hour later.

I saw his chest rising, stuttering. For the second time I worried about his health. He was not in good shape, and the normal strain of skippering a yacht this size would be enough for most people. This was a stress situation, and I wasn't entirely sure he could handle it.

'We got lucky,' he said. 'The damage is far less than I'd feared – it's not structural, and we caught it before it spread beyond the source,' he indicated the black lump on the table, 'which was contained within a storage cupboard on the lower deck.'

I peered at the lump, an uneasy feeling rising in my gut. It looked familiar.

'Burning plastic gives off a lot of black smoke, which is what you saw, and could have been fatal on its own, given the confined areas we're working in.' He sniffed, glancing at Jason. 'The ceiling and walls in the surrounding area have plenty of smoke damage but not from the heat – I expect the owner won't be best pleased, given he's just refurbished the whole lot.'

The crew remained silent, all eyes on Jason and Harriet, who had both joined us, keen to stay involved in events. Jason, in particular, looked seething, and understandably so – his boss's £200 million asset had nearly gone up in smoke. He managed a pained expression, shaking his head.

'What is it?' said Lily, pointing at the table.

Jack scratched the back of his neck. 'It's the hard disk storage for the CCTV system,' he said. 'It was plugged into a power outlet in a storage cupboard on the lower deck. The control console is in the tank deck. It's all wireless, including the cameras, so it was as good a place as any.'

He emphasized this last point to Greg, who narrowed his eyes. I guessed they'd already debated that point.

'Clearly it wasn't,' said Greg. 'It overheated –'

'It *didn't* overheat,' said Jack. 'I keep telling you. The power cable is loose – it arced on to the main board and fried it. I don't know why – maybe the fact we're smashing through ten-foot waves isn't helping.'

'Perhaps it was installed incorrectly?' said Greg. 'Perhaps it was handled roughly from the dock? You tell me, you're the engineer.'

'I didn't carry the damn thing down,' said Jack, his voice squeaking in protest. 'I *told* you. That was the deck crew or the stews.'

The comment prompted an eruption of defence from the rest of them. 'We were short-handed,' said Luan. 'We chucked everything on board to hit our departure time.

Loading is the bosun's responsibility, and we didn't have one.'

I couldn't believe Luan picked this time to twist that knife again. But Dan nodded in agreement, adding his weight to the awkwardness. Arno closed his eyes. Camila shrank away. The moment of silence was deafening.

'Don't blame us for an electrical fire,' said Luan, his voice dropping an octave, perhaps sensing he'd gone too far, again. 'That's all I'm saying.'

'I agree,' said Dan. 'You don't have a full crew, you get mistakes. Simple as.'

'Excuse me,' said Jason. 'Fried it? The disks?'

Jack nodded, tearing his eyes away from Luan. 'All the disks are dead. The power cable must have sparked, caught fire, and the insulation burned all the way out. The placement in the cupboard meant it spread to some cleaning products – cloths, sponges, towels, et cetera. That's what the fire was, mostly. It could have been a lot worse.'

A *lot* worse. An echo of Camila's comments. They were both right, but my stomach flipped anew. This was my domain, the CCTV provided by Mitch's company. I hadn't even considered its placement on the ship – it was already installed when I boarded. If it were the cause of the fire then eyes would surely be on me.

'The footage?' asked Jason.

'Erm. Gone,' said Jack. 'The disks are charcoal.'

I saw Jason glance at Greg, then at me. He chewed his lip.

'That's not good enough. It's an insurance requirement,' he said. 'You're telling me it's out of action?'

'That's hardly the important –' began Greg.

'No,' said Jack. 'I mean, the actual console is OK, and our security contractor,' he nodded my way, 'provided backup disk units. I can replace them, move the disks into engineering with me, where I can keep an eye on it all. As I said, it's all wireless, doesn't matter where it is.'

Jason nodded, seemingly placated a fraction. But a few glances around the table suggested not everyone was happy. I caught Luan staring at Greg, his eyes flashing.

'So that's all great,' said Greg, spitting the sarcasm at Jack and Jason in turn. 'We can watch each other on TV again, but this,' he indicated the blackened lump of melted plastic and metal, 'could have killed us all.'

I waited for it, and it came: Greg's glance at me, not accusing, not yet, but he couldn't hide it entirely. Silence descended, as I felt other eyes on me. For a moment the sun broke through a gap in the galloping clouds, shining through the window, bathing us in light. The *Escape* forged ahead at full throttle, smashing through the waves, the deep throbs sending shivers through my spine.

'Why didn't the sprinklers go off?' said Lily, in a small voice, speaking before I had a chance to. She looked at the ceiling, at the subtle pipes, impotent in their inaction, the nozzles sealed and dry. 'Why didn't they go off?' she repeated. 'And what about the smoke alarms? I had to hit the fire alarm myself. Aren't they supposed to be automatic?'

'She's right,' said Arno. He looked tired, worn out. 'Why didn't the fire suppression system work? The first hint of an uncontrolled flame should have bathed that deck in water. The smoke alarms should have sounded throughout the yacht. The fire alarm should not have had to be manually triggered by any of us.'

Greg indicated that Jack should answer, but kept his gaze elsewhere, as if he couldn't bear to look at his engineer. Jack stared at the table, his own expression one of guilt, of second-guessing. I could imagine his mind whirring at the thought he'd screwed up somewhere, and the reason why.

'I'll get to the bottom of it,' he said, nervously glancing up at the crew, perhaps looking for support. He didn't find it.

'And I need to check out that unit,' I said, 'call my boss. I've never heard of this happening before.' The truth, but a little weak. I wasn't about to accept any blame, but nor did I want to see Jack taking it all.

Greg looked at me, nodded. 'Camila,' he said.

Camila looked a million miles away. She'd been quiet since walking back from the bow with me. She blinked a couple of times, back in the room. 'Yes?'

'There seems to be a general feeling that we need a bosun for this trip.' He glared at Luan and Dan in turn, before turning back to her. 'So you're it. Consider this your promotion. You have the deck crew and, if you need them to help clean up this mess, the stews.'

Dan opened his mouth to protest – Luan and Lily were his staff – but, perhaps wisely, shut it again.

Camila appeared to regain her composure. A flicker of a smile passed over her face, but she hid it well. Ambitious. I couldn't blame her. She looked at Arno. As the other deckhand, he would be the obvious alternative – just as experienced. But I saw him nod his approval. Good for him, I thought, and for her – it must be nice to be promoted ahead of her male counterpart, even under such drastic circumstances.

'Right,' she said. 'No problem.'

'The rest of you,' said Greg, appearing to relax a fraction, 'thank you for your actions this morning, particularly you, Lily. Your quick thinking means we're all still standing here. No Mayday call necessary. Let's get the rest of the mess cleared up, quick as you can. I'll be on the bridge if you need me.'

14

We dispersed, the mood subdued, mirrored in the worsening weather. Grey clouds and dark minds, each reflecting on what could have happened had the fire been discovered a few minutes later, or started a few minutes earlier.

I watched Arno out of the corner of my eye. He'd showered, come through the event unscathed, with even his humour intact. He saw me looking, cocked his mouth into that annoying grin. He tossed me a Coke before being called away by Camila to help on the lower deck. He backed away, pointing at me with a wide smile that said *we're not done.*

Jack balanced on a stepladder, precariously swaying from side to side, checking the sprinkler pipes, his timid nervousness at breaking point. He couldn't offer any conclusions yet on why the fire suppression pumps hadn't activated – they didn't use the main water tanks but a separate grey-water system, so should have worked.

Jason and Harriet watched us all, sipping their coffees nervously from the lounge, sunk into the dark leather sofas, deep in conversation. They moved themselves away from the open areas to continue in private, and I found myself following, surreptitiously creeping across the carpets, ostensibly on some other errand, just close enough to listen in.

Harriet still struggled with the motion, her awkward

stumbling betraying her lack of sea legs. I thought perhaps she was telling Jason off – this was her yacht, after all, her estate. Jason, for all his arrogance, was just a lackey when it came down to it. He worked for her. We worked for him. But when I got closer, it seemed to be the other way around.

'What have you told people?' Jason's voice, hissing at Harriet.

'Nothing. But I didn't know it was a secret,' replied Harriet. 'How could I?'

'It's probably nothing. Just . . . maybe keep your head down, stay in your cabin.'

Harriet huffed, turned away, stormed off.

I kept my eye on her, made sure Jason wasn't watching, and then followed. She almost made it to her cabin before I caught her.

'Hey,' I said, grabbing the wall as the *Escape* lurched to port.

Harriet turned, her light dress swirling, circling her tiny body. Mere skin and bone. A half-remembered maxim flashed through my mind: you can never be too rich or too thin. A shame, but not my primary concern.

'Oh, hi . . . Sarah, isn't it?'

I nodded. 'I wanted to check you were OK.'

Partly true.

She shrugged. 'Thank you for asking. As well as I can be. It hasn't exactly been smooth sailing, pardon the cliché.'

'We'll find out what happened. Greg has already filed the report. He'll get a lot of shit . . . sorry, I mean a lot of *flak* for this. The insurance will go nuts.'

She sighed, shaking her head. 'How long until we arrive? Where are we, anyway?'

'You can check on the bridge,' I said, 'but roughly . . . fifteen hundred miles from home, two and a half thousand to go. Ish.'

'Christ,' she said, frowning.

'This is your first crossing, I take it?'

Harriet nodded. 'I spend a lot of time on each circuit – the Med and the Caribbean, but never this. This weather, the motion . . . never again. This was not the time out I needed.'

Nor me, I thought, but at least you get a luxury cabin. 'I don't blame you. You're feeling OK? No seasickness?'

She shrugged again. 'A little. It's . . . not going to get any worse than this, is it? The storm? It's scary looking out at that, like something out of a movie.'

What could I tell her? It mostly depended on what Greg did, but yes, it could get much worse – we could be racing down waves the height of two-storey buildings, deafened by the screams of the wind, confined to cabins, lying flat on our backs when not on shift. I seriously hoped not, but it wouldn't be the first time for me.

'I doubt it,' I said. 'The storm will probably pass us by – the seas should calm in a day or so.'

She smiled, nodding to herself. 'Thank you,' she said, turning back to her cabin door.

'Can I ask you something?' I said.

'Of course.'

'Do you know why we left in such a hurry? It was on Jason's instructions. And now Greg is powering us along at top speed.'

'Have you asked him?'

'Jason said it was a business decision. Greg said he follows orders – we must hit the schedule.'

Harriet's eyes narrowed, briefly, but noticeable. 'That sounds reasonable,' she said, sounding unconvinced. 'Why?'

'Jason seemed concerned when I mentioned Nikolas. I only mentioned the name because you did, remember? I thought it might be something relevant to our speed of passage – something that I should know.'

Harriet held my gaze, her eyes flickering, but recovering instantly. 'Nikolas is a cousin of mine,' she said. 'Second cousin. Not relevant, I'm afraid.'

Her answer was quick and dismissive. If she knew anything different, she clearly wasn't going to say. And perhaps there was nothing *to* say, nothing to learn. I was used to rigid timetables, rules, and a decent amount of honesty from my superiors. I guessed this might just be civilians doing what they do – muddling along and dealing with things as they screw them up, not before. I should let it go.

'Thanks anyway,' I said. 'You have a rest. I'll see you around.'

Next stop, engineering.

On my way down, I passed a storage area near the laundry, stopping to see if I could grab a fresh towel. But I paused, hearing a blast of static, a radio. It was faint, the voices weren't English, and I couldn't make them out. I stepped into the laundry, only to find it empty, the washers and dryers off – no water for washing, nothing to dry. The radio noise faded, and all I could hear was the steady background thrum of the engines, the distant crash of the water.

I stepped back out into the long corridor, to see the solitary figure of Dan at the far end. He turned into the next stairwell and out of sight. I cocked my ear. Nothing.

I flashed back to the first night, after the dinner, padding the corridors. The same noise – a pocket radio, perhaps, picking up the fragments of broadcasts from the coast. Is that all it was? Dan, the closet foreign radio enthusiast? Doubtful – and more likely he was watching porn on his phone – but something about it bugged me, the distinct tone of the static, the bursts, it conjured uncomfortable memories.

It was probably nothing. I shook it off and turned back towards the engine room.

Despite the constant whirring of the air circulation, the air was stuffy as I entered Jack's domain. Body odour, fumes, and the other thing. I found Jack at the bank of screens set into the port side, powering up the replacement for the charred lump of plastic which sat on the floor next to his feet. He was hunched over, his hair greasy, clothes sweaty and stained. Engineers needed a couple of showers a day at the best of times, but with the water rationing he was lucky if he got to wash the oil off his hands each night.

'Got a minute?'

He turned to me, eyes bloodshot, hurt. No wonder. He'd taken the brunt of the blame for the fire, and I wanted to at least support him, rule some things out.

'Sure,' he said. 'As long as you aren't here to shout at me.'

'That depends,' I said, smiling. 'I need to put in a report to my boss. Can you show me what exactly started the fire? I heard you upstairs, but I'm not sure I understand.'

'Well, that makes two of us,' he said, indicating for me to come closer, pulling the box-shaped unit towards us across the desk.

'This is the replacement. Identical model. I grabbed it from your storage cupboard – signed it out.'

I nodded.

Jack popped the case open and one side came away. 'It's pretty basic. Like a desktop computer. Power supply, motherboard, the array of disks . . .' He counted out the six of them. 'This,' he said, wiggling a rubber-covered thick wire, 'is the internal power cable.'

'And it came loose?'

'God knows how,' he said. 'It's screw-clipped in at each end, but one end was loose and frayed – bits of wire exposed. I never checked it. Why would I? Greg seems to think I'm responsible for every microchip on this yacht. I tell him that most of it comes sealed and all I do is plug it in. He doesn't listen. Lately he's . . . well . . . a loose cable shouldn't have caused a fire. But what else could it be?'

I peered in at the cable. I was no electrician or engineer, but I failed to see how, even in rough seas, the small but high-voltage cable could come unscrewed and fray itself, not unless it had been tampered with.

My heart hammered at the thought, a brief thump, trying to make sense of what I was seeing.

'So you're saying the electrical damage was one thing. A frayed cable would wreck the unit, wipe the disks. But that's it?'

'In a nutshell,' said Jack. 'Even if it was bouncing around shorting out everything else, a loose cable wouldn't normally cause a fire. I think it was all just extreme bad luck. What else could it be?'

I watched him for a moment, a few answers spinning in my head, but decided not to offer any of them. I thanked him for his time, left him to it.

What else could it be?

I waited until I was outside before I hammered out a quick message to Mitch on my phone. I gave him a brief report of what had happened. I finished with my question: *But have you ever had one of the CCTV units fail? Overheat, electrical short, that sort of thing?*

He came back to me within minutes, expressing his shock, checking I was OK. He was also probably busy emailing our suppliers, screaming at them, checking the insurance. His reputation was on the line here. Starting fires on superyachts was probably bad for business.

His answer: *No. Categorically. Those units are installed on boats the world over — yachts, cruise ships, ferries in the back of beyond. I've never heard of that happening. It's not impossible . . . I guess. Anything with a power source can spark . . . Listen, I'll take it up with the supplier, see what else I can find. Take care. How's the hot tub?*

I thanked him, assured him the hot tub wasn't on fire, leaned for a few moments against the cold wall, mulling over what I'd seen. My gut told me there was nothing wrong with the equipment Mitch had provided.

And why, of all things, the CCTV hard disks, containing footage of our journey so far?

15

I headed down towards my cabin, pausing against a bulk-head in the crew quarters, trying to make sense of the gnawing anxiety in my gut. Why was the CCTV so important? That's what it came down to, wasn't it? Was it really about insurance, just as Jason had said? He did seem *awfully* keen to get it working again.

I wasn't always one for instinct. I preferred evidence, but I couldn't shake the growing unease, and the frustration that came with it. The snooping in my cabin, the water tanks draining themselves, an electrical fire . . . not to mention all of the interpersonal fighting and grudges. Luan's anger – how was it channelled? Just in childish tantrums, or something more? *He's got it coming* – Luan's words, but did that extend, by accident, to the rest of us?

But then I considered Jack. His obvious flaw – his alcoholism – and the very real fact that he could be responsible, *still* responsible, for the majority of the engineering screw-ups, of which this was just the latest.

But I didn't really know any of the crew, did I? This group went back years, and I was an outsider, not even a yachtie. My job was to protect against the threats from outside, not inside.

Another thing bugged me. I pulled out my phone and tapped in a quick search: *DeWitt-Fendley*.

Mitch had been adamant we didn't pry into the client's

identity or business. They were paying for the privilege of anonymity, and we should respect it. However, it seemed to me that Harriet turning up out of the blue had rather spoilt that premise. Whatever privacy she claimed, it had evaporated the second she stepped on board.

Lots of results on the web: business pages, stocks, property. A sprawling business empire, most of which I didn't understand. The image search showed a few snaps of the family – a couple where I recognized Harriet, dressed to the nines at some gala event. Nothing interesting.

I searched again: *DeWitt-Fendley, Nikolas.* More prying. My soldier's something-not-quite-right-with-this-shitshow instincts firing.

Fewer results. A series of *Financial Times* articles, restricted behind a paywall. More of the same from *Business Insider*. Then one. A single result: *Nikolas Aubert.* A member of the DeWitt family empire. A photo of him shielding his face against the photographer outside a high-rise development in Canary Wharf. A stock market gamble, millions lost. Outrage and suicide – not his, but one of Nikolas's employees taking his own life. Bingo.

Shit, I thought. Family scandals don't get much worse. I flicked through the article but it was mostly hyperbole and lacking in detail. Just another day in the lives of the megarich. Everyone profits, except the dead. No more search results, and I tucked my phone away, that particular alarm quenched, at least for now. What I'd read might explain Jason's reluctance to talk about him, and Harriet's concerns were probably for her privacy and reputation.

Nothing much I could do about it – and as I thought, not my business, anyway.

I rubbed my eyes. Tired. The pills not doing a good job. I needed distraction, and not the sort that involved fire extinguishers or relationship counselling. The failures of this yacht aside, Mitch would be pissed if I completed the trip and returned to his doorstep just as screwed up as when I left. He was paying for my therapy, and I appreciated it. I should try to make it work.

Kay told me that you regret the things you don't do, not the things you do. I *think* he said it to get me into bed, but I readily agreed. We laughed about that one. No regrets.

Not until the day I destroyed it all.

Afghanistan, a little over twelve months ago. We'd raided at first light. Coming into the shore, the seas were calm, the Zodiac slicing through the glassy water with barely a shudder. I was almost two years out of training, and this was my fifth deployment, but the first with Kay.

They wouldn't have let us work together if they'd known.

It was stupid, but we were young, excited, caught in the moment – and so we kept going. A flirt turned into a kiss, a kiss into covert night operations within camp, where we attempted to infiltrate each other's sleeping quarters, snatching a few moments where we could.

Kay was one inch taller than me, twice as wide in the shoulders, faster in a sprint, slower to hit 10km. We competed like a couple of schoolkids, and he *never* let me win, not once. His features were rough but mischievous, his hair always messy, his mouth always ready to smile. He'd fallen into the Marines like so many fitness enthusiasts do, when they find the challenges of civilian life not enough, the thrill lacking, a restless taste for more.

He was my soulmate, and I knew it the day he beat me in an open water swim, collapsed on the beach, and accidently elbowed me in the jaw as I helped him up. It was lust at first sight.

Against the advice of my friends, against the rules, we became a couple. A secret couple who pressed our bodies together in mud, sand and freezing water by day, and in hot sweaty sheets by night. The sex was rough, raw, a release from the increasing pressures of our situation and the realities of our deployment into a messy war zone with no end in sight. He'd hold me tight, our grip on each other like vices, moving as one, our bodies surging with pent-up desire and emotion. I'd keep him going until my orgasms blended into a single pulsating wave, a burning surge of nirvana that only he could give me. And then I'd let him go, feel his body shudder, hold him until his muscles relaxed and his eyes closed, withdrawing into a haze of confusing thoughts and dreams – and shared doubts of our future.

Being assigned to the same fire team should have been the final warning to us. We could have fixed it, found a reason to separate.

Because if we had, that day would never have happened.

I wouldn't have screwed everything up.

The *Escape* sensed my mood, my rapid plummeting into the abyss. It yawed and pitched, shaking me back, grounding me in the here and now. *Wake up, Sarah*. How many times can you run through the same story in your head? How many shocks can your system take, wrestling between wanting to remember and needing to forget?

My heart thudded; I wiped my palms on my trousers. Square breathing, cut it off before it happens, keep the panic under, bury it.

This time I was successful.

16

The crew kitchen felt smaller each day, becoming messier, littered with bottles and discarded food wrappings. I guess it reflected the increasingly dishevelled appearance of the crew, none of whom had showered for a couple of days. We kept clean, some more than others, but the strain was obvious. If we couldn't keep ourselves looking presentable, then the crew quarters would surely follow.

I found Elijah, seated alone, braced in the corner, nursing a cup of coffee. He was the best groomed of us all, clean-shaven, hair short enough not to matter. His chef's whites had been discarded in favour of darker clothes – I guessed they hid the food stains better.

I grabbed a glass, a Diet Coke. 'You feeling OK?' I asked.

He nodded. 'I'm fine,' he said. 'No big deal.'

I leaned against the worktop. Maybe not to him. Most of the crew saw it differently.

'So are you any closer to figuring out what started the fire?' he said, glancing up. He fidgeted with his coffee cup, twirling it, scratching at it with his nails.

Interesting question.

'Beyond Jack's explanation,' I said. 'What do you mean?'

He shook his head, shrugged.

I sipped my drink, watching him, his nerves, the fact he was sitting on his own. Stewing about something, or just processing the day?

'Lily was quite upset about the whole thing,' he said.

'I don't blame her. But she did well. Took control, sounded the alarm.' I thought back to her comments on our first tour. Lily was made of sterner stuff than I'd given her credit for.

He nodded again. 'She did.' His face twisted, sulky.

So that was it.

I sighed, wondering at what point I'd changed job roles from security to relationship counsellor.

'You two are . . .?'

'I'm trying. I think we get on well, but we disagree on what happens next.'

'Next?'

'After this,' he said. 'I mean, this is my career – a chef on yachts like this, it's what I've been working towards for years. But Lily . . . I'm not sure. You know what I mean?'

'I do,' I said, surprised he would share his thoughts with me.

It was a universal anxiety – what does the future hold with this person in front of me, this person I think I might love. Can I imagine a future without them? If not, what must I do? But Lily and Elijah were right at the start of their journey, and I already got the sense Lily was on the wrong path.

'Lily is educated and bright,' I said. 'She'll want independence, freedom. I think this job might be a temporary fix for her.'

I watched his frown deepen, wondering if I'd been too blunt.

'Maybe,' he said. 'But it's good work, well paid, allows one to travel, meet people, et cetera.'

'Within pretty narrow confines,' I countered. 'This is a floating hotel, not a wilderness adventure.'

His frown deepened. 'I know. I just . . . I want it so bad. And I really like her.'

I understood, but felt an urge to argue on Lily's behalf. Perhaps Elijah was simply old-fashioned. Forgivable, but not something Lily should necessarily accommodate.

'Then help her figure it out,' I said. 'If she wants to spread her wings, help her fly. But that might not be in a place like this.'

Elijah nodded.

I could see he understood, was wrestling with it, but also cared, deep down.

'I'll try,' he said, grimacing, then another shrug. 'But life is precious. Short,' he said. 'When you find someone, the right one, you try to keep them, yeah?'

I sniffed, drained my Coke, rinsed the glass and left it on the side.

'Life is short,' I agreed.

I headed to the stern, pushing against the wind – stronger than this morning, still picking up, whipping around the fine lines of the *Escape*, buffeting my ears.

For the second time, I found Arno and Camila face to face, and, just like when I saw them in the gym, Camila looked to be dictating the terms of the conversation, instructing Arno, while he kept his gaze lowered, the subtle shake of his head displaying that he was unhappy about something.

But I think I read it correctly this time; her hand on hip was authoritative, not sexual, not flirtatious, just matter-of-fact. She was giving him an order. And he didn't like it.

I waited for the right moment to interrupt.

She stopped, stepped away from Arno, crossing her arms, staring over the gunwale.

Arno watched her, chewing his bottom lip. 'OK,' he called to her. 'Fine.'

She spun on her feet, giving a wide smile. 'Good.' She looked as if she was going to speak again, then she noticed me, the smile thinning, disappearing as she glanced at Arno and headed off, giving me a small wave.

'Trouble?' I asked, approaching, watching her departing figure, marvelling at how far her hips could swing as she walked, rolling in sync with the ship.

The side door slammed and she was gone.

Arno looked flustered; his nostrils flared. 'A disagreement,' he said. 'I think her new job has gone to her head.'

'Oh, of course,' I realized, 'she's the bosun now. Cracking the whip?'

'Something like that,' he said, stretching his arms behind his back, giving his shoulders a crunch. 'Although Dan says Pieter is still the bosun on the roster – that it's not over. I'm not sure what he means.'

'Well, there's not much Dan or Pieter can do about it, is there?' I said, watching him lean against the rail.

He shrugged, broke into a grin. It looked a little forced, but lit up his face all the same.

'I'm glad you turned up,' he said. 'I was going to come looking for you tonight.'

'I'm busy,' I said.

'Oh?'

I chuckled. 'Yeah. I was going to find this goofy South African chap, see if he wanted a drink. A *soft* drink. *Just* a drink. Talk shit for a bit. Try to distract myself from this.' I indicated the back of the *Escape*.

'Well, as it happens . . .'

'But I can't find him. Moody guy, dark horse, shaved head. *Luan* something?'

Arno spluttered with laughter. 'You're so funny, Sarah. I mean it. Stand-up quality.'

The *Escape* rolled, shuddered, catching me in the moment. I staggered forward, with no place to go other than Arno's chest. I put my hands up and they hit hard muscle. I fell forward until our faces were inches apart.

His grin intensified. 'I have this effect,' he said.

The *Escape* saved me, lurching the other way. I went with the motion, getting my feet planted.

I let his T-shirt slip from my grip. 'I have that effect,' I laughed.

He screwed up his face. 'How about the sun deck bar?' he said. 'I can open it, grab some . . . lemonade. It'll be chilly but quiet.'

'Perfect,' I said.

It was a mistake, perhaps, but an experiment. I knew my memories would forever cycle until I did something about them. The therapist told me that, Mitch told me that. Amy would tell me that, if she knew the truth. This was *something*. A test, a gentle prod at the most solid of walls I'd erected inside me.

I'd decided on a whim, after leaving Elijah in the kitchen, wondering what the hell I was doing here. It was a choice of going to my cabin, sliding into bed, and reliving those moments again, watching the visions in my head projected on to the ceiling, as my eyes burned with tiredness and my mind refused to give in. Or I could do this.

I chose the cute South African with buns of steel.

Life is short.

He pulled open the door to the sun deck bar. It still smelled new, of polished hardwood and fragrant fabrics – the rich smell of leather from the sofas, the floor unmarked and delicate.

'This morning,' he said, 'when the alarm sounded in the corridor, you –'

'It was nothing,' I said, pushing in ahead of him. I grabbed a couple of Cokes out of the fridge – in case he had ideas of getting drunk – and tossed him one. Could I ever tell someone like Arno what went on in my head? Why certain combinations of light, sound and motion triggered me? What it felt like to have a panic attack of that magnitude, when I thought my heart was going to punch a hole through my chest, and my mind wanted to curl up and die?

Mitch knew what it felt like, because he was one of us, had lived through the same things. The shrink knew, because . . . well, I had no choice but to tell him. But how could I ever make it part of a casual conversation? *Hey, I did something terrible, and my subconscious will never let me forget it until the day I die.*

'It didn't look like nothing,' he said, grabbing two chairs, unfolding them, placing them a little too close together.

I kicked mine a few inches to one side.

'Just . . . memories,' I said. 'Stuff.'

'Stuff?'

'Uh-huh.'

Arno sniffed, leaned back in his chair. 'I get it,' he said. 'We all have our *stuff*.'

'Like what?'

'Oh, so I'm supposed to tell you mine, but you won't tell me yours?'

'That's exactly right,' I said. 'Take it or leave it.' He'd already seen me at my worst – as vulnerable as I could get. I needed to see some of him. Balance it out a little. 'Come on,' I said. 'Tell me what makes Arno tick. What are you really doing so far from home?'

He chuckled, cocking his head, peering at me. 'Not much to tell, I'm afraid. My bro and I . . . let's just say we escaped South Africa, rather than left it.'

'Criminals on the run? Great,' I said. 'Bank robbery? No, wait, fraud?'

'Ha. I meant when we were young, much younger. A lot of families like mine in SA are very old-fashioned – full of toxic masculinity, you might say.'

I made a point of looking him up and down. 'You mean there's a modern man in there screaming to get out?'

His smile thinned. 'You joke, but it was horrible. My father was a drunk and a chauvinist. Still *is*, I expect.'

'You don't keep in touch?'

Arno shook his head. 'They separated. Eventually. I visit my mum when I can.'

He drained his can of Coke. 'Sure you don't want anything stronger?' he said.

I shook my head. 'You feel guilty?'

He shrugged, dipped his head, nodded. 'Terribly so. I let my mum put up with it. Year after year. As for my brother – I know he's a grumpy fucker, but give him a chance – he came to blows with Dad about it. I stuck up for him.'

'How old?'

'Fifteen, Luan just fourteen. Don't get me wrong, we were both big guys even then, could look after ourselves, but you know ... it's still son versus father. The family always loses. Mum, she ... I wish I could take her out of there. Save up some money, give her a decent retirement somewhere else.'

I tried to imagine what it was like. My own parents were a rock – a launch pad for Amy and me. We were told we could do anything, be anything. I wasn't stupid – I knew Amy and I had to punch twice as hard in our fields of work to get the same result as our male peers, but we got there. Attitudes were changing ... just not universally at the same pace.

'So you broke out into the big bad world,' I said.

'After trying to join the military,' he said. 'They told me to come back in a few years, when I'd dealt with my issues. Luan didn't even pass the written test.'

I wondered what they'd seen in him. Anger was useful in a soldier, if channelled correctly. What wasn't useful was locked-up rage.

'Have you dealt with them?' I asked. 'Your issues?'

Another shrug. 'We left SA, went to the States on student visas, worked our way around, became yachties.'

'That doesn't answer my question.'

'It's probably your turn,' he said. 'Tell me why you had a panic attack when the fire alarm went off.'

He fixed his gaze on me. It was gentle, not demanding,

but knowing. He'd obviously known pain in his life, seen trauma. I owed him something.

But I couldn't tell him.

The words bubbled to the surface, ready, an avalanche of emotion backing them up, ready to bury the both of us. It was too much, too soon.

I stood, crumping my Coke can, tossing it to him. 'This was nice,' I said. 'Let's do it again.'

I headed to the stairs. Arno stayed put. I felt his eyes on my back.

'Sarah,' he called. 'I may be young, perhaps inexperienced compared to you, but I know the feeling when the world wraps itself around and tries to crush you. Talking doesn't make it any worse, is all I'm saying.'

I paused. Please stop, I thought. You *don't* know what it's like. You can't. This wasn't what I had in mind, what I planned. Arno was supposed to be a distraction to lift my mood, not a therapist to examine it. I couldn't even get this right.

'I did something stupid,' I called over my shoulder, 'and I lost someone I loved. There's nothing else to talk about. Nothing else to say.'

'Sarah, I –'

'Goodnight, Arno,' I said, entering the stairwell, closing the door behind me before he had a chance to respond.

17

I heard thunder as I crawled out of bed, a deep rumbling through the charged air. It was close, by the sound of it, and the floor throbbed and lurched with the swell. The storm wasn't getting any kinder, and Greg must be sailing us straight through. I hoped again that he knew what he was doing.

It was late in the morning of the fifth day, the sleeping tablets keeping me under. On waking, my mind was as groggy as my body. I changed into my gym kit and drank a bottle of water, checking it off in my head. Rations were holding, though I'm glad I had a cabin of my own. The guys would start getting a little whiffy soon unless they were willing to take saltwater showers.

I headed along the crew corridor, replaying my brief drinks date with Arno. You couldn't even call it that. We'd spoken. He'd talked. I'd shut it down and left. Brilliant going, Sarah. And yet the thought of him still gave me a tingling feeling – new territory waiting to be explored. It was so simple in my head, when he wasn't there. As soon as he appeared, my defences went into overdrive, the walls came up.

I saw Kay in him, and it scared me.

I took a breath, pushing the thought away. Deep vibrations in my feet – the *Escape*'s hull battling against the swell as we headed further into the storm.

I noticed Lily's cabin door was open, and poked my head through.

She was lying on her bunk reading a book. I peered at the cover – a Clive Cussler titled *The Rising Sea*. I smiled – another action thriller fan. I'd brought a few novels with me – a couple of Ludlums, le Carrés and a Forsyth. I'd read them all multiple times, but that was the point – familiarity and comfort – old novels I'd read over and over. I'd brought them on this trip to help soak up the dead hours, to distract me when my head spun into a frenzy, when thinking became too difficult. It hadn't worked.

'Is it good?'

Lily tucked a bookmark in and dropped the novel to one side. A flash of lightning filled the cabin, illuminating her face, her pale skin. She looked so young, so pretty. A keeper. Elijah's comments preyed on my mind.

'Sorry,' she said.

'For what?'

'For hiding in my cabin. I'm just . . . exhausted, I guess. What with the fire and everything . . .'

Another flash of lightning. I sat on the end of her bunk and she tucked up her legs, her eyes sparkling in the light.

Thunder cut through the air as she bit her lower lip. 'This yacht isn't where I want to be,' she said. 'At least, I don't think so. Not once this trip is over.' She shuffled up against her pillow, pulling down her skirt, giving me a smile. 'Oh, I don't know. I see you and what you've achieved – independence, a first career in the military, already on your second. I think . . . there's got to be more than this,' she indicated her cabin. 'This job, this life. All the problems with this particular trip aside, I want more. I wanted to see the world, but not by serving rich assholes and sleeping in a cupboard.'

'There are some good things, no?' I said. 'You like *some* of the crew.'

'You mean Elijah? He's great, I really like him, but . . . we want different things. That's clear, and I see it. But I'm not sure he does, and I don't want to hurt him. Maybe we can make it work – a long-distance romance, something like that. But I can't stay on here.'

I smiled – I saw a little of me in her. Only a few years her senior, but I'd had my maturity beaten into me over that small gap. I could see the fire in her eyes. She could do it. At her age, there was absolutely no reason why she shouldn't.

'Please, don't make a thing of it,' she said. 'Don't tell anyone, particularly not Elijah.'

I nodded, thinking of Elijah's conflict in the kitchen – how to pin Lily down, keep her here with him. She didn't yet have the resilience, the guts to say *no man tells me what to do*. I still had a few days with her, though. Perhaps I could teach her.

She reached over, taking my hand. She gave it a small squeeze.

'It's good to have you here, Sarah. I haven't had a decent friend on board for months. Particularly in this,' she indicated the window, the storm outside. 'I've never been in anything quite like it.'

I smiled, surprised my natural defences hadn't sprung up with a sarcastic response, something to deaden the moment. She was right, though; at that moment it did feel good to be here. I savoured it, knowing it could be lost any second, waiting for my brain to catch up.

Waiting for the punishing memories to arrive.

I leaned against the wall, peering through the window, needing distraction. The glass was streaked with water droplets, running sideways, blurring the greys of the water and sky together, the darkness of each indistinguishable. I braced myself against the side of the bunk as we lurched to port, the *Escape* seeming to roll to an unrecoverable angle, before it settled, sinking back again, taking my stomach with it. We were firmly in roller-coaster territory now, racing up and down each wave, screaming and shuddering – the thousands of tonnes of metal hull, its majestic and imposing stature, meant nothing out here, not when the ocean had more energy in each wave than the *Escape* could ever exert in its lifetime.

I watched the sky fill the window, seeing the racing clouds, a flash followed by a deep rumble. And then it was gone, we rolled again, and all I could see were the white crests dancing across black water, so close, leaping up to fling themselves across the glass. Mesmerizing, dangerous.

The water drops on the outside of the glass flashed, blinding points of light. I focused through them, saw the fork of lightning stabbing into the ocean. The boom followed, trembling through the air.

Then another, further forward, closer. A blinding tear in the sky, a triple fork of light hitting the water, the scream of it hitting my ears at the same time. There was no distance now, the storm was on top of us, surrounding us.

And then it happened.

I felt it before I heard it, the bang in Lily's cabin as loud as a grenade, a shockwave of sound travelling through the air and hull in a fraction of a second. My heart stopped, my natural instincts took over, ducking, grabbing Lily's hand, finding the low ground.

The cabin lights went out, the power sockets on the wall flashed, the chargers plugged into them popped. I winced at the sight of Lily's phone – a small wisp of smoke coming from the side of it.

Lily yelped, tugging herself away from my grip. 'What the fuck?'

I recovered, shook my head, kept myself from sinking inwards.

I took a breath, listening for the inevitable – it took a few moments before I was sure, but the low throb of the engines dying was unmistakable to me – 'We've been hit.'

'Hit? Was that lightning?'

The *Escape* shuddered as it slowed, the thrust of the two engines no longer pushing us through the rising walls of water. We yawed slowly, side-on, the wind taking us. It had only ever happened to me once at sea, and on that occasion we'd been in a flotilla of six Navy ships.

The *Escape* was a flotilla of one.

'Find some torches,' I said. 'I have one next to my bunk. There'll be some in the crew kitchen.'

'Where are you going?'

'To the bridge,' I said.

To listen to the latest set of excuses from Jack and Greg. To hear first-hand how fucked we really were this time.

18

'The hull is intact.'

Jack paced to and fro, right hand shaking as he stroked his chin. His eyes were wild, his body wired with adrenaline, withdrawal, disbelief.

On the bridge already were Greg, Jack and Camila. Dan sat in the observer's couch. Camila gripped the lifeless wheel with both hands, breathing heavily, jaw clenched. I could feel the tension in the air.

The *Escape* wallowed and lurched, at the mercy of the raging storm, impotent, helpless.

'Get them to check it again,' said Greg, staring at the bank of screens on the cockpit, all dark, not a single LED to break the harsh reality. His head and clothes were soaked – he'd been outside in the rain, examining his ship from every angle, staring at the masts as the sky hurled all it could down on him. I could see his chest rising and falling. This wasn't some interpersonal drama he could shout about and make things right. This was serious, and I got a jolt of nerves, a feeling I hadn't experienced in a while – the possibility this could all go south, and there'd be no happy ending, no laughing about it over a beer. This was real, and Greg knew it.

Jack's rapid explanation revealed the lightning had struck the highest point, the VHF antenna on the radio mast, which in turn was surrounded by the radar and communication domes. The lightning *should* then have travelled down the conductor – a thick protection system designed to carry the huge current through to sea level, where the approximately three hundred million volts would disperse through a metal grounding plate into the water.

Standard protection. No yacht of this size worth its salt would sail without it.

Except it soon became clear this wasn't the path the lightning bolt took. The lightning protection system on the *Escape*, like many other systems, was revealed by Jack to be offline, not connected, not installed. The metal rod terminated behind the mast on the sun deck, awaiting parts and inspection before being signed off. The electrical charge was therefore left to find its own way to the ocean. Through whatever route it could find. And when left to its own devices, lightning has a way of destroying everything in its path.

The radar and communications domes were wiped out within the first fraction of a second. Then, forcing itself along the path of least resistance, the lightning hit the main wiring system, reaching the switch panels, which distributed current to every working electrical system on the yacht. It took out every connected electrical device – from the spotlights in the crew cabins to the TVs to the fridges to the computer systems in the tank deck – and there it caused the greatest damage of all, blowing every major computer system, from the GPS to the radar to the basic radios.

Those essential systems that kept everything running – the guts of the *Escape* – flicked off within a second, damaged beyond repair. All communications obliterated in an instant.

There was nothing it didn't touch, nothing it didn't destroy. Lightning is ruthlessly simple in that regard. No prejudice. Admirably powerful.

Finally, the force of the bolt exited the hull. In many cases, this meant punching a hole straight through it. Fibreglass hulls would shatter and tear, wooden hulls would often superheat and explode. The *Escape* was steel, and while not immune, the thickness had provided a degree of protection.

When Jack said the hull was intact, it meant he and the deckhands had crawled along every inch of the tank and lower decks, looking for an exit point, looking for damage. So far, so good.

'Have we managed to get a distress call out? Any comms at all?' I said.

Greg shook his head. 'I've sent Karis to gather the handhelds.'

He meant the EPIRBs – the Emergency Position Indicating Radio Beacons, capable of sending a rescue signal from anywhere in the world using a satellite system – plus the normal satellite phones and battery-operated GPS and radios for emergency use. I just hoped they weren't all sat in the charging dock when we were hit – if so, there was a good chance they'd also be fried.

'Personal devices?' I asked.

'A lot were charging,' said Jack, 'because crew aren't allowed their phones on duty – they leave them in cabins plugged into the wall sockets. I haven't checked Jason and Harriet yet. They're in the main lounge asking for coffee.' He rolled his eyes.

I thought of my own iPhone, currently plugged in

under my bunk. I hadn't even checked it, but I suspected it would be dead, a few thousand volts having run into the charging port and across its delicate microchips. It would only have been good for GPS anyway, having no way to communicate. There was no mobile phone signal in the middle of the Atlantic, and all internet traffic was through the VSAT dish – one of the first things to fry.

'Generators?'

Another shake of Jack's head. 'I haven't had a chance to assess yet,' he said, 'but it's all connected. The generator circuits were hit with the same charge. I'll see.'

I nodded, taking a slow breath, watching Greg, watching Jack. Worst case, we were alone, no communications, no power. The consequences of such an event, given we were already on rationed water, did not need spelling out.

I watched, keeping a tab on my own rising levels of anxiety, feeling my throat running a little dry as I observed Greg and Jack run through checklists and proper procedure. Dan excused himself, ostensibly to take care of the guests, though I think even his natural machismo was struggling under the circumstances.

It didn't take long before Greg's own fears and impatience began to surface.

'How could you, Jack?' he said, quietly, but with menace. He thumped the checklist on to the navigation table, where Jack was scanning a manual, following wiring schematics, looking for answers to the myriad questions Greg kept throwing at him.

Camila remained at the wheel, for no useful purpose other than perhaps to give her a small sense of control over the rising crisis.

Jack couldn't find an answer to this one.

'I thought we were protected,' said Greg, staring at the cockpit. 'I went through this storm *because* we were protected. You never told me. Dammit, Jack! After *everything* I've let go.' He spun towards his engineer, fire in his eyes.

'I . . . I . . .' Jack spluttered the beginning of his defence. 'I tried, Greg. I asked to speak to you yesterday, and the day before. I said –'

'You didn't say anything, Jack,' shouted Greg. 'Nothing. You knew our heading, knew the weather. It's your job to advise me, I –'

'I did advise you! I asked to speak to you. I *told* you running her full throttle was a bad idea!'

'Engine problems, you said. Fuel. Overheating. Not this.'

'I never said that. I asked to *talk*. I have a whole load of things . . . but you dismissed me. You –'

'Because I can't talk to you when you're drunk! For fuck's sake, Jack. I was waiting for you to sober up.'

Jack opened and closed his mouth like a guppy. His secret that was never a secret. Greg knew, I knew. How many of the others? And yet he was allowed to get away with it. Part of me was glad Greg had finally said something. Another part was furious it had taken a disaster to make him speak out.

'That's . . .' Jack looked pleadingly at Greg, glanced at Camila, who kept her back to him. 'This wasn't my fault,' he said. 'It wasn't. I –'

The rear door burst open and Karis stormed in. She paused, seeing Greg and Jack's red faces.

She narrowed her eyes before speaking. 'They're gone,'

she said. 'EPIRBs, sat phones, GPS units, I think we had three VHF radios.'

Greg took a second to respond. 'What do you mean?' he said. 'They're down in the –'

'No, they're not,' she said. 'Not in the radio room, not in the crew mess, not in engineering. The docking station is there, still smoking, I might add, but the devices aren't.'

I stepped forward, watching her face, the stark message in her eyes.

'And that's not all,' she said. 'Life jackets are all stowed, but none have personal locator beacons attached. We can't even use them to get a satellite signal out.'

'Were they there when we departed?' asked Greg, closing his eyes, pinching his temples.

Jack shrugged.

'I don't know,' said Karis. 'We departed in a hurry. Did anybody do the full checklist?'

Greg's chest rose, he looked about to explode, but he stopped, breathed out slowly. 'The refurb company managed all the subcontractors, but we followed the correct departure procedure, Karis,' he said. 'I'm not sure what you're insinuating.'

'I'm not insinuating anything, Greg,' she said. 'But I'm saying we don't have any hand-held comms or emergency beacons. We have no ship comms. We have no way of contacting the outside world, period. No way of getting help. We're powerless, rudderless, and entirely on our own.'

19

Camila remained on watch, which meant staring at blank screens and watching the waters ahead for any sign of other ships. Arno and Luan were told to do the same, scanning the water in all directions, gathering the flares, setting three off at fixed intervals, preserving the rest, only to be fired on Greg's orders.

I accompanied Jack to the tank deck, as much to occupy my mind as to help. I had a rudimentary engineering knowledge – like how to fix things fast in a gunfight, but I doubted it would be much use against the computerized *Escape*.

The deck itself was eerie in its relative silence. The outside world hammered at the hull, but the lack of mechanical noise – the engine throb, the whine of the fans – was stifling in its absence. The air was thick – even worse than before, no longer ventilated properly, and the fumes lingered.

'We should never have sailed through this,' he muttered, switching on a couple of battery-powered lights. They cast a dim hue over the machinery and metal floor. 'Never. What was he thinking? That prick Jason does nothing to help. This isn't some jaunt around the islands, this is open ocean – the *Escape* wasn't ready. Greg should have my back, not this –'

'Jack,' I said. 'Stop a minute.'

Jack turned to me.

I watched his expression, his eyes, the nervous tremor in his lips. Another crack of thunder seeped through the many layers above, sending vibrations through my feet, my calves.

'Take a breath,' I said. 'Sit down.' I indicated the swivel chairs next to the engineering console – another bank of black, inoperable computer screens.

Jack paused for a moment before collapsing on a chair, taking his head in his hands, planting his feet wide to brace his body against the motion. I let him breathe, hoping he'd settle. He was no good to us in this state, and no matter how frustrated I was, I needed him to be focused over the next few hours and days. Greg, in his anger, had torn him down. I needed to bring him back up again, tease the qualified engineer out from under the angst and the addiction. We were unlikely to survive without Jack, and everyone needed to recognize it.

'Are you sober?' I asked.

He pulled his hands away, dragging his palms down his face. He nodded.

'How long?'

He shrugged. 'Last night.'

'And –'

'But this wasn't anything to do with that,' he said, the pleading tone returning. 'The lightning protection system was disconnected. It was on my engineer's report – it was one of the many reasons I said we had to delay sailing. Greg ignored it, and me.'

'But you knew we sailed without it working.'

'We don't usually sail straight through fucking thunderstorms,' he said. 'The chances of being hit by lightning in a normal year are infinitesimally small. It wouldn't have mattered. I don't know what's got into him.'

I nodded. There was no use arguing about what Greg did. Foolish, perhaps, but not illegal, and not unheard of. Despite Jack being compromised by the alcohol, I failed to see what he could have done to prevent this.

'So what do we do?' I said.

'We?'

'You. Me. The crew. Where do you start, Jack? I'm not spending the next few days drifting through a raging thunderstorm, and I'm not jet-skiing my way home.'

That got a smile out of him – small, but a crack in his wallowing anguish.

'The switch panels are both blown,' he said. 'I have a spare panel. If I can get that to work . . .'

I raised my eyebrows.

'Don't get too excited,' he said. 'It'll take hours, maybe through the night. Also, I still need engines and generators.'

'Can you get the engines working?'

'Maybe. As for the steering . . . if I can get the engines started, I might have enough power for the hydraulics. I'm not sure. I won't know for a couple of hours.'

I tried to give him a reassuring smile, and I hoped by the tentative glint in his eye I was having the desired effect. He might be damaged and irresponsible, but in my experience, engineers thrived in the detail – ask them what needs doing, pay some interest, then leave them to it.

'Greg's angry, but he'll get over it,' I said. 'Until then, you need to focus. I trust you, Jack.'

I hoped it sounded sincere. I left him with it, watching

him take a deep breath, dragging folders from the overhead lockers, opening the tool station and preparing his work.

Did I trust him? No. Not because I thought he was fundamentally incompetent, but because he was an addict. Addicts are untrustworthy by definition. Knowing how to manage them was key.

So I left him to it, ensuring he had enough cans of cola to keep his caffeine levels up. Another deep rumble accompanied my exit, a snap in the air, reminding me we were a long way from safety.

And even further from home.

The bridge was busy when I re-entered. The voices calm but urgent. Greg and Karis were huddled over the navigation table with paper charts and two smartphones. Jason sat on the sofa, sipping a diet soda, trying to catch it in his mouth as the furniture rocked in front of him. I should tell him to stand up, that it was easier to steady yourself when upright. I didn't.

Camila remained at the wheel, Dan and Lily perched awkwardly near the rear door, perhaps eager for news, but unable to offer much in the way of help. I guessed Arno and Luan were on deck watch, still scanning the ocean for help.

I sidled over to Jason. 'Harriet OK?' I asked.

He nodded.

I noticed a sheen on his forehead. So even Jason was nervous. It shouldn't have pleased me quite so much, given I was literally in the same boat.

'She won't leave her cabin,' he said. 'Locked it and stuck a *Do Not Disturb* notice on the door. I don't blame her.'

'Her sickness?'

A brief shake of the head. 'Just scared. Angry. I think we all are. I'll keep checking on her, make sure she's OK. I've told Dan and the others to leave her alone.'

Jason providing his own personal service now, it seemed.

I saw his eyes dart to Greg. 'I'm told we have no communications at all,' he said. 'Another of Greg's oversights.'

He looked to me, perhaps for a response. But my trust in Jason was a fraction lower than in Greg.

'Perhaps if he wasn't being pushed to such a rigid schedule,' I said, immediately regretting it.

Jason's eyes darkened. The sky rumbled. He made to say something, but stopped, giving a thin smile instead.

I saw Greg and Karis break away from the navigation table, heading to the back of the bridge, through the door into his personal quarters. He stopped, searching me out, beckoning me to follow.

I glanced at the charts as I passed.

Greg closed the door to the bridge, blocking out the sounds of the wind and rain, the nervous chatter of the crew.

I hadn't been in his quarters before – it was a modest space, decorated in clean whites and blues, with plenty of daylight from two large windows, a darn sight roomier than the crew cabins. There was an office area leading through to the bedroom. He offered us chairs, while he remained standing.

Karis spoke first.

'Why not the Azores, Greg?' she said. 'If we can get the engines back, they're less than two days away.'

I'd never stopped there, the small group of Portuguese islands, some nine hundred miles west of the mainland. It would mean turning back, but surely the safest plan, *if* Jack could get us power.

Greg chewed his lower lip. 'I told you why,' he said.

'Yes, the *schedule*,' she replied. 'But that's blown, isn't it? We're drifting in a storm well outside the shipping lanes. We're in a serious situation, Greg. This is protocol.'

He winced. 'Don't quote maritime protocol at me, Karis,' he said. 'I know my job.'

'Your job is –'

'My job is to get this yacht to its destination. I understand the seriousness of what just happened, but sailing to the Azores will result in weeks of delay while we await parts. I can't –'

'You can,' Karis butted in. 'I mean, I don't want to sit in the Azores for weeks either, but seriously, Greg . . .'

Greg looked ready to snap, stared at both of us, perhaps thought better of it. I kept my expression neutral, ready to back Karis if she needed it.

He took a breath, glanced at the closed door. 'Any news from Jack?' he asked. 'I fear my temper may have got away from me.'

I shrugged. 'He's at work, seems cautiously optimistic. I couldn't say what he'll be able to do.'

Greg nodded, taking a moment, lost in thought. He walked over and grabbed a third chair, dragging it across the carpet. 'I knew him before his wife died,' he said, glancing at me. His face looked suddenly older, perhaps in the change of light, the bags under his eyes pronounced, his cheeks sagging. 'Brilliant,' Greg continued, 'focused, a killer sense of humour. I always kept him on my crew – knew we were in good hands . . .' He tailed off, took a breath, sitting heavily. His body looked weary, worn out.

'A part of him died when Sally passed away. Throat cancer, rapid and violent. I saw the light in his eyes extinguish overnight. His confidence and exuberance replaced with the nervous tics and anxiety you see today. He's still brilliant, mind you, but you've seen what happened. How he copes.'

'He needs help,' I said. 'What he doesn't need is for the people close to him to ignore it. Or blame him.'

'Is that what you think I'm doing?' said Greg, with a hurt expression. 'Believe me, I've tried, Sarah. And failed, for the most part. Keeping him employed is about all I can do. What do you think would happen if he worked on another yacht, under a crew that didn't understand him, didn't know him?'

I understood, and tried to choose my words carefully. 'We don't know how much of our current predicament is due to Jack,' I said. 'The water tanks, the fire, the lightning protection. I could go on. What else, Greg? What will we find when we wake up tomorrow?'

Greg sagged, nodding to himself. 'I know, Sarah. I'm working on it.'

'There's something else,' said Karis, her face twisting with concern. 'The hand-held emergency beacons – the EPIRBs.'

Greg shrugged. 'There should be at least three on board, placed in the obvious locations – one on the bridge, one in engineering. One somewhere in between, usually out on the main deck. You can't find any?'

'None. I asked the rest to keep a lookout, but no sign.' Karis looked flustered, and understandably so. The first mate would have to accept at least some responsibility for essential safety equipment going missing. 'The only thing I can think of is that they were taken off for service and not replaced,' she said.

Greg screwed his face up. 'Makes no sense.'

I watched him, seeing him glance again at me.

'What are you thinking, Greg?'

Greg paused, kept my gaze for a few seconds.

Was there another explanation? My thoughts danced around, *still* dancing, trying to make sense of the myriad oddities that had befallen us prior to the lightning strike, and now this. But none of it made sense.

'It's not beyond the realms of possibility some incompetent engineer dockside forgot to replace them,' he said, 'it's just very unlikely.'

About as unlikely as all the other failures, I thought, and even more dangerous. The beacons were our final lifeline, and without them we were closed in, cut off. Alone until we found our own way out of this; or fought our way out.

Greg stared at Karis for a few seconds before taking a deep breath, pushing himself to his feet. 'The reason I brought you two in here was to ask for your support. If Jack can get the engines started, and it's a *big* if, it'll be self-steering from here on, rigid shifts – Karis, Camila and me. It'll be tough.' He turned to me. 'Sarah, you seem to have the calmest head on this yacht – and considering we're in emergency procedures, it makes sense to have you in the loop.'

'The crew are pissed off, Greg, not mutinous,' I said.

He smiled. 'I didn't say they were, but I'd value your support all the same.'

'You've got it,' I said, wondering how bad he thought it would get. Much worse, if we were drifting for long.

Things would go downhill fast, and Greg knew it. I knew it. I wondered how many of the crew did – they were used to luxury charters, no more than a few hours from land. It would come as a shock – and in my experience, there was no limit to the depths to which humans could sink when desperate.

I also couldn't shake my growing unease, the gut feeling, a primal reaction to too many coincidences, too much bad luck. But why?

'We do need to plan for the worst,' I said. 'But not yet. Let's give Jack more time.'

Greg nodded.

'In the meantime, Arno could help?' I offered. 'I know you gave Camila the bosun's job, but Arno seems capable?'

Greg huffed. 'Maybe,' he said.

I narrowed my eyes, couldn't keep my expression neutral. 'You don't like him?' I asked.

Greg stared at me for a moment, before his face softened. 'They told you?' he said, sighing. 'Bloody bankers. That was supposed to be confidential.'

I raised my eyebrows.

Karis cleared her throat, intrigued.

'What can I say?' said Greg. 'Yeah, I refused to give Luan a reference. Those two might make decent deckhands and stews, but they should keep to that level. Arno is . . .' He tailed off, awkwardly, glancing at me.

My cheeks flushed. 'What?'

'I mean, *Arno* is OK, but Luan is immature and reckless – needs watching over. I thought long and hard about it, but I couldn't have my own reputation tarnished by recommending them. I just couldn't do it. So yes, I told the bank they were unsuitable candidates, in my opinion as a captain of twenty years, to take on a huge marine mortgage. I'd do it again.'

'Your reputation,' said Karis. 'Making it about you again. Why does that not surprise me?'

Greg waved her away with a flash of irritation. 'It's hardly the most pressing issue right now, is it?'

'It'll come to a head,' said Karis. 'That sort of thing festers, Greg. You shouldn't have done it.'

I took a long breath. Shit. Luan's anger wasn't useful, but hardly misplaced.

'Perhaps reconsider?' I said, trying to choose my words carefully. 'Arno really is a good guy, and I'm sure Luan will grow up. It's all a bit fraught out there – they'd welcome some support from their captain.'

Greg nodded unconvincingly. 'Later, Sarah. They'll keep. And I'll bring in Arno if it gets too much, yes?'

'Up to you,' I said.

We exited his cabin on to the bridge, immediately hit by the sounds of the storm, the rain lashing against the windows.

Luan and Elijah had joined the others, nearly a full house. All eyes turned to us, expectant, as if we'd hidden away for five minutes to formulate a master plan. No such luck, but I'd leave it to Greg to disappoint everybody. He seemed to be good at it.

Greg's brief motivational speech consisted of telling everyone to keep working and to stand by for instructions – Jack had everything in hand, the emergency was temporary, fixable. But his voice betrayed his emotion, and his final action, perhaps subconsciously, as he assured everyone that we would come through this, was to place his hand on Karis's, as she stood beside him at the navigation table.

Karis let it rest for a few seconds before pulling her hand away. Her cheeks flushed; she kept her smile fixed. The crew nodded and filed out. A few murmurs, a few raised eyebrows.

Greg was preoccupied, obviously so. Karis, too. Our leadership was focused, but perhaps not on the right things. I subconsciously checked my pulse, finding it racing beneath my fingers. I tried to force my breathing to slow.

Only Jason lingered in the doorway, his eyes remaining on Greg, narrowed, angry. He finally glanced up, saw me looking at him, and stormed off, the door slamming in its frame.

20

Jack worked through the afternoon into the early evening. Torches came out, battery lighting strung in the corridors and cabins. The *Escape* wandered in its misery, pushed by the high winds, carried by the current, plotted on the chart by Greg, our coordinates entered into the logbook.

In the dining room, the chandeliers swung overhead, the cut glass catching the beams from LED lanterns on the table beneath, unable to cast any of their own.

I sought out Lily, remembering her face on the bridge, the look of contained fear – nervously looking at each of us, not finding the reassurance she needed. Comforting her might be just what I needed, a way to pause the spiralling anxiety in my gut, the uneasy sensation that things might get worse before they got better.

Tucked in the farthest corner of the main lounge, close enough to see other people, far enough for some solitude, Lily read another of her novels, sipping at a can of lemonade mixed with ginger – Elijah's natural seasickness remedy. Her hair was tied loosely, kept out of her eyes. She looked small, childlike in the dim light. I sat next to her on the leather sofa, sliding over, nudging her with my shoulder.

'Hey,' I said.

She closed the book, dropping it to her lap.

'You're getting through those quickly,' I said.

'I'm not really reading it,' she said. 'I can't concentrate.'

Her eyes darted through the lounge towards the dining area and kitchen. Elijah was back there somewhere, busying himself preparing dinner. He'd made it clear, with a certain pride and arrogance unique to chefs the world over, that his job didn't stop just because the *Escape* did.

'We'll get through this,' I said. 'A huge ship like this . . . no problem.' I hoped my voice sounded more confident than I felt.

Lily nodded. 'Has this happened to you before? I suppose it has, all the adventures you've been on. What happens? How do we get rescued? Dan said something about the beacons going missing?'

What to tell her? I didn't want to lie, but revealing the extent of the hole we were in wouldn't help her either.

'We're struggling with comms at the moment. But Jack will get to it.'

Her face dropped. 'Struggling, as in, we don't have any?'

I pulled a tentative expression.

'My phone's dead,' she said. 'My laptop is OK, but I can't get the internet. It's not just me?'

'No,' I said. 'We can't get anything at the moment, but we will. The beacons might be found somewhere. If not, maybe Jack can get one of the radios working on the bridge.'

I thought back to the blast of radio I'd heard in the laundry, not long after the fire. And before that – the first-night dinner, in the aft corridor. Was that really Dan on his phone, on a pocket radio, or someone on one of the

VHFs? If so, where the hell was it? And *who* the hell was on it?

'And if he can't?'

'Then he'll get the engines started,' I said. 'And we'll get under way again.'

She looked sceptically at me.

'This is as bad as it gets,' I said, contradicting my own thoughts just minutes ago.

Lily bit her lower lip, nodding to herself. She wasn't stupid, and not having an engineering background didn't stop her from understanding the seriousness of what we faced. I wasn't sure who was revisiting the calculations, but we would have to face tightened water rationing within the next twenty-four hours. It would be on Greg's ever-growing list of bad news to dish out.

'How is everyone else holding up?' I said. 'How about our hunky chef?'

That got a confused smile. 'I don't know. We might have had a bit of *us* time during all of this distraction,' she said. 'Which probably wasn't the right thing to do, but . . . I think he's the only person apart from you I trust on this boat.'

It was a strange way to describe things.

'Trust?' I said.

Lily turned on the sofa, keeping her feet braced to stop herself sliding around on the polished leather. She checked over my shoulder, frowned. 'I don't know. People are acting a bit weird, that's all,' she said. 'I mean, I know we're in the proverbial, but before that.'

'Hmm. Before we caught fire, or before we ran out of water?'

She chuckled. 'I don't know.'

'The crew on this boat – current company excluded –' I flashed her a warm smile, 'is weird, full stop,' I said. 'I've never met such a bunch of schoolkids.'

'It's the most dysfunctional group you'll ever meet,' she said. 'I don't know. I can't put my finger on it. You expect a certain amount of gossip and whispers . . .'

I watched her innocent face contorting in concern. Lily was a people person, emotionally intelligent, sharper than I was on that front. For her to emphasize her dislike of the others was one thing, but her distrust . . . The more I watched her, the more she furthered my unease; the warning was already there, lurking in my subconscious.

'Everyone is under a lot of stress,' I said. 'Even from day one – you told me that. The rushed departure, the constant issues with this hunk of junk.' I slapped the sofa with my palm.

Lily nodded, her face relaxing. 'You're probably right,' she said. 'I'm sure it's nothing. My imagination running wild.'

'Too many high-concept thrillers,' I said, unsure who I was trying to convince. It certainly wasn't working on me. I tossed her book on to the coffee table.

She tried to grab it, smiling, nearly tumbling off the edge of the sofa as the *Escape* rolled sharply to port. 'Wait,' she said, holding the glass tabletop, putting her other hand up, cocking her ear.

I felt it at the same time.

Vibrations, a deep rumble. A pushing sensation in my inner ear, causing a moment of vertigo. A deep throb as the two diesel giants sprang into life three decks below.

I slid off the sofa on to my feet in one quick movement, letting the next roll push me upright. The radio crackled as I did so, Jack's voice coming over loud and clear.

'*Captain to engineering, please,*' he said. '*We have power. We've got our fricking engines back!*'

21

The engines ran through the night at half power, celebrations paused until we were sure it wasn't a fluke. Jack had been awake the whole time, running the engines and steering from the engine room, unable so far to establish any control from the bridge. The steering was locked on our heading, and we proceeded at ten knots, barely chasing out the wind and currents.

The morning of day six saw a brief lull in the weather, the worst of the storm appearing to move to the north, leaving behind a fresh wind and choppy seas, but without the heavy swells of the day before. The water had changed to a deep blue, the wave peaks appearing to chase us before racing off in all directions. I woke at the crack of dawn, restless, anxious, seeing sunshine through brief cracks in the clouds, wondering if it also signalled a break in our bad luck. If, indeed, luck was in control.

I was in the gym – using the weight machine, enjoying the feeling of my back muscles straining as I pulled down on the lateral bar – when Jack called me. The running machines were silent – we may have had engines, but electricity was confined to the closed circuit of the engine room and hydraulics. The main switch panel was yet to be replaced, the main systems and wiring still damaged to the extent that it didn't matter how much current we pushed through them. They were dead until we reached port.

I heard Jack's voice in my ear. I checked the radio – engineering channel, not open to the crew.

'*Sarah, can you come down here, please?*'

'*What is it, Jack?*' Karis's voice.

A pause. '*I need to speak to Sarah.*'

Silence from Greg.

'I'll be right there,' I said. I towelled my neck, passing Arno on the way out. 'Can't stop,' I said. 'I'm in demand.'

'Shame,' he said. 'I was hoping we could work out together.'

Ever the optimist.

I'd yet to find a moment alone with Arno since before the lightning strike. I wasn't avoiding him, but it seemed the more distance I put between us, the more he came looking. I'd found him hovering around my cabin, the kitchen, and now the gym. He maintained his signature smile and stared at me with increasingly puppy-dog-like eyes. Despite everything, he still managed to distract me, ruin my train of thought, challenge my promises to myself.

He was slowly and surely wearing me down. And I was letting him. Though playing hard to get was quite good fun.

'I have to see Jack. I'll find you in a bit?'

Arno's face fell, a mock sulk. 'So you like Aussies now, huh?' he said. 'I have bigger muscles than him, you know?' He flexed his biceps, striking an outlandish pose, swivelling on his feet into a lunge.

'They could do with a bit of toning,' I said, eyeing him with mock disdain. 'I think you need that workout.'

He jumped over and flicked his towel at me. I dodged and walked off, giving him a wave, hearing him chuckle as he entered the gym.

My smile lasted for three flights of stairs, until I entered the rear of the tank deck and found Jack slumped against the engineering console, face in his hands.

'Shut the door,' he said. 'Please.'

I nudged it shut, casting my eyes around the gloomy interior. The dull throb of the engines travelled through the air and hull, vibrating through my heels.

'You look like shit,' I said, examining his face, his dirty clothes. Even over the smell of fumes, I detected his body odour, and the sour smell of spirits. 'And you're wasted,' I added.

He shook his head, sniffing, coughing up what sounded like a lungful of phlegm. He grabbed a dirty cup from the console and checked the contents before taking a slug.

'Not any more,' he replied, his voice coarse. 'I . . .' He pushed himself away from the console, the chair screeching on the slatted floor. 'Sarah, can I trust you?'

This didn't sound good. 'Of course,' I said.

'I think maybe I did something. I think this was all my fault.'

He looked at me with bloodshot eyes. I saw a weight of responsibility behind them.

'Tell me,' I said, perching on the side of a huge metal pipe. It ran from the low ceiling over to a lump of metal I assumed was an air-conditioning unit – it too was silent, and the pipe felt cold through the seat of my shorts. 'What do you mean?'

He sighed. 'I don't actually know. But last night I . . . drank a lot. I think I blacked out around three a.m. Might have been earlier. I think . . .'

'And?'

He took a couple of shaky breaths, chewed his lower lip. I imagined this was a lot like trying to extract information from a toddler. A hung-over one.

'I think it might have happened before, I don't know. Something she said.'

'Who?'

He rubbed his face again with his palms. I could see the grease glistening in the light of the lamp above.

'Camila,' he said. 'She visited me last night, we had a drink.'

'What sort of drink?'

He gave me a sheepish look. 'She doesn't know about my drinking . . . I guess you do. *Obviously*, you do. She was just being nice. Told me to ignore Greg, that I was doing a good job, et cetera.'

OK. A nice gesture from Camila, acting as a proper bosun should, though bringing alcohol to the engineering deck was a mistake.

'You got drunk together?'

Jack shook his head. 'No. I got drunk. I think she was humouring me, trying to be nice.' He blushed a little. 'I was flattered, OK? She's, you know . . . smoking hot. I'm not a fool, but I wasn't about to send her packing.'

I gave him a curt nod. 'So what did she say?'

He shook his head. 'Nothing. It wasn't what she said. It's what I realized while I was talking to her. I explained what I was doing – stuff I hadn't shown her yet – electrical systems. The autopilots and switchgear. I showed her where we'd moved the CCTV console – it's switched off now, clearly, but it isn't damaged – it's on a separate circuit and was still unplugged when the lightning struck. I'll turn it back on if I can get the power back. The new hard disks are fine.'

I tried to follow his stuttering account, losing patience. If Jack had called me down to bemoan his evening drinking with Camila, I wasn't interested. 'So?'

'After she'd left . . . that must have been around two a.m. . . . I was pretty drunk. I went back to check a few other settings on the switchboard, ready to replace it today.' He took another slug of whatever was in his mug. He cringed, pulling his knees together. 'The main breaker for the fire suppression system was switched off,' he said. 'Off, and the fuse had been taken out. It wasn't broken.'

I shook my head. 'OK, so?'

'So? It was on when we left port. I could have sworn it. I must have . . .'

'Must have what? Switched it off? Pulled the fuse?'

He shook his head, gritting his teeth. He shrugged. 'Maybe. I don't know. That's the thing. I can't *remember*, Sarah.'

'So what if you did? You said yourself, even if you ballsed up the CCTV installation, caused the short – and I'm not saying you did – the fire was completely unforeseen.'

'It *is* my fault! I'm the engineer, and I never even looked. Yeah, the thing might have ignited by itself, but the sprinklers should have worked. The electricity powers the pumps. The gas bulbs on the ceilings blew, as they're supposed to, but no water came out.' He rubbed his eyes, hard, scratching his face.

'But we're OK, Jack,' I said. 'We caught it in time.'

'That's not the point,' said Jack, voice straining, up an

octave. 'The point is, I fucked up, Sarah. The fire system should have been switched on. That's on me. But if I forgot that, then what else? The lightning protection? The water tanks? What if this was all me? I thought I had everything under control – I *thought* I had myself under control. I know what I am, Sarah, and believe me I hate myself for it, but anger is all that keeps me going sometimes. But what if I blacked out before and did something to them? What if I do this all the time?'

'What are you saying, Jack?' I shuffled on the pipe, feeling my bum going numb on the cold metal. 'Have you ever blacked out before?'

He looked at me in confusion, his brow twisted with worry. I saw his hands shaking. He clasped them together, which only served to make the rest of him shudder.

'I . . . No. I don't think so. But –'

'Jack,' I said. 'Look at me.' I pushed myself off the pipe, rubbing my backside to get the blood moving. I walked over, crouched in front of him. 'You're suffering hangover anxiety. You're hyperventilating. I'm guessing you've still got a shitload of alcohol in your system.'

He met my eyes. His were watering, pleading.

'It's not real,' I said. 'This state you're in. You're exaggerating your role. You screwed up, yes, but I don't think you caused the malady of disasters that have hit us so far.'

'You don't know that.'

'I know what I'm staring at. Believe me. I've spent enough time with guilt-ridden squaddies the morning after. It isn't real. You're beating yourself up for something you had no control over.'

My legs started to cramp and I pushed back, sitting

on the floor, replaying my own words in my head, thinking how good I was at dishing it out to other people. Poker face on, Sarah. Keep him from descending into a useless mess.

I watched him for a few moments, waiting for his breathing to slow, for him to naturally ease out of his anxious state. He wasn't too far gone to do it himself. He just needed a few minutes, and a friendly voice to reassure him he wasn't a total screw-up.

'Jack, you're doing well,' I said. 'You have a problem, let's not pretend otherwise, but right now you have to focus. I meant what I said last time. Do what you do, and do it as well as you can. The blame can be shared, you don't deserve it all on your shoulders. Got it?'

Jack took a deep breath, puffing his chest out, trembling, unconvinced.

'This is what you do, Jack,' I said. 'You're good at it, and you know it. You wouldn't be working on a yacht this size if you weren't. Greg wouldn't have hired you.'

He tilted his head, a small shake.

'No, listen to me,' I said, shuffling forwards. 'It's the truth. We *need* you, Jack. I need you. Electrics, engines, comms . . . it's all you. You can be the difference between cruising home with a good story and sitting out here for weeks watching our rations run out. Pick the former, Jack. Do it for me. Don't make me regret sticking up for you.'

His eyes flickered, but I saw it, the distant and damaged pride. It was still there, and I'd hooked it. He took a deep breath, then another, sucking the air between his parched lips. The trembling subsided. He sniffed, reaching for his mug.

'That had better be lemonade in there,' I said, 'or I'm going to swing for you.'

He grinned, pausing with the mug to his lips. 'Coke, without anything added. I promise.'

'Sure?'

He nodded.

I pushed myself to my feet, stretching the stiffness out of my legs. 'We'll keep this chat to ourselves, Jack,' I said. 'No need for the others to know, yeah?'

'Thanks, Sarah,' said Jack. His expression had already changed, grateful, more positive, his body recovering from the depths. 'Lily was right about you.'

'Oh?'

He shrugged. 'You're one of the genuine ones. Trustworthy. Not many of those around here.'

Jack kicked his chair back and stood, heading towards the tool station. He had another day of hard graft ahead of him. I left him to it.

I emerged on to the bridge deck, feeling exhausted, the early hour and lack of proper breakfast after my workout taking its toll. I thought about Jack's final words – *trustworthy*. It bothered me – the same turn of phrase Lily had used.

My head was muddled, spinning. That bloody CCTV. Had someone wiped the disks by sabotaging the cable? But why? And in doing so, accidentally started a fire – that was a freak outside chance, according to Jack. A fire could have killed us all, no question.

But at the same time, someone had turned the fire suppression system off.

But what the hell did any of that mean?

Unless Jack was right, and he was responsible for the whole bloody lot of it. But I wasn't so sure.

I saw Arno as I walked, through the reflection of the lounge window, his clothing camouflaging him against the dark mahogany of the lounge walls and dresser. I went to call out but held my tongue, seeing another figure behind him. Camila, again, playing with her hair, talking as Arno listened, their conversation playing on mute as I stood the other side of the glass. Bosun and deckhand. Perfectly normal, and *none of your business, Sarah.*

I headed straight past, nipping along the side of the deck towards the bridge. If Arno saw me, it would have been a brief glimpse of me disappearing behind the entrance to the gym and gallery. He didn't call out, didn't follow.

'Karis,' I said, entering the wheelhouse. 'Is there anything I can –?'

Karis looked up from the nav table, her brow furrowed with worry. She clasped two battery radios, one in each hand.

'What's up?' I said.

'Have you seen Greg?' she asked.

I shook my head. 'Not since last night. Why?'

Her breathing was heavy, fast.

'I can't raise him on the radio. I can't find him anywhere.'

'Can't find him?' I said, puzzled.

It was a big yacht, but you couldn't lose a captain on it. As I stared at Karis, her eyes widening, her lips trembling, a renewed sense of fear tickled down the back of my neck.

'Nobody's seen Greg since last night,' she said, slowly. 'I assumed he'd taken the morning off. He's not in the skipper's cabin, and I've asked all stations to report in.'

'And?'

'We can't find him, Sarah. Greg's missing.'

22

We started on the sun deck, arranging ourselves into groups of two. Jack killed the engines, our position was marked, our course and drift plotted and calculated.

We scanned the water first, each with a pair of binoculars, working methodically. The darkness of the storm still hovered to the north, and Karis eyed it warily. The seas were restless, choppy, a fresh swell hitting us side-on. The horizon was clear on all sides – no sign of any other vessels, and we didn't expect there to be any. We weren't in the clear by a long way, and the ocean reminded us of it with every turbulent second that passed.

Karis checked the radios – we were running low on batteries, unable to charge any of them until Jack got us some power. It was one between two.

Jason joined Karis, making it clear Harriet would remain in her cabin, and only he would give her an update, once we had something to say, other than *we can't find the captain.*

Camila selected Arno to search with her. I grabbed Lily. The others paired and we split up. The sun deck was clear – there was nowhere Greg could have got himself trapped, snagged in a rope, otherwise injured. We moved to the bridge deck.

Twenty-five thousand square feet of yacht, and yet there was a limit to the number of places where a person could disappear. With each passing minute I could feel the anxiety rising, taste it in the air, hear it in the voices of the crew.

Nobody wants to utter the words 'man overboard' on an ocean crossing. If you see it happening, you have a good chance of rescuing the unfortunate sailor. If you don't, the protocols are clear, the search pattern is calculated, the ever-widening area piloted, until you have a result, one way or the other.

The reasons can be many and brutal. I remembered an incident on board a Navy destroyer some five years ago – a rating got his hand tangled in a winch while operating the drum end. He tried to free himself but was thrown clear over the stern. Some screw-up had meant he was working on his own, without a tether, and by the time anybody realized, he'd drowned before he had a chance to bleed to death. They recovered his body and his right arm, separately. Heads rolled, but the poor sailor paid the ultimate price and reminded us all – it only takes a second. The ocean is unforgiving and will take you in a heartbeat.

But Karis hadn't called it yet, and I had to let her take command – it was her ship until we found Greg.

The bridge deck was cleared within five minutes, the gym and art gallery searched by the interior staff – Dan and Luan – the lounge and outer decks by the rest of us.

'Check for anything on the gunwales,' I said, examining the railings and even the deck for scuffs, signs of damage, anything that might give a hint to indicate an accident or misstep. The railings were high, and even with the motion, it would be hard to imagine Greg falling over the side.

The lounge was clear – cupboards, kitchen, fridge,

freezer, everything was checked. The decks had huge lockers for the storage of rope and fenders – the huge fixed and inflatable cushions that protected the sides of the *Escape* in dock. All were emptied, unpacked, repacked.

We moved on.

Down from the bridge to the owner's deck. Jason searched Harriet's main room – with some degree of reluctance and protest, though Karis insisted she be allowed to check the office and accompanying outer rooms, wardrobes and bathrooms.

Nothing.

'Did you see Harriet?' I asked as Karis rushed past me.

She shook her head. 'No. And I really don't need to right now.'

The lounge, kitchen and bars were all clear, and I entered the forward port stairwell, Lily right behind me – the other pairs all taking alternative routes. It would be just our luck to miss Greg crumpled at the bottom of a staircase that nobody used.

I'm not sure if it was one of the stewards I heard calling, their voices echoing through the interior, or my imagination, but the *Escape* shuddered at the same time, rolling over a rogue wave. My vision flickered, narrowing as I descended.

A fresh wind howled down the stairs, salty, cold. It took me back to the Zodiac, cutting through the water, that day, that morning.

Not now, Sarah. I repeated it in my head, even as my chest tightened, my face flushing.

'You OK?' Lily, right behind me.

Her voice was distant. My ears were popping. I stared

out from the bottom of the stairs at the narrow corridor leading to the central foyer.

Take a breath.

Heart thumping.

Lily bumped into me, the motion causing her to stumble on the last step. The jolt caused my vision to right itself, sound flooded my ears, the galloping thud of my heart retreating into normality.

'I'm fine,' I said, shaking my head.

A near miss, not as bad as the last one. Was that a good sign? Or was my brain storing it up for later? I gulped, trying not to worry that my panic attacks seemed to be increasing in frequency.

'Let's start in the guest rooms,' I said, stepping forward, ignoring Lily's concerned expression.

We didn't have time for my fucked-up head right now. After this, it was just engineering – the lower and tank decks, which had already been swept by Jack, Camila and Arno. My heart faltered at what we might face in the next few minutes.

We raced through, swapping one room for another, passing Elijah, Arno, Camila and the rest as we tag-teamed through the entire length and breadth.

The lower deck was called all-clear, then the tank deck, the latter revealing a surprise to most of us, but not the one we'd hoped for.

We gathered as a group, the whole crew, near the central staircase. I pushed my way to the front as Dan punched a reinforced metal door, sandwiched between the infirmary and the engine room. It was designed to look like part of the wall, invisible.

'A safe room?' said Dan. 'What the fuck?'

Jason appeared behind the group, nervously glancing around. 'It's not uncommon,' he said, 'on a yacht this size. A bolt-hole for the owner in case of piracy or hijack. I can't tell you much about it, because I don't know. Sarah might . . .'

'Sarah might, if Sarah had known about it herself,' I said, trying to keep the frustration from my voice, not quite believing Jason hadn't told me there was an armoured safe room on board. Mitch can't have known either, which meant it wasn't on the blueprints. It was precisely hidden, tucked away in a place where the crew would never venture. On a ship this size it might never be discovered.

'Why didn't you tell me?' I said.

'It's not in use,' he said. 'It was irrelevant.'

Dan pushed the door, leaning into the heavy reinforced metal. It swung open, revealing a very cramped cabin which looked remarkably like mine, containing a narrow bunk and a connected bathroom. A metal desk was fixed to the wall, housing a radio and three LCD screens.

'Not in use?' Dan pointed at the desk.

Stacked at one end were cartons of soup, bottles of water and energy bars. The seals had been broken on all of them, items missing. He ducked under the desk, pulled out a waste bin, fished out a used food wrapper and an empty water bottle.

'I'd say it's in use,' he said. 'One of you lot has been in here.' He laughed, a short burst of disbelief, as he turned to the rest of us.

Jason's face dropped. He barged past Jack and me, joining Dan in the cramped room.

'What the hell?' he said. 'This room was out of bounds.' He spun to challenge the group. 'Who's been in here? Who collected this food?'

I cast my eyes around the bewildered group. Frowns, murmurs, but no admissions. I looked at each of them in turn, searching, watching for a second more than they expected me to. Nothing.

Lily reached out, grabbed my arm. 'Someone . . . else?' she said, her face twisting in confusion. 'But –'

'Like who?' said Dan, thumping the door again, the sound reverberating into the corridor. 'Some illegal pricks from Palma, hitching a lift? It's a big boat, but not that big. Besides, we've just searched the whole fucking thing from end to end. It's just us.'

His attitude to migrants aside, I wanted to agree. It would be near impossible for any stowaways to be living in secret on the *Escape* without us knowing, six days in.

And yet the thought sent a little shiver down my spine. I suddenly recalled Karis's comment about Pieter, *I hate to think of what he might do*. I didn't know Pieter from Adam, but were we dealing with a stowaway? What if Pieter had silently refused Greg's dismissal, and instead decided to join us? As bosun he'd know where to hide, how to stay out of sight. The shadows, the snooping in my cabin . . . the radios. Was it Pieter? Christ. My mind starting spinning.

'Who else knew about the safe room?' I said, my eyes resting on Jason. 'You did, Jason. What about you, Jack?'

Jack shuffled his feet, nodded. 'I knew. It never occurred to me anyone might use it. But it's in my contract NDA – I couldn't tell anyone. And Greg knew, obviously.'

Camila caught my eye, raised her eyebrows. She mouthed 'Greg?' at me.

Greg? Was that it? But what the hell was Greg doing in the safe room? Privacy? Solitude? There were plenty of places for that without coming here. His own cabin for a start. Unless he had a good reason for wanting to lock himself in. Away from someone else. The thought jarred.

Or else one of the others was lying. But what did they want with it? The same? A quick bolt-hole for a secret liaison, or a bit of solo time?

Jason paced back and forth, in and out of the engine room. We all stood, alone with our thoughts – whirring minds running through the possibilities. The *Escape* creaked and groaned, the floor pushed upwards beneath our feet, shuddered back down.

I couldn't shake the feeling. This was odd, bizarre, but equally inexplicable. I kept scanning the crew's faces, looking for clues. Still nothing. My gaze settled on Karis.

She sighed, a long, shuddering breath. 'Jason?'

The suave appearance of the New Yorker had long since faded. Jason's skin was pasty, his clothes creased, hair greasy. 'Karis?'

'Are there any other cabins or compartments not on the plans?' she said. 'Tell me the truth, please.'

Jason stared at her for a moment, before shaking his head. 'No,' he said. 'That's it.'

'Then . . .' She closed her eyes, squeezing them tightly shut for a moment. 'I don't care. I don't know what's going on here, or who's been shagging or sleeping or eating in secret, but it ends now, you hear me?' Her voice cracked, barely controlled, her glare landing on each and every one of the crew.

Nobody nodded, because that would have been an acceptance of guilt. Everybody's expressions remained neutral, cautious.

'Greg has to be here somewhere. We must continue searching. Arno, Camila, have you checked the garage? The tender? Underneath the tarps?'

They both nodded.

I watched Karis.

'Jack,' said Karis. 'Engine room . . . fuel tanks . . . what about the water tanks? Any chance he might have slipped under the grates? The bilge? Have we . . .'

Jack nodded. 'He's not here, Karis. This is the last place on the ship he could have been.'

Karis looked from each of us to the next, shaking her head, unwilling to call it.

'Life jacket count?'

'All present and stowed,' said Arno. '*All* of them . . .'

'But . . .' She trembled, clenching her fists, holding one of them to her mouth.

I saw it coming, and stepped forward, taking her arm as she started to hyperventilate.

'He can't have,' she whispered. 'It can't . . .' She turned to me, eyes filling up.

'Come with me,' I said, guiding her past the rest of the crew, through the foyer, past the staircase, the bulkhead and into one of the guest rooms. 'Give us a minute,' I called behind me.

Karis perched on the end of the bed, staring at the floor. Her chest rose and fell in stops and starts.

'We can't get any emergency comms out,' I said. 'We will, just as soon as we can, but right now all we can do is search.'

Karis glanced at me, face white as a sheet. 'He'll be somewhere,' she said, nodding, wiping her eyes.

I shook my head, crouched in front of her. 'We have to assume he's overboard, Karis. I don't know how, but it's the reality.'

'No,' said Karis, raising her voice. 'No. That's ridiculous. He's the captain. Captains don't fall overboard. He's experienced. He's a . . . he's a good man, Sarah. He's my . . .'

The tears returned and I jumped up, cradling her as she crumpled, holding her tight against me. She felt frail in my arms, her face suddenly old, sunken and lost. A far cry from the future 'Captain Karis' we'd talked about on the sun deck a couple of days before.

She shook, sobbing. I let her. A few more seconds wouldn't change things, and she needed to get this out before she pulled herself together. I needed that drive from her – that leadership quality I knew, or hoped, she possessed.

'I haven't seen him for hours, Sarah,' she said, sniffing. 'Hours. Last night. Eleven? Camila and I took turns on watch. I slept. I haven't . . .'

'We'll speak to everyone,' I said, 'get an accurate time. Plot our speed, drift, wind direction. You don't need me to tell you this, Karis, but we need to start now. Jack can steer the *Escape* from engineering. I can take the tender. Arno can launch a jet ski.'

I doubted myself as I said it. The tender, maybe, but the seas were too rough for the jet skis. We'd never get them in the water.

But what Karis needed was a plan. I just worried she wouldn't be able to take command of it.

The minutes ticked by. Karis didn't pick up as I'd hoped. If anything, she spiralled downwards, the crying intensified.

'He and I . . . I told you . . . we *were* going to sort it out, Sarah. Everything. We'd made plans. He meant them. I –'

I swallowed down my own surge of emotion. Had Karis's future with Greg just been snuffed out in equally brutal fashion? I knew what she was going through, the flashes of a thousand thoughts, a thousand possible opportunities reduced to nothing.

'We haven't lost him yet,' I said, knowing it was a chance in a million that he was still alive if he'd fallen overboard during the night. The futility of our search would soon become apparent, but we still had to do it. You don't give up on people while there's still a chance, however small.

She looked at me, eyes bleary. 'Will . . . you?' she said. 'Organize . . . everything. I need a minute . . . some time.'

'Time's what we don't have, Karis,' I said, feeling the pressure bearing down on my shoulders like an avalanche.

Was she seriously delegating her command to me?

Her answer was to bury her face in her hands again. Her shoulders shook, her chest heaved.

I had no choice.

'Stay here,' I said. 'When you're ready, head to the bridge. We need eyes up there, scanning with the binoculars.'

She nodded.

I closed the door behind me and ran back to the assembled crew. Their faces were hard to read, the tension seizing the air around them.

'OK, everyone,' I announced, feeling the nerves kick in as all eyes turned to me. 'Karis has asked me to organize the MOB procedure. You all know what to do?'

Nods all round, narrowed eyes from Jason.

'What's the last time anybody saw Greg?'

A brief discussion revealed that Elijah had seen Greg shortly after 11.30 p.m., grabbing a snack from the pantry. I checked my watch. 10 a.m. Nearly eleven hours had passed.

I turned to Arno. 'Take Luan and see if you can get the tender launched. Plot your search radius, and life jackets all round.'

They nodded and headed off.

'Jack,' I said. 'You and Camila plan the *Escape*'s movements. Pick a trackline search or expanding square . . .'

I referred to two commonly used search methods. The first involved travelling back and forth along our trackline, adjusting a little wider each time. The other involved making right-angle turns in an ever-increasing square pattern.

'You'll be in engineering?'

Jack nodded.

'Fine. Camila, you take the bridge. Everyone else, get throw lines ready, and prepare to enter the water if you need to.'

I paused, my mind flashing back to the safe room, the desk, the food wrappers. 'Keep checking on each other. Got it? And keep me posted.'

More nods. I saw fear, but also grit, a determination in the faces in front of me, matched by the adrenaline which flooded my body. The reality was that Greg would have survived a few hours at most – in calm waters maybe longer, but not in this. Not without a life jacket. The best open water swimmers would struggle in these white-capped ocean waves, and Greg was far from an athlete.

And surrounding our task was the veil of unspoken tension – too many unanswered questions, the unravelling of relationships peppered with anomalies. Did one of the crew know more than they were letting on? If they did, then where did that lead me? Was Greg's disappearance, in fact, a terrible accident, or had something else transpired here?

I had no choice but to set them all to work, and start preparing myself for the next decision – the one where I called off the search, and we resumed our fragile journey, with our captain lost at sea.

23

It came earlier than I expected. Jack appeared behind me as I scanned over the bow with a small pair of high-powered binoculars. The *Escape* was surging through an ever-growing search pattern, which had revealed nothing. Not that I expected it to. A body would sink after a few hours. Fish food within ten. We might find scraps of clothing, but unlikely. I found myself assessing these facts dispassionately, conscious of my growing responsibility.

'We have to stop soon,' he said.

I checked my watch. We'd been unable to get the tender or the jet skis in the water – the motion was too great and the winches had slammed them back into the launching platform. Arno had tried, but injured his arm as a result. I called it off – there was nothing to investigate at that level in the water. We'd end up losing another person if we risked it.

'We've only been going five hours,' I said. 'Not long enough.'

'Five hours at full throttle,' said Jack. 'It's not that. It's the fact Greg had us on full power for the first few days – our fuel load is precariously low. If we don't stop soon, we'll have another problem.'

'You think we might run out?'

'We're literally bang smack in the middle of the North Atlantic. Azores are maybe a thousand miles, Cape Verde the same. Antigua thirteen hundred,' he said. 'If we spend another day out here, burning this amount of fuel, we risk ending even further from help than we are now. The water won't last, either – people are being lazy on rations.'

Typical.

'How much?'

'It's not an emergency, yet,' he said. 'But . . . we can't circle here for much longer. You have to make the call.'

Jack looked at me for instruction.

Me. I had to do it.

Karis had dragged herself to the bridge but, so far, she just stared out of the windows, lost in a daze of grief. Denial was crowding her mind – I could see her heart breaking with each passing moment, and I had to check my own in turn.

Memories of Kay flashed in and out as I watched the water. Karis and I were in very different situations, but I could already see the signs – the guilt, blaming herself – though she couldn't yet put her finger on what for. She jumped, startled, every few minutes – adjusting her binos, taking a breath, sagging uncontrollably when a perceived object turned out to be nothing – just a strange-shaped wave, a shadow, a burst of white water creating shapes in her head.

After Kay, I remembered being OK at first. Shell-shocked, perhaps. It wasn't until a week later it hit me. The nightmare woke me in the early hours, the crippling anxiety following well into the next day. I shrugged it off, throwing myself into exercise, drinking a little more – someone always had a stash. I was doing anything to avoid thinking – I needed to push the grief anywhere but front and centre.

The numbness didn't hit for another week. The feeling of complete detachment, walking on another plane of existence. I walked right out of the base and sat in the middle of the road. It was my friend Becks who found me, who walked me back, face twisted with concern, keeping the others away. She marched me to the unit's medical officer and had a quiet word.

The talking started the next day.

PTSD.

It wasn't your fault, Sarah.

Karis might follow a similar path. At the moment she was shell-shocked, and I had no idea how long it would take for her to regain some semblance of control. I forced another hour before putting my hand on her shoulder.

'It's time,' I said. 'We need to stop.'

She turned to me, without protest. The blood had drained from her face and she just stared – eyes hollow and dry.

'Will you give the command,' I said, 'or do you want me to?'

An offer, but one I shouldn't have to give. I formed no part of this crew's hierarchy, and yet I couldn't in all conscience refuse. The rest of the crew were a mess, and no obvious leader came to mind. I'd always been task oriented. It was the Royal Marine way – give me a job and I'll do it. If Karis wanted me to run things until she could, I'd do it without question. Perhaps it was the only way – I was still an outsider, could move around without the baggage they all carried.

And yet it still made me uneasy. I was no yacht master, no captain. I could make people move, through sheer stubbornness and rudeness – Mitch hadn't hired me for my politeness and charm. Hopefully, they'd respect me enough to follow. I wouldn't ask them to do anything other than their jobs.

And hopefully I could keep my own shit together until Karis found hers.

'I talked to him,' she whispered. 'I fought for him, like you said.'

Her lips moved, but couldn't quite form the next words. She muttered, and I had to get her to repeat it.

'You want to know why Greg was in such a rush?' she whispered.

I tilted my head, nodded.

'He told me last night. It was the bonus – much bigger than usual. Huge – a surprise. It would have covered his divorce, all his debts, the lawyers, everything. It was enough for him to start again . . .'

I held my tongue. From the conversation I'd heard between him and Jason before we set off, I'd suspected Greg's motives were money-driven – though it still only explained Greg's actions, not Jason's.

'He forgave me for Pieter. All of it. He was trying to hit Jason's schedule so we could have a new life,' she said. 'He actually meant it, this time. We were planning to stay in the US at the end of the season, a fresh start.' She sniffed. Her eyes began to fill up again.

I saw myself, twelve months ago. My own dreams smashed. The tentative plans, that realization when you've found *the one*, the gathering of thoughts, all creeping towards that master plan. The life plan with your life partner. Maybe not shared – or only with yourself, in the quiet hours, when you stare at their sleeping body, knowing that this is it. You've found them, and all you have to do now is keep living.

'What on earth happened to him, Sarah?' she said.

I gripped her shoulders with both hands. 'Lily will sit with you, OK? Give the order, and I'll sort things out. I'll be back very soon.'

'Are you sure?' she said. One last burst of hopeless optimism.

'I'm sorry,' I said. 'I'm sure.'

She nodded. 'Then do it. Please.'

She stumbled away towards Greg's cabin. I heard her cries as she shut the door.

'Jack, Camila,' I called.

They'd remained across the wheelhouse while I was with Karis.

'That's it,' I said. 'Log everything. Prepare the statement for when we have comms back. Camila – notify the crew, please. I'll talk to them in a minute.'

'Are we resuming our prior heading?' said Jack.

I could see he was struggling – Greg was his friend, despite their recent conflicts – and I admired his professionalism. I couldn't have him falling apart as well. Not yet.

'You don't want to try for the Azores?' he said.

'The storm is behind us and to the north,' said Camila. 'We risk heading back into it. Antigua is further but the chances of good weather are better.'

Jack nodded. 'That's a good point. It could be unpredictable. But there may be storms ahead. Without weather radar we don't know.'

I thought for a second. 'Better to avoid the storm we know about rather than the ones we don't?'

'Agreed,' said Jack.

Camila nodded. 'And let's take it steady?' she added. 'Reduced power, no more racing across this ocean, *non*?'

Jack considered the fresh water issue, but agreed.

I nodded, thinking there were a hundred things I was probably missing, but relying on these two to help me.

'Let's do it,' I said. 'Resume previous course and heading. Twelve knots if you can make it. Arrange the watch rota with any qualified crew.'

I watched Jack exit the bridge, thinking he had a puzzling spring in his step – sober for a few hours now, a drastic difference to when I'd seen him earlier. I would talk to him when I got a chance, check a few things out. His suggestion of a blackout in the night might be accurate, given the state I found him in the following morning. But had he seen something? Heard something? I'd detected nothing off about him, other than the obvious – his guilt-ridden torrent suggesting nothing to do with our captain's disappearance. But still, it niggled away at me.

And it wasn't the only thing. Far from it.

There should be a rational explanation for Greg's tragic end – it was rare, but it happened. Transatlantic sailing carried an intrinsic risk, and sometimes shit just happened – a rogue wave, an attempt to perform something you shouldn't – lean over a little too far, go for the rope that's just out of reach. I didn't think Greg drank, but he might have had a night off, spent a few moments alone on the lower deck, on the tender platform – no railings, nothing to stop you slipping, hitting your head. It would have been stupid, but sometimes good people do stupid things.

Gone forever.

But I thought about the rest of the crew, the issues so far, the barely contained resentment. So many reasons to lash out. So much still hidden – I'd hardly scratched the surface.

This was the point in any mission where I'd turn to a mate and say, 'Does something feel odd to you?' Perhaps our entry point was off, the target buildings weren't where they should have been, our native contact a little too talkative, or not talkative enough. We'd smell a rat, talk it through, evaluate, get a consensus, call for intel if we could.

Except I couldn't. There was no one I could call, no military know-how but me – a washed-up marine with an attitude and enough mental health issues for the rest of the crew put together.

Was it all in my head? The spooks, the shadows, the combination of isolated incidents – what did they add up to? Circumstance and bad luck, or something more sinister? Too much had happened, too much remained unexplained. My gut continued to scream at me. I just wished it gave me more answers.

The door closed behind Jack. I tried to wind my thoughts in. Failed, but figured at least he'd done well. He hadn't fallen apart. Whether that remained the case for the rest of the trip . . . we'd all find out soon enough.

I knew that, despite Jack's initial professional demeanour, he'd crash too, they all would, once they processed what had happened. The death of a friend was tragic, of a colleague more puzzling – sometimes harder to deal with, because you didn't know how to react. In a crew like this it would range from nonchalance to disbelief to anger. The more emotionally intelligent would grieve simply because a human life had been lost. The others would box it up, tuck it away. Perhaps it would come out some day. Perhaps not.

Assuming they all mourned his loss.

Another shiver down my spine.

Camila hovered next to me. She gave me a small smile of encouragement, though her expression was hard to read. Reality was hitting her, too, her perfect calm disrupted by the day's events, her make-up smudged and her hair windswept. Her promotion was putting her in a place of visibility, of responsibility.

I patted her on the arm. 'Thanks, Camila,' I said.

She glanced at me. Her smile faded, an uncomfortable twist of her mouth replacing it. She turned, stared straight ahead, out to sea.

'I'm doing my job,' she said, rather more bluntly than necessary. 'I just hope everyone else can do theirs.'

I left Camila on watch. She was suffering from normal stress and fear, certainly a little grief. She knew Greg as well as any of us, better perhaps, after her extended watches on the bridge. But I needed her to keep going, to keep that stoic bluntness and turn it into pragmatism, alternating on the bridge with Karis – who I suspected would need most of my sympathies.

The rest of the crew had congregated in the main deck lounge. There was no time for pleasantries, and I stood by the rear glass doors and repeated our intentions. My words came out subdued, lacking in certainty, the sight of everyone watching me draining my self-confidence.

They were silent for a few moments when I'd finished, glances exchanged between them, eyes darting, too fast for me to catch. I reminded them about the water rations. Lily stood, the first one to show her support.

'We'll help,' she said. 'Anything you need, just shout.'

Elijah echoed her. Arno nodded to me.

Dan shrugged with his usual attitude. 'I'll take care of Jason and Harriet,' he said.

'How could it happen?' Luan asked.

A reasonable question, although I questioned his motives for asking it – or how much he cared.

'Are we doing this now?' said Arno, staring at his brother with surprising vehemence.

Luan shrugged. 'I'm just saying.'

'We need to do another sweep,' I said. 'Look for damaged railings, gates, check the rear garage, the launching and swimming platforms. Anything that might have caused an accident.'

Luan pulled a face.

'Do as Sarah says,' said Arno. 'Stop asking stupid questions.'

'Hardly stupid,' said Luan, squaring up to his brother.

'He's right,' said Dan. 'What are we supposed to be looking for? I'm just saying. Greg was going through a divorce, struggling – we all knew that. He'd also screwed up his only good relationship.'

Arno shook his head, slowly.

'He wasn't suicidal,' said Elijah.

'How would you know?' said Dan. 'You hardly knew the man. You don't know anything about any of us.'

'What the fuck is that supposed to mean?'

'Nothing,' said Arno. 'He's being a prick.'

'Fuck you, Arno,' said Dan. 'He had a few enemies, but I'm not one of them.'

Arno shuffled his feet. His face was red. Angry, or embarrassed. He glanced at me.

'A few?' I asked.

'Pieter, for one.'

'Pieter's not here.'

'I've seen Jason ripping shreds out of him.'

'Stop this,' said Arno. 'I –'

'*Enough!*' I shouted, surprising myself with the ferocity of my voice. 'Shut up, all of you.' I couldn't let this descend into chaos, not if it were just me in charge. Even if I wanted answers to these questions myself.

I faced each of them in turn, trying to project calm authority, control, even though I felt nothing of the sort. 'This has to stop,' I said. 'Please. Wind it in and calm down. Do as I ask – check everything again. Stay out of each other's way, if you have to. We've still got five days or so together, maybe longer, depending on what Jack can squeeze out of the engines.'

I took a deep breath, then another. Everyone sat there, nobody challenged. Luan stared daggers at the rest of the crew, Arno had one of his huge arms against his brother's chest, holding him back.

'If you have anything to say on the matter,' I said, 'anything at all, please talk to me in private.'

Lily got closer, placed her hand on my back, showing

her solidarity. A small gesture, but welcome. It showed she had guts. The testosterone in the rest of them was simmering, threatening to boil over, and perhaps we were the perfect pair to keep it in check.

'I'll check on Harriet,' she said. 'If Jason will let me.'

Dan nodded.

I hovered as the rest separated, getting themselves into pairs, mapping out the areas they'd be searching again.

I kept my eyes on Arno, and I think he took the hint. I waited until it was just the two of us. We sat in silence for a few minutes. He lifted his huge bulk out of the sofa with ease, coming to perch next to me.

'You OK?' he said.

A brief moment of panic hit me, one of those fleeting and all-encompassing waves of dread that made me want to stop, crawl into a dark corner – ask someone else to take over, deal with Karis, get us home safely. Arno would, from what I knew of him. But I couldn't give in, and the wave quickly passed, followed by a surge of determination, the grit I once prided myself on. How long it would stay with me was anyone's guess.

'I will be,' I said. But the talking caused another wobble.

I didn't quite lose it. *Shit.*

'I'm right here with you, Sarah,' said Arno. 'You hear me?' He gripped my arms, two small vices against my muscles, his chest so broad it filled my vision, his tender, serious face. 'You tell them what you want, and they'll do it,' he said. 'If they don't, I'll make them. OK?'

The way he said it caused a flashback to my former life.

He sounded just like Kay, like a soldier – standing before me giving me his unwavering support. My enforcer, should I need it.

I nodded, trying to keep the lump out of my throat. He kept his hands where they were, and my emotions flipped, veering from the nerves and anxiety of a few minutes before, to a rush of closeness, a hot surge of desire for this man who'd managed to break down my playful resistance, and still remained here when it mattered.

I leaned in, smelling his body, tasting his breath. I suddenly needed him more than anything, wanted him, all the while my brain was screaming I couldn't have him. I was falling, letting him guide me. I raised my mouth to his, and he brushed it with his lips.

I waited, imagining him pushing his tongue into my mouth, forcing me hard against the wall, running his lips and tongue across my neck. I wanted his hands on me, firm, controlling, letting me know his desire was as strong as mine.

Our eyes met. I don't know what mine revealed, but his were troubled, his face flushed, brow furrowed. He didn't kiss me again, and I pulled away, sensing the moment had already passed.

'I'm sorry,' he said. 'That was inappropriate of me.'

Of him? No, it wasn't. I *wanted* him to kiss me, to take me away from this chaos, if only for a moment. I'd regret it afterwards, for sure, but that wouldn't stop the pleasure of the moment. It never did.

'I –'

The radio crackled in my ear. It was Dan. His voice was raised, strained.

'*Sarah. It's Dan. We need to gather everyone back again.*'

My mouth remained open. Arno stood back, apologetic, frustrated.

Before answering the radio, I whispered to him. 'It was entirely appropriate,' I said. 'And next time, don't stop, you idiot.'

He chuckled, closing his eyes for a second, rubbing my arms as he released me.

'I copy you, Dan,' I said, my heart thudding as my brain scanned the possible reasons for Dan's call. 'OK . . . All crew, back to the main lounge,' I said. 'Immediately, please.'

24

Dan lurched through the rear doors of the lounge, wrestling Luan behind him. Elijah followed close behind, pushing Luan as he attempted to break free, the three of them tumbling into the room. It played in slow motion, my eyes trying to make sense of the fight, my body tensing, preparing to retreat or throw myself into it.

Arno got there first.

'Take your hands off him,' he shouted, leaping forward, grabbing Dan's right arm and thrusting it away. He pushed him in the chest, sending Dan staggering backwards, before turning to Elijah, who kept his hands out, palms open, but blocking the exit. Dan backed away from Arno's challenge, leaving Luan crouched in the middle.

He looked up, red-faced, teeth bared.

'What the fuck?' said Arno. 'What are you doing?'

'Him,' said Dan. 'It was him!'

My heart skipped a beat. I think Arno's did, too. He paused. I found my voice.

'Explain,' I said, for the first time wishing I had some form of weapon on me. The taser wouldn't be a bad idea in this situation, where I had no idea who I could trust. What was I looking at?

'The water,' shouted Dan. 'It was Luan. The water tanks.'

My breath caught in my throat. I was aware of the rest

of the crew approaching from the deck and from the dining area, hearing my radio call. No sooner had they all been dismissed than we were back here fighting again.

'The water tanks?' Lily's voice, from behind me. 'What did you say?'

'What do you mean?' Elijah asked, right next to her.

Arno stepped back, turned to his brother. I could see a renewed fire in his eyes.

Luan cowered, lowering his gaze. He was sweating, beyond the exertion of the fight. I suspected we were about to find out the cause.

I saw the danger in his eyes, the pent-up aggression, a pressure cooker ready to blow. This man had anger issues. I'd seen it before, not in the heat of battle – my squadron was far too professional for that – but in training, in the dead time, when people had too much opportunity to dwell on the darker moments, the evil which pervaded the theatre of war, waiting in the shadows.

I saw that same darkness in Luan, and it worried me. Rage like that always came out, one way or another. I should know.

'I found him on the tank deck, trying to put these back on the water tanks.' Dan produced two pipe valves with small taps on the top. 'He must have raced straight down there, trying to cover his tracks. The missing valves, yes, Jack? The ones that left the tanks draining themselves into the bilge? He'd kept them in his locker.'

I hadn't noticed Jack to my left. He nodded, shaking his head at Luan, his own anger evident. He'd been blaming himself.

'Luan?' I said, trying to keep the weariness out of my

voice, trying to rewind the trip to that night. 'Make this easy for us? What were you doing?'

Luan clamped his eyes shut; his fists were tightly balled. He stood, and I saw Dan position himself, ready to take him if he made any sudden moves. Arno stood to one side, eyes flicking between Dan and Luan – I'm not sure who he was most angry at.

When he spoke, Luan's normally gruff voice was surprisingly calm and conciliatory. Caught, with nowhere to run.

'I don't know what happened to Greg,' he said.

An odd way to start a confession, but guilt talks in funny ways. Luan had a story to tell, and apart from the details, I think Arno had already told me what it was. My only question was how far Luan had gone.

'But he was a fucking asshole,' continued Luan.

That got a gasp from Lily.

'You should have some fucking respect,' said Dan. 'The man's gone, and you still bad-mouth him.'

'It's the truth,' said Luan.

'No, it isn't.' A small voice, coming from the dining area. Karis walked forward, her eyes fixed on Luan. 'Please don't say that about him.' She opened her mouth, closed it again.

'What did you do, bro?' said Arno, his voice low, simmering.

'This isn't . . .' began Luan. 'That wasn't . . . I still don't know what happened to him. OK?'

'Keep talking,' said Arno.

He'd assumed my role of interrogator. Was that a good idea? Could I stop it?

'This was ... you know he ...' Luan struggled for words. 'I overheard him talking on the phone, before we left Palma ...' He paused.

Arno's hands were on his hips.

'He was talking about his bonus — I don't know, to his solicitor or someone. Boasting about how much it was.' Luan shook his head. 'I ... Christ! This sounds bad, but all I tried to do was screw his bonus up. Any sane captain would have turned around after the tanks emptied. I didn't think for a *second* he would continue. The water would cost the rest of us nothing but time, but it would cost Greg his fat stack of cash. It was his *greed* that forced us —'

'I said don't talk about him like that,' said Karis. Her voice trembled, the hurt evident on her face. Her eyes were still glazed, the shock maintaining its grip. 'He wasn't greedy, just stuck,' she said.

What did I believe? Was this a full confession, or only a partial one, the rest of it far more serious?

'Did you confront Greg?' I said to Luan. 'About the reference? I know you were angry.'

Luan narrowed his eyes. 'How did you know?' He realized before I answered, sneering at Arno. 'Oh, right,' he said. 'Of course. So much for family business, hey, bruv?'

'Watch your tone,' said Arno. 'She heard you mouthing off. I didn't tell her, but even if I did, it's because I'm worried about you.'

'About me?' Luan chuckled. 'Fuck, brother, you should be worried about shacking up with her. She's your boss now, it seems. Everyone's boss. Although I can't remember any of us agreeing to that.'

I swallowed, waiting for the response of the crew,

worrying for a split second I'd misjudged everything. That I was, in fact, unwelcome in this screwed-up family.

'Because I said so,' said Karis. Staring beyond Luan, somewhere through the glass, out to our stern and the dark waters. 'I asked her to, Luan, because our captain is dead, and I'm first mate, and Sarah's the person I trust to run things. Is that a decision I should have run past you?'

Luan paused; his face was twisted in frustration. The crew stared at him, waiting for an answer. They'd taken my side, it seemed.

'CCTV,' said Elijah. 'Maybe if Luan's memory is failing him, we can check.'

'We can't,' I said, turning to Jack. 'It's still not online.'

Jack shook his head. 'I can't get anything working at the moment,' he said. 'I need more time. The wiring . . . I'm working as fast as I can.'

'You don't need CCTV,' protested Luan. 'I told you what I did. You don't seriously think I had anything to do with Greg falling overboard?'

Nobody responded. Eyes darted nervously.

Arno moved towards Luan, closing the gap, his face red, muscles tensed. He looked ready to hit him. 'You fucked up, brother,' he said. 'You're really gonna pay for this.'

'*Stop!*' I said, seeing Arno's fists clenched, feeling my own anger rising. If this were my squad, we would have knocked heads together by this point. The sheer folly made my blood boil.

I put my hands against the back of one of the sofas, feeling the expensive leather – it was hard, unworn. I squeezed, casting my gaze around at the assembled crew, then wider, taking in the luxurious furniture, the side-boards still dressed with fresh flowers, the scattered pieces of artwork and colourful wall panels. The majestic grand piano stood to one side, its polished lid down, stool tucked underneath.

I saw everything in the room differently now – the lustre of my first impressions dimming, tarnished by the stress and tragedy of the last few days. The crew themselves – what a contrast this gathering was to the first night, when we'd assembled outside for dinner, full of enthusiasm for the trip ahead, although even then the underlying tensions were simmering close to the surface.

How much of what had happened since was human stupidity, how much driven by some unknown ulterior motive?

What was rotten at the heart of this trip?

Jack had so far been blamed for so much, yet Luan's temper was responsible for the water. Did I believe he was also responsible for Greg's death? The CCTV sabotage? I didn't know him well enough to say – but in my career, I'd seen the worst in humans, and the best. Tempers get messy, things escalate, one step too far, and suddenly it's too late, everything changes – lives altered, history fixed. Luan had it in him; an accident of rage, a second of mis-judgement, blinded by the red mist. It wouldn't be the first time a jealous colleague hit out in anger.

Or maybe not an accident at all. Was this exactly what he wanted to achieve?

His actions so far had proved he was capable of screwing things up for himself and the rest of us. But had it extended beyond that? I had no experience to draw on.

People died in the military, both friends and enemies, but it was a different type of aggression: controlled and planned. We were sanctioned, our actions a matter for our commanders and those they answered to. That didn't stop the guilt – we'd all seen those crosshairs in our dreams, the body of an enemy combatant, the screams of a human being in pain – but it did justify it, and the only stories we had to invent were for ourselves.

But if it was all just fuelled by anger, then who else fitted the bill?

Elijah was new, and an outsider – not even Lily knew him that well, her romantic intentions already strained. Dan was another angry soul, ready to lash out at everyone – his friendship with Pieter, how close and deep did that go? An argument, a fight – Dan certainly had it in him – a ball of anger waiting to explode. Did Dan assume every woman was his for the taking? Had his misogyny towards Karis and the others driven a fight with our captain? Or was my outlandish theory about Pieter real? Had he been hiding out in the safe room, stalking the corridors, waiting for his chance? It was insane, and I couldn't honestly entertain it, but the use of the safe room remained a mystery.

I also hadn't forgotten Jason and his shady excuses – his demands on Greg had taken us through the storm, I was sure of it – why else would Greg have risked it? But he was unlikely to reveal anything else, and I could hardly interrogate him, much as I'd like to. Since the lightning strike, he had withdrawn, focusing on the reclusive Harriet, on himself – perhaps giving up on whatever his financial agenda might once have been – but his part in our misfortune, even if simply the arrogance of his position, was equally disturbing.

I wasn't the police, and I couldn't investigate properly. All I could do right now was maintain control, protect myself and those around me. If things weren't as they appeared, my only option was to watch and wait.

If one of the crew in front of me had done something terrible, it would come out, one way or another. When it did, I'd be ready.

'Enough,' I repeated. 'Disperse. Do your jobs. Look after our guests. Avoid each other if you have to.' I turned to Karis. 'I suggest we ask Luan to remain in his cabin, on restricted duty. He only leaves if supervised – perhaps Arno and Dan can take care of that?'

Luan looked ready to explode afresh, but Karis nodded.

'I agree,' she said, and then, without another word, turned and left.

I followed. I managed to make it to the nearest bathroom before the attack came on.

I staggered inside, closing and locking the door. The shakes hit me first, followed by the inevitable crushing sensation in my chest. I held myself upright in front of the mirror, willing my reflection to fight back. The more I stared, the more my focus suffered, small lights dancing in my peripheral vision, vertigo threatening as the yacht shifted and my inner ear compensated.

I looked old, tired, eyes sunken, jaw hanging loose. My hair was pulled back but the grease shone in the light from the small porthole.

The low ceilings and narrow corridors of this yacht conspired to take me back to that place. The darkness came quickly, and as it did, my knees buckled, sending me sliding to the tiled floor.

I gasped, but all I could taste was the desert dust, the heat of the compound, the chemical haze of rounds being fired, and the metallic tang of blood in the air.

I heard the crunch of the gravel underfoot, my own boots making the sound, before entering the building, the walls enveloping the noise around me.

I glanced back. Where was he? I smiled.

All clear. I called it, keen to see his face.

The man at the table repeated the whisper to his wife. I didn't understand Pashto, but Kay did. I turned, cast my eyes around, let myself become distracted by a vision of the night before – of Kay's body and mine, entwined in heat and passion. I felt him inside me, the throbbing urgency, the screams of relief, the laughter that followed. I stared at him and lost myself.

The thought of him. That brief moment, that lucid daydream, was all it took.

It was enough to distract me for a split second. The most important second of my life.

My guard down.

Kay entered. My weapon was lowered, my smile giving Kay the assurance he needed.

No threat here.

Neither of us saw the shadow emerge from the back room.

The thumps were deafening, pulsing through the air, echoing in the confines of the room.

'Sarah.'

The voice wasn't Kay's. Again, deeper, a banging, pounding at my side.

'Sarah, open the door.'

I watched Kay's smile fade, the dirt turn white, the heat dissipate, my hands cold on the tiles. Part of me wanted to stay there, with him, to watch his smile. But the picture of his perfect face flicked out in an instant.

I pulled myself to the toilet and vomited, heaving until I was dry. I flushed, scrambling on the floor, pushing myself to my feet.

'Sarah –'

'I'm OK,' I called. I put my hand to the door, leaned in for the count . . . four in, hold, four out, hold. I unlatched the door and swung it inwards.

Arno stood outside, alone; his face was creased with worry.

I wiped my mouth. 'I'm OK,' I said, pushing past him.

Arno couldn't help me, and I didn't want him to see me like this, to witness my weakness, my failing. What if he could read it in my eyes, saw my history as clearly as I did?

He followed, running to keep up. Part of me wanted to sprint, to lap the boat and keep going. But there was no escape, not yet. Not from my guilt or my dreams or the reality of what I'd done.

The attacks were coming nearly every day. Note to self – *your mind is fucked, Sarah*. The shrink reckoned they'd fade, and with each passing month, with appropriate help, I'd start to control them, catch the pain before it swallowed me whole.

This trip didn't exactly count as *appropriate help*.

'Wait,' he called.

By the time I hit the bridge deck my heart rate was still pumping, but at least for the right reasons, my thighs burning from leaping up the stairs so fast. Arno lumbered behind, not too shabby, hitting the deck a few seconds later.

'Sarah,' he yelled this time.

I had my hand on the wheelhouse door.

He bent over, catching his breath. I glared at him for reasons he didn't deserve, at the same time still wanting that hug, that kiss. I wanted this man to grab hold of me and tell me everything would be OK. I wanted him to give me that sense of absolute escapism, of total release from this world and all the pain within it.

But all of my body language told him the opposite. He shook his head.

I pushed open the door.

Karis and Camila were standing over the navigation table. Karis held her binoculars, scanning to our starboard side. She huffed. The tears had stopped; she was trying. Deflated, but doing her best.

She caught my eye, a glimmer of appreciation. 'Thank you,' she mouthed at me.

Camila smiled at us – a fractional curl of the lips. 'Anything from Jack?' she said. 'Night will be on us soon. The batteries are running low on everything – we'll have to start saving some of the lamps. Half the radios are dead.'

I shook my head, catching my breath, calming down. 'He's working on it,' I said. 'Still . . .'

The euphoria which had met the restarting of the engines had long since worn out. Jack was taking longer than he'd expected, and we were all suffering until he figured something out.

Camila nodded. I saw her eyes dart to Arno, then away.

'Are the crew OK?' said Karis, her voice small, tentative.

'Leave them to me,' I said. 'You stay here, do what you can.'

Another nod, her chest shaking with each breath. Just about holding it together, but it wouldn't last.

'Camila can take longer watches,' I said, glancing her way. 'We can drag Luan out of his cabin and –'

'We don't need anyone else,' said Camila, keeping her gaze fixed outside. 'I'll do it.'

'I'll help,' said Arno. 'We'll get through.'

'We don't have the weather on our side,' said Karis, checking her binos again. 'The storm is turning – looks like a one-eighty, coming straight back for us. As if it hadn't done enough damage the first time.'

Karis couldn't hide her bitterness, and I didn't blame her. It was easy to see motive in Mother Nature. Her relentless attacks often seemed intensely personal.

'What's our speed?' I said. 'Can we outrun it, this time?'

'No,' said Camila, rather abruptly. She cleared her throat, turned to offer another smile – thin, forced. 'Jack advises we don't push the engines. Safer that way, even with the storm.'

Jack had said a similar thing to me. I didn't push it – she was right. Better to keep going, even if the storm swept us up in its new path. Overwhelming the engines now might mean a far worse position in twenty-four hours.

'Have you checked on Jason or Harriet?' said Karis.

'They haven't come to see me . . . not even a word about Greg . . .' She swallowed, clenching her jaw.

I shook my head. 'I'll speak to Jason when I get a minute, but they'll have to fit in with us. They might own this yacht, but they aren't in charge at the moment. Got it?'

Nods all round.

Camila leaned forward, putting both palms on the black screens of the console, peering out at the vast ocean in front of us, the thousands of miles between us and safety.

'Got it,' she said.

25

The storm caught up with us through the night. By the morning of the seventh day the wind raced across our stern, the white breaking swell attacking the *Escape* with a fresh vigour – the warm waters and pressure conspiring to deliver a surge of energy, directed at us, following our path.

The engines thundered, their deep throb surging and waning as the yacht pitched, reminding us that some of our luck still held, and the steering directed us on our approximate heading, but the darkness of my cabin told me the electricity was still elusive. Jack was struggling. If he failed, we all failed.

I shook the sleeping tablet-induced grogginess from my head, the nagging anxiety biting as I grabbed breakfast – dry cereal, two slices of bread. My stomach churned, the relentless rise and fall of the ship even giving me a fleeting touch of nausea. The fresh food was almost out, the fridge in the crew kitchen as warm as the air out-side. We had plenty of supplies, but I'd need a can opener for most of them.

I saw Arno in the corridor and learned the cabin arrangements had all changed since yesterday. Lily and Elijah had bunked in together – which made me distinctly uneasy, my confidence in everyone failing, though I guess I preferred her not to be alone. Arno and Luan were also together, but the others had spread out, taking individual cabins. The close-knit bickering crew had overnight adopted a *trust no one* approach, locking doors, keeping their distance.

The tension still crowded me; my chest tightened, my jaw and neck ached, with no respite. On impulse I closed my cabin door, reaching under the lower bunk, dragging the hard gun case into the open. I paused, turning over the emotions in my mind – the sudden desire for another level of protection. I unlocked the box, checking both the Glock and the APC. The magazines and ammo were slotted into their compartments, the shoulder and leg holsters folded.

What threat did I seek to mitigate by carrying one of these? The impression on the others would be immediate and lasting – resentment, panic? And for what?

I swallowed, taking a deep breath, closing the case. Everything remained strapped inside. Locked and hidden, I decided there was another option, less extreme.

There was nobody in sight of the storage room on the main deck, and I unlocked the door, closing it behind me. Fumbling around in the dark, I found the small box holding the tasers. The batteries all read as full, which was fortunate. I was thankful I'd checked them every day – a discharged taser is about as useful as a wooden spoon in a fight. The pistol was small enough to slip into my shorts pocket without creating too obvious a bulge.

I paused again, wondering if even that was necessary, but I replayed yesterday's scene in my head – how it might have gone differently, how we might have discovered something that forced one of the crew to act out of desperation.

I logged my actions on the paper chart on the black clipboard and slipped out of the room before I changed my mind. I sincerely hoped I'd check the taser back in again unused, but I couldn't shake the prickles of unease. I still hoped they were fragments of my imagination, driven by my own damaged and twisted mind. But they felt real enough to keep me alert.

I stepped out, feeling the weapon in my pocket, the muscles tightening in my legs and shoulders. I shook the tension out, trying to relax, knowing if I remained this uptight, I'd plummet soon enough, the darkness would come looking, and I'd find myself waking up on the floor somewhere.

Drag yourself out of this, Sarah. If I couldn't get a grip of myself, I couldn't expect it from the rest of the crew.

I raised Lily on the radio, drawn to my new friend – to check she was OK. *Going soft*, is what Mitch would say. But I couldn't imagine Lily having any part in the damage that had befallen us. She was a constant, her natural optimism shining through. I should tell her I appreciated it.

'Main deck galley,' she responded over the airwaves. 'I'm helping out.'

I arrived to find her and Elijah rearranging the kitchen, or rather, unloading produce from the freezer, stacking it in neat rows along the worktops.

'Most of it is ruined,' said Elijah, eyeing the lumps of meat and fish, sealed for the freezer, limp and dripping with water. 'I left them in there as long as I could, but we don't have any gas to cook on, so it's going overboard. We start on the tinned food today . . . we have about a month's worth, though we'll be sick of it within twenty-four hours.'

Lily hefted a box full of tired-looking green veg to the sink. 'Can you use any of this?' she said.

Elijah shrugged. 'If you fancy a mouldy asparagus sandwich on dry bread, sure.'

Lily screwed her face up, dumping the contents of the box into a bin bag, before pulling a stool next to me. 'You OK?' she asked.

'I came to ask you the same thing,' I said. 'Both of you.'

Lily shrugged. 'We're fine, I –'

'Are we?' said Elijah. He continued to grab packets of food from the fridge, slamming them on the worktop with increasing force. 'We slept last night with the door locked. I've never done that before in ten years of working yachts.'

Lily tucked her arms around herself, glanced at me. 'What do you think, Sarah? Are we imagining things?'

I looked her square in the eye, wondering if I could hide it well enough to answer.

'There's no reason for you to worry, I'm sure. What's done is done. What happened to Greg . . .' What could I tell them? That the police in Antigua would swarm over this boat on arrival and question every one of us? They must know that.

'I don't believe he jumped,' said Lily. 'Have you spoken to Karis? They were happy, or trying to be. There's no way he'd throw it all away.'

Elijah paused, before joining us, dragging a stool across the wooden floor. 'He wasn't himself,' he said. 'You can't deny it. He was a troubled man.'

'So what?' said Lily. 'We're all troubled. It doesn't mean we throw ourselves into the ocean.'

Elijah frowned. 'I agree, and much as I can't stand some of our illustrious crew, I can't honestly see them having anything to do with it. It's too . . .'

'It's crazy,' said Lily, turning to me. 'Don't you think?'

'Sarah thinks it was an accident,' continued Elijah, looking at me. 'I can tell by your face. You don't think we should be worried?'

'I –'

'You've gotta admit, something on this yacht stinks, and it isn't the rotting fish in my galley. Take Jason, for example. The man gives me the creeps. He wouldn't even let me take Harriet a hamper for her room.'

'Elijah is very attentive to the guests,' Lily explained. 'It's what marks him out.'

Elijah smiled, put his hand on hers. 'Fat lot of good it did me, Jason snatched the hamper and told me to leave her alone.'

I watched the two of them – understandably nervous, echoing my thoughts and probably those of the rest of the crew. The shock of Greg's death was compounded by the uncertainty – however small – that something had transpired with Luan. But neither he, nor anybody else, was acting with the sort of guilt I'd expect, had they committed such an act.

'Jack,' I said, calling over the radio. 'It's Sarah. Come in.'

'*Hi, Sarah.*'

'Any idea how long until you get the CCTV back online?'

He paused.

'*I sent Karis a status report a few minutes ago. It's not good news for the main systems, but I'm hoping to get some of the non-essentials online later today. CCTV will be one of them – seems everyone is asking.*'

'Everyone?'

There was a crackle as Jack switched to the engineering frequency.

'*Jason came to see me again,*' he said, in a hushed tone. '*He wanted to know before I switched the CCTV back on. Told me to report directly to him.*'

I paused, trying to be careful how I framed my next question.

'The coverage of the cameras,' I said. 'Would it show us the obvious areas on deck? Landing platform, side passages, tender garage?'

'*Erm. Yes.*' He knew what I was asking. '*It should have been recording all the natural exit points – gates in the gunwales, swimming platform, anywhere an accident was likely to happen.*'

'OK,' I said. Better not to question Jason's motives over the airwaves. I hoped I'd earned Jack's trust enough for my second question. 'Can you do me a favour? Call me first?'

Another pause.

'*Sure thing.*'

'Thanks, Jack.'

I ended the conversation and turned to my worried couple.

'We might never know what happened to Greg,' I said. 'But my guess is he slipped. The seas are rough; this boat is bouncing around like a rubber dinghy on rapids. It wouldn't take much to send a person over – even someone with

Greg's experience. Mentally, he knew what he was doing. Physically, he . . . may have been a few years out of shape.'

My heart hammered, my body objecting to the unease of such a dismissive statement when my mind was still racing with every possibility, and acutely aware of my responsibility in finding the truth.

Lily smiled. It was sad, but warm. Providing her with some reassurance was important to me, and I wasn't sure how else to give it.

'If you need anything – shout,' I said, feeling an unfamiliar surge of closeness to her. 'I'll be with you like a shot.'

Her smile expanded. 'Why don't you join us for dinner later?' she said. 'It'll just be us two – the rest of the crew are choosing to eat alone in their cabins, with Harriet and Jason in theirs. Karis and Camila are staying on the bridge. Elijah's going to rustle us up something from the dry stores. It'll be delicious.'

Elijah snorted. 'It'll be awful, and I hate to serve it. I might have to drag one of these ovens downstairs if Jack can't get the power up here.'

I left them to it, deciding to spend a few hours patrolling the *Escape*. My presence might reassure the others, or it might unnerve them. Either way, I needed to do it for myself.

I spent the next few hours in a daze, walking circuits on each level, nodding my presence but not engaging in any conversation. The crew diligently performed their tasks before retiring to their separate rooms, books and magazines providing the only leisure distraction in the storm – the decks were cold and wet and inhospitable to even the most hardened sailor. The only person I didn't see was Harriet, whose door was closed, the *Do Not Disturb* sign still hanging on the silver handle – I tried it. Locked, and I honoured her request.

I watched Jack hard at work, the engineering deck a mass of wires, as he tried to fit the new switch panel in the semi-darkness, amid the pitch and rolling of the storm, cursing to himself as he discovered one problem after another. I caught another whiff of alcohol as I stood there, pausing, deciding to move on without passing judgement. I hated to think it, but in our predicament even a drunk engineer was better than no engineer.

As I arrived on the bridge deck, I paused outside the gym, noticing the door to the art gallery was ajar. Curious, I pushed it open, slipping inside.

About the same size as the gym – some forty feet long and almost as wide – the windows had a darkened film over them, restricting most of the light. The floor was tiled, plain and white, and against the windows a number of wooden crates were stacked, with rolls of packing material next to them.

I closed the door behind me, letting my eyes adjust to the gloom, trying to make out the contents of the other three walls. They held what I assumed to be the owner's private collection, referred to and revered by Jason. I moved closer, trying to make sense of the first picture.

Amy had what she described as an amateur passion for art – no proper time to immerse herself, but enough to appreciate some of the contemporary artists who exhibited in the galleries around her corner of the UK. I considered myself an art ignoramus – not a proud one but, like most people, never given the opportunity of an education in such wonders. I did know the art *market* was not the same as art *appreciation* – that the owners of valuable works bought them for very different reasons. Did the owner of the *Escape* value these pieces in dollars or on some scale of transcendental enlightenment? Hiding them away in their own private gallery seemed selfish, but in keeping with the rest of the place – superyacht ownership was not a public service.

Two huge canvases stood against the wall, perhaps six feet high and four wide, the frames fastened in brackets, sturdy clips, with a clear plastic shield a few inches in front of them. Two plaques at the bottom of the plastic read: *Rembrandt van Rijn (1606–1669), Portrait of Marten Soolmans, 1634* and *Rembrandt van Rijn (1606–1669), Portrait of Oopjen Coppit, 1634.*

I stood back, squinting in the light, trying to remember what Jason had told us. Wedding portraits of the happy couple. He hadn't given a value, and I could only guess. Were these one million, ten million, one hundred million dollars' worth? Did it matter? Not to me. Perhaps not to the owner.

Amy once tried to describe Baroque art to me – the drama and the action, the intent to evoke emotion and passion. That's the only reason I'd heard of Rembrandt, and seeing these portraits up close I hoped would conjure something of a revelation, a wave of emotion which might tug at something deeper within. But the overwhelming sensation was one of faint bemusement. I had no reference point to judge the quality or impact of the two paintings – this famous couple. I had no judgement, period. They were intricate, grand in scale – a moment in history captured with such skill and dedication – and yet I had no words, not even to myself.

I moved back, disappointed, suspecting my uneducated appraisal would fail to make sense of any of the surrounding pieces.

In doing so, I noticed a smallish flat crate against the far wall, no more than three feet high, perhaps two wide. It was still sealed, security tape covering all the edges of what looked like sturdy reinforced plastic. On closer inspection, I noticed the crate was hinged and padlocked, fastened with heavy-duty fabric straps connecting to hooks in the wall. A metal plaque to the left of it was blank.

A small but priceless work, I guessed. This one too good to be on show. Too risky to let us riff-raff see it – or worse, *appreciate* it.

I sniffed, noticing the room had a strange odour. Looking up, I saw two large vents, silent, of course, and realized this room would be kept at a precise humidity and temperature. I had a sudden fear that the works would be forever damaged from this period of unconditioned air, even the mysterious painting crated and sealed from view.

Not your problem, Sarah. Worry about the people first.

I backed out of the gallery and began to pull the door closed.

'What are you doing?'

Dan's voice startled me and I jumped, annoyed with myself. If anyone was going to make me jump it shouldn't be this idiot.

'Doing my rounds,' I said. 'Why?'

Dan indicated the bags he was carrying. I spied more packing materials, tape, straps.

'Jason wanted me to start crating some of it back up again. Protect it from the elements. He's coming to *supervise* me.' He peered past me, frowning. 'I left the door unlocked?'

Jason seemed to have his priorities in order – protect the art, protect the money. Did I blame him? No, but I wished I could.

'You did.'

It seemed to surprise him, but he nodded over my shoulder. 'Gonna let me past?'

I paused for a second, for no particular reason than because I could. 'Sure,' I said, 'but be careful in there. Some of the paintings are worth a bob or two.'

He snorted, giving me a wide berth, before entering the gallery, shutting the door without another word.

I returned to my cabin, washing and changing for my dinner date with the lovebirds. As I thought about Lily and Elijah, I couldn't help but picture the couple in Rembrandt's paintings – their faces etched in my memory, my recollection of their posture and expression captivating me in a way I couldn't describe. Perhaps they had a more lasting effect than I anticipated. I wondered if I might get to view the portraits again, before they were locked away.

I was still in a daze as I left my cabin. I found Arno loitering outside.

'All dressed up and nowhere to go?' he said.

I eyed him suspiciously. His shirt was clean, his chinos fresh from the drawer. Even his flip-flops looked clean.

'They invited me too,' he said, with an overenthusiastic wink.

'Fuckers,' I said, feeling my stomach tingle and flutter. I couldn't stop my smile.

'I might have nudged them,' he said.

I let out a long sigh, feeling a smidgen of tension leave my body with it. These moments were fragile, important, and I missed them. Losing myself in the company of someone like Arno was possibly the only thing that might keep me sane on this trip.

'I'm glad you did,' I said, returning the wink, clasping his arm, and marching him towards the stairs.

We got as far as the kitchen before his radio went off.

'*Arno, I need you on the lower deck. Head to the bow, please,*' said Camila. '*I'll meet you there.*'

Arno stopped, his face fell, his normal shine and enthusiasm evaporating. He appeared to consider her request.

I gave him a nudge in his ribs. 'I'll save you some dried cereal,' I said.

He nodded.

But I could tell he was troubled. Was dinner with me that important? A part of me hoped so. The part that was trying to ignore the warning bells.

'What's wrong?' I asked.

He glanced at me, held my eyes for a second before forcing a smile, carving his goofy grin into his face. 'Nothing,' he said. 'I was looking forward to dinner, that's all.'

He held my arm, caressing it under his fingers for a moment, before turning and striding back the way we'd come.

26

'Delicious,' pronounced Lily, licking the long-life cream from her spoon, before dunking it back into the bowl of tinned peaches.

'You're an animal,' said Elijah, leaning back in his chair, eyes darting to the stairs and the wide glass doors. We'd relocated to the sun deck for dinner, the uppermost part of the *Escape*, also the smallest, with near-panoramic views of the ocean – though at this point in the storm, visibility was close to zero, and all we could see was the rain and wind lashing against the glass. The occasional white-tipped wave broke through the gloom, a flash of lighter clouds in amongst the grey. So far, there was no hint of thunder or lightning.

Lily and Elijah did a good job of not making me feel like a third wheel. They kept their hands to themselves and the conversation stayed light-hearted, given the circumstances – a welcome respite from reality. I took the opportunity to quiz Lily, perhaps be a little provocative. It was what friends did, wasn't it?

'You still never told me why you started working on yachts,' I said, scooping the remains of my own bowl on to the spoon. Elijah had made an interesting concoction out of what was left of the fresh food – his own Jamaican-style seasoned wraps heating my mouth from the first bite. Dessert was Lily's contribution.

Lily narrowed her eyes at me for a second, but smiled. Wistful, tinged with regret.

'I graduated with a first,' she said. 'English Literature, not that anybody on here cares.'

Elijah put his hands up in apology. 'You're too bright for me,' he said. 'If I asked you about it, I wouldn't understand the answers.'

Lily gave him a sarcastic smile. 'Most of my friends found corporate jobs, climbed the ladders, planned their next mortgage payment or house flip. Me . . . I couldn't motivate myself. I did some agency work, stared at the rain through a drab office window in Birmingham, questioned whether I wanted to do the same thing for the next fifty years. I didn't think it was as appealing as the career adviser at university made it out to be.' She glanced at me. 'On a particularly rainy day I signed up to a crewing agency – a random advert on Instagram – and hit the sunshine of the Mediterranean a few weeks later.'

She sighed. 'In the last four years I've been to more countries than all of my friends combined. I've basked in the Italian sun in the hot tub of a £250 million yacht – even bigger than the *Escape* – scuba-dived off the back of a sailing catamaran in the British Virgin Islands, and played water sports with a Middle Eastern prince . . .' she cocked one eye at Elijah, 'who happened to be smoking hot and offered me a permanent position.'

Elijah threw his napkin at her. 'Doing what?' he said.

'Exactly,' she said, laughing. 'I politely declined and came back to the UK for a bit. And now . . .' She cast her eyes around the dim interior, at the battery lanterns which were already fading, and the eerie grey glow framing the three of us. 'I'm here. I'm a glorified waitress and chamber maid, and I don't even have a tan.' She stretched her bare legs out to illustrate the point, resting one on Elijah's thigh.

'They look good to me,' said Elijah, grinning, making me wish Arno were here.

I thought these two would be ready for their cabin soon.

'I've never worked a delivery run before,' she said. 'And I sure as hell won't again, I –'

'But you like the life, yeah?' Elijah frowned.

There it was – the same look he'd given me when I'd spoken to him in the kitchen. Desperation, trying to keep hold of her. He could see it as clear as day. But did I blame him?

Lily huffed. 'I like *you*,' she said, smiling, ever the pleaser.

'That's not what I asked.'

Her smile dipped. 'I'm not spending my life as a dozy stewardess, Elijah,' she said. 'Not when there's a whole world out there.' She glanced at me. 'Look at Sarah. She's travelled the world, fought the world, but her job had *meaning*. Now she has a kick-ass job in security. I want . . . I dunno.'

'You're going to join the army?' said Elijah, chuckling. 'I'm not sure you're cut out for that, Lily. You stropped when Greg said you couldn't wash your hair.'

Lily's smiled disappeared altogether. I saw a flash of irritation, of hurt, but also defiance. I tried to bite my tongue, but I hoped she wouldn't hold hers. Intentionally or not, Elijah had just hit a raw spot.

'Lily can do whatever she wants, Chef,' I said, forcing a smile as I said it. 'And signing up wouldn't be the worst –'

I stopped, seeing the deep frown on Elijah's face. I heard it at the same time.

'Damn,' said Lily. 'Is that what I thought it was?'

I nodded, adjusting my earpiece.

'Jack,' I said, over the engineering channel.

I waited a few seconds.

'Jack?'

No answer. Silence on all channels.

'Jack,' I repeated. 'Why have the engines stopped?'

I staggered, the motion of the *Escape* wild and unpredictable, the lack of forward motion once again causing us to wallow and race into the trough of each wave, hurtling downwards before being pushed violently on to the next crest.

'Karis, this is Sarah,' I called on the bridge frequency. 'What's going on?'

'*I can't raise Jack*,' came Karis's response. '*I'm alone on watch. Can you head to engineering?*'

'Already on my way.'

The dim interior spoke to me as I descended, whispering and teasing, drawing me in. I resisted, focusing on each step, pushing my breaths out with ever-increasing force, holding them while my heart bucked and danced in my chest, matching the shuddering movements of the hull.

I raced along the crew corridor, nearly hitting Arno as he stepped out of one of the cabins – my cabin – in front of me.

He looked startled, flustered, a holdall slung over his back. 'I was looking for you,' he said. 'I heard the radio call.'

'I've been with Lily,' I said, glancing towards my cabin. 'Have you spoken to Jack?'

Arno shook his head. 'I've been running errands for Camila,' he said. 'I felt the engines go, though.'

'In my cabin?'

He paused, shuffling his feet. 'You got me. I, err . . . I was hoping to catch you after your dinner.' He pulled a deflated expression.

I smiled. 'Hold that thought?'

He nodded. 'Do you need me? To talk to Jack?'

'No,' I said, thinking that if Jack was in an alcohol-induced mess, it might be better if I discovered him alone. 'I'll keep you posted.'

I raced forward and down at the next stairwell, trying, and failing, to raise Jack on the radio. Entering the tank deck, I scanned the machinery and the metal steps into the engine room. The engineering console was still a tangle of wires, the replacement switchboard on the floor next to the cabinet where it should be housed.

Jack's mug rested on the console. I checked it, half full, the smell betraying its contents.

Jack's domain, his work, his badly kept secret. But no Jack.

'Jack?' I called again, louder, my voice reverberating off the metal walls and ceiling, my ears ringing. The only response I heard was the rhythmic, deep thumping as the waves pummelled the outside of the hull, knocking, as if the ocean also waited for an answer.

I started a slow search, engine bays first, careful with my step as I staggered through, minding my head on the low-hanging ventilation shafts. It would be easy to knock oneself clean out on this deck. I hoped Jack's silence was as simple as that.

The air was warm in the engine room, the diesel giants ticking and banging as they cooled, the metal contracting. The engine control panel was alive with red LEDs, flashing at one-second intervals, adding an unwelcome tinge of warning to the air.

I circled the engines, checking the fuel tanks and the entrance to the bilge.

'Jack?'

I pulled myself up, back out to the tank deck, standing on the spot, staring at the machinery. Huge, complicated, yet not exactly full of hiding places. It was possible Jack had incapacitated himself clambering behind the electrical trunking, but unlikely. In the corner was the CCTV station. All screens still black, the hard drive bay open – the hard drives which held all of the footage weren't even plugged in. Where were they?

'Karis,' I called, careful to remain on the bridge radio frequency, 'it's Sarah. I can't see him. Jack's not here.'

I paused. Could this possibly be happening? First Greg, now Jack, the two most important crew members on the *Escape*. The chances of it happening once, with Greg, were remote. The chances of it happening again . . .

'*What do we do, Sarah? Where is he?*' Karis's voice over the airwaves.

Once again, a question we should all be asking her. First mate, in charge of this vessel. But her voice was tense, breaking. If Karis had held it together until now, this might be enough to finish her. We had no choice but to search until we were sure, then perform the 'man over-board' procedure until Karis called it.

And then what?

'I need to think,' I said, as if by uttering those words my brain would somehow formulate a crisis plan. 'There's nothing . . . I think we have to –'

'*I called Camila,*' said Karis, '*sent her to Jack's cabin. Are you there, Camila?*'

'*I'm here.*' Camila's voice, clear and strong. '*And I think you should see this.*'

'What?'

'*Just come. It might explain things. It might not.*'

'Stay on the bridge, Karis,' I said. 'I'm on my way.'

The radio clicked off. I headed forward, leaving the chemical smells behind me as I raced past the infirmary and the laundry, the safe room, reaching the spiral stair-case in the centre of the yacht. I held myself against the bannister as we rolled to port, hearing another thump, smaller, accompanied by the howl of the wind down the stairwell. It sounded eerily like a cry – apt, I thought, that the *Escape* itself was calling out to me.

I found Camila standing over Jack's bunk. His cabin was much the same as the rest of ours, just a little larger to incorporate a desk and PC, but still a cramped box.

She turned to me with an expression of fatigue and contempt. 'Look at this,' she said.

I tried to count the vodka bottles laid out on his sheets. Some were still full and sealed, others half empty. She'd arranged them in rows. The number was surprising, but not the contents. Camila must already know about Jack's drinking problem.

'I found them under his bunk,' she said, 'but also these.' She handed me a white paper bag; the type used by UK pharmacies. I opened it to find twenty or so small boxes of Zopiclone, three of them empty, the blister packets still in the bag.

'Sleeping tablets,' said Camila. 'Prescription. Strong.' She sighed. 'A fucking alcoholic *and* a drug addict.'

She said it accusingly, and I saw the frustration on her face, which would no doubt be shared by everyone else in due course.

'How does someone like this get a job as first engineer?' she asked. 'Is it common practice in your country – to put addicts and idiots in charge?'

I didn't answer. Her insult was worsened by the fact Zopiclone was the same brand of sleeping tablet I was becoming increasingly reliant on. I wondered at what point it became an addiction – when I couldn't sleep without them? Check. When I normalized it, when I accepted my life was only bearable with the help of the small white pills in the dead of night? Also check. Did that make me an addict?

'Jack is more than this,' I said, feeling an urge to defend him; to defend *us*. 'Sure, he has issues, but he's valued on board, well liked . . . I –'

'Explain this,' Camila said, handing me a folded piece of paper.

It was headed by the logo and company address of the *Escape*'s owner, with a couple of lines of handwritten scrawl, and a stapled payslip in the centre.

'Final payment,' I read, confused. 'As agreed. Thank you for your understanding . . .'

'Severance?' said Camila.

I scanned it again. It appeared to be Jack's last payslip, along with confirmation of prior termination of his contract – apparently decided before the trip, signed by somebody in HR. The company was letting him go. Jack was a grieving addict on his last trip – doing the one thing he loved, and failing at it. And he'd already been sacked.

'Where was this?' I asked.

'In the top drawer,' she said. 'I wasn't prying, but . . . Karis asked me to look around.'

Her voice was softer now, perhaps sensing my discomfort. Her own frustration had been aired, and slagging off Jack wouldn't get us anywhere.

The letter wasn't signed, only finished with the company footer.

'So this was Jack's last trip?' asked Camila.

I shrugged, but seeing the way Camila looked at me, it was possibly the most important question of all.

'That doesn't mean . . .' *Shit*. What did it mean? Had I read him so wrong? I thought Jack had been open with me about his issues. He never showed even a hint of resentment towards Greg. No . . . that wasn't quite true, but only in those first couple of days, when Greg overruled his advice, told him to follow orders. Not since. Not to me.

Or had I missed it? Wrapped up in the drama, had Jack been simmering away, seething, spiralling? I imagined him sitting here in his cabin, reading that letter, despairing at his future, outraged at the cause – where would his suspicion and anger fall? His mind was already in such a dark place, it wouldn't take much to send him over the edge.

But would he seriously take Greg with him?

I already doubted Greg's part in this. He hadn't given any hint he wanted to be shot of Jack. On the contrary, he'd openly acknowledged Jack's failures to me and Karis, the secret drink problem, and his willingness to keep Jack on when nobody else would. Was that a lie? Had he said one thing to us, and another to Jack?

None of it made sense, but we needed to figure it out, and quick.

'We need to talk to Karis,' I said. 'But we also need to search. Same procedure.'

'Man overboard?' said Camila. 'We have no power, and night is falling. If Jack isn't on board there's nothing we can do.'

She was right. Sending anybody out on the tender or jet skis in this weather was reckless, lethal. And I knew the futility of such action, with the sheer distances involved, but it wouldn't stop the events of the next few hours. We still had to search. We were duty bound.

'Karis,' I called. 'We need to gather everybody. We need to do this again.'

We had already climbed to the main deck before she responded, simply.

'*Do whatever you think.*'

Not the words of a captain in charge, but rather the words of a grieving partner – someone who has given up all hope, and must drift through this crisis, turning inwards to protect themselves from further harm.

I was not sure I was ready to do that. Not yet.

The crew sat in pairs or alone – Elijah and Lily huddled together, Arno and Luan united as brothers. Dan and

Camila sat apart, and Jason hovered on the periphery, his face paler than usual, his dress shirt creased, sleeves rolled up. I spoke to him outside – he couldn't confirm or deny Jack's firing, said it would have been up to Greg. Karis remained on the bridge. Harriet, I assumed, was remaining locked away.

I figured honesty was my only option, and relayed what we knew – what Camila and I had found. I left the possible implications hanging.

'He wouldn't,' said Lily. Her face was pale, clammy. 'Not Jack.'

'Does this mean I get an apology?' said Luan, his voice low. He scratched his chin – the few days of stubble gave him a sour and menacing appearance.

Nobody responded.

'He wouldn't,' Lily repeated. 'Not Jack. What you're saying, it's madness.'

'Jack is missing,' I said. 'We don't know what happened to him. Let's not jump to conclusions.'

'Because of what you told us,' said Luan, 'you think he couldn't live with the guilt of what he'd done. This is your conclusion. Isn't it?'

The bulge of my taser pressed against my leg. It provided an odd reassurance as I cast my eyes around, looking for a hint – something, anything. But all I saw was confusion and worry – and with good reason – the engines were off and we had no engineer, no captain. I didn't need to emphasize how much more serious our situation had become – our water rations were dwindling, our progress slow, now halted, at the mercy of the wind and the ocean current.

'Jack had been fired,' said Camila. 'He blamed Greg. He blamed himself.' She shrugged. 'Is it that simple? I've seen men lose their minds over far less. If he really did push Greg, the guilt would have got to him quickly, wearing him down. A bottle of vodka and a few of those pills . . .'

Nobody wanted to accept it, yet nobody offered their thoughts, or suggested any other possibilities. Camila caught my eye, questioning, waiting. She, along with the rest of the crew, was looking to me now. And I had zero answers.

'We search,' I said, trying to inject energy into my voice, attempting to quell the tightness in my throat, the bile in my gut. 'Same as before. I want every corner of this yacht turned over. Then . . .' I glanced out of the windows at the failing light, the dark waters, turning from grey to black as evening approached.

I looked at Arno. He gave a slow shake of his head.

'Whatever battery spotlights we've got – I want them manned on the sun deck. Tomorrow morning, at first light,' I said, 'we run MOB procedure. I –'

'What's the point?' said Luan. 'He's long gone. Same as the captain.'

A little too sure? Or stating the obvious. But why speak up unless innocent? Why make things even more uncomfortable?

'Because it's procedure,' I said. 'We can't leave this position without searching, whatever we might think happened.'

I meant it. There was comfort in the rules – we'd follow them and log that we had done so. To do otherwise was negligent and criminal. How would any of us face Jack's friends or family if we hadn't tried to find him – or, in the worst case, tried to recover his body?

'I'll take the tender out myself,' I said. 'Camila, I need you to calculate our drift. I want it all plotted by morning.'

She nodded, excusing herself.

Arno looked relieved. The others simply stared at each other, judging, watching. Whatever suspicions each might have entertained before, they were now amplified. As the lights dimmed and the energy of the storm rose, the thundering reality began to hit us.

I had nothing else to offer.

Night drew in. The search was conducted in silence, by the book, nobody expecting success. No sign of Jack was discovered – not a scuff, not a mark, no hint of what had conspired to make him leave his station. Nothing was visible in the waters around the *Escape*, all life jackets accounted for. After three hours, in darkness, we assembled back in the lounge. It would be impossible to sleep, and nobody seemed willing to venture below decks, into the darkness.

I agreed with Arno that we'd sleep in shifts. He wasn't the only one I thought I could trust, but he was the only one who might handle himself, and others, if it came to it.

'I'll take first watch,' he said to me.

I searched his eyes, but the warm reassurance was missing, the smile absent. He looked in shock, calculating, readying himself for the unknown. I understood the feeling – the rush of cortisol, the stress hormone, preparing our bodies for fight or flight. And yet, in this situation, it was useless. There was nothing obvious to run from, and nowhere to run to. And nothing to fight.

Was there?

I tucked myself into the corner of the room, playing the events over and over in my head.

Was it as grotesquely simple as Camila suggested? Luan in the clear, and in his place a sickening murder-suicide born out of Jack's mental health crisis and misdirected rage? Would Jack do that to his fellow crew, strand us out here on the ocean, knowing where it left us? I doubted it. I refused to believe it. But did any of us know Jack? I thought I did, but in these few days I'd only scratched the surface of his troubled and grieving mind.

Which left what? Two accidents. Two men overboard, the chances of which were so unlikely as to be absurd.

And so I found myself fitting the pieces together, *willing* them together. Humans hit out at each other for far less, killed for far less. I nodded, hoping by some miracle to shake my mind into accepting it. I needed the explanation to fit. Because otherwise, the reality was something I'd never faced before.

It meant one of the crew had a motive to harm both Greg and Jack. And they'd followed through on both.

And they were still on board the *Escape*.

27

Morning couldn't come soon enough. Arno and I had taken four-hour caffeine-fuelled shifts, my body wired and restless. The others had too – each watching the others, any last fragments of trust evaporating as the sunlight forced its way through the windows. Nobody gave anything away, although any comfort they took in viewing Jack as the perpetrator seemed wafer thin. But if they didn't believe it, what did they believe?

Dan broke out the alcohol through the night, followed by Luan. Even Elijah took a glass. Wine and beer, whatever was easiest at the bar, along with a bottle of Jack Daniel's. A few shot glasses still lay on their sides, rolling across the thick carpet, spilling their last drops. Nobody protested, nobody dared. I hoped they knew when to stop, wondering if I had the energy to challenge them.

In the brief scraps of sleep, my mind had tried to process not just the shock but the new situation. Eighth day at sea, drifting in the midst of a relentless storm with no power, and little chance of recovering it. Our water would last several more days, but we'd need to ration it further. We needed a complete crisis plan, and I couldn't conjure one in my dreams.

And that was before dealing with the possibility that one of our crew wasn't who they claimed to be.

'Stay here,' I told Arno, pulling myself up. 'I'm going to see Karis.'

Arno rubbed the sleep out of his eyes. 'I'll come with you.'

'No,' I said, 'I want you to . . .' I darted my eyes to the others. 'Keep an eye?'

He nodded, but didn't follow my gaze, instead staring at his lap, tapping his left foot, nerves as fried as mine. I watched him for a few moments, noting the visible sweat stains under his armpits and around his collar, before leaving, taking the stairs two at a time.

I marvelled at how claustrophobic the interior of the *Escape* had become to me, how the opulence and grandeur had faded with the ever-distant sun, how the constant wrenching of the hull over the waves felt more akin to a ship at war than the simple passage of a superyacht.

Nothing about this trip was simple.

The footsteps behind me were light, but as I reached the top I spun around, nearly knocking my shadow flying.

'Lily . . . are you OK?'

She raised her eyebrows.

'OK, stupid question. But you're holding up?'

'I feel like I should be doing something,' she said.

I nodded. 'I get it, but we need to plan out the next twenty-four hours. I need to speak to Karis first. It might be safer for you to stay with the others.'

'You just want me to sit around in the lounge?'

'I don't want . . . I'm not in charge, Lily.'

Another raise of the eyebrows, but this time sympathetic. 'Some have greatness thrust upon them . . .'

'Huh?'

'*Twelfth Night*. Shakespeare ... sorry. You might not have wanted it, but Karis was right to put you in charge. You're the only one who can keep things under control.'

I smiled, hoping it masked the fact I was barely keeping control of myself, let alone the crew or the *Escape*. 'One thing you could do,' I said. 'Jack's room ... Camila searched it, but it might need another going over to see if we missed anything. Would you mind? But take Elijah – don't do it on your own.'

She nodded. 'Sure thing. What are you looking for?'

Good question. 'I don't know. Probably nothing.'

Lily rubbed my arm, leaning in to give me a hug, crushing me in her small arms. Her chest trembled.

'Thanks, Sarah,' she said.

Karis stood alone at the dead wheel. I think, like the rest of us, she'd slept in her clothes; her hair was unbrushed, her gaze vacant.

'I'm going to launch the tender as soon as I can,' I said.

Karis turned to me, nodded. She squeezed her eyelids closed for a second, took a deep breath. 'I'm sorry, Sarah,' she said. 'For letting everyone down. I just can't ... I can't do it – the crew need a natural leader. I'm not it.'

'I think you are,' I said, 'or can be. But you're grieving, Karis. This is an extreme situation. Nobody blames you.'

She shook her head. 'A good leader would have done it anyway.'

Maybe. 'You'll get through this,' I said, biting down on the hypocrisy before it had a chance to show. 'Time heals.' I winced at the cliché.

She chuckled, sad and drawn out. 'Maybe,' she agreed.

We stood in silence. My knees trembled as the ocean pushed us up, paused for a second, sucked us back down. My stomach followed, my breakfast churning with each movement.

Karis gestured through the window. 'You can't go out in this,' she said. 'Not in the tender, not on anything. It's too dangerous.'

I stared at the driving rain. It was joined by the wind and the crashing waves, warning us it was still in control, that it would take another of us without a moment's hesitation.

I relented. Back in the day, my squadron might have launched RIBs in these conditions – in fact, I could recall several training exercises off the Devon coast in similar conditions, in the depths of the UK's winter storms. But that was with my team and the backup of a full squadron. Launching on my own in these conditions was crazy, even by my standards.

'We'll wait,' I said. 'This storm can't last forever. It's not like we're going anywhere.'

'The engines?'

I shook my head. It wasn't good. It appeared that Jack had kept them running through constant tinkering and adjustment – without him they quickly shuddered and died, and we couldn't figure out why. It would be up to me and Arno to try, if I could drag him out of his stupor.

'We'll search first. We could spend days down there trying to figure out what Jack was doing. The more eyes looking outside today the better.'

Karis nodded. 'Then we sit it out,' she said. 'Watch and wait. The storm might pass us by in twenty-four hours.'

Too late for Jack, and we both knew it. If we launched a search later today, we'd be looking for a body. But we had no choice.

The time dragged, the morning ticking slowly past, second by second. I remained in the observation sofa on the bridge, checking in with Arno every twenty minutes. The crew remained in the lounge, tense, waiting. Nobody left except to eat or get changed. I tried to engage Karis in conversation – to distract us both – but she withdrew even further as the clock ticked.

My pulse kept time, and I focused on my breathing, remembering the long waits on patrols, sitting on operations arse-deep in the mud and cold, watching targets for hours, sometimes days. I used to control the inevitable anxiety by repeating my objectives, checking my kit, even relacing my boots. Drifting into a daze was easy but unacceptable. It meant the difference between seeing and relaying a vital piece of information, and sleeping through enemy troop movements. People died when you did that.

I drank another can of Coke, feeling the acidity burning my stomach. 'Do we have any flares left?' I asked.

Karis shrugged. 'Arno will know. There should be several stowed on each deck. I . . . can't remember how many we launched on the first night – after the power died.'

I tapped my radio. 'Arno?'

I heard a scuffling. '*I'm here.*'

'Can you do a scout for flares, please? Gather as many as you can, bring them to the bridge?'

'*Sure thing, Sarah.*'

I worried we'd been too relaxed about broadcasting our

position with lights and flares. By day we should also be firing smoke signals – on the off-chance there were aircraft in the vicinity, US Navy, perhaps. None of the flares were visible much beyond thirty miles or so, and it was a long shot, but our options had got a whole lot fewer with the breaking day.

It wasn't long before Arno stumbled into the bridge carrying a pitiful assortment of what was left. He was followed close behind by Lily and Elijah, who had a package of their own.

Elijah dumped it on the navigation table. 'Are you going to tell them?' he said to Lily.

I stared at the cardboard box. 'Tell us what?'

Elijah opened the top and began unpacking the contents. I counted the items out – two satellite phones, a portable GPS, two high-powered VHF radios and three bright orange fist-sized devices.

'EPIRBs?' I asked, taking one.

Karis nodded, blinking a few times before grabbing one of the others. She flipped the catch and manually activated it, frowning, turning it over in her hands.

'It's broken,' she said, trying the third, then mine. All with the same result. 'These are tough to damage,' she said, running her thumb over the bottom.

The thick plastic cover was cracked, whitened, as if by a sharp impact. The other two looked the same. Multiple points of impact.

'They look like they've been hit by a hammer,' offered Elijah.

I grabbed a sat phone.

'They're all dead,' said Lily. 'We tried them. They've also

been damaged – the batteries have even been removed from the radios.'

She hugged her arms around her stomach. Elijah pulled her close.

'Where did you find these?' I asked.

They looked at each other.

'Behind a wall panel in Jack's room,' said Lily. 'We missed it first time. I went back because I'd forgotten my water bottle. It had fallen on the floor – rolled under the bunk. I crawled under, saw this panel was loose, and . . . well. This lot was behind it.'

'Anything else?'

Elijah shook his head. 'I ripped the rest of the panels off. Nothing we could see.'

'This is all of them,' said Karis. 'I think. I mean . . . this is what we'd normally sail with. This is what we were looking for.'

As we stared at the sabotaged devices, my legs started to tremble, not just from the motion. A fresh surge of adrenaline – God knows how I had any left – flowed through my weary body. My heart took up the signal, surging into my throat, unpleasant, nausea-inducing.

Calculating, swallowing, spinning it around in my head, breathing . . . *slow it down, Sarah, you're on the edge.*

'It was Jack,' said Lily, decisively, still holding herself tight. 'It *was* him. How could he . . .' Her own throat refused to let any more out. She sobbed into Elijah's chest, her knees buckling as he held her.

I picked up the EPIRB again, feeling the weight, examining the damage. 'Why?' I asked.

Arno looked surprised. 'Why what? They were in his room.'

'No, I mean, why would Jack do this? What did it achieve?'

He blew his cheeks out. 'I don't think any of us knew what was going on in his head, did we? This was . . . well. He sabotaged everything, didn't he?'

'I don't know, it's why I'm asking.' I tried to hide the irritation in my voice, but it simply didn't stack up for me. 'These were removed before Greg disappeared,' I said. 'Before the lightning struck. All this did was remove our chances of getting help. Why would Jack want us stranded with no communications?'

'So he could have it out with Greg?' said Arno. 'Take his revenge, and then . . . I don't know. The guilt afterwards made him take his own life?'

I frowned.

'Then he's trying to kill us, too,' said Karis. 'Is that what you're saying, Arno? Leaving us stranded in the middle of the ocean – no engines, no power, no comms. Sarah's right – why would he? What did any of us do to Jack to deserve this?'

'I don't know,' stressed Arno, 'but these were in *his* cabin, *deliberately damaged*. I can't explain his actions, but they're the most obvious motives, aren't they?'

I glanced at Arno; his mouth was twisted in concentration. The stress was getting to us all, and stress can do funny things to reason and rationality. Arno was convinced of Jack's guilt – though his body language didn't quite tally with his argument. He was ready to draw a line under the events of the last few days and face whatever came next.

But I wasn't. There were ramifications I'd yet to process. Whatever was going on in Jack's head, I didn't believe he'd want all of us stranded mid-point across the Atlantic. If he'd killed Greg, it was an act of madness, but risking all of us – that was another level of psychosis. I wasn't buying it.

'Don't tell anybody about this,' I said, indicating the devices. I collected them all and placed them back in the box. 'Not yet. And don't tell Jason or Harriet.'

I expected an argument, but they all nodded.

'Good idea,' said Arno. He looked relieved.

'And you may disagree, but we must still perform a search for Jack,' I said. 'As soon as the conditions allow, I'm taking the tender out. Got it?'

I'm not sure what I hoped to find. It was a long shot, but if we did recover a body, it might shed some light. Suicide would be hard to prove one way or another, but if something else had happened to Jack . . . some obvious injury to his body . . .

More nods, except from Karis.

'You can't, Sarah. You're needed here. We'll find someone else.'

'I won't ask anyone –'

'No,' she repeated. 'We can't . . . I won't risk you out there.'

I understood. Karis wouldn't cope if I weren't by her side. Her troubled eyes pleaded with me.

'We'll figure it out as soon as the weather breaks,' I said. 'Let's try to get some rest and some food. Arno, take another look in the engine bay, see if you can figure out any way to get them started? Take your brother.'

He gave a reluctant shrug. 'I'll do my best.'

I paused, taking a breath. 'Will you be OK if I leave you for a bit?' I asked Karis. 'Ask Camila to join you?'

Karis nodded absently, searching Camila out on the radio.

'*On my way*,' said Camila. Abrupt, stoic. Professional – one of the few we had left.

I found Jason in his cabin. The door was closed and locked. I hammered until he answered.

His eyes were bloodshot, face drawn and suspicious. He held the door ajar.

'Yes?'

'Can I come in?'

He sniffed, still maintaining a degree of aloofness. The door opened wide enough to let me in. He shut it quickly afterwards, flipping the catch. I tensed, keeping my distance, casting my eyes around his room.

The four-poster bed was unmade, the sheets tangled at the foot. A number of plates and cups lay stacked on a tray against the wardrobe, next to a pile of dirty white shirts. Jason had lived in here for the last few days, hardly venturing out.

Dressed in black chinos and a matching shirt, his feet were in trainers. An odd combination for a man who always dressed in suits, and I guessed even Jason was affected by events. He stood away from me, his eyes darting, finally resting on my face. His cool demeanour was breaking. About fucking time.

'I came to see if you were OK,' I said.

He sneered. 'OK? How the hell would I be OK?'

I nodded. 'I'm doing my best,' I said, before giving him a detailed update on our plans – keeping any confusing suspicions about Jack to myself. As the owner's representative, Jason had a right to be kept informed about what we were doing, the status of our failing crew, and the seriousness of the *Escape*'s position. He nodded, listening to everything without comment. I noticed he hadn't mentioned Harriet at all so far. I'd half expected to see her in the cabin, perhaps in the bed, but there were no signs of female company.

'We'll start the search soon,' I said. 'Then we'll take a look at the engines.'

His eyes narrowed. 'Why are you really here?' he said.

Not even a word of sympathy about Jack. Same as with Greg. A heart of stone, or of money.

'I told you.'

Jason paced in front of the bed, keeping his eyes on me. I watched his hands shaking. He saw me looking and plunged them into his pockets. His chest rose and fell rapidly.

'Try to calm down,' I said, feeling my own breaths, shallow and staccato, and wondering how hard to push him. 'Is there anything you want to tell me?' I said, staring him in the eye, waiting for his response.

It was a useful question, the phrasing of which had been described to me by Amy as one of the best interrogative questions of them all – although I think she meant it for husbands and lovers, not dishonest businessmen.

Watch them closely, she told me. *They'll reveal the answer.*

'Tell you?' He raised his eyebrows.

I caught the flicker of his eyes, up and to the right. Thinking, creating? Lying? Unfortunately, that particular tell had been debunked years ago. Liars were no more likely to look to the left or right. The hands were a good sign, so Amy said, although in this case useless – Jason's were still planted in his pockets.

Perhaps it was a combination of all his small body movements that did it, but Jason paused, swallowed, pursed his lips, breathed at the wrong moment, stepped too far as he switched his feet and paced the other way. It was clumsy, caused by a momentary lapse in his concentration, as his mind tried to calculate something else.

It was enough to raise the hairs on the back of my neck.

I shrugged. 'Anything at all that might help,' I said, choosing my words carefully, knowing he wasn't going to tell me whatever had just raced through his mind. 'We're not quite sure what's going on here.'

He swallowed again, a big gulp. Obvious, perhaps done for my benefit.

'No,' he said, biting his bottom lip. His shoulders had sagged, he was relaxing.

Didn't see me as a threat. Should I see him as one?

'Two men are dead,' I said.

His eyes widened, his gaze piercing. 'I'm well aware of that,' he said. He opened his mouth to continue, before clearly thinking better of it. 'All I need our first mate to do is get us to our destination,' he said, in almost a whisper. 'Can you help her do that?'

I frowned, wanting to shout at him, but not clear what I'd say, or what it might achieve. He was still my employer – Mitch's employer – and if we got through this, his opinion would matter.

In the end I simply nodded. 'I'm trying.'

Jason closed his eyes, squeezing them for a second. When he opened them, his gaze met mine.

'Then please,' he indicated the door. 'Get on with it.'

28

The atmosphere inside the *Escape* seemed frozen in time even as the afternoon raced by, the clock ticking faster, my pulse beginning to race. Uneasy after my conversation with Jason, and none the wiser, I perched again on the bridge, watching Karis surge in and out of her personal trauma, keeping an optimistic eye on the storm, eyes glued to the binoculars, watching the changing colour of the sky. It took a few painful hours to be sure, but I wasn't imagining it – by late afternoon, the precipitation had diminished from heavy rain to driving drizzle. Visibility was still poor, but the waves, while significant, no longer thrashed against each other in white-crested battles. The storm, while still upon us, offered a brief respite.

'It's time' I said. 'We have an hour or so of daylight left.'

Karis nodded. 'Tell them to be careful, whoever you send.'

'I will.'

I summoned Arno by radio and asked him to meet me at the tender garage on the tank deck. Situated behind the engine room, the garage was a low-ceilinged but cavernous area packed full of water sports toys – scuba equipment and inflatable paddleboards, kite surfing boards and small laser sailing dinghies. At the centre, an eight-person tender and two jet skis were tethered to metal rails, sloping towards the rear door, which opened on to a moveable platform on the stern. The jet skis would slide straight into the water; an extendable crane would lift the tender over the lip, dropping it away from the hull.

But you'd never normally launch anything in this weather – the jet skis were dangerous, the tender might just about work with a skilled pilot. As I hit the button to open the rear door, I was blasted by the warm wind, laced with salt, howling into every crevice and corner. At sea level, the waves looked much bigger and more ferocious – the distance on the upper decks giving an unfortunate illusion of calm.

'Sarah?'

The *Escape* leapt into the air. Arno shouted. Cold on my feet and legs. The waves had started to break over the rear platform, sweeping into the garage. We'd have to be quick.

'I'll go,' I said, taking a life jacket from the rack. 'I'm the only one who –'

'No.' Arno grabbed the jacket, shaking his head. 'Karis told you to stay on the *Escape*. For good reason. Besides, we have volunteers.'

I shook my head, looked into his eyes. I wanted to ask him not to go. But who could I send in his place?

'We're going.'

I turned to find Luan and Dan zipping up their own jackets, throwing ropes and flares into the top of the tender. Arno manned the crane, winding the cable with a hand winch, straining as the ratchet caught.

Luan pulled me to one side. 'I know what you think of me, Sarah,' he said, shouting over the wind and waves, his voice whipped away, lost in an instant. 'I've been an idiot, a fool. My anger . . . it led me to do something stupid, but I never hurt anyone.'

'Luan, I –' My words were swallowed up by the storm. He didn't hear me.

'I screwed up,' he shouted. 'But I'm going to put it right. We failed to find Greg, and I never got to apologize to him – I'll forever regret it. But if we find Jack . . . that's something, isn't it?'

I nodded, confusion taking the place of my suspicion. Was Luan finally showing his true colours? A flash of honesty in the anger?

I turned to Dan; his face was locked in grim determination. He glanced at me, approached, leaned in.

'I don't *care* what you think of me,' he said, whispering into my ear. 'I've done nothing wrong, and I don't shy away when the serious shit needs to be done. Why don't you watch a couple of men at work?'

He pushed himself away, striding to the open door, guiding the tender as it slid along the metal rails.

I noticed that his posh accent had given way to a more normal tone. Finally at the point where he didn't even care about that. Fucking macho asshole. That sort of attitude would get them both killed. And yet, the act of them both jumping into the small boat at least *hinted* that neither of them had anything to do with Jack's disappearance. Why would they offer to search if they had? Unless by some twisted plan they were in it together, and only sought to waste our time?

Genuine human beings, or great actors, I couldn't be sure.

Part of me wanted to overrule both of them, to cancel this search, to call it off. And yet I had to believe that finding Jack's body might reveal what we needed to know. I glanced out at the sea. Rough, dangerous, but not extreme. I'd allow them an hour on the water, two at most. It was a manageable risk. A necessary one.

'You have working radios?'

'One each,' said Luan.

'I want a running commentary,' I said. 'No silence. Got it?'

Luan nodded. Dan ignored me.

'OK, then.'

The tender slammed twice into the platform as it launched, the motion unpredictable. Arno wrestled with the cable, waiting for the right moment to release it, struggling to keep the boat away from the edge.

The engine started on the first try, and Luan gunned it, propelling the boat away from the *Escape*, achieving a safe distance before he spoke.

'*We'll track first.*' His voice crackled over the airwaves. '*I have Camila's calculations. We'll be out of visual contact but we'll radio for flares if we need them.*'

'Roger,' I said.

Good luck, I thought.

The first hour raced by. Luan and Dan relayed their movements, tracking further behind the *Escape* with each pass. I heard them battling the waves, the brief burst of radio transmissions confirming the strain and difficulty they faced trying to manoeuvre the small boat in such heavy seas. Arno fired flares from the sun deck at twenty-minute intervals, checking the tender could still see us as they searched.

I took a break from the bridge, deciding I had another visit to make – one I'd left long enough, too long, for which I irrationally blamed Jason.

The owner's deck had a large al fresco dining area with settee lounge. Through the doors, the interior comprised a private salon with entertainment centre, bar and games table area. Beyond this was the main cabin – private study, master suite and bathrooms.

The cabin door was closed and locked with a *Do Not Disturb* sign hanging on the door handle. There were other entrances, but I suspected they'd also be locked. I knocked gently, then again, louder this time.

'Harriet, it's Sarah,' I called. 'Can you open up for a few minutes, please?'

Nothing.

'Lily,' I called on the radio. 'When's the last time you serviced Harriet's bedroom? Took her some food?'

My radio crackled and hissed. The battery must be almost dead. 'Lily?'

'*I'm here,*' she replied. '*Um. The day before yesterday. Jason was taking her food yesterday. And this morning, I think.*'

Jason didn't have a radio. Typical.

'Can you grab Jason, please, and both meet me at the owner's stateroom?'

'*Sure.*'

'Bring Elijah,' I said, conscious I didn't want Lily wandering the corridors alone.

They arrived within minutes. Lily was hitting her radio. 'They're almost out of power,' she said.

'She won't answer,' I said to Jason. 'Can you . . .' I nodded to the door.

Jason sighed, looking a little sheepish. 'She hasn't answered for me, either.'

'Since when?'

'All day. Last night. I don't know. I saw her yesterday morning. I think.'

I closed my eyes, squeezing them in exasperation, counting to ten. 'You didn't think it was important?' I asked him. 'Harriet?' I called, thumping at the door.

Jason's lips clamped together. 'She owns this yacht,' he said. 'If she wants privacy, I don't argue, neither should you.'

'We're not on a fucking charter in the Caribbean,' I said. 'She doesn't get privacy on this trip. Not any more. I *thought* you were looking after her!'

'I was. She felt safer in there. Can you blame her? I . . .' Jason's face flushed. He leaned into the door, tapping feebly, looking at me with an air of frustration.

'Harriet?' he called, with a subtle change in the pitch of his voice. An arse-licking voice, not altogether sincere. 'Miss DeWitt-Fendley?'

No answer.

'Get out of the way,' I said.

'Why,' he said. 'What are you –?'

I took three steps back, strode forward and stamped against the door handle, wincing as the pain shot up my leg. The doors on superyacht cabins are delicate and soft and not designed to stand up to that sort of force – the lock snapped out of the door; the frame bent open. I pushed the door.

'Harriet?' I called.

The entrance hall was quiet, private study off to the left,

wardrobes and dressing area to the right. We cleared them and moved forward to the bedroom and bathrooms. I remembered Karis's description when I first boarded – the stateroom was another level of luxury, and yet, even as my boots sank into the rug and I stared at the roll-top bath with gold fixtures and a panoramic view over the bow, it all disappeared in a sense of dread. The colours were dampened, the sparkling taps dulled as the sun already started to set, hanging low in the grey skies. This opulent space was merely a hollow container where our owner should be enjoying her trip, ordering the stewards around, calling the captain to check if we had enough champagne to last the voyage.

But apart from her luggage – four Vuitton suitcases stacked in one corner – an array of magazines and novels scattered on the queen-sized bed, the silk sheets tangled on one side, Harriet was nowhere to be seen.

I pulled one of the magazines towards me – it was open at a centre-page spread showing Monaco, an editorial piece on next season. Harriet was keeping up on society news – her society. And she'd left the article open and gone . . . where?

The four of us faced each other across the room. Lily's hands went to her mouth, staring at me. Elijah's expression was stony, a deep frown, eyes on the empty bed. Jason backed away, eyes darting between us all. He stopped against the dresser, muttering to himself before turning and hurrying out.

'Wait,' I called.

He ignored me. I heard the outer door slam.

My hand slipped into my pocket, fingering the plastic

casing of the taser. Follow him or not? But the moment had passed. Chase him and do what? My other hand went to the radio.

'All stations. Report if you've seen Miss DeWitt-Fendley. Harriet. Has anyone seen her?'

Silence.

'Karis, come in.'

'*Go ahead.*'

'Harriet isn't in her room.'

The hiss extended for several seconds. I gave the radio a tap.

'Did you hear me?'

'*I heard you.*'

More silence. Was that it? What did I expect?

'Karis, I want you to stay on the bridge with Camila. I'll be there in a minute.'

'*It's getting dark, Sarah,*' said Karis. '*We need to get the boys in, soon.*'

Did she even hear what I'd said? Her voice was dead, devoid of understanding or emotion. Shutting down, blocking it out.

Or something else? She didn't even sound surprised.

My heart leapt, thudding in my ears, my throat, my head. Lily moved forward but I shook my head and she stopped. I was in a nightmare, a surreal trance, locked away on this bizarre floating palace, this luxury vessel of death.

Jason? Karis? What the fuck were they playing at?

I backed away towards the entrance hall and door.

'Stay together, you two. I'll call you.'

I walked the first few steps, ran the rest, to the aft

stairwell, straight down, three at a time, doing my best not to stumble. Lower deck, crew cabins. I threw open the door to mine, slammed it shut and locked it.

I clamped my fists together as I breathed, sucking the air in through my swollen throat. My chest tightened; stomach twisted. No time.

I switched frequencies on my radio.

'Dan, Luan, come in, please.'

Were the only people I could trust, in fact, on that little tender, bouncing around on the open seas, a mile behind us? Just my fucking luck. I waited. My heart ticked with the passing seconds. No. Stupid. Lily and Elijah had given me no reason to be suspicious. Arno had done nothing but help me – going over and above, each day – he had my back. The others? Shit. I had no idea.

'*Here, Sarah.*' Luan's voice. '*We're done on this pass. We're a few miles behind you. I . . .*'

The radio cut out.

'You need to come back,' I said. 'That's an order. Cancel the search and head back.'

The pause between transmissions was infuriatingly long.

'Dan,' I shouted, hitting the radio button.

'*We hear you,*' said Luan. '*Hang on a minute.*'

I swore under my breath, knelt, reached under the bunk. All I grabbed was air. I got down on to my stomach, pushed forward, stared at the empty space.

My gun case was gone.

I scrambled around, looking behind me, in case – as if by some miracle – it had appeared on the floor of the en-suite.

Shit, shit, shit.

My guns. My Glock and APC9K sub-machine gun. Taken.

I touched the leg of the bunk. Solid. I ran my hand over the floor. Gritty, sharp. Iron filings. The chain had been cut, and both the chain and the case had been removed. When was the last time I'd checked it? Not since yesterday morning.

'Dan, Luan,' I said, trying and failing to keep the trembling from my voice.

'*Roger, Sarah,*' said Luan, '*we're turning. Oh, wait.*'

'What?'

'*There's something . . . hang on.*'

'What is it? I need you to come back, Luan. That's an order.'

Silence. White noise, a crackle. Too far away, the radios were struggling.

'*Oh.*' Luan's voice. '*What the hell?*'

'What?' I shouted. 'What is it, Luan?'

'*Oh, shit. Sarah, we –*'

A burst of static finished his sentence.

'Luan,' I said. 'Luan? Dan, come in. Can either of you read me?'

I repeated it over and over, checking my radio. Had the range been exceeded? Was the battery dying?

'Arno?'

'*I'm here.*'

'Can you raise Luan and Dan?'

'*No,*' he replied. '*I heard their last broadcast. I'll keep trying. Have you seen Lily?*'

'She's with Elijah.'

I pushed my forehead against the inside of my cabin door, trying to squeeze some sense into my brain, to come up with some explanation. But I had none.

What the fuck was going on? Who and why? First Greg, then Jack. My guns had been taken *after* both of those events.

And now Harriet.

I pulled the taser from my pocket, checked the charge, opened my door. I listened first, creeping along the corridor, pistol by my side. I paused next to each door. I didn't think anybody was on this deck, but I nudged each door anyway.

The corridor shrank and pulsed in front of me. Blood pressure, adrenaline, my body reminding me how much it could take, and how close I was to my new limit – the limits my mind would allow before it withdrew and closed down – protecting itself, protecting me. As a soldier, *before*, I believed I was invincible, my abilities the pinnacle of soldiering. It's what I'd been told and what I believed.

But *after*, my reactions were slower, my muscle memory weaker. I guessed and second-guessed. I was a shadow of my former self.

And I was armed with a plastic taser against the unknown. I could trust nobody, not even myself.

I reached an empty cabin, pausing, slamming into the wall as a wave hit us, jarring my elbow, feeling the pain shoot up into my shoulder. As I pushed myself away, I heard a second thump. Lower, fainter. Something loose, rolling against the wall inside? There it was again, muffled, scuffling.

I kicked, low down, my boot causing a dull thud, leaving a black mark on the white paint.

Another thump immediately afterwards. A response, a reply.

I stepped back, nudged the door open with my shoulder.

'Hello?'

Thump.

The wardrobe. The door moved. I leaned forward, pulled the catch, stood back with my taser raised.

The wide eyes of Harriet stared at me. She wore a thin nightgown, her feet bare. Her mouth was gagged, and blood matted her hair, dripping on to her forehead. Hands and feet were tied with rope. She'd been placed curled in a foetal position, stuffed into the bottom of the empty wardrobe.

I dropped the taser and crouched, cradling her as I pulled her out on to the floor. Her eyes rolled – groggy, struggling to focus.

I eased off the gag, feeling the blood at the back of her head sticking to her hair as I pulled. She groaned and I sat her against the wall, keeping her upright with my body as I tried to untie the ropes. They were tight, a sailor's knot – she'd never have loosened them herself.

'Harriet,' I said, holding her, bringing my face to hers. 'Harriet. Can you hear me?'

She panted, blinking, and started to struggle, pulling her arms away, thrashing her legs. One of them kicked out, caught me in the upper gut, right in my solar plexus.

'It's Sarah,' I gasped, trying not to vomit. 'I'm not going to hurt you, Harriet.'

I wrestled her legs down, holding her tight until her surprisingly strong writhing faded. She opened her eyes;

with each blink she seemed to adjust, her vision returning.

'It's OK,' I said. 'Everything's OK. I'm here.'

Was it OK? Far from it, but I wasn't going to let any more harm come to this poor woman. I felt behind her head, my fingers gently probing in her sticky hair. Halfway down, on the back of her skull, I found a lump the size of an egg. She groaned as my fingers brushed it, her body shaking. I touched below it, judging the seriousness. The bleeding appeared to have stopped, which was good. I wondered how bad her concussion would be; how long she'd been unconscious.

'Can you hear me?'

She nodded, a small jerking movement.

'Do you know where you are?'

Another nod. Small gasps of breath.

'The yacht.'

'Which yacht?'

'*Escape* . . . the Atlantic.'

'What's your name?'

'Harri–' She turned and vomited on to the floor, coughing up thin bile and water.

I stopped her falling forwards, pulling the hair away from her mouth as best I could. A moderate concussion, at the very least, possibly more serious. And not much I could do about it.

I let her cough and spit for a few moments. When she sat up, her face looked clearer, her eyes focused, though her face was white and clammy.

'Who did this to you? Tell me, Harriet,' I said, throwing a towel on the floor to cover the mess.

She shook her head, slowly, eyes searching, widening, suddenly alert, suddenly remembering.

'The black dress,' whispered Harriet. 'Le Bar Salle Blanche, Monte Carlo. She looked so radiant, she stood out, even there. I remember telling Daddy. He knew her. He *knew* her.'

'Who?' I asked.

But she winced with pain, a sudden convulsion. My hands slipped away and she lurched backwards, her head hitting the wall.

'Harriet,' I hissed, scrambling, trying to catch her body, but too late.

Her eyes rolled back and she slumped to the floor.

29

I checked her pulse. Slow, but steady. I ran to my cabin and grabbed two bottles of water, returning quickly, using one to make a cool compress with a flannel, holding it against the back of Harriet's head. It wasn't cold enough, but it might offer some small comfort, reduce the swelling a fraction. I watched her carefully for a few minutes, recalling my field training on concussions, knowing none of it would help. She was in and out of consciousness, had received an obvious impact to her head, and carried severe nausea.

She needed to rest and be monitored until we could get her to a medic.

I nudged the cabin door closed and locked it, planning my next move, my next conversation. I had to tread very carefully.

'Karis,' I called over the radio, attempting to keep all emotion out of my voice.

'*Yes, Sarah.*'

'Just checking in. Are you two OK on the bridge?'

'*It's only me. Camila went to help Arno with the flares. Anything from Luan and Dan?*'

I paused, taking a deep breath. 'No,' I said. 'And Karis?'

'*Yes?*'

'I'm on my way up. I'll be there in a minute.'

I needed to marshal my thoughts. I cleared my throat.

'Arno,' I called. 'Can you see the tender yet? Are you OK?' The radio hissed and crackled. My hands trembled. 'Arno?'

'*I'm here,*' he answered. '*Nothing. I'll keep trying.*'

'Is Camila with you yet?'

A pause.

'*No. I think she's on the bridge.*'

I flicked off the radio.

The black dress, Harriet had said.

I tried another frequency. 'Lily,' I said. 'Come in, please.'

Another hiss. Silence.

'Lily?'

Nothing.

'Elijah,' I tried, my voice wavering, the pitch rising with each word. 'Come in, please.'

More silence. Hiss and static. No answer.

She looked so radiant. Harriet's words.

I couldn't risk saying more on the radio, but my mind was a whirring mess, trying to rewind everything that had happened – Greg, Jack, Harriet. Was the same person behind all of it?

But this wasn't an end game. Barring some deranged psycho on a killing spree, whatever they were doing wasn't over. Harriet had been brutally attacked and stuffed in this room, in what could only have been intended as a temporary measure. Were they coming back to finish things?

Was *she* coming back?

'Harriet,' I said, sliding next to her on the floor, ignoring the pungent smell of vomit in the close confines of the room. I tapped her cheek gently, calling her name, massaging her hands. 'Wake up,' I said.

She stirred, tossing her head from side to side.

'Harriet,' I whispered. 'We need to move.'

She looked up, pupils dilated, struggling to focus.

'Can you walk?'

She gave a feeble nod, and I helped her to stand. She wobbled, struggling to hold my arm. It was unwise to move her, but with my firearms gone, my best defence was to find somewhere else to hide Harriet while I figured out what to do, found some answers. Nobody would know Harriet had been discovered, not yet, which bought me some time. Twenty-five thousand square feet of deck was a lot, but difficult to hide in. For any of us.

What were my options?

'This way,' I said, taking her towards the central staircase.

We'd nearly reached it when I received a burst of radio static in my right ear.

'*Sarah, it's Lily,*' she said. '*Sorry. I had my earpiece out. We . . .*'

'We?' I crept forward.

'*Sarah,*' Elijah's voice over the radio. '*It was my fault. We're at the rear port stairwell. We haven't seen any sign of Harriet so far. What do you need?*'

I closed my eyes. Any remaining doubts I might have had disappeared. The little pieces, the signs. All there – if only I'd been looking. But who the hell was? Harriet had already known who it was. Before she was attacked. She'd recognized her at the beginning of the trip.

'Stay together,' I said. 'Head to the bridge. Find Karis.'

If I'd got the call from Lily a few seconds earlier, it might have affected my route through the *Escape*. It was a one in five risk when deciding on which stairs to take, and without any other information to help me, I'd taken the most direct.

But as we entered the foyer, my mistake glared at me from above, the svelte figure rounding the staircase, slowly descending, holding my Glock pistol in one hand, a large satellite phone in the other.

And there Camila stopped, pivoting on the white marble.

'*Je te rappelle dans dix minutes,*' she said into the phone. '*Non. Très bien. Á bientôt.*'

The phone burst with static for a moment, before she ended the call, glancing at the phone's screen before clipping it on to her belt. I managed two steps back, shielding Harriet, before she spoke. A sat phone, a burst of static. Not radios, not VHF.

It was Camila.

'Stop,' she said. 'Don't make this any more difficult.'

She gripped the pistol, practised, keeping her distance above us.

'Do you have any weapons on you?' she asked.

A fucking cheek, I thought, given she was holding mine. A fire ignited in my gut, not a soldier's rage, just my normal reaction when people messed with me – my natural inbuilt *fuck-you* reaction. I hoped she couldn't see the small bulge of the taser in my front pocket. She was within range, just about, but it would take maybe two seconds to withdraw and fire. Long enough for her to pull the trigger on the Glock and for the bullet to hit me or Harriet. One life would be lost before the electrified darts made it across the short distance.

'No,' I said. 'But I see you have mine. Why is that, Camila?'

I shuffled my feet as I said it, keeping myself between Camila and Harriet. I'd take the first bullet. Harriet might escape if she was quick enough, back along the corridor, one of the aft stairwells. Up or down. But then where?

Camila didn't smile, her jaw clenched, frustrated, her eyes fiery and full of hate. Who did she hate, and why?

'No,' she said, her eyes darting upwards at a brief sound from above, a door opening and closing, the howl of wind at the top of the staircase.

Uncertainty, I knew that look. If she fired, everyone would hear it. They wouldn't know who, or where, but it would be the end of any secrecy.

Another door slamming. Caught in the wind – or somebody above? She shook her head, appearing to reach a decision.

'What did you do with Greg?' I said, trying to buy a few more seconds, still shuffling to the right. I was off-centre, and Harriet could make the cover of the corridor, if I gave her a hard shove. 'And Jack?'

Camila rolled her eyes, lifting the pistol in a two-handed grip.

Shit. My muscles tensed.

I saw it in her eyes before her finger moved.

Time slowed. The door at the top of the staircase banged for the third time. I forced my hand downwards to my pocket, at the same time pushing Harriet hard with my shoulder.

Camila's eyes darted upwards to the sound, her arms and aim followed. She saw my movement in her peripheral vision but it took her another second to react, by which time the taser was out. I fired as accurately as I could while still pushing sideways.

Camila fired a fraction of a second later, the recoil forcing her arms up and to the right, the bullet grazing my left shoulder, ripping the skin and outer flesh as it passed, sending a shocking stab of pain down my arm.

Time sped up. I crashed against the wall of the corridor, keeping my feet. Harriet hit the floor but somehow managed to push herself up. Out of Camila's aim.

'Run,' I screamed, grabbing Harriet and pushing her in front of me, back along the crew corridor, weaving left and right.

Harriet was weak but found the strength, summoning it from somewhere – her body strung out but knowing that survival required her to move. I forced myself to shield her, sprinting behind, waiting for the impact of the next bullet in the middle of my back, my head, my legs.

Any second.

But it never came.

All I heard was a scuffling and a thump from the staircase. A small, frustrated scream. '*Merde!*'

We reached the end of the corridor.

'Left,' I said, guiding Harriet into the rear left-hand stairwell. 'Up, fast as you can, don't stop.'

Harriet tired quickly, her initial burst of energy fading. By the time we reached the bridge deck I was propping her up, holding her body against me, her arm over my shoulders. I kicked the door open, checking the route.

'Sarah to all stations,' I said into my radio, ensuring I was broadcasting on the crew channel. 'Listen carefully.

Camila is armed, dangerous, and responsible for Greg and Jack's disappearance. Do not approach her. Gather on the sun deck. I'm armed. I can protect you. Please hurry.'

My eyes watered at the pain and the lie, and I could feel the hot blood flowing on to my hand.

The radio hissed.

'Don't waste time responding or gathering anything,' I shouted. 'Just run to the sun deck. I'm armed – I'll cover you.'

I hoped they'd all run, not think, or pause or question me. I prayed they had all heard me.

Gathering everyone in one place was necessary to protect them, and I had no quick way to do that other than by advertising it across the airwaves. I gambled that, by claiming I was still armed, it might dissuade Camila from following. She'd somehow stolen my primary weapons, but she didn't know what else I might have. I hoped she didn't realize the taser was a single-shot device.

If she chose to call my bluff, then it was unlikely we'd survive the night.

'Keep going,' I said, urging Harriet forwards.

The reason I chose the sun deck, apart from its commanding views, was because there were only two entrances to the enclosed area. One through the centre, the other from the outside jacuzzi area, through the glass doors. I didn't know yet how I might secure them, but it was better than waiting on the lower decks, where she could come at us from any direction.

We arrived to find Arno at the railing, binoculars in hand, empty flare cartridges by his feet. His face was stricken, alternately scanning the sea for his brother and the deck behind him. He saw us coming and raced over, helping us inside, pulling the heavy glass doors closed as we slipped in. I rested my palm against them, leaving a bloody handprint, a smear against the flawless glass. Behind me I'd left a trail of drops on the wooden deck, already diluting under the light rain.

Lily and Elijah were inside. Whatever questions they had remained on their tongues as they registered our injuries.

'Here . . .' Elijah took Harriet, lifted her in one movement and carried her to a sofa. He placed her on her side, seeing the mat of blood in her hair, rushing to the bar to find water and napkins. 'What happened to her?' he said.

'Head wound,' I said, holding my arm, trying to see the damage. The bullet had taken a good chunk off the outside of my shoulder, hard to see through the ripped fabric. 'She has a concussion; she needs to stay still.'

Lily grabbed a bar towel, folded it over and came to help, wincing as she examined my arm.

'Just tie it,' I said. 'Hard, over the shoulder, under my armpit.'

Lily wrestled with the fabric, surprising me with her strength. I bit down the scream as she pulled it tight and tied it off with a double knot.

'It needs cleaning,' she said.

'Not now.'

The inner door crashed open. Karis entered, white-faced, the tears still in her eyes, her face streaked with moisture. 'What happened?' she said. 'I heard a gunshot.'

'Shut the door,' I said. 'Where's Arno?' I turned.

He was outside, launching another flare. I could see his lips moving, calling into the radio. Luan and Dan were nowhere to be seen, but I could only process one emergency at a time.

'Arno,' I shouted. 'Come back inside.'

'What's going on?' Karis demanded, her voice trembling, trying to assert some sort of control, perhaps only over herself. 'What's this about Camila?'

'Where's Jason?' I said. 'He doesn't have a radio. Where is he?'

Lily shrugged as a thought struck me. Was it possible Jason was working with Camila, on whatever twisted endeavour she'd planned?

I knelt next to Harriet. She'd been sick again.

Elijah was mopping her brow. 'She's not good,' he whispered.

'Listen to me,' I said to Harriet. 'Why did Camila do this? I need to know everything. Anything you can tell me.'

Harriet frowned, a small shake of her head. 'I have no idea.' As she leaned over, the colour drained from her face. 'Sorry,' she said. 'Nausea.'

'Try not to move your head,' I said.

'I told her I recognized her,' she whispered. 'She came to my cabin, yesterday. I told her –' Harriet grabbed my forearms, 'I was right.'

'From Monte Carlo,' I nodded. 'The dress. What does that mean?'

Harriet took another sip of water, rinsing it around her mouth before swallowing. She closed her eyes. I gave her the time, though painfully conscious of the seconds ticking by.

'Nikolas,' she said, finally. 'My second cousin. The family outcast – the pariah. She was with him.'

'Camila?'

'Yes. In Monte Carlo. At the bar. Last season. I saw them more than once together, in all the trendy places – even at the yacht club. They were berthed near us. I can't remember the name of the yacht – it wasn't one of ours.'

'You mentioned your dad? He said something?'

'He ushered us away. Didn't want us talking to him. Nikolas had been involved in some shady business – serious stuff. He and Daddy had words, but I didn't see him again for the rest of our stay.'

'But Camila was with him? With your cousin.'

'Second cousin.'

I waited for more, but Harriet dipped her head, panting with shallow breaths.

'So what?' I said. 'So Camila knows your family. That still doesn't explain what she's doing here'

Kidnap. I managed not to say it, but it sprang to the front of my mind. Kidnapping the niece of a billionaire was a pretty serious crime, but it didn't make any sense. Why would they wait until Harriet boarded the *Escape* on a transatlantic voyage? It would have been much easier to grab her on land.

'He's not family,' she said, wincing, stretching her legs out. 'But he's destroyed plenty of lives. Businesses went under, and the usual people suffered – normal people. Three managers at the Tokyo exchange took their own lives – that was the rumour.'

I nodded, remembering the news article I'd looked up. 'Who was he involved with?' I said.

Harriet shrugged. 'I really don't know. There was something in the international financial press. Insider dealing, or something even worse. But . . . it was all hushed up — these things often are, especially in families like mine. The bad press is worse than the crime itself. Nikolas was silenced, cast out, family ties cut forever. He doesn't have a penny, as far as I know. Not from my family, anyway.'

Cast out and broke. Nikolas sounded like a prize asshole, but that didn't tell us why Camila had attacked Harriet in such a violent fashion. It didn't explain what she might have done to Jack and Greg. If this was kidnap, whatever the unusual circumstances, I'd already failed to protect two lives, and I genuinely didn't know how many more were at risk.

'I came on this trip to get away from all of the family drama,' said Harriet, reaching out to hold my arm. She looked as if she was going to vomit again. 'It was so stressful at home. This was my peace and quiet. Looks like the drama found me anyway.' She managed a small wince of a smile. 'I'm sorry I can't tell you more,' she said, 'but I know who can.'

'Who?'

'Jason Chen.' Harriet blinked, focusing on my face. Her lips were chapped, her breathing still shallow and ragged. Getting away from Camila must have taken every last ounce of energy she had.

'Do you trust him?' I asked.

She shook her head, a small movement, involuntary. 'I don't know,' she whispered. 'He's known my family for years, been in business with my uncle since I was a little girl, but . . . I don't know.' She closed her eyes, shuffling her hips to get comfortable.

'Don't let her fall asleep,' I said to Elijah, resting my hand on Harriet's shoulder for a moment, feeling her chest rise and fall.

Elijah nodded.

Lily joined him, crouching on the floor in front of Harriet. 'We'll take care of her,' she said. 'But what's going on? Camila did this to her? She shot you?'

Arno opened the glass doors and stepped through, sliding and locking them in place.

'She has my weapons,' I said, glancing at Arno. 'Firearms – a pistol and an APC.'

Arno's eyes were wild, widening, his face flushed. He shook his head, turning against the glass. 'This isn't –' he started to say.

'What? Isn't what?'

Arno turned. 'Sorry,' he muttered. 'Isn't happening. Luan is still out there. My brother. He can't be . . .' Arno spun again, facing away, hands against the glass.

'I get it, Arno,' I said. 'We'll find them. But we have a bigger problem.'

'Camila has your weapons,' said Karis. 'What do you have?'

I tossed out my used taser. 'There are two more in the storage room on the main deck. A few other non-lethal weapons – nightsticks, pepper spray.'

'Against a gun?' said Elijah. 'What does she want?'

'I don't know,' I said. 'We need Jason up here. I think he knows. Camila was talking to somebody on a sat phone. She had one all along.'

'Who was she talking to? You think Jason might be working with her? Camila?'

I shrugged.

'I'll get him,' said Elijah, standing, his frame large and imposing, his usual friendly face twisted in anger. 'He'll be in his cabin. I'll drag him up here by his scrawny neck.'

'No,' I said. 'It has to be me.'

'You've been shot.'

'I'm fine,' I said. 'And this is my job. It's what I do, OK?'

They all turned to me, except Arno, who kept his gaze trained outside, searching through the glass, in the direction of where his brother should be.

Nobody argued, nobody spoke.

'That fridge,' I said, pointing to a ceiling-height unit behind the bar. 'Does it move?'

'I'll make it,' said Elijah. 'Why?'

'The internal door,' I said. 'Barricade it, wedge the fridge into the frame and stairwell. I'll use the external doors, you can lock them, pile up the sofas and bar furniture behind me.'

'You sure?'

As sure as I could be with ten seconds' worth of planning, no weapon and an armed assailant prowling on the decks below.

'I'll be back in five minutes,' I said.

30

Elijah slid and locked the door behind me. I didn't hang around, racing to the outside stairs leading to the bridge deck, pausing at the bottom, crouching in the rain and wind, thankful that night was falling and my movements would be hidden.

I paused, watching the waves, the way they danced unceasingly in their random patterns, circling the *Escape*, teasing us, perhaps already knowing our fate. The visibility was worsening, the light drizzle turning heavier, the encroaching darkness giving rise to a cloak of claustrophobia. I'd trained for so many battle scenarios, and yet I felt unprepared, always one step behind – the motives of my enemy unknown. The weight of responsibility had found me and I couldn't do anything but accept. I must go with my instincts, minute by minute. Survival took priority over everything else.

I took the rear starboard stairs to the main deck and stopped, nudging the door to the rear lounge open, controlling my breathing, scanning the area, listening over the noise of wind and water crashing against us, the dull thumps causing a cacophony of misdirected sounds.

Keeping to the windows, I edged through the lounge and dining area, pausing again at the kitchen, straining my ears to hear.

Nothing.

The *Escape* was eerily devoid of human sounds – the

bustle of daily activity I'd grown used to stifled, my crew contained within one small area two decks above.

My main hope – that I'd hit Camila with the taser – was dashed the second I peered into the foyer. If I'd hit Camila in the chest, there was a chance she'd still be incapacitated. But my quick scan up and down the stairwell revealed it to be empty. She'd cried out as Harriet and I ran away, which I suspected meant I'd hit her – perhaps in the leg, in which case the two darts might only have paralysed the muscles for a short time. She'd have been able to drag herself away – injured for a short while, but it wouldn't be long before the effects wore off.

I had to risk it. Jason's cabin was down another flight of stairs and forward. But first I slipped into the storage room and retrieved a few items – a nightstick with belt, plasticuffs and pepper spray. I also opened the taser case and retrieved another pistol.

I crept downwards. The guest foyer was clear, and I wondered where Camila would retreat to. Lower deck? Forward cabins?

It would help if I had any idea what she wanted; what she hoped to achieve.

I watched Jason's cabin door from behind a large wooden dresser covered in multicoloured glass sculptures, the light bending and creating rainbows on the white-tiled floor. I wished I had longer to think, to evaluate what I knew about Jason, what I knew about Camila. But the answer was *not much*. Not enough.

I strode forward, trying the handle. Locked. I knocked, softly at first, then louder, feeling increasingly anxious as I stood exposed in the corridor.

I heard footsteps on the other side.

'Who is it?'

'Me. Sarah.'

A pause.

'What do you want?' He sounded scared.

It could be an act, but I had to take the risk. If Camila was also behind that door, I was dead already.

'Are you alone?' Worth asking.

'Yes.' No hesitation.

It didn't mean much, but I couldn't judge it through the door.

'I need to come in.'

Another pause. The lock clicked open. I raised the taser.

As soon as the door moved, I kicked it with force, stepping forward. Jason staggered back as I scanned the room, aiming across, towards the en-suite, then back to Jason, who was empty-handed, arms half raised, an expression of chewed-up fear on his face.

'What the hell?' he exclaimed.

I kept the taser level, dead centre with his chest.

'Come with me,' I said.

I covered Jason from behind as we made our way to the sun deck, taking the same route in reverse, my skin crawling at the thought we were being watched, covered by a gun, *my* gun. But if Camila was watching, she let us go.

Elijah and Arno heaved the furniture to one side, pulling the door open. I shoved Jason ahead of me.

He spun on his feet, eyes darting at each of us, taking in the barricaded internal door, the glass bi-folds with my bloody handprint still on the outside. 'Harriet!' he said, leaping forward, crouching in front of her.

I didn't stop him, curious at his reaction, puzzled, reassured.

'Are you . . . who did this?' he demanded.

Nobody answered, instead turning to me. Arno, once again, stared outwards, fidgeting, pacing back and forth. I tried to take his arm, but he shrugged me off. His face was twisted with angst, flushed. He was panicking and I needed him to calm down.

Harriet was groggy, but conscious. She tried to prop herself up on one arm, failed, and instead cradled her head, turning to Jason. She relayed what had happened, while I watched Jason's expression. Deep in thought, calculating.

He glanced at me. 'She shot you?'

I nodded.

He put his head in his hands. 'Oh my God,' he said.

'What do you know?' I said. 'About Camila, about what she's doing.' Once again, I held the taser outwards, ready.

Jason rubbed his face, sat on the floor next to Harriet, an impossibly vulnerable position. He let out a deep breath. Any final remnants of the snobbish VP who had stepped on board several days ago had disappeared. As human as the rest of us.

My hand wavered.

'I don't know Camila,' he said, shaking his head. 'Never met her, never seen her before. But if what Harriet says is true, then . . .'

'It *is* true, Jason,' said Harriet. 'I saw her with Nikolas last season. What was she doing with him? How does she know the family? You've known something all along, haven't you?'

More shakes of the head from Jason.

'You need to start talking,' I said, waving the taser, 'or you're getting a shot of this and will spend the rest of the trip tied up against that bar.'

Jason didn't get up, didn't look scared. He looked puzzled and confused, which worried me even more.

'Nikolas Aubert . . .' he said. 'The family pariah. What Harriet says is true. He gambled a lot of family money on the markets, lost most of it, destroyed a string of businesses – and people – in the process. All perfectly legal, by the way.

'But he was always a snake, no moral code or compassion. A sociopath, I think you'd call him, manipulative, deceitful. He could have slunk away after losing the DeWitt-Fendley millions, but instead turned to alternative sources of funding in an effort to recoup his losses – private banks linked to criminal enterprise – specifically the South American drug cartels. A funding source of last resort, these banks launder drug money through legitimate investments – property, stocks, what have you . . .'

Jason looked uneasy talking so openly in front of the crew. I gave him an encouraging glare.

He nodded, turning to Harriet. 'Your uncle found out what Nikolas was doing and cut all ties, financial, legal . . . Nikolas was no longer part of the family business. I urged caution, advised we should leave him with something – some small property or investments – but your uncle wanted to take a hard line, send a message to the business and the rest of the family. Nikolas was left with nothing – not a cent.'

He paused. We waited. The *Escape* tossed us around impatiently.

'It's only rumour,' he said, 'but I heard Nikolas reached out to new associates, undesirable businesses we'd only ever dealt with on the periphery – a French syndicate fronting a European cartel, ruthless and feared, responsible for controlling western Europe's narcotics and weapons trade. Your uncle ignored it, told us to stay away. If Nikolas wanted to self-destruct in the criminal underworld, let him. He was now a stranger to us. Let him be. We wanted no part of it –'

'So where does Camila fit in?' I said. 'Harriet saw her with this Nikolas. Who is she?'

Jason chewed his lower lip. 'Where did you find her?' he said, aiming his question at Karis. 'Did *you* hire her?'

Karis shook her head. 'Greg did. I didn't think anything of it – the captain can hire who he wants. But . . . shit.'

'What?'

'It was Camila who told Greg about me and Pieter. Something Greg said shortly after departure – that he felt he could really *trust* her. It was a dig at me, but she must have done it to get rid of Pieter so she could have the bosun's job. It meant she'd be on the bridge most of the time.' She squeezed her eyes shut, the pain evident.

I glanced up at Arno. His eyes were fixed to the binos, staring out to sea. 'What happened in France, Arno?' I said. 'Where did you meet her?'

He turned; eyes glazed. 'The sailing clubs . . . we got talking. She knew I was working white boats and she introduced herself, said she was looking for her next step up . . . I introduced her to Greg. That's all. I only saw her a handful of times, and then there she was, at Palma.' He gave a feeble shrug, apologetic, guilty. He turned back to the glass.

'Greg's bonus,' I said to Jason. 'You were paying him a stupid amount of money to keep to the schedule. How much?'

Jason took a breath. 'Fifty,' he said.

I heard Elijah swear under his breath.

'You offered Greg fifty thousand to leave on time and keep to the schedule. Why?' I said.

Jason squirmed on the floor, his face flushing even brighter. 'Because we'd heard something. We didn't know the details, but it had to do with the family assets. We got wind of a group linked to the French syndicate taking an interest in us . . . they specialize in asset retrieval.'

'Asset retrieval? In English, please?' I said.

'They *steal* things,' said Jason. 'People, money, weapons, anything. That's *why* you were hired. But we couldn't tell you. Couldn't risk a leak.'

'That worked out well for you,' I said, glancing at the room around me. 'The *Escape*? Is that what they're stealing?' I had a horrible thought, a repeat of when I'd found Harriet in the wardrobe. '*Harriet?*'

But Karis was shaking her head. 'No,' she said. 'Greg said he was getting seventy-five thousand if we hit the schedule. Seventy-five, not fifty.'

Jason frowned. 'Not from us. I offered him fifty for swift passage. If he got paid anything else, it was for another purpose.'

The realization slowly dawned.

'Shit,' said Jason. 'So Greg was *paid* to hire Camila.

Twenty-five K. Christ. What the hell did he think he was doing?'

'I doubt he thought much beyond the money,' said Karis. 'He was desperate and broke. And it's not the first time some rich family has paid to get their kids jobs. I've had requests like that before myself. Obviously, you're supposed to turn them down.'

I thought on Jason's comment, turned to Harriet. 'When did you decide to join us?'

Harriet sniffed. 'A day before we left. I didn't tell anyone.'

'Then it's not you they're interested in,' I said. 'Camila only attacked you after you recognized her and told her so – she didn't expect you to be on board. Which leaves the *Escape*. So they're stealing this yacht?'

Jason sniffed, more shakes of his head. He glanced at Harriet, frowning.

Harriet raised her eyebrows, letting out a groan. 'Tell me it's not on board, Jason,' she said.

Jason's eyes shot to her, then to me. I think he sensed he was out of options.

'OK . . . I mentioned the owner's art collection, yes?' he said. 'Perhaps I was a little loose with my tongue, in fact. I let myself go a little that first night at sea.'

'Rembrandts,' I said. 'Two of them. I've seen them . . .'

Jason took a deep breath, preparing himself. 'The Rembrandts – and everything else, in fact – are dwarfed by a single piece. Crated up securely in the gallery, we have possibly the most expensive work of art in the world. The *Salvator Mundi* by Leonardo da Vinci. To give you an idea, it last sold at Christie's in 2017 for £450 million. My employer – Harriet's uncle – bought it.'

He left it hanging while the number computed in our heads.

'Fucking hell,' I said, remembering the small, reinforced crate strapped to the wall of the gallery, padlocked and taped. Four hundred and fifty million. No wonder it wasn't on show. Jason winced at my language, but it was all I could do, the amount becoming meaningless. I waited for it to sink in, as more rational thoughts presented themselves.

'We have some of the most precious art ever created on board,' he continued, 'in total valued at approximately £750 million. Hence my rage after the fire,' he glanced at me, 'it could have been the end of it all. I wasn't angry at the damage to the *Escape* – yachts can be repaired, replaced. But those pieces of art . . .'

He paused again, letting it percolate. The art gallery was worth almost four times the yacht itself. I remembered Camila's behaviour in the immediate aftermath of the fire – she did a good job of covering her anger, her shock – and I remembered Jack's comment that a frayed wire shouldn't have caught fire. Did her own clumsy act of sabotage risk her entire heist? But it didn't make any sense, and it bothered me.

'Then why on earth would you transport it on the *Escape*?' I said. 'Are you mad?'

Jason gave a small chuckle. 'Because it's the *safest* way,' he said. 'At least, that's what the insurers calculated. A superyacht like this is tough, can go anywhere in the world, and, most importantly, it's under our direct control. If something comes up, I mean customs or a trade issue, or *anything* else, we can just turn around, go somewhere else, or wait it out in international waters.

'Once I got wind of Nikolas's activities, I moved the most valuable pieces of our collection on to the *Escape* and scheduled our immediate departure. We *had* to hit that date – we had to be out of the country *before* the customs paperwork was processed, which would reveal which pieces were on board. It was worth paying Greg anything to get him moving.'

'But your plan . . .' I said. 'Someone found out.'

Jason nodded. 'Someone found out. And so I wanted us to sail as *fast* as possible to Antigua to offload the assets – secure them. I pressured Greg to do it – through storms, water rationing, lightning, anything. But I didn't know what the threat was, exactly. My interest in the CCTV . . . I didn't know who to trust. I wanted to look for anything out of the ordinary. I'm sorry I hid that from you.'

I paced back and forth, the room shrinking, trying to fit the pieces together.

'So they steal the *Escape*, with the collection on board. And take it where?'

'You can't steal a yacht this size,' said Karis. 'There's nowhere on earth you could take it. No port would have you. Too large to hide away.'

'And presumably *their* plan went to hell when Greg raced us through the storm,' said Lily.

It was a good point. 'But they must have some backup, some way of getting the *Escape* to port,' I said.

'The family would pursue it,' said Jason. 'The police, Interpol.'

'Private collectors would buy the art,' said Harriet, her voice straining to be heard. 'It's always been the case, which is why it's kept so secure. The art can disappear in a heartbeat, the transaction hidden through people such as Nikolas's contacts.'

'But not the *Escape*,' I said.

'No,' she said. 'Not the *Escape*.'

We circled back around, talking through each point in turn, looking for holes. The obvious one was that Camila's plan had gone awry. The storm and lightning strike was an act of God; drifting powerless would mean she couldn't take the *Escape* anywhere.

So what was she doing now? It wasn't the whole story, and Camila's isolated role on board bothered me.

'She was talking on her satellite phone,' I said, trying to remember her words. My French was poor. I hoped Harriet's was better.

'I didn't hear her,' said Harriet, 'I'm sorry. Only the last phrase – it was when I saw her, her lips moving. *Á bientôt*, she said.'

'See you?' said Lily.

'See you *soon*,' said Jason, correcting her.

Soon. As in a few days? Weeks? Or . . . a fresh memory struck me – one of my first years out of training, working in the Caribbean on joint ops with the US Coastguard. The Royal Navy led dozens of drug busts in the western sea, using commandos as the raiding teams. One of the challenges we learned was how the traffickers rapidly moved shipments from one vessel to another – exchanges at sea, ship to ship, spreading a container across multiple smaller vessels, even small submersibles. We could only ever catch one or two, the rest getting away at high speed.

The ludicrous profit margins meant the narcos could simply write off our haul as the cost of doing business.

I heard Luan's voice in my head – his last, confused words over the radio. He and Dan had seen something. Found something. Or something found them.

Could it be that simple?

'We need to get the engines started,' I said. 'As soon as possible. Arno?'

He dragged himself away from the glass doors. 'Now?' he said.

'I don't think Camila was talking to somebody on land,' I said. 'I think she was talking to another ship.'

See you soon . . .

'I think we're going to be intercepted. And I think it's going to happen tonight.'

Arno's reaction surprised me. While the rest fired questions, he stared at the floor, his mouth twisted, bottom lip chewed to the point of bleeding.

'Arno?' I said. 'Please. We have to try and get the engines started.'

He glanced at me, at the rest of the crew, gave a small shake of his head. 'I'm waiting for Luan,' he said. 'I don't know . . .'

And neither do I, I wanted to scream, *but we cannot stay here while another ship bears down on us.*

'We might not have long,' I said. 'We have to try. The rest of you, barricade the entrance as before, and take these . . .' I handed Elijah the pepper spray and nightstick, leaving me with the taser.

'If Camila comes up here?' said Lily.

'Don't let her in,' I said, knowing the absurdity of such a statement. But I also thought, and *hoped*, she wouldn't venture up. She'd be preparing for her friends to join us. No point risking it all now.

I wanted to buy some time, that's all. If another ship boarded us, there was no telling how many other hostiles would join her. Until that time, we had to run the risk of getting this hunk of metal moving and keeping out of Camila's way in the process.

'Try not to use the radios,' I said. 'Only contact me if

you must. Listen, but don't say anything that might give us away.'

Lily and Elijah took the sofa with Harriet. Elijah continued to mop her brow, while Lily tried to get her to drink from a water bottle. Karis sank into a chair, while Jason hovered behind, separating himself off, standing at the doors. His posture had slumped, his impeccably groomed exterior finally giving way. He looked almost normal.

Once we were outside, I stopped Arno.

'We'll find Luan and Dan,' I said, taking the opportunity to scan a full 360 degrees with the binoculars. It was useless, the visibility closing in, the lenses covered with raindrops.

He shook his head. 'They should have been back by now,' he said.

I didn't want to reveal my other suspicion, one which had dawned on me minutes before – that Luan and Dan *had* found something. Just not Jack.

'Come on,' I said, taking my previous route.

'No, this way,' he said, heading forward. 'There are plenty of ways through the yacht. This is less frequently used.' He shrugged. 'Safer.'

I followed Arno on what became an increasingly roundabout route, taking one flight of stairs, across the bridge deck, weaving in and out, down again. I resisted my urge to take control – Arno knew the *Escape* better than I did – but I followed with an increasing sense of anxiety. We stopped on each deck, scanning the water. I tried to listen above the sound of the driving wind, straining for the telltale throb of an approaching vessel – a marine diesel engine or two chugging their way towards us. But I heard nothing except the relentless force of the storm, the energy of the waves, singing and dancing at us, and so we kept descending.

Arno kept muttering to himself, stopping along one corridor, turning, and taking another. Worried for Luan, or for himself. I realized this wasn't a vast departure from his normal behaviour. In the few days I'd known him, he seemed to have a somewhat distracted focus one minute, a grim determination the next. He'd amused me on a daily basis, appearing with his winning smile and flirtatious comments – a borderline sex pest, except I *was* interested and smiled along with him, forgetting myself, heading towards the inevitable.

I'd dreamed of his arms around me, his muscular body on top of mine, watching me with those cool eyes, that lopsided grin, taking me to a place where I could forget all the rest – a place where the guilt couldn't find me, at least while the pleasure lasted.

If we lived through this, perhaps the dream would become reality. There were worse places to find denial, worse men I could shack up with. Amy would be proud of my pragmatism.

But I worried for his state of mind. None of the crew had received the training I had – most would buckle under pressure, when faced with a fight. I couldn't prop them all up. But I only needed one. I needed Arno. And I could feel him slipping away.

He stopped again, as if sensing my discomfort, hearing my mind spinning its multiple threads, balancing its plates, one wrong decision away from dropping them all.

'Where do you think she is?' he said.

I'd thought about it on the way down, and while there were several places she could hide out, one was safest of all. I'm not sure if I'd injured her at all with the taser, but if I had, she'd be recovering, perhaps more cautious about her next move.

'The safe room,' I said. 'She's been discovered, but doesn't have complete control over us. She doesn't know if we have weapons – and if the other boat is nearby, she might as well wait for them to arrive before coming out. They can storm the bridge, take control by force. If I were her, I'd be holed up in there.'

He nodded, seeming satisfied.

'Why not let her?' he said, leaning against the bulkhead, staring me in the eye for the first time since I'd staggered on to the sun deck with Harriet.

'Let . . . what do you mean?'

'Why not let her do whatever she's doing?' he said. 'Steal some shit that was probably stolen in the first place. I –'

'What?' I said. 'Are you serious?'

He shrugged. 'Come on. Nobody gets this rich,' he indicated the *Escape*, 'by being honest. Harriet and her family fleeced their money from somebody – lots of people, over the years.'

'I'm not sure what you're getting at,' I said, taking a small step back.

What he said was true, in the broadest sense – old money and capitalism conspired to suck money from 99 per cent of the population and give it to the super rich, who used it to increase their own fortunes, never the other way around. But that couldn't justify a Robin Hood approach to putting things right, particularly when cousin

Nikolas wasn't even poor – he was just another rich entitled asshole who wanted his share of the spoils. And Camila was just a mercenary for hire, probably wealthier than all of the crew put together.

It also couldn't justify taking two human lives, and perhaps countless more, before she got what she wanted. That seemed to have escaped Arno's reasoning.

'We don't have to get in her way,' he said. 'Let her take what she wants and let us go. It's not ours, right? Why do we care? At least we'll *live*.' He stared at me with a pleading look in his eyes.

But as I watched, preparing a hundred reasons why he was wrong, my thoughts were overtaken by another, more immediate realization.

'Harriet said the art can disappear in a heartbeat,' I said.

Arno nodded. 'So? So let it go. We'll be on our way. I don't care if they take it. I want my brother and I to live through this.'

'But . . .'

Was that it? Was that what had bugged me since Harriet made her statement? A sneaking, terrifying thought: a simple heist would never work. With a haul of this size, £750 million, it would get political. Interpol, the local and international police forces would never stop hunting, and while Camila and her group might hide away, Nikolas never could. Not unless . . .

'What is it?' said Arno, peering at me, shifting from one foot to another.

My gaze travelled down his face to his body, his grubby T-shirt stained with oil and dirt, his rough hands flexing and fidgeting. Still wired.

'The *Escape* . . .' I said. 'They're not interested in the *Escape* at all.'

'We know *that*,' he said, shaking his head.

'But how would Camila and Nikolas ensure the art isn't pursued after the heist?' I said.

Arno shrugged. 'Disappear? Lie low for a bit. I don't know how these gangs work. I'm sure they have a way.'

I shook my head. 'It would never be long enough. Not with this much money. It would never end.'

He frowned. 'Then what?'

I swallowed. Heart thumping. Pins and needles in my head, crawling over my scalp. It was obvious to me now – it explained everything, even why the loss of Greg and Jack didn't matter.

'The authorities wouldn't pursue any priceless artwork,' I said, 'if it was all lost at sea.'

I watched Arno's eyes darting, calculating.

'We're going to be intercepted,' I said, 'the art offloaded. A heist at sea.'

Arno nodded.

'But I think I know how the plan wraps up – how Camila's heist ends. How it *must* end.'

'We'll get picked up,' he said. 'Rescued . . . someone will find us, we –'

We were interrupted by a blast from the radio.

'*Sarah, it's Karis.*'

The bridge frequency. Was Camila listening? Did it matter at this point?

'What is it, Karis?'

'*It's here, Sarah. The ship. I can see it. Please, you have to come back up. It's too late.*'

I could hear the desperation in her voice, on the brink of hopelessness. My chest hammered at the sound of it, the anxiety creeping, ever creeping. I thought we'd have more time, that I could buy us some, or some distance.

But I was wrong. This was it.

'We're coming,' I responded, turning to head back.

'Wait,' said Arno. 'Let me go for the engines.'

I shook my head. 'Too risky. Camila's down there. You're not trained, you're not –'

'I might still be able to do something.'

'No, I –'

'Please,' he said, the sweat dripping over his brow, his eyes burning, bloodshot, as desperate as the rest of us. 'Let me *try*. I have to try. Luan's out there . . .'

I swallowed. I didn't have time to argue, and whatever Arno could do might be the one thing that saved us. Even to limp along at a few knots would make it much harder for them to board us. I watched his face, that goofy mouth, torn by anguish now, but still full of warmth, of promise. If I let him go, it was on me.

I handed him the taser. 'Take this, point and shoot. If you can't fix the engines, hide, and stay hidden. OK?'

He took the pistol, stared at it for a few moments, a flash in his eyes, a deep intake of breath. He raised his hand, turning to me.

'Sarah, I—'

I grabbed his head with both hands, shoved my mouth against his, tasted the salt, the heat, broke away before he could reciprocate. A moment. Just a moment. But I needed it.

He gasped, licked his lips, shock and confusion.

'Go,' I said, pushing him away, spinning on my feet. I didn't look back, pounded the corridor, running towards the exterior door, the panic growing as my realization of just a few minutes ago took hold.

Camila's plan.

I knew what she intended.

There would never be a heist, not officially.

The *Escape* would never arrive at port, never arrive anywhere. All cargo and all souls, with £750 million of artwork, lost at sea in a tragic accident.

It's the only way it could possibly work. The *Escape* would be scuttled and go down mid-Atlantic. Never recovered, the insurance would write it off. The art would be sold to a private collector and stay hidden for years, perhaps forever. Nobody would live to tell the tale.

They couldn't.

Because the plan required that the crew all die.

Camila planned to kill us all.

32

The panic caught up with me as I ran, the hours and days on board the *Escape* piling up on top of one another. Flashes, short stabs behind my eyes, the onset of combat, my mind preparing for my body's screams, the surge of adrenaline which had carried me through the last hour replaced with the telltale narrowing of my vision, the galloping from within my chest.

I forced it back, kept moving. I couldn't stop.

I had my job. One job. To protect this crew.

Just like before. My job. Do it properly and nobody gets hurt. Screw it up and people die.

And you failed.

What have you done, Sarah? They're all going to die. And you with them.

My footfall echoed, hollow in my ears, steps that pulsed with my heart, deafening thumps of guilt and failure.

The crew trusted me, relied on me. People with futures, with families, with friends. Their loss would cascade outwards, the grief rippling, becoming a tsunami, hitting everyone they touched. I saw Karis's face, the deep trauma that could never be fixed. The loss of a loved one before you've even had a chance to properly love. Her living shock was a spiralling list of questions that would never be answered.

And it was about to be repeated many times over.

Your job, Sarah. Why didn't you see it?

The *Escape* bounced and surged, the motion travelling through my feet, through my muscles into my thighs and hips. My body compensated, on autopilot – even in these rough seas the human body adapted. I could run without a stagger, my inner ear tuned to the roll and pitch.

Outside, my feet pounded the deck. I paused, staring out at the black expanse. The visibility had closed right in, and all I could see were the white-tipped crests of the waves as they pummelled our hull. I couldn't see the other ship. Karis would have the high-powered binos – so it must be several hundred metres away still, a mile perhaps.

But approaching.

Boarding us would be hard – they'd be out of sync, moving several metres in all directions – potentially lethal for those having to make the jump. But of course Camila never anticipated the storm. She would have chosen a quiet, calm stretch of water, made a distress call, perhaps – to bring them alongside without any suspicion or chase.

Whatever went down tonight was a deviation in the plan. Rough seas, high winds, the crew against her. Camila would have a lot of things to think about – and a lot of opportunities to make a mistake.

But her intention was clear.

I turned towards the interior, but as I did, a moving shadow caught my eye, even in the harsh driving wind and the rain which stung my eyes. Over the gunwale, in the water to my left.

I pulled out my torch, searched, the small beam reflecting, casting a sparkling array of light in the droplets that blew off the top of each wave.

My stomach sunk further, my throat constricting with the taste of bile. My breath escaped in a hiss.

A body. Floating, lifted up by the swell, presented to me, then sucked away, before being hurled against the side of the *Escape*, the faint thud lost immediately in the wind, inconsequential.

Unmistakable shaved head, black T-shirt under the life jacket. It was Luan. Arno's brother. Face down, floating, lifeless. His clothing torn, small pockets of damage. I couldn't see the blood that I knew was there, the marks unmissable to anyone who'd lived the battlefield. The darkness swallowed the details.

I'd blamed him. Suspected him. But his anger and behaviour, driving us all to distraction, had been reasonable, in his own head. I'd thought the worst of him, making my failure all the more abject, because nobody deserved this. To die like this and be discarded as a piece of meat.

A costed casualty in an operation driven by profit. His life was worthless. As were the rest of ours.

I kept the beam on his torso, transfixed, watching him tossed repeatedly against the side. I raised my finger to my radio, instinctively, but released it. There was nothing I could do, nothing Arno could do. Telling him now wouldn't help anyone, least of all him.

Another death, Sarah.

I spun on my feet and ran.

By the time I reached the sun deck my chest was cramping, my breaths coming short and fast. Worse than before, worse than ever. I staggered into the door frame, hitting my shoulder, the pain a dull stab through my upper body, but not enough to shake the descending darkness.

I held my shoulder; it was slippery with fresh blood, my wound reopened. My palm against the glass, I pushed.

They were waiting for me. Elijah threw open the door, pulling me in, before slamming it closed. The furniture was piled behind me as I caught my breath.

And it wasn't until I saw their faces that my mind caved.

The expressions – shock, disbelief, *expectation*. They crowded me, and I buckled.

'Where's Arno?' said Karis, staring at my bloody clothes, my hands.

I raised them up in front of my face, the dark red flickering in the light. My vision wavered, the sound of the wind surging and fading, the sounds of Lily and Jason calling my name, looking at my body, my arms, my neck, asking me question after question.

What are we going to do, Sarah?

It's coming.

But I didn't hear any of it. The panic was upon me, and their words drifted into the wind and became nothing more than white noise against the pounding in my chest, my heart breaking all over again.

There was nothing I could do, my knees buckling and my body sliding to the floor as my throat constricted and my lungs clamped themselves closed.

'He's dead,' I whispered, as the panic attack took hold.

Karis crouched in front of me. I could see her face but it was backed by a flickering image of the dusty corridors, the rooms we'd cleared, the Afghan compound in the early morning. Where it had all ended for me.

'Who's dead?' she said. 'Arno?'

I shook my head, saw Luan's body, lifeless, discarded. I imagined the flash of pain as he took his last breath. Another life, paid for with my failures. My indecision. All because of me. I imagined Greg's body in the same position. Then Jack's. Face down in the limitless ocean. The faces in front of me blurred together. Each of them would join the dead before the sun rose.

'No. He's gone,' I repeated, as if it explained everything.

Luan's face disappeared, the metal floor of the *Escape* turning brown, dusty orange in the morning light. I saw Kay instead, still alive, watching me, knowing what had happened, already at peace with it.

Karis held me. I curled up against her.

Too much. I'd been so close to breaking. The final straw was a man I thought was my enemy, dead in the water.

'Kay,' I said. 'Kay's gone.'

And then it all came out.

Disordered, a rambled and feverish account of that day. The day my world fell apart. My memory, my dream, my waking vision which played on repeat, night and day. I held Karis to me as I told it, scared that if I let go of her, I'd also let go of him, of the moment. Of Kay.

Because Kay died in my arms.

And it was my fault.

I was distracted, completely and utterly, by the thought of him walking into that room and smiling at me, the same way he'd smiled the night before, when we'd made love under the Afghan stars. He'd leaned in to kiss me, whispered the magical words.

'I love you.'

Those words replayed in my ears all night, all morning. Even as we raided the compound. A brief moment, a brief daydream, was all it took. I planned to say those words back. The first time in my life I'd ever uttered them and meant it. Once we were back at base – that night.

But I'd never get to say them, not to Kay.

The compound in the Helmand province hadn't been empty, after all.

It only took one man. The man in the shadows of the room, hiding, waiting. He didn't hesitate, firing an uncontrolled burst into Kay's torso, sending him crashing into the wall. I shouted in surprise, opening up, two bursts to the man's chest, taking him down. I saw him fall – he wasn't even a man, he was a boy, a jihadi warrior, delusional and deadly.

I'd swept back to the two at the table. They both screamed, pleaded. The room filled with the others from my fire team. The woman kept screaming as I ran to Kay, cradling him in my arms, trying to apply pressure to the gaping holes in his chest and back. The screaming continued, until I realized it was my own voice, screaming his name. I held Kay while the blood poured out of him, his eyes locked on mine. No last-minute smile, no words, no wink.

Just shock, and pain, and a desperate body failing. Kay died in my arms.

The medivac came in, seconds afterwards, and the rest of the compound was swept again, secured. One lone warrior. One marine dead.

I had called the all-clear. It was my fault. My lack of attention to detail, my professionalism, my judgement. And Kay paid for it with his life.

That was it. Over in a flash. After four years of preparing – one of the first female Royal Marines to hit the ground in the Middle East, having trained my ass off, and then some. I couldn't go on another mission. Wouldn't. They wanted me to stay, my CO almost begged me – I was a 'bundle of highly trained potential'. Destined for great things, he said. Special Forces selection could be mine. Everything I'd dreamed of.

Except my dreams were now single-track. I watched the scene on repeat. I watched the boy appear, rifle raised, the flash of the muzzle as he fired. The vision filled with Kay's face. His beautiful, pain-stricken face.

And I'd broken inside.

Please don't throw it away, said the medical officer. We can get you through this. But I refused everything they offered, for months, except the discharge.

Marine fire teams function because everyone knows their shit, and has it together. I was a liability – I'd put the whole team at risk. More deaths, more friends, maybe my own. I left to save myself, but also to save the others. Kay deserved better than me, and so did the rest of my squadron. They deserved a soldier who didn't wake up screaming every night, who could pull the trigger when it mattered.

I was a failed Royal Marine. I was done.

I could still feel his chest. Taste the blood. Smell his body.

I was done.

I came to, a short while later. Karis still held me, Elijah paced in front, gradually coming into focus as the haze lifted. The room followed, the sound of the storm crowding my hearing as if someone had just turned up the volume.

My body jolted; I checked my watch.

'How long have I been out?' I said.

Karis shook her head. 'A few minutes. You hyperventilated so hard you passed out. I'm sorry, Sarah. I'm so sorry. I had no idea, you –'

I pushed myself up, out of Karis's grip, pressed my hands against the glass, gazing out to sea. The night sky greeted me, the sun low and disappearing, the clouds covering any trace, rain pelting down upon us. The sea maintained its vicious battle of white crests, hurling them at us, shoving us across its path, like a predator teasing its prey. It was only a matter of time before it consumed us.

'Luan's dead,' I said, the words tumbling out. 'I saw his body. Floating . . . I figured –' I cut myself off.

Did they need to know what he looked like? Clothing torn; flesh ripped apart by high-calibre rounds? Would it help matters, knowing that's what they all faced before the night was out?

'Sarah,' said Karis. 'We . . .'

All eyes were on me, terrified, full of doubt. I realized what I must look like, covered in blood, collapsing in front of them, pouring my soul out to a bunch of strangers, hanging my weaknesses out for all to see. Why should they care about my past? I was employed to protect them, and now look at me.

'Where's Camila?' whispered Harriet. She was curled in the foetal position, knees tucked to her chest.

I shook my head.

'What are we going to do?' said Lily.

Another shake. I didn't have any more answers. The anxiety gripped me, my hands trembling, my teeth chattering. I could feel it coming on again, my throat swelling, my energy being sapped away.

'Sarah.' Karis stood, rubbing her eyes, taking a deep breath as she approached me, gripping my shoulders. 'Listen to me.'

I let her hold me, watched her piercing eyes lock on to mine. Her fear was evident, her own grief raw, but I could sense that her courage wasn't entirely extinguished. There was a spark in there, she hadn't given up, even after seeing my failure, even after hearing the burden I carried – what I'd done. How I'd killed the one person I loved.

Her voice was firm, commanding. She held herself upright, body taut. I saw the same Karis who had invited me on board just days before, slowly emerging from her grief.

'You're a soldier, Sarah,' said Karis. 'What you just told us – it's a nightmare I can only ever imagine – but whatever blame you have put on yourself wasn't justified. The burden you carry isn't yours.'

I shook my head. She meant well, but she was wrong. I didn't have the energy to argue.

'And I'm sure everyone who has heard your story has told you the same thing,' she said.

I paused. Touché. Although very few people had heard it. It wasn't the sort of story you told at parties.

Hey, everyone, I killed my boyfriend. What do you think of that?

'But that was then, and this is now, Sarah. Whatever you believe, we *need* you. I need you. We need the soldier, the kick-ass piece of attitude who boarded eight days ago, the one I handed command to after I failed you all.'

'Karis,' I whispered, 'you didn't –'

'I *did*. I can't make you feel better, or take the pain away, or even keep the panic from overwhelming you. Our futures are altered, Sarah. Neither of us are getting our happily ever after. But I've cried myself to sleep ever since Greg disappeared, and now I know who is responsible. And along with the grief and the guilt I feel *anger*, Sarah. Camila chose this yacht, this crew – and so far, I've failed.'

I shook my head.

'I was captain the second Greg died, and I failed to step up. I'll do whatever it takes from this point forward, but I'm not a soldier, Sarah. You are. Without you, we're at the mercy of Camila and whoever else you think is out there. You're the only one who can help us get through this. As the captain, I'm *ordering* you. Tell us what to do.'

She held my shoulders, fingers digging in tight. Her eyes kept their grip on mine, and I couldn't avoid it, her stare, her words, her projection of confidence. I knew what she was doing because I'd done it myself a hundred times. I'd held Karis in this way not two days ago, given her the same pep talk, told the same lies.

I broke away. It was too much. I couldn't take a gushing display of fake confidence in me, the begging, and the naïve belief I could simply flex my muscles and make everything OK. I was a soldier, so what? I failed then and I'd fail now.

I pushed her away, turned towards the glass, closed my eyes. And yet, all I could see was Kay's face. He looked different to my normal picture. Dressed in the crew clothing of the *Escape*, sitting in this room, across from us at the bar, watching this conversation, judging my response.

And I could hear his reaction.

He was flinging playful insults, like he did in training, goading me on, teasing me each time I stumbled, cursing each time I pulled ahead of him. He'd dissect what had happened so far, picking me up on every little detail I'd missed – every opportunity I'd had to save Greg, to save Jack, to uncover Camila's deception. He'd laugh, poke fun at my mistakes, raise his eyebrows when I swore, push me to the next challenge.

He was reminding me of our encounters in the first few days and weeks, after we'd met on the beach. When my squadron competed on the firing range in the pissing rain and my gun jammed, putting me into last place, and I stormed off in a rage to the sound of hollers and jeers. When he came to find me, dragged me back, watched me painstakingly pull apart the rifle, clear the stoppage and restart the course. And again, because my score wasn't good enough. And again, until it was. He didn't let me stop until I'd beaten his score and the score of all those fuckers who'd laughed me off the range.

Only then he'd give a little smile, a twisted grin. *That'll do*, he'd say.

Because Kay never let me fail. He'd demand I pick myself up. You fall, you get back up, you're a fucking marine, Sarah. Not just any marine, either. Whether you like it or not, female marines have more to prove than the rest of us. So stop bitching, and prove the naysayers wrong. Show them you don't give up when you're down, drowning, hurt, dazed, shot, screwing everything up . . . What marks the very best marines out from the rest is that, after *all* of that, they get back up, drag themselves to the front, and keep fighting.

Where are you, Sarah? Are you still fighting?

He'd swivel on the bar stool, order another drink – a pint of whatever the cheapest lager was, followed by a Scotch, and turn back to me.

Besides, he'd say, sipping his beer, your average marine lives for scenarios like this. You've trained for it, performed it in the daylight, in the dead of night, in the baking heat of the desert. In the freezing waters of the Arctic, the calm waters of the Mediterranean or the huge untameable seas of the Southern Ocean. You've done it all, Sarah. A hostile force taking another craft at sea is a Royal Marine's bread and butter.

I squeezed my eyes together, heard his voice, clear as if he were here with me.

Go and fucking get them, Sarah. Kick their fucking asses and don't come back until you're done.

P.S. I love you.

He finished his beer, necked the Scotch, and disappeared.

'You bastard,' I whispered, opening my eyes, seeing Karis's confused expression, reaching out and holding her arm. I took a deep breath, then another. My lungs released, and my throat relaxed. I was in the moment. I was here.

For you, Kay.

33

'There.'

I shielded my face from the driving rain as Elijah passed me the binoculars. I'd put him on watch while I made one final trip to the main deck, sprinting with as much stealth as I could muster to the storage room and back again. I'd unpacked the device on the floor of the deck and slotted in the battery.

'Show me,' I said, wiping the lenses. Sure enough, in the distance, some five hundred metres off our stern, I saw the unmistakable hull of a small cargo vessel emerging through the darkness, illuminated by a dozen spotlights and searchlights. No longer concerned with staying hidden, it was lit up like a Christmas tree, approaching at a crawl, keeping a constant distance.

I scanned the side of it, noting the rust-red colour, the length, maybe ninety metres, slightly smaller than us, it struggled in the heavy waves. The name *Nakatomi* was stencilled across the bow. I swore under my breath, remembering the last time I'd seen it – following us out of Palma marina and west, trailing us for several hours before disappearing to the south.

They'd been following us since we departed, in contact with Camila the entire time, and now prepared to make their move, execute their heist. It would be violent – they'd move fast, securing our crew with overwhelming force and aggression – exactly the way I'd do it if the roles were reversed.

Except they planned on killing us all – I'd bet £750 million worth of art on it.

I couldn't see any crew, so couldn't judge the threat, but I already knew it would be better to take the initiative. My plan was quick and dirty. It would take every ounce of training I had, and then some – but it was also the only plan I could possibly conceive of. I wasn't part of an organized group with months to plan. I was a lone foot soldier, a marine, and what I knew was fighting – quick, dirty, aggressive, causing maximum damage in the shortest time.

My plan was to play the *Nakatomi* at its own game.

I issued the two remaining working crew radios – short-range VHF units – to Karis and myself, pausing for a moment before making a tactical call.

'Arno,' I whispered across the airwaves.

The seconds he took to respond felt like an age.

'*Still here. No luck. The starters won't turn. I could do with a hand.*'

'I'll be there shortly,' I said, the lie hurting, but necessary. I had to keep Camila thinking I would remain on board. 'Radio silence until I get there.'

His radio clicked off. I had to push the thought of him out of my head. There was an outside chance he might get the engines working. His choice, his decision. I just hoped to God Camila wouldn't go hunting for him. I prayed for his success.

I sealed my radio in a plastic kitchen bag I'd found under the bar, tying the top before putting it in my pocket, along with the taser, also bagged. A small torch completed my equipment.

Karis had taken charge in the bar, her grief parked, her anger focused. She figured that, with all of the furniture combined, along with some strategic damage to the precious floorboards, they could create a barricade preventing any single person from breaching the glass doors, armed or not, at least for a while. They had the pepper spray and the batons. I didn't pretend they were safe, but they were in the safest place I could think of.

She gave me a quick embrace, then set to work. I stepped outside with Elijah, who'd volunteered to man the device I'd grabbed from storage – the sound cannon. This would put him outside the barricade, in harm's way. He offered. I accepted. I didn't have time to describe the risks of being a solitary figure on the top deck – a sniper could zero in quickly, and although even the most skilled marksman would have trouble hitting anything in these seas, Elijah was still a sitting duck. It was a brave thing to offer, and I told him so.

'You have to wait until they're closer,' I said, showing him the controls. 'Aim at their bridge, any crew you see on deck. It'll mess with them for a bit, until they decide to pull back. If you see any small boats – inflatables, anything – aim it at them as best you can.'

I saw the fear in his eyes but also the stubbornness, not like Dan's – not macho – but still a weight of responsibility. His love for Lily was deep in his core, and he felt his role was to protect her. I couldn't argue with that, not now, and there wasn't much else to say. Point and shoot, hope it hits the mark. As soon as the battery was flat,

Elijah would head to the bridge deck and hide in Greg's old quarters. We both knew how effective that would be.

'One more thing,' I said, handing him the last flare I could find. 'Wait five minutes, then fire this. It'll confuse them, and they'll be looking at the sky, not at me.'

'Where are you going?' said Elijah.

I nodded to the gunwale. 'Over there,' I said. 'I'm going swimming.'

Now

At this time of night, and in other circumstances, the superyacht
Escape *should have been illuminated with a dazzling array of
lighting – a shout-out to surrounding vessels, to aircraft, and to the
crew and guests. Spotlights, deck lights, LED walkways. Underwater lanterns and multicoloured lasers, turning the water every hue
under the sky. Fireworks were a regular evening spectacle on a yacht
this size, though perhaps not in weather like this.*

*Tonight, the only glow was from a dying flare – the last one,
launched in desperation. It glided towards the water, dancing as gusts
of wind took it this way and that, before it was extinguished, unseen,
under the black water of the Atlantic.*

*The superyacht drifted, thousands of miles from land, rising and
falling in the white-crested swell. Water crashed over her bows and
stern, swamping the lower decks, swirling into every corner. The
metal hull shuddered under the strain, vibrations travelling deep
inside the vessel. Thunder rumbled as wind screamed across every
surface, with no sign of relenting.*

*Outside, battling the wind and rain, Camila limped along one of
the side decks, pausing to peer into the swirling waters below, holding
tight to the rail. The floor was slippery, the yacht's motion uncontrolled, unpredictable. She shivered against the wind, tasting the salt
spray, feeling the drop in temperature the storm had brought with it,
tugging at the zipper on her jacket. Was that movement – footsteps,
a splash in the water? In this weather, it would be a miracle to hear
anything useful at all.*

She remained motionless for a few seconds, ensuring she kept to the darkness, out of the range of any feeble lanterns swinging in the windows, avoiding the probing search of a flashlight from above. Satisfied, she headed forward, ducking inside, towards the stairwell.

34

I waited for Elijah to launch the flare before dropping over the side of the bridge deck, hitting the water with a practised feet-first surface dive, creating as small an impact as possible. The water wasn't cold, and I went deep, pushing away from the hull.

I kicked out, surfacing on the crest of a wave, which showered my face in froth, hitting my nose and mouth, causing an involuntary gasp. But I held it back, keeping my mouth closed, my breath in. I'd trained in seas like this until swimming in them was second nature. A frightening hell for most normal people, the fifteen-foot waves peppered with heavy rain were simply inconvenient to me, hiding my target with each peak and trough, causing me to guess my heading in the darkness – in this case, the rear launching platform of the *Escape*, and the tender garage.

Jumping had been the quicker option, and with the *Nakatomi* this close, I needed to be fast, and stealthy. I also wanted Camila to believe I was hiding with the others.

I swam to the rear of the *Escape*, timing my approach before grabbing a side rail on the launching platform. It lifted me clear of the water on the next wave, and I grabbed with my other hand, pulling myself on to the deck.

I crouched, checking my surroundings, keeping against the wall. I hoped the *Nakatomi* didn't have night-vision equipment, or if they did, that they wouldn't wear the goggles until the assault. That said, I made haste towards the side garage door, popping the catch and swinging it open. The interior was pitch black and I switched on my small torch, moving around the empty space where the tender had been stored, and training the beam on the two jet skis, neither of which was feasible. Even if I could launch one of the jet skis myself – doubtful in these waves – I'd make a noisy target for any trigger-happy crew member on the *Nakatomi*, not to mention Camila. My plan would be over before I started.

I was after something much slower, something I'd seen when I first boarded. In amongst the scuba equipment was a pair of scooters – submersible swimming propellers, small battery-powered devices that could drag me through the water faster than I could swim. All I had to do was hang on to the handles.

I unloaded one of the scooters and checked it worked, before placing it to one side.

Next, I stripped to my underwear and selected a light-weight wetsuit, pulling it on, along with booties with decent rubber grips. Grabbing the largest dry bag I could find, I scoured the shelves for anything else I could use. Two bundles of 4mm rope, another torch, and a diving knife in an ankle sheath. A scuba mask and snorkel went over my head, and I threw a pair of fins next to the scooter.

As I turned to the exit, the torch beam glinted off something hanging on the wall on the far side of the garage – hidden behind a bunch of buoyancy aids I found a pneumatic speargun along with two spears and tethering lines. Not the most practical of weapons, and useless in close quarters, but I unhooked it all the same, checked the pressure, and slung it over my back. Spear fishing was not my forte, but the gun was sharp and deadly. I had very little else. The biggest drawback was the bright yellow handle, and it took a bit more searching before I found a roll of black duct tape, which I used to cover the offending colour. I dropped the roll of tape into the bag.

There are those moments – the precious minutes after you formulate a plan and before you execute it – that are filled with nerves and indecision. But experience told me the longer I delayed, the more doubts and questions would present themselves, none of which would have ready answers. I might live through the next hour, I might not, but it wouldn't be for lack of trying.

My plan was to board the *Nakatomi* with the element of surprise, something I'd lost with Camila. There was very little I could do with her barricaded in an impenetrable safe room holding both my Glock and APC. She could sit tight and wait for reinforcements.

But we couldn't.

If an armed crew from the *Nakatomi* reached us, we were finished, I was sure of it. Trapped on the sun deck, we could only watch as they took their loot and either executed us or scuttled the *Escape* and left us for dead.

The only way to change the tide was to take the offensive, and board them first – stop them ever reaching the *Escape*. I didn't know how I'd achieve it, yet, but they wouldn't be expecting me. Offence rather than defence – that was my hope, putting myself on an even footing with whatever came next. I had to assume they'd be highly trained, but so was I. And I was a vicious opponent when I put my mind to it. I'd do whatever it took.

I fixed my fins and mask, tested the scooter once more, before pushing off the platform. I kicked furiously, keen to get a decent distance before the next wave hurled me back again. The scooter's propeller bit into the water, and I steered towards the *Nakatomi*, taking a straight line. The speed was slow, the low-powered motor struggling against the force of the waves. Although I was only making one or two metres per second, it would still take me less than five minutes to cover the distance between the two vessels.

I settled into the motion, fitting my snorkel, clearing the water from it every few breaths, keeping myself low in the water. The bag dragged, the speargun twisting itself awkwardly, but I steadily approached the towering hulk of metal.

The *Nakatomi* was sitting high in the water – no doubt devoid of any cargo – the Plimsoll line high above the surface, and bouncing around like a rubber duck in a bathtub. It would make it more difficult to board, but I relied on them having a smaller vessel at the rear – a tender or RIB, ready for launching against the *Escape*. It would be difficult, though not impossible for the *Nakatomi* to pull alongside the *Escape* and offload the art, but in these seas the risk of damage was surely too high.

I scooted along the port side of the hull, keeping myself hidden, though the spotlights weren't searching the water around the hull – they were directed high, towards the *Escape*, which at this distance was barely visible – the battery lanterns and lighting casting only a very faint glow, dampened by the rain. The dying flare was barely visible. I didn't have long.

As I approached the stern, I could see not one but two small boats. The first, a large rigid inflatable already in the water, was still attached by ropes to a crane on a launching platform some three metres from the surface. I switched off the scooter and let it glide, kicking my feet until I could grab hold of the rope on the RIB's collar.

It was then I identified the second boat behind, and my heart skipped a beat. The *Escape*'s tender, the one Dan and Luan had launched just hours before, was also tethered to the *Nakatomi*. I dropped back into the water and swam to it, finding the steps at the rear, climbing slowly on board.

I knew what to expect, but it still turned my stomach. Dan's body, face down on the floor. Even in this light I could see the ragged holes in his life jacket, the dark stains of blood on his clothes, the crimson splatters across the white seating. Hit by multiple large-calibre rounds. Luan had gone overboard, drifted, but Dan took his last breaths here, in the cramped bottom of the tender.

I knelt, checking his pulse, but he was cold, long gone. Slaughtered by the crew of the *Nakatomi*, left alone and exposed, undignified in death. The controls had been shot to pieces; the fuel tank ruptured. The tender was useless, and yet they kept it, like a trophy, probably planning to sink it later, when they were clear.

I paused, feeling my heart hammering with fear and rage, fuelled by adrenaline. I was a civilian, and my actions from this point forward would break the law in every country which might prosecute – the notion of inter-national waters was fine until one country took an interest, and in this case, a few might come looking. But it was act, or die – and it wasn't only my life I was saving. I had to proceed as if I was a soldier with a job to do, and that meant no hesitation.

The platform above was bathed in light, and I could see one solitary man dressed in black oilskins working the crane, hunched over the mechanism, shielding his face from the rain. The two crane ropes were thick, climbable, but it would take me at least a minute or two to grapple my way up. Better to climb the tender's single rope. Harder, but not impossible.

I waited, gripping the gunwale of the tender, letting it take me as it thrashed around. One minute, then two. The man remained where he was, hunched over. He spoke into a radio, the outline of the walkie-talkie visible in the light, but the sound muffled by the wind. I was perhaps five metres from him, and he was side-on to me, but not looking my way. He seemed more concerned with shielding his face from the rain and wind, tucking his hood over his eyes. I guessed he had been told to stay on the crane and watch the RIB until they were ready. Guard duty. We'd all been there. I'd almost sympathize in other conditions.

But I couldn't wait much longer. Once they decided to board, I'd have to kick off and hide, and miss my chance. I pulled myself to the bow of the tender, keeping low, pushing my bag ahead of me, my black wetsuit hiding my movement.

Kicking my fins off, I tucked them in my bag and slung it over my shoulders. I did the same with the scooter, feeding a rope through the handle and attaching it to my waist.

The tether holding the tender was thin and slippery in

my hands but I pulled, inching upwards, using the rubber grip on my boots against the hull. As I was about to reach the platform, a sideways wave yanked the tender away, the rope whiplashed in the air, taking me with it. I dropped two feet, hands sliding against rope – the burn ripping the skin from my palms. I bit down on the pain, used my feet to clamp the rope, take my weight.

I thudded against the hull, my breath knocked out of me, blood dripping from my hands, the ache from my shoulder wound permeating my chest.

Digging deep, I pushed down with my feet and pulled with my injured hands until the edge of the platform was within reach. Gripping with my fingertips, I performed a pull-up of the sort that always impressed my PT instructor – a rock climber's pull-up, almost impossible for most people, the strain on the hands unbelievable, even if you had the upper body strength. I didn't think, I just pulled, shoving my elbows on to the platform and kicking my feet against the hull to get me over the edge.

I'd hoped to land quietly, but the man turned, three metres from my position, and pulled his hood back. Dark eyes and a darker beard, his surprise was evident, and it gained me the vital seconds I needed. Pulling the diving knife from my ankle holster, I lunged forward, landing on him before he had a chance to speak.

He saw the knife and dodged, but I was smaller, nimbler, and threw my left arm around his neck, grappling so my body was behind him, on his back. He pushed himself backwards, thumping me against the wall, knocking what little breath I had left out of my lungs. But I held on. Taking somebody out with a knife can be a messy, violent and drawn-out action – nothing like the smooth one-stab death you'd get in a Hollywood movie. I held on as he threw himself around, gripping his neck as tightly as I could, waiting for the moment.

He was trained, knew my intentions, closed his chin to his chest, shoving me into the hard metal until the back of my head hit something solid and I nearly blacked out. I released my grip a fraction and cried out – a feint, and he took it, leaning back to throw me off. But his movement was all I needed. I tucked my knife under his chin, into his exposed neck, and sawed back and forth. The knife was sharp enough, cutting through his windpipe first, then both arteries. I held on, kept sawing until I hit bone, as the blood spurted over my hands and his knees buckled and we both went down.

I lay on top of him until he stopped moving, before pushing myself away, lying on my back, heaving the air back into my chest, trying to stabilize my vision after the knock to my head. My upper arms and shoulders screamed pain like they'd been wrenched from their sockets, the muscles torn and shaking.

The rain helped, pelting my face until I heaved myself upright, facing the body, soaked with blood and saltwater. He didn't even have a weapon. Just the radio, a set of keys, a packet of Marlboro cigarettes and a Zippo lighter. No wallet, no identification. I dragged him to the edge and kicked his body into the water.

One down.

I hesitated before venturing further into the ship, deciding I should take whatever opportunities presented themselves. The tender was useless, full of holes, so I cut the rope, letting it drift away. Disabling the RIB was next. I could climb back down or winch it up. The former didn't fill me with enthusiasm, given the state of my hands, and winching it might create a noise – the crane looked antiquated and might scream my presence when I switched it on.

Instead, I untied the scooter from my waist, then pulled the speargun from its strap and rested the barrel on the crane's controls, aiming at the RIB. It wasn't a long shot, but the motion meant I'd have to time it perfectly. It took five waves before I pulled the trigger. The gun fired with a dull thump and a hiss as the spear shot forward. It hit the side of the RIB and pierced the inflatable skin. I heard the rush of air escape and took the line, giving it a good tug, ensuring the barb took hold, ripping the fabric, keeping the hole open.

Down one of my two spears, but I was satisfied. The RIB wouldn't sink immediately – they were designed to float low in the water in the event of a puncture, but not in heavy seas – the amount of water already in the fibreglass hull, coupled with the weight of the engine and fuel would work to my advantage.

Cutting the two ropes was easy, and the deflating RIB followed the tender, disappearing off behind us, already swamped by the huge waves as it sunk lower into the water, the outboard dragging it down by the stern.

Leaving the *Nakatomi* without its boarding vessel.

35

The *Nakatomi* was an old freighter, a stark contrast to the *Escape*, no plush decks, or lounges with a choice of pastel-colour stairwells and marble fittings. The towering bridge was at the bow, on top of basic living quarters and cabins, and behind it, the rest of the hull was open, with space for dozens of metal shipping containers. Except there were no containers – just a cavernous hollow, too dark to see the bottom. The entire ship was steel, painted and rusted; a narrow walkway ran along the starboard and port sides, joining the rear platform, where I'd boarded, to the rest of the ship.

It lurched and wallowed, a deep throb signifying the engines were running, but only to maintain a static distance from the *Escape*. The bridge was alive with lights, and I scanned the walkways and windows, holding the guard's radio close, monitoring any chatter. It was silent, and remained so for several minutes, not even a buzz.

Time to move.

There was no cover on the exposed walkway, but I didn't have time to climb one of the many ladders down into the open hold, to try to find a way along the bottom, risking getting lost or stumbling upon another crew member in the dark.

I took off at a fair pace, covering the seventy metres or so in under thirty seconds, clasping my bag and the speargun to my chest. As I reached the bridge tower I slowed, counting the entrances – four at the rear, probably another couple on the sides.

I chose one at random – the furthest right – and approached it, holding the speargun in front of me until I was upon it, before switching to the taser, which I ripped out of its sealed plastic bag. The light flicked on – it was still operational, and charged. The speargun went over my shoulder.

The door was unlocked – no reason it wouldn't be – and swung open, the hinges greased and well used. I stepped inside, taking a breath, preparing to adopt a standard board and search procedure. We excelled at this – I *had* excelled at this, when I was serving. My skills and memory hadn't departed yet, and I swept the first corridor and adjoining rooms.

The first deck appeared to be empty of crew, used for storage, unmarked crates and boxes stacked floor to ceiling. I paused, my boots squeaking on the metal floor. Nothing. No sign of life. I completed a circuit, noting the layout – it should be the same on each deck, the bulkheads and structure repeated for simplicity and strength.

The port stairwell was clear and I proceeded upwards, wishing I at least had a proper pistol. The taser felt like a toy in my hands. The door to the next deck opened, and I was hit by heat, the smell of cooking. The lights were brighter on this deck, offering less cover. I crept forward, clearing the first two rooms – cabins with metal bunk beds and not much else. I tried to judge the number of sailors on board, but the cabins were clean, tidy – just narrow hard mattresses on wire frames. No way to tell.

Judging by the smell, the kitchen and mess were at the end of the hall. I continued, then froze, hearing the unmistakable sound of heavy boots. I slipped back into one of the dark cabins, hard against the wall, as the footsteps approached. Two people, their voices clipped and harsh.

'*Quand?*'

'*Bientôt.*'

'*Jusque là.*'

'*Nous attendons.*'

The voices thundered in the corridor, outside the cabin. I held my breath, feeling the water dripping from my hands on to the floor. The droplets made a low tapping sound as they hit the metal.

The men didn't stop, pushing open the stairwell door. I thought their footsteps went upwards, but couldn't be sure. What were they saying? Waiting for something? Waiting for Camila, perhaps?

I risked poking my head out. All clear. I listened for thirty seconds, steadying my breathing and my hands, before I stepped out, heading towards the kitchen.

There were two doors, one at each end of the long room which housed a mess table with benches, and a serving counter on the far side, behind which a chef in grubby whites stood with his back to me, cleaning a set of stoves with a dirty cloth. At the table, one man was hunched over, slurping food out of a bowl, pausing every few mouthfuls to tear a chunk of bread from a wholemeal loaf. The man wore black, and the condition of his clothes triggered a memory – the jacket was new, expensive. I flashed back to the quay in Palma. I'd watched the pilot boat passing me, a group of what I'd thought were fishermen on board, dressed in black, who'd stared at me for a little longer than necessary, a little longer than complete strangers taking a polite interest.

The man was heavyset, but not armed, no sign of holster or straps. I backed away. I couldn't take him out without alerting the chef, and it wouldn't gain me much. I had to hope he'd be eating for a little while longer.

There was nothing else on this deck, so I took the nearest stairwell and kept on heading up.

The noise of voices flooded the air from all around as I opened the door into a dark corridor. Deep laughter and multiple conversations, some in English, some in French. I heard a few German shouts from the end of the corridor. I paused, checking the doors – five along the corridor. Two on the right, three on the left. The left was where most of the noise was coming from, and I risked glancing in the first.

It was a huge common room with a widescreen TV at one end attached to an old DVD player, playing some fuzzy soap opera. I counted fifteen men, many facing the TV, slouched on sofas or folding chairs. Against the chairs rested all manner of long assault rifles – I could see Chinese-made AK47s, American AR15s and a couple of smaller SMGs I didn't recognize. Several of the men had grenade belts across their chests, all wore the same black combat clothing. A small group of four at one end were playing cards, throwing notes on to a battered plastic table.

Fifteen armed men were more than I'd been expecting, hell, more than Camila could possibly need. I backed away, checking the passageway, checking my hiding places – the room immediately behind me was pitch black, affording more storage. I entered and tucked myself into a corner, catching my breath. I could cut and run now, but I'd achieved nothing yet, and I needed to know what was in the other rooms – I needed to find the armoury, give myself an advantage, figure out some way of securing the bridge.

Sucking in another deep breath, I checked the corridor, hurrying past the first common room and towards the second door. I poked my head around the frame.

I wished I hadn't.

Smaller than the first, the second room was empty of furniture apart from a central table around which another five men huddled. Dressed and armed like the others, they faced each other, absorbed with whatever was on the table – I assumed a chart or perhaps schematics of the *Escape*, planning their attack. Their voices were low, broken English, French and German accents, deep in discussion.

'Time?'

'Within the hour.'

'The primary is on board?'

'*Ja*. A complicated passage. The storm almost fucked things for us.'

'She should have called it off.' The third voice was English, thin, cockney. 'We're skirting the limits here. Boarding is gonna be a fucking nightmare.'

'Don't ever repeat that.' The second voice again. 'She's running the show. All of this, the ship, the money, the weapons. It's all her. You make a comment like that, and someone talks, you don't get another chance. She has a long memory.'

Camila. The *primary*.

Camila was the mastermind, not the hired help. The primary, on board the *Escape*. My heart thumped a little faster.

The first guy agreed. 'Remember that guy in Mexico? Who had his arm cut off at the elbow with a saw?'

A pause.

'That was her. He pissed her off once. Never again.'

'OK. Fuck. I didn't mean –'

'We do what we're told, and if she wants this yacht disappeared, then it disappears. Got it?'

Clearing his throat. 'I got it. No problem.'

'Likely resistance?' The first voice.

'None. The crew is incompetent and reckless. No end of problems. She was forced to dispose of a couple ahead of schedule. The captain caught her on the sat phone. The engineer saw something he shouldn't have on the CCTV. She's been playing them while trying to secure things, a little misdirection. I think she enjoys it.'

'Fuck. Sounds like she's had fun and games.'

'Makes it easier for us.'

'Security?'

'One. A woman. Some washed-up soldier. Unarmed.'

A couple of them chuckled, low, sinister.

'Perhaps you can show her your gun, Gustav. Something for her to suck on while I find some proper ass.'

A burst of laughter.

I felt my temperature rise, partly anger, partly fear.

I knew about such operations. *Asset retrieval*, Jason had called it. The people who did the jobs the big crime syndicates couldn't or *wouldn't* do themselves – the wet work that was messier than most. For that, Camila would claim a big cut, a huge percentage. And when we're talking £750 million, even taking off the expenses of the *Nakatomi* and its private army, it would be huge.

I had a fair idea what would happen if this group of men caught and overpowered me – the rules of war didn't apply to mercenaries out here, and I knew the stories of female captives in the lawless oceans. I shuddered at the thought, but knew I couldn't let the fear overcome me. Not now. I was dead anyway, so I may as well go down fighting.

'Orders?' the first voice.

'Waiting for the final call. She's been holed up below decks – she'll stay hidden until we approach, then meet us at the stern platform. We clean up, level by level. OK?'

'And the friendly on board? Are we off-loading them?'

I froze. *Wait.*

Another chuckle. 'Shit. Friendly goes the same way as the others. We offload the primary only.'

A chorus of OKs around the table.

'Get your teams ready. And radio Franz, will you? He's pissing about with the RIB outside. Probably fucked off for a smoke.'

'Will do.'

I paused, my limbs reluctant to move, my injured hands shaking, but I managed to back into the room opposite, across the corridor, pushing the door half closed behind me. Darkness and silence. A moment to catch my breath.

A *friendly*? What the fuck? Camila had a *friendly* on board? My skin crawled, pulse thundered. Sarah, you *fucking idiot*.

Once again the guilt piled on, the panic rose up. It dawned on me, that I'd been played all this time. That's how she was able to dispose of Greg? Jack?

So who? I struggled, cycling through everyone, looking for the signs, came up wanting.

I rummaged in my bag, pulled my radio out of its plastic bag. Raising the mic to my lips, I paused. Who would answer? Karis? And could I trust her? For all of the events so far, how was I to know what was real? Did she really love Greg, or was it all an act?

You can't have two captains on a ship, Sarah.

No, not Karis. Please. I tapped the mic. But who else might hear the broadcast? This wasn't military encrypted radio. Anybody scanning the airwaves would hear me.

Shit, Sarah. Think. You can't know who it is, you don't have time to figure it out, not until you get back on the *Escape*. If Plan A was storming the bridge, you'd better think of a Plan B pretty fucking quickly.

Focus. I could hear Kay in my head, clear as day. Task by task, Sarah. You've been thrown a shit-ball. Deal with it when you can, not before. Right now you need to focus on the immediate threat.

I'd seen twenty armed men – more, if you counted the one in the mess and whoever was on the bridge. With a four-person Royal Marine fire squad, weapons and surprise, my team might have succeeded in taking this lot out, but it would have been bloody and risky. On my own . . . no fucking way.

I sucked in a breath. If those mercenaries were right, and Camila had a partner on board, then I needed to execute my next move even more ruthlessly, and faster than ever.

Kay was correct, as usual.

'Shit, Kay. I wish you were here.' My voice hissed into the darkness, and his response was instant.

I'm right here, Sarah. Do what you do, I'll be watching.

Four deep breaths, heart rate down. Another four, clear your head.

Don't let him down.

My eyes adjusted to the dim light of the room, my gaze landing on a fully stocked gun rack and crates of armaments. I'd backed into an armoury with enough munitions to start a small war. It should have been a relief, and yet the sight of it made my stomach turn. This operation must have cost millions, which, when you considered the prize, was small fry. But it meant it was expected to work. These men weren't returning home until they had what they came for. They weren't going to let a few inconvenient crew members get in the way – or one washed-up marine.

I pushed the door closed – leaving an inch or so to hear if anybody approached – and checked out the gun rack. I scanned the rifles before selecting a modified AR15 with optic sights and folding stock. I released the bolt and checked the chamber – it looked brand new, never fired. I placed it back on the rack and grabbed the next, an identical model but with some signs of wear – I'd always favour a gun that's already been fired over one straight out of the factory.

I opened the ammo crate beneath the rack, grabbing several 30-round magazines. I took an ammo belt and loaded it full – four across my chest, another two magazines into the dry bag. I loaded one into the rifle and flicked the safety off, selecting the 3-round burst. I checked the door, scanning the room to see what else I might use.

A SIG pistol and holster were next, tight around my waist, one magazine loaded and another in the belt. I clipped it against my body before crouching next to a large crate with a familiar warning stamp on the outside of it.

The crate was full of what we called C-4 demolition blocks, plastic explosive ready moulded and packaged into big enough lumps to blow a bridge, a building ... even a ship. Was this destined for the hull of the *Escape*? A few of these would make short work of that delicate white hull. I had a brief bizarre vision of the grand piano from the lounge exploding in a flash of white faux-ivory keys and splintered hardwood, the strings creating a death cry of sound as it disintegrated.

Each demolition block had an electronic detonator on the side with a digital readout and two buttons – one to set the delay, the other to start or stop the timer. The last time I'd seen this much explosive was back in basic training, and my heart skipped another beat, the tendrils of anxiety only kept at bay by the constant flood of adrenaline, and the imaginary words of Kay teasing my ears.

Keep going, Sarah. You probably know what you're doing, and if you don't, you'll figure it out.

And it was the memory of Kay that suddenly made everything so simple – of an exercise where we'd calculated the charges wrong and blown not just the doors off the training building, but the frame and most of the front wall. We'd got in the shit for that one, but at least we'd know for next time. You could do a lot of damage with a small amount of explosive.

As I lay four charges out at my feet, I examined the

detonators for breakages or anything which might signify a fault, before pausing, catching my breath, calculating.

It might just work.

I knew what I must do.

It took all of thirty seconds to prepare the blocks and place them into my dry bag, one on top of the other. Four was overkill, but I hefted the bag on to my back, grabbed my rifle and headed for the door.

My timing was off. A few seconds earlier and I might have made my exit without a fight. But the door opened and a thick bearded man walked in, heavy boots, wearing an ammo belt, a side holster with a pistol. He had his head down, staring at the screen of his mobile phone.

I had nowhere to go.

The man looked up. He took a second to register me – a dark-haired woman in a wetsuit with dripping hair and speckled with blood, a rifle aimed at his chest.

Our eyes met. The surprise in his was resolved quickly, as he made a judgement – the correct one. We both knew only one of us was leaving the room alive.

He dropped the mobile phone and went for his gun, swift and practised, arm slapping to his side. But my finger was already on the trigger, and the three rounds hit his chest before he'd even closed his hand around the pistol grip.

The sound was deafening in the room. My ears rang, the smell of cordite filled the air as he staggered backwards, hitting the wall, slumping to his knees, pirouetting on to his back.

His gun remained in the holster. I didn't wait to see the result, didn't look him in the face, didn't see the shock and pain in his eyes, or give him the courtesy of another human being's hand to hold in his final seconds of life. I had no choice but to leave him staring at the ceiling, gasping his last breaths as I jumped over his legs, throwing the door open, sprinting into the corridor and towards the left-hand stairwell.

The first bullet hit the wall above me before the door closed.

Two steps at a time, I raced downwards. I heard shouts from above, doors slamming, heavy boots pounding the floor – sending vibrations through the stairs. The door to the corridor on the next floor opened. I sent two bursts into it, not looking as I hurtled past. A scream followed me, more shouts from above. I heard two shots, two rounds whizzed past my head, ricocheting off the cold metal of the floor.

I was outside, into the driving wind, forcing myself to stop as I surveyed the exposed walkway towards the stern. How long did it take me to cover it? Thirty seconds? Longer, carrying all the explosives. Too long. I'd be cut down in my tracks.

No time, Sarah.

I ran to the first ladder and slid down it, into the depths of the hull, as the door crashed open behind me.

The *Nakatomi* was not only more basic than the *Escape*, but smaller, the maze of walkways at the lower levels providing little cover. The crew knew where I'd gone, and the searchlights lit up the floor around me as they tried to locate their unwelcome guest.

The walkways at the bottom of the hold – those which ran alongside the rusty and pocked flooring where the shipping containers would normally be stacked ten high – were below the waterline, and I kept to the sides, where the floor of the hold met the hull, nothing between me and the ocean but half an inch or so of old steel. I could feel the trembling water behind it, waiting for its chance.

I didn't hesitate, tucking the first charge against a welded seam and bulkhead, pushing it against the metal, wanting to check and recheck before I hit the button. But a searchlight hit my face a second later, the bullets peppering the floor in front of me. I triggered the detonator and ran, counting the seconds and the distance. More shouts, single shots, controlled. These were no cowboys or jihadi child soldiers – they sought out their target before firing – the rounds hitting the walkway barely inches away from me as I sprinted. I adjusted my speed, weaving, creating as difficult a target as I could, keeping myself low and in the shadows.

I placed the second charge behind a pile of discarded metal cylinders halfway along the length of the ship, adjusted the time, and pressed the button, counting the seconds in my head as I raced towards the stern. Not far to go, but the shouting was closer and louder over the wind, and as I looked up, I could see three figures stalking the passageways above, high-powered torches attached to their rifles, all aimed downwards.

As I watched, one of the figures crouched, dropping his rifle, holding his hands to his ears. He shook his head vigorously. The man next to him did the same. We must have been close enough for Elijah to give them a blast of noise. Not enough to disable, but to disorientate, which was more than I'd hoped for. I thanked him under my breath, using the distraction to shoulder my rifle and take aim, squeezing off three bursts before moving forward. It would give away my position, but I couldn't risk them reaching the stern before I did.

I was dismayed to find the walkways in the hold curved inwards, away from the outside of the hull, over the engine bays, giving me nowhere to place the third charge. Should I head back, look for a way down even lower?

The clock in my head answered, screaming at me I didn't have time. I stared at the charge, then over the side of the walkway, made a quick adjustment to the timer and dropped it over the side. I didn't hear it hit the hull, and hoped it hadn't landed in a foot of bilge water – which might screw with the timer and detonate too early . . . or not at all.

Almost at the rear platform, I crouched down to unpack the final charge. I set the time and placed it at the foot of the ladder where it was welded to the hull.

Four charges, timed under gunfire, the delay relying on my mental clock. What could go wrong? All I had to do was climb the ladder, grab the scooter – if it was still there – and throw myself off the stern.

I'd placed my foot on the bottom rung when the searchlight found me again. Two rounds hit the rungs above me and I dropped off, rolling into cover behind a thick ventilation shaft, squeezing myself between it and the hull. It was hot – exhaust from the diesel engines – and I burned the outside of my hand, yanking it away before the skin stuck to the metal. Turning to my left, I could see the brick of C-4 at the base of the ladder, the red light flashing, just out of reach. I couldn't cancel the timer, or grab the brick and throw it further away.

The seconds ticked away in my head. More rounds pelted around me. The crew had my position and didn't intend for me to leave it. Twisting around, I tugged my rifle into a rough aim and fired until the magazine clicked empty. I loaded a new one and kept firing, counting down in my head. It would be a close call – far too close for comfort – but I didn't have much choice about what I did next.

The alarm went off in my head two seconds before the first charge detonated, with a deep thump which sent vibrations through the entire ship. I couldn't see the blast from where I was hiding, but I heard a fresh rush of water, the sound of screeching – metal upon metal, the seam of the ship being ripped open.

My counting was off – too fast – and the second charge exploded after my count, this time close enough for me to feel the shockwave reflecting off the inside of the hold, a rush of noise and chaos and uncontrollable damage.

The firing stopped. The shouting intensified – panicked and urgent – the crew's priorities shifting as they realized my intent, and that they'd been too late to stop me.

It was now or never.

I pulled myself out from behind the exhaust vent, firing more rounds towards the walkways before climbing the ladder as fast as I could, waiting for the retaliation, for the bullets to hit me – my back, my legs, raining death from above.

But the only thing that hit me was the shock from the third charge – a deeper boom, guttural, and ground shaking – sending painful tremors through the metal structures, nearly knocking me from the ladder. My left foot slipped and for a moment I was hanging by my hands, the pain from my torn and damaged palms registering as a dull and distant trauma, my body reminding me I could only keep going for so long.

I reached the top of the ladder and hit the ground, rolling to my left, on to my feet.

Tick, tock, Sarah.

I was in single figures now.

Five seconds before the final charge went up.

I scrambled to the loading platform, feet sliding on the deck.

Four.

Past the crane, I grabbed the scooter, pulled the fins out of my bag and hurled them into the water.

Three.

Grabbed my snorkel and mask, yanked it over my neck, slung my rifle on its strap.

Two.

I leapt into the darkness.

36

Shards of metal fired past my head as the rush of air flipped me, tumbling me forward into the crest of a wave. I emerged too close to the *Nakatomi*, and turned, kicking as hard as I could, looking for the scooter. My fins floated a few feet away and I swam to them, jamming them on to my feet.

I kicked on the spot, searching in vain, but the scooter had disappeared, dipping beneath the waves. Trying to keep my head above the white crests of each wave, I filled my lungs, over and over, feeling the strain in my chest, the scream of my muscle fatigue, the mental triggers telling me I was almost done, that I couldn't make the final few hundred metres, that giving up was my only option.

Slip beneath the waves, close your eyes, the pain will be over soon.

But I heard my own scream of defiance above the waves and the wind and the increasing pitch of the *Nakatomi*'s engines as the ship listed to starboard, lifting one of its propellers half out of the water, firing a horizontal blast of white water towards the stern. I clamped down on it, slipped the mask over my face, and kicked forward, away from the sinking hulk of the freighter, and towards the *Escape*.

I didn't look back, focusing instead on the swim, getting in the zone, pacing myself as the distance closed, my chest heaved, cramps threatened in my calves and thighs.

I thought I heard shouts, isolated cries, whistles blowing. I tucked my head into the water and kicked.

The swim took me a little over twenty minutes, by my internal count.

The *Escape* was perhaps five hundred metres from the stricken *Nakatomi* and drifting, taking it further away with each passing minute. I stopped twenty metres from the launching platform, keeping myself low, out of sight, trying to scan the darkness. It might have been a trick of the light, but the platform looked closer to the water than before. It was hydraulic, so could have been moved, but as I closed the distance, I thought the *Escape* was sitting lower than it should be.

I kicked, bobbing in the black water, waiting for each wave to toss me up and drag me back, searching for any sign of life. Satisfied the stern was clear, I approached the platform and heaved myself up, rolling over until I was safe.

My body screamed stop, but my mind overruled it. *If* my plan on the *Nakatomi* worked, I still had a long way to go, facing not only Camila but an unknown foe. For the latter, I'd withhold nothing in my retaliation. I'd been fucked over enough by the woman in charge. My trust was shattered. Her crony would face deadly resistance without a moment's hesitation.

I only hoped I could do it without hurting the rest of them.

My rifle came off my back first. I gave it a shake, knowing it would be fine – designed to work in all theatres of war, a brief submersion in saltwater wouldn't hurt.

Kicking my fins to one side, I took stock, casting my gaze towards the *Nakatomi*. It was hard to see at this distance the damage I'd caused. The lights flickered all over the bridge and along the hull, but the darkness hid its position in the water. I wondered if that would work to my advantage now – whether Camila was in constant radio contact, whether she knew, yet.

It wasn't a question of *if* it sank, but *when*. The four charges of C-4 between them would have created catastrophic damage at each detonation point in the hull. No amount of bailing or pumping would fix that. I'd give them a few hours at most.

Rifle up, I nudged open the door to the tender garage, creeping in, thankful for the grip and silence of my rubber boots. I didn't use the torch, my night vision honed after the long dark swim back – but the garage was empty and I continued forward.

Through the bulkhead, keeping my rifle up. I couldn't have predicted what Camila might do while I was gone, but I'd been forced to make the choice – take out the bigger threat and come back for her. I hoped I wasn't too late.

Tank deck, engine room, I stepped over the threshold to the sounds of a muffled voice up ahead. Female, high pitched. I froze, listening.

Again, I heard it, coming from the far door, outside the engine room.

I took my eyes off the shadows, raced forward.

My mistake.

Straight into a wall of pain.

My muscles tensed, a full body cramp, my legs dropped from under me as my fingers lost their grip. My rifle hit the ground a second before I did.

I lay on my back, the metal slats digging into my spine,

the pain unbearable, until it wasn't – the cramps suddenly dissipated, my fists unclenched. *Shit*. I'd only been hit with a taser once before, in training, and I already knew I'd lost the advantage.

The shot had given my assailant what they needed. I heaved myself into a seated position on the metal floor, watching as they swung the barrel of my rifle to point at my chest. My hands remained in front of me. I couldn't pull my pistol out of the holster in this position.

I swallowed.

'You,' I said, feeling the emotion bubbling up, the recognition, the humiliation. My cheeks burned.

'I'm sorry, Sarah.'

He still looked at me with those puppy-dog eyes, except this time they were full of shame – wet, blank against his reddening cheeks. His hands trembled as he clasped the rifle.

'Why?' I kept my voice calm, but my insides were torn up, my own eyes filling.

How stupid could I be? Of all the bastards on this yacht, I'd got close to this one. I almost begged him to convince me I was wrong, I'd made a mistake, that in fact the one person I'd trusted, got close to, wasn't a murdering rat. I let him in. I *kissed* him, for fuck's sake, let myself imagine more, dreamed of him around me, on me, in me.

'You betrayed us,' I said. 'All of us. Greg, Jack . . .' Alongside my humiliation I could feel the rage building. At myself, as much as at him – that I'd let my guard down and been blind to his advances. Those warning signs when I saw him and Camila together – they weren't lovers, they were conspirators. But I wasn't looking for it – why would I be? I'm just the fucking security guard. Stupid and blind.

I tried to keep my peripheral vision clear, scanning the engine room. 'Where is she? Where's Camila? What have you done with the others?'

'Nothing,' he said. 'They're safe. Look. Nobody has to get hurt. She promised nobody else would get hurt.'

I saw the honesty in his eyes, but the conflict in his face. He believed what he was saying. But the gun, *my* gun, remained trained on me.

'Oh God, Arno, you fool,' I said. 'What have you done?'

'I need you to stay down,' he said. 'Please. She'll be coming in a minute.'

He bent over, sucking in a large breath. I thought he was going to vomit, but he managed to keep it in. More pleading in his eyes.

'All I need is for you to comply,' he said. 'When she's done, you'll be free to go, I promise.'

I saw the uncertainty even as he said it. What tale had he been told, what string of lies from Camila? How did he ever think this could be resolved?

I needed time. A few seconds to pull my weapon – but it was impossible, sat on my arse. I'd be dead before my hand hit the holster. If that's what he intended. Did he have it in him? I had to assume he did.

'Tell me,' I said, shuffling my bottom forward, keeping my hands by my knees, wary of the way the rifle was trembling in his hands. If he weren't careful, that trigger finger could end everything in an instant. 'Why did you do this, Arno? Help me understand.'

I didn't much care, but I tempered my anger, knowing

I needed to break him down. He sniffed, shook his head, turned behind him. My eyes followed, but there were only more shadows. Wherever Camila was, she chose not to show herself.

'I didn't . . .' he started, stuttering the words, eyes watering. 'I don't . . .'

A recent memory clicked into place. Arno leaving my cabin with a heavy holdall, the night Jack went missing. Running errands for Camila, he'd said. He hadn't lied. That was exactly what he was doing. My first days on board, the snooping in my cabin. Sizing up the task.

'My weapons?' I said. 'It was you, wasn't it?'

He paused, nodded. The gun wavered. 'To avoid people getting *hurt*, Sarah. She said I . . .'

'Money?' I said, shuffling slightly on my rear. 'Is that it? Is that why you did this? How much is she paying you?'

Another nervous look behind him. He lowered his voice to a whisper. 'You don't know what it's like, Sarah. Please understand. I didn't intend for any of this –'

'You didn't intend? At what fucking point did you try and stop it?'

He sniffed, sucked in a breath. 'I can't explain, Sarah. I'm sorry.'

'You're sorry?'

Dammit, Arno. I needed time. My hands slid slowly upwards, a millimetre.

'Tell me, Arno, seeing as I'm dead already.'

He screwed his face up. 'I'm not going to *kill* you, Sarah. You're going to be free. As soon as this is all over. I just need you to stay the fuck down, stop causing trouble.

I *told* you, just let them take what they want – all you have
to do is let them, and you live.'

The poor deluded prick. Arno had been down here the
whole time. He obviously hadn't seen the *Nakatomi*, and
Camila wasn't sharing her plans. He really thought he'd
still be getting away with a fat wad of cash. For him and
his brother. His dead brother.

Another flash of memory. How mad Arno was after
Luan's stunt with the water tanks. Luan had been trying to
sabotage Greg all on his own – he had no idea what Arno
was doing. It was desperately sad, and Luan had paid the
price for Arno's deception. We all had.

My hands were at my thighs. My right one crept up, just
an inch.

He saw it, raised his gun, pointing at my legs. 'But I will
hurt you. I don't want to, but I will.'

Fuck. My hand slid back down.

'Easy, Arno. Easy. Just talk to me. Tell me why. Help me
out here.'

He shook his head. 'It's gone too far. You have to
believe me when I say I didn't want to hurt anyone.'

'You killed Greg?'

'No! God, no,' said Arno. He shook his head vigorously. 'No, no, no. I had nothing to do with it, or Jack. I
swear.'

I stared him down. I didn't know what to believe.
'You're an idiot.'

'Look . . .'

He glanced behind him, just a split second, but enough
for me to shift my elbow an inch or so, no more.

'Camila . . . she's just a low-level member of some

recovery firm, employed to do a job. Asked me if I wanted in. She said there was money in it for both of us. Luan and me.'

Low-level, I thought. Camila was at the top, not the bottom. She'd played him well.

'You know what we're after. It's a job – a routine trans-action, nothing to worry about – and it was supposed to be non-violent. I'm not entirely stupid, I knew it was theft, but nobody was supposed to get hurt. She *promised*.' He winced as he said it.

'She promised?' I said. 'She killed Greg and Jack. Injured Harriet, shot me.' I stopped short of telling him about Luan and Dan. Not yet. His hand trembled, his fin-ger on the trigger. I couldn't risk his reaction. 'Where are the others?'

My hands moved again. Imperceptibly. My right thigh shifted, outwards.

'Still up on the sun deck. I think . . . I think they're OK.'

'It's not too late, Arno,' I said. 'Put the gun down, I can get you out of this.'

Arno was shaking his head, chewing his lips, his expres-sion a mess of guilt and confusion. I saw the turmoil. He was so out of his depth, drowning in lies, and yet he still couldn't see the end point.

He didn't know that Camila was going to kill him, too.

'I tried,' he said. 'After Greg went missing – I suspected, but didn't know. Camila came and saw me. Told me it was an accident.'

'And –'

'And I was terrified, and angry. I told her I was out. Done. She'd lied to me, and whatever she was doing, it wasn't worth this. That I was going to tell you and Karis everything.'

I watched him, confessing, the guilt pouring out. The tough guy with the gun, compelled to explain himself, even as he held me captive, awaiting his master's judgement.

But I could already guess what had happened next. People like Camila didn't offer deals like that without a little guarantee to go with them. Arno was fucked the minute he agreed to her initial offer.

'What does she have on you?'

He shook his head, surprise in his eyes that I knew, the anger and fear twisting his mouth, his jaw jutting out.

'I was set up,' he said. 'Long before this trip. Saint-Tropez. Last season. We met. We . . . you know. We shared information – about our homes, our families. She offered me money, *so much* money, and all I had to do was recommend her to Greg, do a few jobs on board, turn a blind eye. When you turned up, I was told to keep you out of the way . . .'

I swallowed. And I fell for it. All the little things that, with more focus, I might have figured out. But not when I was running around with a stupid crush in my head.

'After Greg . . . she showed me a picture of my mum's house, back in SA. A recent picture, time stamped. She said I must keep doing what she wanted, or my family home gets burned to the ground with my mum inside it. There'd be a fresh photo showing her charred remains. I had no choice, Sarah. *None.*'

So Arno was always her target. I wondered what Camila had on the rest of the crew, what else she might have used.

'After Jack, I –'

'You set him up,' I said.

He shook his head, trying to protest.

'The letter, the resignation, made it look like poor Jack was overwhelmed and chose to end it. It's fucking disgusting, Arno. Sickening.'

He swallowed, chewed his lips. No retort to that.

'You're an accessory to two murders, Arno. More. Perhaps all of us – but that won't matter, will it? Because you'll be dead, too.'

The blood drained from his face. 'Luan?' His expression was twisted, confused.

I heard a noise, from behind Arno, the far door. A door opening, then closing again, a latch being thrown. I listened, the silence of the interior contrasting with the churning water outside, thuds against the hull, vibrations in the floor, the whole yacht waiting for action.

'You still think you're getting your money, Arno? You think this ends well for you?'

He shrugged, his shoulders sagged, defeated. 'What else do I have? My mum, Sarah. I'm sorry, but it's you or her. Just stay down, or I'll be forced to make you.'

I shook my head, teeth grinding. His behaviour – acting just like the rest of us, with our suspicions and fears and barely contained panic – I should have seen his feelings were real, but caused by altogether different reasons. Arno had been carrying this burden, his belief that if he let Camila take what she wanted, we'd all go free.

But his story was enough. His confession buying me the minutes I desperately needed.

Enough for my right hand to reach my hip, enough for me to pull my pistol from its holster and at the same time scramble sideways on to my feet. My muscles protested after the taser shot and the exertion, but I reached the cover of one of the generators, a huge metal block four feet high. I adopted an aiming stance around the side of it.

Arno jumped backwards in surprise, his eyes meeting mine. He wasn't trained to react like I was. I raised my pistol, aiming at his chest. I stared into his hollow eyes.

I hesitated.

'*Enough!*'

A scream from the far doorway, followed by a short burst of automatic gunfire. The small-calibre rounds rattled off the metal wall behind my head; a ricochet caught my left hand, punching out a chunk of flesh. I felt the blood ooze out, dripping to the floor. My knuckles were numb, fractured, my ring and pinkie fingers throbbing and torn.

Camila appeared, with Lily in front of her, shuffling forward, using her as a shield. Camila's right hand held my Glock pistol with the barrel against Lily's right temple. Her left hand held my compact APC sub-machine gun, the barrel still smoking. We were twenty feet from each other, across the engine room.

I tried to keep my gun hand steady, controlled, covering the new threat. Arno ran back, but there was nowhere to go. He stood at the centre, spinning on his feet.

'You were supposed to knock her out,' snarled Camila, 'not fucking pillow talk her.'

Arno remained between us, awkwardly in the way, his head spinning back and forth, his rifle grasped inexpertly. Camila didn't have a clear shot at me. But neither did I at her.

'Christ,' said Camila, 'you can't get anything right, can

you? You were supposed to seduce her, fuck her, enjoy I don't care what with her, but at the very least keep her out of my way. Why is she still here, Arno?'

Arno took a breath, staring at Lily, whose face was pale, streaked with tears. She trembled, gasping for air with small shallow breaths.

'Camila,' he said. 'Please. I –'

'Shoot her,' said Camila.

Arno glanced at me, shook his head. 'But,' he protested, 'you said –'

'Fuck what I said, Arno,' ordered Camila. 'You fucking moron. Just shoot her.'

'Get out of the way, Arno,' I said, keeping my head down, trying to peer around the generator, finding a line of sight to Camila. But the room, though large, was full of machinery. I couldn't see her clearly; I couldn't see Lily. I couldn't risk firing.

'You said nobody else.' Arno's voice came out as a whine, desperate. Still in denial, he turned from Camila and Lily to me, and back again.

'It's over, Camila,' I shouted, 'they're not coming.'

'Arno,' she said. 'Do as I tell you. You'll go free. You and your brother, your family, as promised, with a fat wad of cash behind you. Think of your mother, Arno.'

'She's lying,' I called. Time to tell him about Luan. This was about to descend into a close-quarters gun battle, and if even one of us came out alive, we'd be lucky.

Arno paused. He took a tentative step back, towards Camila, turning to me, raising his gun. I could see his expression. I couldn't take both of them, no way. A sustained burst from that rifle and I was gone, cover or not.

'He's dead, Arno,' I shouted. 'Luan. I saw his body floating in the water. They killed him in cold blood. There is no money, no escape, Arno.'

'Don't listen to her,' screamed Camila. 'She's a liar. Shoot that fucking bitch, Arno.'

I peered up, risking a look. I needed to see his eyes.

'She's not taking you with her, Arno. You're done.'

His gun was raised, he saw me, and if he'd pulled the trigger in that instant, it would all have been over. But I held his gaze, watched his eyes sink, the spark go out, the wall of denial shatter.

He knew I was telling the truth. I saw the shock and the hurt and the betrayal all boil into one moment of fury. His body tensed, those huge chest muscles jumping as he gripped the rifle.

I saw what he was going to do, and I was too late to stop him, even if I'd wanted to.

With a scream he turned towards Camila, swinging the rifle around with him.

But he was never going to make it. Camila already had the APC raised, aimed. While Arno had to shift his entire body, all fourteen stone of muscle, all Camila needed to do was pull the trigger, a feather's weight of effort.

The gunshots reverberated, the sound wave excruciating. My ears popped, rang like a bell.

I screamed, watching in dismay as Arno staggered backwards, a simple look of disbelief on his face. He made it to the corner before sinking to his knees. The bullets had entered mid-chest, piercing his heart, his lungs, the small hollow-point bullets expanding on impact, destroying everything they hit. I watched in slow motion – the blood pumping out to the rhythm of his heartbeat, his body in shock, the confusion on his face, his eyes searching me out, locking on to mine in desperation.

I resisted the urge to race forward, forcing myself to watch helplessly as the blood emptied relentlessly from his chest. He was already fading, and I knew the outcome. I'd never be able to stop the bleeding, and even if I could, he needed surgery, an ER suite, a team of doctors. He'd never survive out here. He was dead the second she pulled the trigger.

One more face to add to my nightmares.

I stepped slowly out from behind the generator, pistol raised and aimed.

Camila appraised me, didn't laugh, snarl, show any outward emotion at the fact she'd just gunned down another human being.

'It's over, Camila,' I said, my eyes darting between her face, her left hand holding the APC, and her right hand holding the Glock against Lily's head.

'Let her go,' I said, trying to sound reasonable. 'Every person you let go works in your favour. They'll take it into account. It's one less life sentence.'

That got a laugh. A short burst of contempt. She twisted the barrel of the Glock, causing Lily to squirm, the tears in her eyes spilling over. Camila held the APC a little higher, a little steadier. One blast and I was gone. I couldn't say the same for my chances of hitting her. My pistol was aimed at the few inches of torso I could see, but the bullet could easily go left or right, taking out Lily, or missing altogether.

'The *Nakatomi*'s gone,' I said. 'It's just us.'

She'd failed, lost, her heist over. I think she knew it. The only question was how many people she killed before surrendering.

Her expression hardened again, her eyes betraying something I'd rarely seen before. A deadness, a void. I realized it had always been there – the absence of empathy or remorse – Camila's complete disregard for the rights of others, a master manipulator, unconstrained by the weakness of the human condition.

She was the perfect person for the job, exactly qualified to run an organization which stole, extorted, murdered, tortured and trafficked in order to secure their bottom line. I'd seen all manner of horrors as a soldier, the results of human anger up close – the actions of a determined mind perpetrated against the fragility of the human body. And yet in all my years on the battlefield, I'd never experienced the same shiver down the back of my neck, the same dreaded understanding as I now felt when looking into Camila's eyes, alien and bleak, realizing she didn't care one iota how many people suffered, how many died. They were incidental to her, a distraction.

Part of the job.

And with that realization came the knowledge that I'd still lost. I couldn't reason with her, appeal to her better side – there was no better side, or rather, both were the same. Both sides saw no issue with blowing Lily's brains out in front of me. Both sides would neither enjoy nor regret such an action. She would press the trigger, just as she had with Arno, and move on.

Did Camila fear death? She must know it was close, and yet she behaved as if she was invincible. But how much of that was her unwitting façade, the wall propping up her broken psyche, protecting her to the end?

I didn't know, and it was too late to find out.

My hand trembled, my aim dipped.

Camila tilted her head, pulled a thin smile. 'I think you understand,' she said, and pushed Lily forward. Shifting the Glock to the back of Lily's head, she pressed the trigger.

I drew breath.

The movement of time in a firefight slows and warps, each second drawing out as the brain goes into overdrive, every snippet of sound and vision extending. The effect of adrenaline in the brain, or perhaps just an illusion, we all experience an altered passage of time. It is this phenomenon which allows the formation of extended and detailed traumatic memories – each moment recorded in explicit and unwanted detail. These memories can often come back to haunt you. These memories will often cause post-traumatic stress. I was a case study in such matters.

But the effect gives you no edge. No superhuman ability to react. No *Matrix*-style dodging of bullets. In my experience, it just plays out in agonizing detail.

The trigger click of Camila's Glock pistol should have been inaudible over the sound of the 9mm round igniting and propelling the bullet at two and a half thousand feet per second out of the barrel and through Lily's head, past where I was standing, to embed itself or ricochet off the metal wall behind me.

But I heard it. Not a clean click, but the sound of a stoppage – every soldier's worst nightmare. The trigger had jammed, or the round hadn't loaded properly. The round didn't fire, the bullet didn't exit the barrel, Lily's life didn't evaporate in a bloody instant.

After the empty click . . .

Camila hesitated.

Her eyes moved to the Glock. It took her a full second to comprehend the stoppage, and her mistake.

In that second Lily dropped, letting her knees collapse, falling forward, exposing Camila's head and body.

I dragged my eyes from the Glock to Camila's other hand, the one holding the APC, saw it wobble, saw her finger move.

Lily was halfway to the floor when we both fired, Camila's finger against the trigger of the APC on full auto, my finger against the trigger of my single-shot SIG.

Then time sped up, our actions complete, our moments recorded.

It was just as well.

The burst from the APC hit me in the left shoulder. I spun a full circle as I collapsed, my head smashing against a metal bannister as I went down.

My single bullet hit Camila in her throat, tearing through the flesh on one side, sending a spray of tissue and blood behind her.

We hit the floor at the same time. I collapsed on to my side, facing Camila. Her eyes moved around before finding me, locked on to mine, her jaw trembling in spasm as the blood pumped from her throat, dripping through the slatted metal floor. Alive, I could feel her alien mind still calculating, still judging, still planning her next move.

As my head throbbed, my vision faltered and the shock

gripped my body, I wanted something from her, anything, an acknowledgement. A scream would do.

But she gave nothing away. There would be no apology, no recognition. No words of wisdom from this psychopathic killer. Not to me.

There would be no final words. Not from either of us.

Because I could already feel the pain seeping away, a deep cold settling in my bones. I shivered once, then uncontrollably, shaking as Camila's face began to fade and the colours blended from the white walls to a misty grey to a dark blood red.

I think my eyes closed before hers did. And I let the darkness take me.

Escape.

At last.

Epilogue

The daylight hurt my eyes. The blinding white of the room gradually came into focus and I squinted. My ears followed, registering a flood of deep vibrations and a closer, more immediate sound of hisses and beeps, of footsteps, a pen against paper, a clipboard being snapped against the end of the bed.

'Oh, you're awake.'

An American accent, young, southern, dressed in what I thought was a US Navy corpsman's uniform.

I blinked a few times. 'Where am I?'

'The USS *Sampson*, ma'am,' said the young medic. 'You had us worried for a little while – you'd lost a lot of blood.'

I stared at his freckled face, waiting for my brain to catch up, before glancing to my left and right – I was hooked up to a drip and an ECG, my left arm and shoulder were bandaged, my right leg elevated. My scalp felt tight and both of my hands numb. I lifted them – both wrapped in gauze and tape.

'What the . . . where's the *Escape*? Where's Lily? Karis?' My heart started to hammer, the ECG machine beeping its displeasure.

'Whoa there,' said the medic. 'The captain asked that he be notified the second you woke. It's not my place to answer your questions, ma'am. Please try to relax until he gets here.' The medic opened the door and left, closing it behind him.

I stared, letting my eyes adjust. The room was approximately twenty-feet square, an upgrade from my cabin on the *Escape*, but a lot more clinical. Sunlight bathed me, streaming in from the two large portholes to my left.

I shuffled upright in my bed, wishing I hadn't, as the room spun and I thought I'd vomit. Realizing my head, too, was heavily bandaged, I forced it back on to the pillow, waiting for the nausea to pass.

My thoughts competed for attention and I drifted, trying to recount those final moments on the *Escape*. Camila's parting gift, to execute Lily in front of me. The gunshot, the sound of the APC bursting with fire, the shooting pain as a bullet hit my left chest, shoulder, the force with which I fell.

Then the picture darkened. Arno. A red-tinged nightmare, a desperate feeling, scrambled thoughts as Camila and I both lay on the slatted metal. Together and apart, eyes locked, blinking, her expression, even then, unreadable, a hidden world of malice and evil.

But the image snapped away, with nothing beyond. Nothing until now, waking in this room. Safe, but in an unknown refuge.

The door clicked open and I did a double-take as a man entered – so similar in looks to Greg, I nearly called out to him in surprise. But as he came closer, I saw a stranger, dressed in whites with US Navy epaulettes. He sat on the end of my bed, offering a warm smile.

'Sir,' I said, on reflex.

I tried to lift my arm, but he grabbed it gently and laid it back down.

'Whoa,' he said. 'You leave that where it is. No saluting for you, you're a guest. I'm Captain Atherton, by the way, and the USS *Sampson* is mine. You've been on here for nearly forty-eight hours.'

Forty-eight. Shit. I nodded, wincing at the pain.

He looked me over, glanced at the ECG, at my bandages.

'Welcome back to the land of the living,' he said. 'I was worried. We –'

But my head was filled with questions and I struggled to filter them, blurting them out in rapid succession.

'The *Escape*?' I said.

The captain paused. 'Following us.'

'How did it? They? The crew?'

'OK – they're OK, Sarah. The ones we found. There'd been quite a fight on the upper decks. The chef was shot, but –'

'What? Elijah? Where –'

'He's OK,' he said. 'In the adjacent room to yours. The others took a beating, but they're recovering – clamouring to see you, by all accounts.'

'Karis? Lily?'

He frowned. 'Karis looks like she's been in a bare-knuckle fight, but she's OK. As for the young stewardess . . . apart from the scare of her life – her words, not mine – she's fine. She was asking some of our ratings about life in the Navy, as it happens. She said she might have had a bright idea about her future career.'

I chuckled, in spite of everything, feeling the throb in my forehead. I thought of everything Lily had been through, as the youngest member of the crew, the most inexperienced. What Camila had put her through at the end. Good for her, I thought.

'What happened?' I said. 'Camila . . . ?'

'Your friends stabilized you – stopped the bleeding. The bullets didn't hit anything major, passing straight through, missing your left lung by an inch. It was the knock to your head that took you out – a nasty concussion. You woke just as we arrived, told our marine boarding team to fuck off, then lost consciousness again.'

I paused, bit my lip. 'That doesn't sound like me at all,' I said. 'They must have spoken to somebody else.'

Captain Atherton laughed. 'Don't worry. Since they heard you're an ex-Royal Marine, they've been lining up outside, waiting to check on you.'

'But the *Escape*,' I said, 'Camila planned to scuttle it . . . was it –?'

'Yes, a little low in the water, by the time we arrived. The seacocks had been forced open, it was letting in water, but your crew had the presence of mind to close all of the bulkhead doors – it wouldn't have saved them, but we arrived by mid-morning, got a team of divers in. The pumps we have on board drained that little tub in a matter of hours.'

'So the *Escape*'s OK?'

'Might need some new carpets, I'm told. Plus there are a few bullet holes dotted around. The owner might want to redecorate . . .'

So the biggest question of all. I said it with a sneaking smile.

'How did you find us, Captain?'

Atherton looked at me, a broad grin appearing. 'The emergency beacons on the *Nakatomi* went off,' he said. 'They were automatic, as they are on all freighters. They triggered the moment they hit the water, which was about half an hour after somebody blew a hole in the side of it.' His grin widened. 'But you knew that would happen, didn't you?'

I paused, wondering how much trouble I might get into, admitting to the sinking of a multimillion-pound freighter in international waters. I shrugged. Fuck 'em.

'It was the only way,' I said. 'As soon as I boarded and saw the number of personnel they had, and the firepower, I knew my chances of taking the *Nakatomi* by force were out the window. I'd never make a distress call. I'd never reach anyone. But I still had to stop them – they would have killed us all.'

'So you took the next logical step – you sank an entire cargo ship, knowing their emergency beacons would trigger as soon as it went down, sending a signal out to the global satellites and listening stations, knowing we'd be monitoring them.'

I smiled. 'Too much?'

He shrugged. 'Just enough, I'd say. The *Nakatomi* was a heap of junk anyway. We sent a deep-water camera down to take a look, but I doubt anyone is going to pay to salvage it. Look, I can't tell you what the UK authorities will want to do with you, but the Feds are all over this. Your buddy Jason has been on the phone non-stop for two days. They'll put him in a dark room for a few days and pick his story to shreds, but it all checks out so far.'

I nodded. Taking it all in. So Jason was a good guy all along.

'You're lucky we were in the area. We're on a classified exercise – supposed to be out of all shipping routes. We got relayed the distress notification, tried to hail the *Nakatomi* and got no response, so set a course full steam ahead towards their last known position. You caused quite the excitement, Sarah. I had my marines fighting each other to get on board your yacht. One of them said something about a hot tub.'

I smiled. 'The crew of the *Nakatomi*?'

'We plucked fourteen alive out of the sea,' said Atherton. 'And four bodies. Their lifeboats were blown to pieces and they surrendered without a fight, once we bore down on them. Not even they were stupid enough for that. A few of them were suffering hearing issues – some were foolish enough to swim towards your yacht, and I think that crew of yours blasted them with your sound cannon.

'We don't know who most of them are – they aren't talking. We've identified a few – mercenaries for hire. A few ex-special forces out of South America and Israel. They're not giving up anything, and I doubt they will until the Feds and the DEA get their hands on them, and start cutting some deals. Anyway . . .' he patted the edge of the bed. 'Enough. I just wanted to personally check you were OK and offer you my services – anything at all you need, you just holler, OK? The medic says you need rest. There'll be time for all of this when we reach stateside.'

'No,' I said. 'Wait. Camila? The hostile on the *Escape*? The one who orchestrated all of this. She . . .'

Atherton nodded, a sympathetic smile. 'She died from a gunshot to the throat, bled out within minutes. There was nothing your crew could have done, even if they'd wanted to. Now . . .' He stood, opened the door. 'Rest,' he said. The door closed behind him.

Camila was dead.

I waited for the surge of pleasure, but it never came. Another body, another waste of a life. Camila was a professional criminal, a killer without a conscience. Did that make it easier? No. Not for me. There was no pleasure in taking a life, only another dark notch in my psyche, a growing tally of bodies.

Another face to see in my dreams.

But it had been necessary.

It was her or me. Her or my crew.

And I'd had a job to do.

Lily found me shortly afterwards, followed by Jason, and a rather bruised Karis – one eye was closed and the other had a sutured cut under it.

They hovered at the end of my bed.

'We know about Arno,' said Karis. 'Luan was just a bad egg, but Arno was something else entirely. I'm sorry, Sarah.'

I wondered what they knew. The US marines would no doubt document what they'd found in great detail, and there'd be a trail to Arno's involvement – it would all come out in time. His coercion, the threat to his family. But not today.

'How is Elijah?' I asked.

'The medics say he'll be OK,' said Lily. 'He might need a stay in hospital when we arrive – Camila shot his leg up pretty badly.'

'And you two are . . .'

Lily gave a shy smile. 'Parting as friends,' she said. 'I think I have an idea of what I want to do next, Sarah, and we agreed it just won't work. Elijah's a decent guy. He understood . . . he wasn't happy, but he understood.'

'Good for you,' I said. 'I'll put in a word for you. You'll look cute in uniform.' I gave her a wink.

'Plus he'll be busy now, working for his new captain.' Lily nodded towards Karis.

'Oh?'

Karis gave me a sheepish smile, wincing as she moved. 'Harriet offered me a job – permanent captain of the *Escape*, working for the family. I . . . I haven't accepted yet.'

I watched her face, the spark of hope in amongst the darkness, the glimpse of a possible future, everything she'd dreamed of, yet never in these circumstances.

'You'll make the right choice,' I said, reaching out, taking her hand.

'Another new chapter,' said Karis. 'We'll see.'

'So Harriet's OK?'

A nod. 'Resting. She's been given the all-clear, but they've sedated her.'

But safe. All of them were safe. That's all I needed to hear.

It turned out that Camila knew the *Nakatomi* was going down before our confrontation. They must have been in radio contact, and she went nuts – climbing up the levels and unleashing her anger on the sun deck. Elijah had been exposed and fallen first. The barricade held for a while until she managed to squeeze through.

'We thought that was it,' said Lily, 'but Karis jumped in front of all of us, told Camila to go to hell. Camila beat her to the floor, and grabbed me by the neck.'

I smiled at Karis. She'd stood tall when it mattered,

shielding her crew when all was lost. She deserved to be captain.

'Then Camila said we were going below to wait for somebody, to say goodbye.' Lily swallowed. 'I think she meant you.'

I nodded. Camila's delusion that she could still win. Even in the engine room, Arno's senseless death. She didn't care about the waste, as long as more people suffered along the way.

'The captain said you've been busy,' I said to Jason.

He winced. 'You could say that. Our suspicions were corroborated by Harriet's family – the UK's National Crime Agency debriefed us via a teleconference yesterday – they've already picked up two of the syndicate, caught trying to flee the UK via Heathrow Airport.

'They've cut a deal – spilled whatever they knew, which wasn't much more than we'd figured. Nikolas Aubert hired the Milieu syndicate and Camila to pull off the most murderous heist in recent history. The original plan was for the *Nakatomi* to issue a distress signal – the *Escape* would offer assistance, as is proper etiquette at sea, and they would have boarded us.'

'Then why didn't it?' I said. 'Issue the distress signal?'

'Our speed,' said Jason. 'Greg was pushing us much faster than planned, because of me. His – and my – actions were responsible for so much that went wrong, but what it did mean was the *Nakatomi* fell behind. They were simply too far away – it screwed with their schedule. You might remember Camila urging us to slow down on several occasions. Then the storm hit and . . . well. You know the rest.'

We all did. We'd lived it, hour by hour, day by day.

'But I need to tell you, Sarah.' Jason rubbed his chin, shuffling awkwardly. 'The company and I – that is, Harriet's family – owe you a debt of gratitude. You saved the *Escape*, the near priceless works of art, not to mention the people in front of you. It was all down to you, Sarah, and we'll be forever grateful. You saved our lives. Hell, you saved my life – and I was nothing but an arse to all of you.' He grinned, glancing at Lily and Karis. 'Mitch can expect a pretty good reference, if you need one.' He winked at me.

'You *were* an arse,' I said, as his grin turned to a laugh, 'but thank you.' I twisted on the mattress, trying to shift my bum, which was fast going numb. 'And Nikolas?'

'Disappeared. Interpol are on his tail,' said Jason. 'I guess we'll find out in time.'

I nodded. 'There's one thing that still bugs me,' I said. 'Why did Camila kill the fire suppression system? It made no sense at the time, and still doesn't. The CCTV sabotage was deliberate, probably Arno, but the loose wire wasn't intended to start a fire and jeopardize the heist. I don't get it.'

Jason raised his eyebrows. 'She didn't *want* the *Escape* burning. Not then – not when it happened. We think Arno screwed up while trying to wipe the CCTV disks. He sabotaged the power supply, fried the disks – probably under instruction from Camila – but he got it wrong, or at least, bad luck.'

I thought back to Jack's comments at the time – *bad luck*. No shit.

'However,' continued Jason, 'the NCA gave us a few examples of previous heists linked to the syndicate. It's their MO to incinerate the crime scenes before they leave – high temperature, removing any last traces of evidence – so she probably intended to burn the whole yacht when they'd finished. It wouldn't have mattered much, with the *Escape* at the bottom of the Atlantic, but this group looks long-term. If for some reason the *Escape* was ever salvaged, it would have been burned beyond recognition – and the art, supposedly, with it. A fire at sea, with the tragic loss of all lives. They weren't planning on blowing holes in it. Camila's syndicate doesn't leave traces. They are a professional outfit – the worst, and the best.'

'Until they met Sarah,' said Lily, giving my foot a squeeze, one of the few parts of my body which didn't hurt.

'Until they met Sarah,' repeated Karis, nodding at me, her tired eyes sparkling in the daylight, masking the grief that would pour out in the next few days and months.

But I'd keep in touch with her, check in every now and then . . . I would with them all. I felt a new closeness to these relative strangers in front of me, not unlike the brotherly and sisterly bonds in the military – the knowledge of something you've shared, that nobody else can understand, or ever will. A trauma, a journey travelled. And at the end of it, a sense of understanding, camaraderie. Closure. Others fell, but we survived.

The door opened and my young medic poked his head in.

'I have a call for you, ma'am. On the tablet – says he's your employer. Says to wake you up and give you a strong coffee, make you speak to him . . . I can tell him you're busy if you –'

'No,' I said. 'I'll talk to him. Give him here.'

Lily and the others excused themselves, closing the door softly behind them.

I flipped the tablet to face me and pulled my most sour expression. I was met with possibly the biggest grin I'd seen since I'd departed Mitch's office.

'You fucking beauty!' said Mitch, his face lighting up at the sight of me. He was leaning back in his office chair, creaking away as his eyes darted all over me. 'Look at you. All beat up. You little ripper!'

My sour expression broke in the face of Mitch's enthusiasm. 'Hi, Mitch,' I said. 'How are you?'

'I'm fucking ace,' he said. 'How are you? Got into any gunfights recently? Sunk any ships?'

'You're still not funny,' I said.

'Killed any international criminals?'

'Still. Not.'

Mitch looked down below the screen. 'I have loads more,' he said.

'Save them.'

His laughter died slowly; his smile faded. He looked at me with the calm knowledge of one soldier to another. He wouldn't ask for the actual details of what happened. He'd wait for me to offer, and if I never did, that would be fine by him. Until then, he'd tease, shout, make sure I knew he was there.

'Have the police been in contact?' I said.

He nodded. 'Some detectives from the NCA. I think they'll want a quick chat and a cup of tea with you when you get back. But they seemed nice – pleased, even. They talked about this as some sort of major win for them.'

'I'm sorry,' I said. 'Business might suffer . . . when this

gets out. I'm supposed to keep the boats safe, not sink one and shoot up the other.'

'Are you kidding?' he said. 'The rumours are already out that my security company stopped a hijacking by the French Milieu syndicate. The phone hasn't stopped ringing. I've got every marine security broker trying to book me over the next few years. I've got private owners in Europe asking for my fees. Come next week I'll be hiring like there's no tomorrow.'

'Shit,' I said.

'Exactly,' he said. 'And you know what?'

'No.'

'I want you right here with me, Sarah. I'll cut you in, as part of the company, we'll work something out. You're my star player, and I need you. Just say yes now and we can argue later.'

'Mitch, I —'

'Say yes or I'm hanging up.'

'I . . . would Kay have been proud of me, Mitch? What I did? I didn't save them all, Mitch. I couldn't. I didn't even know —'

Mitch closed his eyes for a few moments, nodding to himself, removing any trace of humour. He opened them, fixed his eyes on the camera.

'Kay would never have pulled off what you did,' he said. 'None of us would. Not in a million years. You're a cut above, Sarah. It's not just physical, even though a lot of us guys like to think it is. It's the mental attitude, the ability to keep fighting when all is lost, the sheer relentless drive and determination to do the right thing, whatever it takes. You've got it, Sarah. Not a lot of people have. Hell, *of course* Kay would have been proud. He'll be smiling down at you now. And Sarah?'

I kept the lump trapped in my throat, feeling the burning sensation at the top of my nose, the tears threatening to flood my eyes. I held on.

'Yes, Mitch,' I whispered.

'He'll be wanting to see what you do next. He'll be expecting a lot. Don't let him down.'

The afternoon waned; the visitors were kept at bay by fresh orders from my medic. The storm had veered to the south and we pushed through summer sunshine, heading for the Florida coast.

Only ten hours away.

The warship became motionless to me, the slow roll almost imperceptible, the warm air flooding my body, my skin, my lungs, until I finally let myself drift, eyes closing, each and every one of my tired muscles relaxing, accepting they had nothing to do but rest.

In my half-lucid sleep I already knew things were different. I was different.

I waited for my dreams of Kay to appear – the steady and familiar film-reel of his final days, his final hours, and the slow, agonizing moments as I held his dying broken body in my arms. I waited for the guilt, and the regret and the second-by-second rewind of my actions on that fateful day. I waited for my body to react, the sweats and the palpitations, the crushing panic as it rose up and demanded that I suffer. I waited for the same nightmare that greeted me every time I relaxed. My torment, seeking me out, reminding me of what I'd done.

But I waited. And I dreamed. And my body followed my mind – and my mind went to a different place. A better place.

In this place, this time, the compound in Afghanistan refused to appear, refused to take over. Instead, my vision was dominated by Kay's gorgeous smile, my ears filled with his booming laugh. My heart melted with his warmth and his charm and his every last word.

Another memory resurfaced. And another. All of our time together – every moment, every laugh, every joke – suddenly erupted into my mind, a new reel of our life together, waiting to be explored again, waiting to be watched in my dreams.

Dreams of how he wanted to be remembered, laid out ready for me to devour them.

The pain would never go away, never be forgotten, but the message was clear, my mind accepting – it was time to move on, and the blame stopped now.

Let myself dream, let myself remember.

Kay smiled, broke away, sat at the bar on the sun deck of the *Escape* in his dress uniform, watching me. He grabbed a shot glass of whisky, raised it in the air before necking it, slamming the empty glass down on the wood.

That'll do, he said.

Acknowledgements

Publishing a novel is a hugely collaborative effort, and I must personally thank a number of people who worked their magic to get this book out of my head and into your hands:

Julie Fergusson at The North Literary Agency is probably the best agent in the world. A brilliant friend and advisor on every aspect of my writing, shaping this novel from idea to finished draft and squeezing the absolute best out of me at each and every stage. Also thanks to Lina Langlee and the rest of the team for their support.

My publishing team: Joel Richardson and Grace Long at Penguin Michael Joseph – the cream of the crime and thriller editorial world. They put such huge energy and expertise into this book, I'll be eternally grateful for the work and commitment they've shown me. The editorial process was intense and delightful – I enjoyed every minute. Also special thanks to Nick Lowndes, Shan Morley, Jill Cole, Eugenie Woodhouse, Lucy Hall, Ellie Morley, Jen Harlow, Percie Edgeler, Jon Kennedy, Deirdre O'Connell, Katie Corcoran, Kate Elliott and Natasha Lanigan.

My film and TV agent: Marc Simonsson of SoloSon Media, who believed in the novel from the outset and secured film adaptation rights in rapid fashion.

My subject experts: Liz and Ryan Brookes. They described what it was like to sail across the Atlantic in a small boat, answered all of my questions and sparked many more. Needless to say I took all of their expertise and butchered it with my artistic license, creating numerous factual errors as a result – I take full responsibility. If you want to go sailing (and survive), go with them, not me. Also thanks to Will Martin, superyacht engineer – my naive questions were answered with speed and accuracy. No doubt I massaged them into complete fiction, but again, all mistakes are mine.

Thank you to the many crime and thriller authors I've had the pleasure of meeting over the last couple of years (Criminal Minds – you know who you are). They are a friendly, supportive group (and extremely talented) and I'm honoured to join the ranks.

A continued thank you to my wonderful parents, my sister Lucy, Tim, Charlotte, Millie, and Alice. To my extended family and friends who are all probably sick of me talking about my latest idea or protagonist, but remain supportive and feign interest regardless.

Finally, thank you to my wonderful wife Kerry, and my daughters Isla and Daisy, who continue to provide the perfect home in which to write, offering love, patience, time and the motivation to keep going.

Did you love

A stranger on board?

Discover the next pulse-pounding
thriller from Cameron Ward.

Coming Summer 2023.

Read on for an exclusive extract...

I picked my way across the garden. Fifty metres from the main house to the firebreak, then another ten to the trees. The air shimmered. The sun was at its peak, the heat already dangerous, coupled with a steady wind from the east, searing my skin, warning me to go back.

I skirted the garages, jumping on to the grass to avoid the scorching tiles, keeping the figure in my sights — an anomaly in the otherwise perfect landscape, a shadow of uncertainty at the treeline, camouflaged by the leaves and bark of the bushland floor. A man sitting against the trunk of a gum tree, hat dipped over his face.

Slowing as I approached, I placed each step carefully, the gravel sharp against my toes. A fresh blast of wind hit my face, tugged at my T-shirt. I raised my eyes, over the treeline to the east. A new haze blanketed the sky, a darkness that crept upwards from the ground to meet the heavens, already changing colour, already too late to stop.

I forced my eyes down, swallowing, trying to conjure some moisture into my mouth. It refused. I tasted grit between my teeth. Bitter and harsh.

Sleeping, or drunk, I recognized the man's clothing, but not his actions. Why would he be out here? I strode forward, grabbed his hat and pulled it off. Stood back. The man's eyes were open, his mouth twisted, a grotesque smile, his swollen tongue hanging to the right. Bile hit the back of my throat, burning as I swallowed again. I leaned in, failed to find a pulse. Not long. No flies. A few hours, six at most.

My knees wobbled, threatened to give way.

A twig cracked in the undergrowth, further to my left, then another. I looked up, hands trembling, eyes searching, but the trees were densely packed, the colours merging into a sea of browns and greens, the hot wind causing my eyes to flicker, lose focus. Besides, the sound was one in a cacophony of insect and bird sounds, the fauna protesting this intrusion, uncertain about the approaching threat, the smell and acrid taste carried on the wind from the east. An impending storm, but not of the survivable kind.

Movement. Crawling across the trunk behind the man's head was a huntsman spider, legs spanning several inches. It froze, perhaps sensing the moment, deciding to blend in, to protect itself from whatever else stalked these forests. Harmless, and certainly not the cause of this man's demise. Further behind, a trail on the ground, leaves scattered — like he'd dragged himself this far and stopped, given up, propped himself against the tree.

I shivered at the sight, backed away, calculating, processing the sudden change to our circumstances. It was what I did — analyse, predict, alert. I'd built a career on it, but hadn't seen this coming. No data, no warning, no conscious choice as my body screamed retreat, away from the scene, across the sharp gravel of the firebreak, to the perceived safety of the house, and to those within it.

The sky had changed again. Before my discovery and after. Altered states, I could smell it in the air, pungent, the taste of no return. Extreme high temperatures, low humidity, strong winds. The colour shifting, deepening. The blues fading, hidden behind the fury of the storm.

I inhaled. A flock of birds took flight in the distance, their wings silhouetted against the orange glow, dipping out of sight before surging upwards, escaping the red sky that followed.

A sky of blood.